Audrey took a step closer and faced him,

the lamps shining a golden, halo-like glow around her head.

She parted her sweet lips and her brown eyes darkened to a seductive shade. "You don't want to leave."

Slowly she reached behind and grabbed the ties of her halter top at the back of her neck. Fascinated and overwrought with desire, Luke couldn't utter a word. He couldn't tell her to stop. He couldn't tell her this was crazy. She was his mystery woman, and he'd secretly hoped to have a thrilling repeat of the night they'd shared.

"I ran away from you once, Luke. That won't happen again."

SUNSET SEDUCTION

BY
CHARLENE SANDS

Published in Great Britain 2013
by Mills & Boon, an imprint of Harlequin (UK) Limited,
Eton House, 18-24 Paradise Road, Richmond, Surrey TW9 1SR

© Charlene Swink 2013

ISBN: 978 0 263 90488 8
ebook ISBN: 978 1 472 00642 4

51-1013

Harlequin (UK) policy is to use papers that are natural, renewable and recyclable products and made from wood grown in sustainable forests. The logging and manufacturing processes conform to the legal environmental regulations of the country of origin.

Printed and bound in Spain
by Blackprint CPI, Barcelona

Charlene Sands is a *USA TODAY* bestselling author of thirty-five romance novels, writing sensual contemporary romances and stories of the Old West. Her books have been honored with a National Readers Choice Award, a Cataromance Reviewer's Choice Award and she's a double recipient of the Booksellers' Best Award. She belongs to the Orange County Chapter and the Los Angeles Chapter of RWA.

Charlene writes "hunky heroes with heart." She knows a little something about true romance—she married her high school sweetheart! When not writing, Charlene enjoys sunny Pacific beaches, great coffee, reading books from her favorite authors and spending time with her family. You can find her on Facebook and Twitter. Charlene loves to hear from her readers! You can write her at PO Box 4883, West Hills, CA 91308, USA or sign up for her newsletter for fun blogs and ongoing contests at www.charlenesands.com.

To Charles Griemsman for not only being my talented editor, a source of great support and a joy to work with, but for being a really amazing person, as well.

One

Usually nothing much unnerved Audrey Faith Thomas, except for the time six months ago when her big brother was bucked off Old Stormy at an Amarillo rodeo and broke his back. He was tossed eight feet in the air and landed with a solid smack to the ground. Casey's injury was severe enough to have Audrey quitting veterinary school last semester to nurse him back to health.

Audrey shuddered at the memory and thanked the Almighty that Casey was alive and well and bossy as ever. But as she sat behind the wheel of her truck driving toward her fate, the fear coursing through her veins had nothing to do with Casey's disastrous five-second ride and resulting retirement from the rodeo. This fear was much different. It scared her silly and made her doubt herself. It made her want to turn her Chevy pickup truck around and go home to Reno and forget all about showing up at Sunset Ranch unannounced.

To face Lucas Slade.

The man she'd seduced and then abandoned in the middle of the night.

Audrey swallowed hard and tried to reconcile her behavior. It wasn't working. She still couldn't believe what she'd done and after repeating her motives a thousand times in her head, nothing much had changed.

Last month, after an argument and a three-week standoff with her brother, she'd left her Reno home and ventured to his Lake Tahoe cabin to make amends. He'd been right about the boyfriend she'd just dumped, and she'd needed Casey's strong shoulder to cry on. But once she'd arrived, Casey was fast asleep on the couch and the last person she'd expected to find sleeping in the guest room, on *her bed,* was Luke Slade—the man of her fantasies, the one she'd measured every other man against. Luke was the guy she'd crushed on during her teen years while traveling the rodeo circuit with Casey—the guy who'd treated her with kindness and the same sort of brotherly love that Casey had.

Seeing him sent all rational thoughts flying out the window. This was her chance. She wouldn't let her prudish upbringing interfere with what she needed. His right arm was in a soft cast. That hadn't stopped her from edging closer.

Luke's eyelids had parted and two partially opened slits of warm blue honed in on her. "Come closer," he'd rasped in the darkened room. She'd taken that as an invitation to climb into bed with him, the consequences be damned. That night, her heart and soul, as well as her body, had been involved.

Well…she'd gotten a lot more than a shoulder to cry on, and it had been glorious and amazing and out and out wonderful. How could it not be? She'd been secretly in love with her brother's good buddy for years.

Audrey sent Jewel, the orange tabby sleeping in the travel carrier next to her, an apologetic glance. "It wasn't like he was some random guy. It was *Luke,*" she told the cat as if that explained it all. Her cat, who hadn't been much company on the drive, opened her eyes and gave her a stare before returning to cat dreamland. Audrey focused her attention back on the winding two-lane road, a shortcut through the Sierra Nevada Mountains to Sunset Ranch.

Audrey lowered the brim of her bright pink ball cap, shading her eyes from the glaring sun, and reached back to straighten out her ponytail. Coming through the mountain pass, she made the turn off the interstate and drove a little farther. As her gaze roamed the road, she recognized wisps of tall grass, purple wildflowers and white fences signifying the manicured property surrounding Sunset Lodge. The up-scale dudelike resort adjacent to the ranch was another of the Slades' prosperous enterprises. Once she passed the lodge, the ranch would be half a mile down the road.

"We're almost there," she told her sleepy cat.

Audrey couldn't relax like the mellow feline beside her. Her fingers curled tightly around the steering wheel and as her doubt and fear doubled, her heart pounded hard in her chest.

She should've stayed with Luke that night. She should've been brave enough to face him in the morning. But every time those thoughts popped into her head, she had images of Casey waking up and finding her in bed with his good buddy. There was no doubt in her mind that Casey would've gone ballistic, asking no questions and taking no prisoners. She'd come to the conclusion that leaving Luke and the cabin had been the only way.

And it was a good thing her brother slept like the dead and hadn't had a clue she'd had a booty call with his best friend.

Two days later, once she'd gotten the nerve to call her brother, she'd learned the reason for Luke's visit. He'd been trampled by a horse in an awful accident. His arm had been broken along with three ribs. He'd come to Casey's Lake Tahoe cabin to recuperate.

Now, she would finally come face-to-face with Luke. She'd confront him about the night they'd shared and confess her love for him, if it came down to that. She wondered if he thought her easy, a one-night stand and a woman who didn't know her own mind. What had he thought about her abandoning him that night?

She would soon find out. She drove deeper onto Slade land and the gates came into view. Overhead, a wrought-iron emblem depicting the sun setting on the horizon marked the east entrance to Sunset Ranch. She slowed the truck to a near crawl, losing some of her nerve.

She could make a U-turn, head home and no one would be the wiser.

Behind her, a driver in a feed truck packed with hay bales laid his hand on the horn startling her out of her reverie. She took it as an omen. *Drive on. Head toward your destiny, whatever it may be.*

She did just that, and a few minutes later, holding her breath and feigning bravado, Audrey parked her truck, grabbed the cat carrier and knocked on Luke's door.

When the door opened, she faced Lucas Slade. A gasp caught in her throat and she swallowed it down with one gulp. She drank in the sight of him, and her heart stirred restlessly, like all the other times she'd been in Luke's company. She was hopeless.

Sunlight played in his dark blond hair and touched his face on a day when he hadn't shaved. Rugged, appealing and so handsome she could cry. He stood a full head taller than she did. As a young girl, she'd thought if she could catch up to his height it would put her on even footing with him on other levels. It had been a silly whim that had never materialized. Luke was tall; she stood at average height. Five years separated their ages, which had seemed like an aeon to a teenager with a crush.

A little dumbfounded, she stared at him, not wanting to blow it by blurting out the wrong thing. She held her tongue and waited for him to say something.

His brows drew together. "That you under that hat, Audrey Faith?"

Heavens, she'd forgotten about the darn hat. She nodded and lifted the brim a little.

A big smile lit his face and sparkled in his eyes. "Well, come here."

He didn't wait for her to move. He stepped forward with his arms outstretched. At that moment, all of her fears were put to rest. He was glad to see her. *Lord, have mercy.*

But when she expected to be swept into an embrace and kissed the way he'd kissed her in the cabin, he bypassed her lips completely. Instead, her face was smothered by his shoulder as he gave her a big welcoming bear hug. There was no doubt about the affection there, or in the two *brotherly* pats to her shoulders, either, before he took a step back to look at her.

"What brings you out to Sunset Ranch?" His gaze whipped over her shoulder. "Did Casey drive out with you, too?"

"Oh, uh…no. Casey isn't with me."

"Okay," he said with a nod. "Well then, come inside, out of the heat. And bring whatever pet you've rescued with you."

She'd forgotten about the tabby in the carrier she'd set down on the porch. "H-her name is Jewel. She was hit by a car two months ago and was in shock for a while. Now she gets separation anxiety if I leave her for too long."

Luke gave the cat a better look through the carrrier's mesh window. "She made the trip from Reno with you?"

Her pulse quickened as his blue-eyed gaze returned to hers. She nodded.

"Lucky cat. I bet you're giving her the royal treatment. You always were great with animals."

She stood there, bewildered by Luke's reaction. He didn't make any acknowledgment about seeing her again. Or about that night that had rocked her world. He didn't seem angry, hurt, relieved or much of *anything.* She hadn't known exactly what to expect when she got here, but his civility clearly wasn't it.

Her feet wouldn't move, and her hesitation didn't faze him. He simply lifted the handle of the cat carrier and swung it along as he walked toward the parlor.

Audrey grabbed hold of her mind, and followed behind.

"You're a sight for sore eyes, Audrey Faith," he said over his shoulder.

So was he. Her throat constricted as she recalled the dreams she'd had of him for the past four weeks. Now she was here with him in the flesh. "I like to be called Audrey now. I dropped the Faith a few years ago."

Luke chuckled, and it was deep and rich and full of raw sensuality, just like she'd remembered. Of course, back when she was a teen, she didn't know much about sensuality. She only knew that she loved the sound of his laughter. "All right, *Audrey,*" he said, softlike.

Mercy. Her belly warmed from the delicious way he said her name.

Audrey gave herself a mental shake as she walked behind him into the house. She managed to keep her eyes trained *off* his perfect butt fitted into Wranglers. Instead, she concentrated on Luke's dark blond hair that reached past his collar to curl at his shoulders. The strands were much longer now. She remembered threading her fingers through those thick, healthy locks. How she yearned to do it again.

That entire night seemed like a surreal dream.

Luke set the cat carrier down on the sofa and turned to face her. "It's really good to see you, Audrey. It's been a long time."

How long was a long time? She'd seen him one month ago.

"Same here," she said. This wasn't how she'd expected this conversation to go. In her wildest imaginings, Luke would have been thrilled to see her. He would have whisked her off to his bedroom, claiming undying love and demanding that she never leave his side again. In the worst-case scenario,

Luke would've scolded her for having unprotected sex with him and then running off in the middle of the night.

But *this* conversation was just plain strange.

"I'm glad you came for a visit," Luke said, gesturing for her to take a seat.

She sat down next to the cat carrier. Luke took a seat across from her in a buttercup-colored wing chair trimmed with round bronzed studs. "You look great."

She didn't think so. When she'd dressed this morning, she'd picked the best her neglected wardrobe had to offer, plaid blouse, baggy jeans and her too-long hair tucked into a baseball cap. She'd been meaning to get a stylish cut but that obviously hadn't happened. The ball cap and casual clothes were Audrey As Usual. "Thanks, so do you. Are you feeling better?"

"I've got no complaints. My arm's good as new now." His arm had been encumbered with a cast when they made love, but that hadn't stopped him from making her die a thousand pleasant deaths that night.

"That's…good."

"What've you been up to?" he asked, being polite.

"I, uh… *Luke?*" She hated to sound desperate, but Luke was avoiding the whole I-jumped-your-bones-in-the-middle-of-the-night subject.

His eyes softened and his voice registered sympathy. "What's up, honey? You have another fight with Casey? Is he still being a bear?"

She leaned back against the seat cushion, rattled. Was he being deliberately obtuse? Surely he had to know why she'd come this distance to visit him.

Luke was a wealthy horse breeder now. Along with his brothers, he owned the biggest ranch in three counties. He had a lot on his mind, and it humbled her to think he remembered her troubles with Casey. It had been years since Audrey had complained to Luke about her brother's overprotective, overbearing nature. She would confide in Luke, because he was the only one who'd really listened to her and treated her as an equal rather than a silly girl with years of growing up to do.

"We still argue," she said, "but it's different now."

"How so?" He seemed genuinely interested.

"He can't ground me anymore, so I really let him have it."

Luke laughed again. "I bet you do."

Audrey forced a smile. She didn't get any of this. Luke acted as if they hadn't been intimate, hadn't steamed up the sheets on that guest-room bed. Was making love to a woman such an everyday occurrence to him that Luke thought nothing of it? Just casual sex with a onetime friend? "Casey knows I'm a big girl now. He doesn't lord over me like he used to."

She wanted to make it clear to Luke that Casey didn't play into the equation. What happened between the two of them wasn't any of her big brother's business.

"So he finally cut the apron strings?"

"He's getting there. It's better than it was."

Luke nodded, and they stared at each other. "Can I get you something cold to drink?"

"No…I'm just fine."

"Okay." He nodded once again and then she caught him glancing at his watch.

"Am I keeping you from something?"

"Nope," he said, sitting up straighter in his seat, giving her his full attention. Luke was the best fibber on the planet. On the rodeo circuit, he used to tell white lies all the time to make people feel better.

Yes, Mrs. Jenkins, your strawberry-rhubarb pie is the best in the county.

Jonathan, you just need another year practicing with that fiddle before you make it to the Grand Ole Opry.

No, Audrey Faith, you're not keeping me from anything important.

Audrey knew it was now or never. She had to speak with

Luke about that night. She couldn't leave things the way they were without clearing the air.

"I actually do have a reason for being here, Luke," she said softly. "I think you know why, but if you're going to make me say it…"

Luke's forehead wrinkled as he gave it some thought. Then it hit him. "Ah…Audrey." He raised his hand to stop her. "Say no more. I should've guessed the second I saw you standing on the doorstep."

Relieved, Audrey let her stiff shoulders relax. Finally, they would get things out in the open.

"You heard about the wrangler job at the ranch," he said. "Casey must've told you I was shorthanded. Come to think about it, there's no one better to help me settle down my pain-in-the-ass, hardheaded stallion. I should have thought of hiring you myself, but we haven't talked in years, so it didn't cross my mind. The truth is, I need to get Tribute in line. He's a big challenge. Casey tells me you're not going back to vet school until the fall?"

Blood drained from her face and a shudder of dread coursed through her body. Her devastation would be visible any second now. She couldn't let that happen.

Get a grip, Audrey. Hang on.

She was finally getting the picture. It was murky at best. "I, uh…y-yes, that's my plan," she managed.

She wished she'd chickened out instead of coming here. She could have done a quick one-eighty on the highway and headed straight back to Reno. Because the murkiness was clearing and the image left underneath was nightmarishly ugly.

We haven't talked in years.

She could take that literally. Technically, they hadn't talked…much. They'd moaned and groaned their way through that night. But she'd be an even bigger fool than she was now if she thought that's what Luke had meant.

The Luke she'd known in the past wouldn't have skirted an issue this big. He would have been up front and honest. He would have probably apologized and felt guilty as hell for making love to his best friend's little sister. There was only one conclusion that Audrey could draw. There was only one reason any of this made sense.

Luke doesn't know he made love to me.

That incredible night of passion they'd shared was one-sided.

He wasn't being obtuse. He was clueless.

If someone plunged a dagger in her heart, the pain couldn't have been any greater.

"What do you say, honey?" The timbre of his deep voice broke through her anguish.

"Want to spend what's left of the summer with me on Sunset Ranch?"

"They're just formalities, Audrey, but we've got to do them," Luke said as he handed her an application for the job on Sunset Ranch.

She sat in the Slade family office located at one end of the sprawling one-story ranch house. Luke had taken a seat at his desk across from her. She felt his eyes on her as she began filling out the personal information on the form. Robotically, she went about accepting the job as wrangler on the Slades' very lucrative horse farm, her mind on automatic pilot as she tied herself to working with Lucas Slade for the next two months.

Audrey wasn't into science fiction, but she could surely relate to anyone who believed in alternate universes. This sci-fi version of her life had her living under Luke's roof and working beside him every day, filling her summer days with something more than meaningless temp jobs back home until she could restart her veterinary education. This universe wasn't ideal, but it was a far cry better than anything reality had had to offer.

Audrey completed the application. As she leaned forward to hand Luke the form, the fresh lime scent of his cologne brought memories of kissing his throat and shoulders and chest. It was the same scent that had lingered on her long after she'd fled her brother's cabin.

Luke glanced at the application for less than five seconds, before smiling and standing. "You're hired. Let me show you to your room."

And within minutes, Audrey stood alone in her new bedroom, slightly dazed by what had occurred during the past thirty minutes.

She'd discovered she'd made love to a man who didn't remember doing the deed.

He'd offered her a dream job.

And insisted she live in a guest bedroom less than twenty feet from his own room.

Audrey glanced at Jewel, who was stretched out lengthwise on the bedspread, a tiger-striped bundle of fur against black-and-bright-yellow flowers. The beautiful space was bigger than any room she'd ever called her own. And yet, as she glanced around the opulent surroundings, she questioned her decision to take the job, muttering, "What have I done?"

Audrey didn't have to wonder for very long. Immediate clarity punched her in the gut. She'd done what she had to do. No way could she have walked out the door, never to see Luke again. The second she'd laid eyes on him today that possibility wasn't an option. She finally came out of her thirty-minute fog and realized she was where she needed to be. She had been given another chance with Luke.

Yes, her heart was broken that Luke had forgotten their night together because her memories of him were profound, unforgettable. Her responses to his heady kisses severed all ties she had to good-girl status. She'd moved on him, mindful of his encumbered arm, in wild, wicked ways that had astonished her afterward. But while in the moment, she'd let go and ridden his tight, hard, muscled body until he was ready to guide her home.

I'll never forget.

A satisfied purr escaped her throat. The cat's head came up.

She stifled a chuckle and walked over to the bed. "Go back to sleep, Jewel," she whispered, taking a seat and stroking the cat's soft underbelly until her eyes drifted closed again.

Oh, to trade places with the cat right now. To have no worries and no heartache and sleep away the day…what could be better?

Audrey allowed herself a few minutes of self-pity and then tried to look on the bright side of things. At least Luke had faith in her. That was a plus. He'd hired her for a job that wasn't easily won on the highly respected ranch, not because of his friendship with Casey, but because she had a way with animals. He trusted her abilities and needed her help with the dang horse that had trampled him and sent him to the hospital.

She would look upon Trib as a challenge that she could conquer.

Getting Luke to see her as anything other than his buddy's baby sister would involve a heck of a lot more work.

"I know we'll be good together," Luke had said, right before he'd walked out of the guest room.

Audrey sighed.

If he only knew how true that statement was.

As soon as Luke showed Audrey to her room, he went back into the office to give her application another glance. Audrey Faith Thomas, half sister to Casey—though nobody much mentioned the *half* part anymore—had had a rough upbringing. She'd lost her parents early on, and Casey had raised her. She'd been the tagalong little sis on the rodeo circuit. Luke thought that Audrey had gotten a raw deal in life. Casey had been overly strict with her. Luke figured her brother was overcompensating, being mother and father to her. Casey had tried hard, but a lot of the time, he didn't know what the hell he was doing when it came to his little sister.

Audrey compensated, too. She took to the animals and the animals loved her in return. They were a good match. Audrey had a special fondness for the rodeo horses. There wasn't a one that didn't temper its wild mood when Audrey walked up.

According to her application, after college, she'd worked for a veterinarian clinic in Reno for a couple of years before deciding to apply to equine vet school. Luke also noted all the charity and volunteer work Audrey had done through the years. She had listed animal shelters and horse rescues, and was part of the Freedom for Wild Horses organization.

Luke picked up the phone and punched in Casey's number. "Hey," he said when his friend answered.

"Hey."

Luke owed his friend a favor for letting him crash at his Tahoe cabin last month. Being with his buddy helped his recuperation move along more quickly. Well, at least it'd been less mentally painful. Luke thought he'd go stir-crazy, not being able to do a dang thing with his arm in a cast and three cracked ribs making it hard for him to breathe. Up at the cabin, it was okay to do nothing but while away the time. Casey made it easy and they'd had a few laughs.

But he would have hired Audrey even if he didn't owe Casey a favor. She was qualified and a hard worker. Audrey was true blue and a nice kid.

"I've got your little sis here. She's working for me now."

There was silence on the other end. And finally "She didn't tell me that."

Uh-oh. Luke didn't like getting in between the two of them. "Yeah, well, it just happened. You must've mentioned that I was shorthanded on the ranch. Anyway, she showed up looking for work, and I hired her as a wrangler for a few months."

"Hell, Luke. I don't recall mentioning any such thing to her. I must be getting old and forgetful."

Luke laughed. Casey was only thirty-three. "Hell, yeah, you are. You see any problem with her working here?" Not that Luke was asking permission. Audrey was twenty-four and making her own decisions now. He'd called Casey for an entirely different reason.

Casey hesitated. "Not at all, buddy. It's just that she's been acting a little weird lately. You know, sort of wanting to be by herself and all. I thought she'd come up to the cabin to spend the summer with me. She had this loser boyfriend in Reno and she finally dumped him. The jerk was cheating on her. My little sis really took it hard. I don't think she's over it yet. It was all I could do to restrain myself from knocking his stupid self from here to Sunday. Jackass."

"Jackass is right."

"Damn straight."

"Well, she's here now," Luke said. "She's going to be staying at the main house. You don't need to worry. I'll look out for her."

"Like you always do. I appreciate it, Luke. And I'll count on you to make sure none of those ranch hands break her heart."

"Hell, she'll be breaking theirs."

Casey chuckled. "That's all right, then."

"Yeah, I hear you. Don't worry about Audrey. And you come up anytime you want to visit. Stay at the ranch."

"What, and leave my cabin? I got me a keg of beer, my barbecue grill and gorgeous women to stare at by the lake all day long."

Luke's mind flashed an image of one gorgeous woman in particular—a blonde with long, slender legs and a dazzler of a smile—who had crashed the lakeshore party Casey had thrown on Luke's last night at the cabin. She'd shown up at his farewell barbecue and had caught his eye the second she'd walked over to join the festivities. She'd been with a small group of people and Luke never did get the woman's name amid the fifty or so partygoers that Casey had invited. She'd come late and left early, but not before giving Luke half a dozen suggestive looks. He'd been ready to approach her, but had gotten sidetracked by someone interested in hearing about his rodeo days.

"You ever find out who that blonde was?" Luke had good reason to ask.

"You mean the stunner?" Casey asked. "I was drunk, but not too drunk to see how fine she was."

"So you know who I'm talking about."

"I found out her name is Desiree."

"And?"

"She's an acquaintance of one of my neighbors. She lives on the East Coast somewhere. She's gone. That's all I know, man. You missed your chance."

Luke wasn't going to divulge what had happened with the blonde to Casey. Luke kept his private life private. But since he'd been accepting his friend's hospitality and living at his cabin for a few weeks, a surge of guilt washed over him for not being completely truthful with Casey. Though having a one-night stand with a stranger, no matter how beautiful, wasn't exactly something to brag about. Not in this day and age. He wasn't eighteen anymore. He was old enough to know better. His only excuse was that he'd been in a haze. Drugged up on pain meds.

Vague memories of that night continually plagued him.

At least now he knew who the mysterious woman was. She'd taken the reins that night, which suited him fine since his injuries prohibited much mobility, and his mind was pretty fogged up. At times he'd thought he'd dreamed the whole thing except that he did remember small details, like her fresh-flower scent, her long flowing blond hair caressing his cheek and his completely sated body and good mood when he'd woken up that morning.

"Well, the mystery is solved," Luke said, thinking it for the best that she lived so far away. One-night stands weren't his thing but neither were complicated affairs. Luke had yet to meet a woman who held his interest for too long. Most of his relationships lasted less than six months before one of them realized that something was missing. Luke never felt the need to explore what that something was. If it wasn't right there, pounding in his heart and making him silly crazy, what was the point of forcing it? He'd done that once with a girl in high school, trying hard to hang on, to convince her it was working, and in the end, he'd been the one who'd gotten his heart shattered.

Usually when he entered into a relationship with a woman, if the flow wasn't smooth and easy from the get-go, Luke was the first one to bail.

"Too bad, though," Casey said. "She was smokin' hot."

Yep, she was. There was no arguing that point. From what he could remember, she'd been a hellcat in bed. But he let the comment drop and turned the conversation to a new venture Casey was thinking about going into since he'd been forced into retirement with his back injury.

After a few minutes, Casey ended the phone call with a last parting remark. "Thanks for helping my little sis out, Luke. You're her second brother. I know you'll look out for her."

"You got my promise on that, Case. I won't let you down."

Two

Audrey grabbed her canvas overnight tote from her truck. She didn't know what to expect when she arrived here without an invitation—certainly not to be hired on Sunset Ranch—but she'd brought a few essentials and a change of clothes with her, just in case things worked out with Luke. A girl could be optimistic, couldn't she? At the very least, she assumed that Luke would've remembered making love to her. It was a given, or so she'd thought. There had been *two* people on that bed, sighing and groaning with pleasure, for the better part of an hour.

Now that she was staying on the ranch *as an employee* for a couple of months, she'd have to do some shopping in town to get a few more changes of clothes. She'd placed a call to Susanna Hart half an hour ago. Her next-door neighbor and good friend back in Reno had the key to her house—technically, Casey's house—where she'd grown up, at least when she wasn't traveling from town to town on the rodeo circuit. Casey hadn't allowed her to stay home by herself much when she was in high school. Susanna's mother would watch out for her when she had a big test at school or something; otherwise, she tagged along with her brother.

Her high school experience had been grim, and she'd struggled to get good grades and keep up with events that were important to her. Senior year had been hard, and though she'd dreamed of Luke taking her to the prom, she'd settled on going with a nice boy who'd also been somewhat of an outcast.

Susanna had offered to pack up her clothes, her laptop, a few photos and Jewel's favorite cat bowl and send them on. Audrey hadn't gone into detail about her situation other than to tell her friend that she'd be working on Sunset Ranch with the horses for the summer.

As she gazed at Jewel snoring lightly on the bed, Audrey wished she could be as oblivious to the world around her as her feline buddy. The bed looked inviting, and she wasn't supposed to officially start her job until tomorrow. But it was the middle of the day and she wasn't much of a napper.

She walked into the bathroom to splash water on her face and then gasped when she looked in the mirror. She gave the image staring back at her a frown. She looked like hell. Her eyes were rimmed with red from lack of sleep last night and her hair, which was badly in need of a trim, was sticking out in three places from under the hat. "Goodness, Audrey, you look a sight."

She worked on her appearance in haste.

Right now, Audrey longed to meet the horses. As she'd driven up, she'd seen the ranch corrals and the dozen or so horses, standing under giant oaks that provided shade from the other side of the fences.

Sunset Lodge had its own stable of horses, Luke had explained, that were primarily used for the lodge's guests. They were sweet, gentle-natured animals that would provide trail rides and hayrides to entertain visitors. But the barns on the real working ranch housed some of the finest stallions, mares and geldings in the western half of the United States.

Casey had always bragged about the Slades's horses until Audrey's ears had burned. Her brother hadn't a clue that hearing about anything regarding Luke gave her a warm, fuzzy feeling in the pit of her stomach. Memories of him, and the fact that Luke had never married, had her daydreaming of him more times than she'd like to admit. It had sabotaged her feelings for most other men. At least until her recent boyfriend. She'd taken a chance with Toby and had really begun to like him, despite his flaws, until the day she'd learned he'd been a cheat with more than one woman.

That had been a hard pill to swallow.

And what upset her most wasn't so much that she was out a boyfriend, but that she hadn't really cared that much. Sure, she'd been hurt by his betrayal and humiliated that she'd been made a fool, but losing Toby wasn't so great a loss. What shattered her was an impending fear that she'd never settle for any man but Luke.

And clearly, he was an impossible dream.

So when the opportunity had presented itself, Audrey grabbed the brass ring. Then fool that she was, she'd lost her nerve and had run out on Luke.

"Idiot," she said, plopping her ball cap on her hopeless hair and striding out the door.

A few minutes later, she stood by the ranch's corral fence close to the trunk of a tree where three horses huddled under the umbrella of shade. One of the horses looked over. He was a beauty, a bay gelding that stood fifteen hands high, his legs marked with white socks.

She softened her tone, "Come here, boy."

The horse wandered over and Audrey put her hand over the corral fence, letting the horse sniff her scent and look into her eyes. "You're a pretty one."

The horse snorted quietly and when she was sure he felt

comfortable with her, she laid her hand on his coat and stroked his withers.

"You and I are going to be friends. Yes, we are."

Another horse wandered over and before long, all three horses were nudging each other to get some attention.

She smiled, realizing she hadn't felt this good in days.

Horses had always been her salvation.

A dog scurried by, barking at the horses for no apparent reason as he ran the perimeter of the corral. Audrey could tell it was a game between the animals. The horses paid little mind to the black-and-white Border collie.

Soon, a small boy appeared, running at full speed after the dog, his little legs making long strides. He came to a screeching stop when he saw her by the tree.

"Hello," she said.

"Hi." He looked at the ground.

"My name is Audrey Thomas. I'm a friend of Luke's. I'm going to be taking care of the horses. What's your dog's name?"

The dog stood twenty feet up ahead, having taken a break from his run to catch his breath.

"Oh, h-he's not my d-dog exactly. I w-watch him for Mr. S-Slade. H-his name is B-Blackie."

Audrey nodded. "Good name. I bet you have a good name, too."

The boy's mouth curled up. "It's E-Edward. No one c-calls me Eddie."

"I won't call you Eddie, either, Edward."

"Thanks." He glanced at the dog, patiently waiting to resume the game of chase. "I havta g-go. My g-grandma's waiting f-for me."

"Okay, nice to meet you, Edward."

The boy nodded and took off again.

Luke found her grinning when he walked up a minute later. "I see you met Edward and Blackie."

The sound of his voice hummed through her body. She couldn't look at him. She stared at the horses, who were still vying for her attention. "Yes. Seems like a sweet boy."

"Yeah, he's a good kid. Ten years old. His grandmother runs the kitchen at Sunset Lodge. It's a long story, but he loves living at the lodge. My brother Logan and I give him chores to do around here. Blackie's one of his *chores with bonuses.*"

"I'm getting the picture." She finally turned to him. His blue eyes devastated her. It was hard looking at his handsome face.

Get a grip, Audrey. You have to see him every day now.

His stomach growled and he laughed. "Sorry. The housekeeper's on vacation and I'm hopeless in the kitchen. I was going over to the lodge to scrounge a meal. You wanna come?"

"I, uh… No, thanks. Look at me. I'm not exactly lodge-worthy right now."

He pulled the bill of her cap down with an affectionate tug, just like he used to do way back when. "Sure you are."

"I'm not, really," she said, her eyes flashing. She looked like hell. She could hardly believe she'd walked up to Luke's door looking like this. "I need a shower and a fresh change of clothes. Besides, I don't want to leave Jewel alone too long. She needs to adjust to her new environment."

Lucky cat was probably sleeping the afternoon away.

Luke studied her face a second. "You still got cooking skills?"

"I can stir a pot when needed."

"I remember. You're a pretty darn good cook. Why don't you shower and change and meet me in the kitchen. Between the two of us, we can probably whip up something edible for lunch. I really don't want to beg a meal over at the lodge. Much rather spend my time sharing a meal with you."

It would hardly be begging, since Luke and his family owned the place. And she couldn't take to heart what he said about spending time with her. That throwaway line, while she thought it genuine, was merely Luke being Luke. He was cordial to everyone.

She should refuse. She should tell him she needed to rest, but who was she kidding? She had enough adrenaline pumping through her veins right now to run a marathon. Luke's beckoning eyes darkened to a deep ocean blue, causing her breath to catch in her throat. Unknowingly, he had powers of persuasion that quelled a woman's resolve. He was everyone's Mr. Nice Guy and he'd been her own private knight in shining armor. It was hard denying him anything—thus her taking up residence here and working for him on Sunset Ranch. "Okay. I'll meet you in the kitchen in thirty minutes."

His stomach complained again and he grinned like a little boy. "I'll be there."

Audrey turned on the faucet, adjusting the water temperature to medium-hot, and stepped inside the shower. As the pulsating spray hit her naked body, she closed her eyes to the warmth and relaxed as she washed away the dusty morning drive. And just like that, memories rushed into her mind of an awkward, lonely time in her life.

She'd been sixteen and upset about missing her high school dance. Not that she was much of a dancer, but she'd missed being with friends who seemed to be moving on without her. She wasn't happy spending most weekends on the road with Casey and this one Saturday night, she'd let her sour mood get the best of her.

Judd Calhoon and his friend were slightly older than she was and pretty much harmless. She wouldn't call Judd her friend. He'd mostly teased her about being scrawny and younger, but they'd shared one common complaint—both would rather be spending their weekends at home. So when he'd dared her to sneak out of the trailer that was her second home with Casey, Audrey had found herself eager and willing to thumb her nose at her big brother's rules. He was her half brother, anyway, she'd thought. And she'd been tired of his demanding, overprotective ways.

She'd met the boys at midnight—Casey, with a Saturday-night drunk on, would never have known she was gone—and they'd built a small campfire in a cleared-out field half a mile away from the rodeo arena. They'd had some laughs, and she'd been feeling really good about her rebellion. She'd even taken a swallow or two of whiskey the boys had brought along. Before she knew it, Judd's friend had passed out, falling into a snoring heap on the ground three feet away from her. Judd had been drinking heavily by then, and his usual mocking tone had suddenly turned affectionate. His hands got grabby and his pockmarked face was suddenly all over hers. Judd Calhoon, the brother of the rodeo clown, was no Romeo, and Audrey had shoved him away, telling him he was stupid for trying such a stunt.

Judd hadn't taken no for an answer. His affection had turned to demand and before Audrey knew it, she'd been pinned to the ground under him. "Get off," she'd said, shoving at him.

He was too big, too clumsy and too strong for her and she'd realized he'd *let* her shove him away the first time. This time, her shove didn't budge him.

"Aw, come on, Audrey. No one will know."

He'd smelled of whiskey and tobacco. He'd kissed her chin, her cheek and kept missing her mouth because he'd been drunk and because Audrey kept turning her face away as fast as he came at her. "I said get off," she'd shouted again, her fists pummeling the wooden block of his chest.

And he'd complied, just like that. Only it hadn't been Judd doing the moving, but Luke, his hands in a vise grip on Judd's shoulders. The next thing she knew, Judd was flying through the air, and Luke's face was red with fury when he'd gone after him. He'd picked Judd up where he'd landed and had held him by the scruff of the collar. He'd spoken with deadly calm then. Audrey, knowing Luke like she did, had realized his great restraint as he'd lectured Judd and placed the fear of God in him.

"You okay?" Luke had asked her after he was through with Judd. He'd helped her up and she'd dusted herself off, grateful to Luke, but fearing what he had to say to her, too.

"I'm f-fine."

"I wasn't gonna do anything to her, I swear," Judd's voice squeaked from the darkness.

Luke hadn't taken his eyes off her. "Shut up or I'll take you to the sheriff."

Luke had taken her hand then and led her to his truck. She'd gotten in and sat in silence on the ride back. She could tell Luke was fuming and part of his anger was aimed at her.

"That was real dumb going off in the middle of the night."

"I kn-know."

"Dangerous, too. Those boys are losers. Stupid to boot."

Audrey had nodded again.

Luke had killed the engine of his truck twenty feet away from the trailer she shared with Casey.

"Why'd you do it, Audrey Faith?"

She'd stared straight ahead into the night and opened up her heart, telling him about her loneliness, her sadness over missing her friends at school and her terrible boredom at the rodeo. She'd told him how Casey was all over her with rules and regulations and that she'd felt like she never fit with anyone, anywhere. How Casey was only her half brother and how she'd had half a life. She was rarely home when it mattered and her only salvation was her love of horses. She'd cried a few times and Luke had leaned over to wipe her tears tenderly with his kerchief.

She'd spilled her guts and Luke had nodded like he understood, giving her words of encouragement for her to let it all out. He'd truly listened to her and in the end, when her body sagged, spent from her crushing confessions and soulful tears, Luke had offered her a compromise. He wouldn't tell Casey what happened, and he'd go back to Judd and his friend and make sure they never bothered her again, if Audrey would promise to come to him when she was feeling like doing something stupid or reckless or dangerous. He'd encouraged her to talk to Casey about everything that bothered her, but told her he'd be there if she ever needed him.

For a girl who'd thought her brother would ground her for life if he ever found out what she'd done, Luke had offered her a dream deal. She'd agreed to his terms and Luke had sealed their little pact with a brotherly kiss to the cheek.

Audrey wasn't sure a girl of sixteen knew a darn thing about love, but she was ninety-nine percent certain that that was the night she'd fallen deeply and wholeheartedly in love with Lucas Slade.

Audrey stepped out of the shower and toweled off vigorously, purging the memory from her mind. She dabbed at her throat, chin and face and talked herself out of any more reminiscing. It wouldn't help her current situation. She was at a loss here with Luke.

And ten minutes away from making his lunch.

"You are in a pickle, Audrey," she muttered as she dressed in her only change of clothes.

She combed her hair, banding it in a ponytail, and glanced in the mirror. The clothes were a slight improvement over the ones she'd worn this morning—new black jeans hugged her hips below the waist and a white peasant's blouse with short sleeves sloped on her shoulders. Her boots were dark tan and well broken in, the most comfortable shoes she owned.

With three minutes to spare, she closed the door on her sleepy cat and sashayed down the hall, heading to the kitchen wondering if the old cliché still held true. The way to a man's heart was through his stomach. If only…

* * *

"Hey," Luke said as she entered the kitchen. His head was poking inside the fridge as he perused the shelves. "We've got leftover roast beef, turkey, ham and three different kinds of cheeses. It figures. I'm in the mood for a patty melt."

As Audrey breezed by him, she picked up the lime scent of his aftershave and refused to let it give her heart failure. Luke smelled good. Period. She'd have to get over it or she'd make a fool of herself. "I'll make you a patty melt. It'll be the rich man's version."

His mouth curved up. "What's that?"

"Wait and see, big man."

Luke laughed and sat at the granite island counter, watching her cook.

She found a fry pan, sweet butter, bread crumbs and sesame seed buns. It wasn't rocket science, but she was pretty darn proud of her creation when she was all through heating small chunks of roast mixed with bread crumbs and layered with melted cheese. The patty came together and she plopped it into a bun with a spatula. "Here you go."

Luke glanced at the dish she slid his way and cocked a brow. "I'm not that rich, by the way."

"Yes, you are." He was wealthy by anyone's standards with his shared ownership of Sunset Lodge and Sunset Ranch and, from Casey's accounting, half a dozen other investments. "But I won't hold that against you. Eat up."

He picked up the bun and dived in, taking a big bite. His eyes closed slowly and his face settled into an expression of sublime pleasure. "It'll do," he said.

"I thought so."

He took two more bites before his gaze slid back to her. "You having one?"

She shook her head. "I'll stick to a cheese sandwich."

He drew his brows together. "That's no fun, honey."

She couldn't get excited about an endearment he'd used in his usual brotherly tone.

"You're doing fine without me." He'd gobbled up the entire sandwich while sitting on a stool at the counter. "I'll make you another one, if you'd like."

He contemplated his empty plate, then gave two pats to a rock-solid stomach a quarter would bounce off. "Tempting, but I'd better not. Sophia and Logan are bringing us dinner tonight. And she's cooking up one of her specialties."

Us? They'd be a foursome tonight, but it would hardly be a double date. "I heard Logan was getting married."

"Yep. My brother's getting the better end of the deal, if you ask me."

She remembered how Logan would come to see Luke at the rodeo and they'd give each other a world of grief. It was all in good fun, for the most part, except when it wasn't. But even though they teased each other unmercifully, Audrey saw the love they had for each other. They'd have each other's backs if there was ever a problem. "Logan's quite a catch. I bet Sophia feels pretty lucky. I can't wait to meet her."

"You will in a few hours."

She placed a bun in the fry pan, then added a slab of cheese and a fresh slice of tomato. Luke walked over to the fridge again and pulled out a pitcher of lemonade. He poured two glasses and handed her one. He stood close, watching the cheese melt onto the bun as he sipped his drink. A trickle of moisture slipped down her neck. Just being near Luke made her break out in a sweat.

"What are you doing after you eat that?"

She shrugged. "I have no plans."

"I was gonna wait until tomorrow, but if you're up to it, I thought I'd take you over to meet Trib."

"Ah…the horse that nearly killed you."

"An exaggeration. There were a few broken ribs."

"He broke your right arm, too."

Luke stared at her. "I see your brother filled you in on my injuries."

Yes, Casey had told her afterward, but she'd also had first-hand knowledge of his broken arm in the cast. But mercy, the man had left-hand skills that satisfied her just fine.

"You had a concussion, too."

"But I'm right as rain now."

It was permission to look him over from top to bottom. Not that she didn't already know how *right* the man was. From the top of his sandy-blond hair down to his black snakeskin boots, Luke was perfect. "I'm glad you've recovered."

"Wasn't ever any doubt, but thanks. Appreciate it."

She took the last bites of her sandwich and rubbed shoulders with Luke, who insisted on helping with the mess. They tidied up the kitchen, cleaned the counters and put the plates away in the dishwasher before heading outside.

A few minutes later, Luke led Audrey to a distant stable, one built for special cases like Tribute, a stallion with great ancestry and beautiful grace, but temperamental as all get-out. The ranch hands had nicknamed him Tribulation for all the darn trouble the horse gave them on a daily basis. One day Luke thought he'd broken the damn horse's barriers and had let down his guard. That was the day Trib had sent him to the hospital.

"I don't want you near him unless I'm with you," Luke said. They walked out of the bright sunlight and into the much cooler barn. Even before he laid eyes on the dang horse, he heard the sound of his shuffling in his stall. "He isn't keen we're here. Darn horse is antisocial."

Audrey's eyes widened as she mentally accepted the challenge that Luke wouldn't let her near the horse until he felt it was safe. He wouldn't put her in danger, and Casey would probably crush him into pulp, anyway, if Luke let his kid sister get injured.

While she was staying at the ranch, Luke was responsi-

ble for her safety. He wouldn't take that lightly. Casey's trust
was one reason, but Luke had always had a soft spot in his
heart for her. If he'd had a sister, he'd want her to be just like
Audrey Faith.

"You know I can't get much done with you hovering over
me, Luke."

"I know no such thing. You can work your magic, with
me *hovering* in the back of the barn. It's the only way I'll
allow it."

"Now you sound like Casey. Bossy."

He had to smile at that. Casey was a pill when it came to
his sister. "Maybe so, but just so we're clear, you're not to
come in here unless I'm with you. Got that?"

Audrey frowned but finally nodded. "Okay."

They came up to the paddock at the far end of the barn
and looked over the half door to see the stallion pacing and
snorting. The space was larger than most, the ground covered
with a bedding of cedar shavings and straw.

"He's a beauty," Audrey whispered in awe. Her expressive
eyes lit with longing and Luke could see her mind working
already. She would find a way to connect with this animal.

"That, he is. I hate to give up on him. I was tempted, believe me. After I tripped in the stall and cursed loud enough
for the next county to hear me, Trib got perplexed, and it was
all I could do to get out of his way before he trampled the
stuffing out of me. He's got heralded ancestry and he'll make
someone a fine horse one day. If—and that's a big if—we can
find his gentle side."

The horse stayed near the back wall, looking at them with
sharp, wary eyes that took everything in. He knew Luke, but
he still didn't trust him. And now Audrey was added to the
mix. "He's better in the corral, but he doesn't play well with
others, so he's pretty much a loner."

"That has to change and it will. In time."

"You have a couple of months."

Audrey glanced at him. "It's a tall order, but I'll do my best." Her eyes deepened in color and her voice rang with sincerity. "I know this is important to you, Luke."

She was sweet, and he was grateful for her help. On impulse, he bent to kiss her cheek, but she shifted her head at that exact moment and damn if he didn't lay a kiss right smack on her mouth.

His senses filled. Her lips were soft and smooth against his rough mouth. She tasted familiar, like wild berries in the spring. She had a scent that lingered, reminding him of something he couldn't quite grasp. She purred deep in her throat, the sound a little startled and a whole lot of sexy. It made him wince and question his sanity as he pulled away sooner than he would've liked.

It was a short, quick kiss, but he'd learned this much: Audrey wasn't a delicate child. She was passionate. But when he wanted to explore a little more, the words *CASEY'S SISTER* flashed through his mind like a banner being pulled across the sky by a plane.

What was it Casey had said? She'd had a loser boyfriend and was feeling a little low right now. He couldn't take advantage of that.

"Sorry," he said quietly.

Audrey's expressive eyes stayed on his as seconds ticked by. Silence filled the barn. Not even Trib made a sound, and then finally she whispered, "No need to apologize."

"I meant to kiss your cheek."

"I know."

It had been an awkward head-shifting and lips-meshing moment. He couldn't put his finger on what niggled at him, but there was definitely something rattling around in his brain. He took a deep breath, noticing for the first time how unique Audrey's scent was. "Are you wearing perfume?"

She shook her head. "Lip gloss. It's called Sweet and Wicked."

Luke zeroed in on her mouth. He should've known. He'd taken a sip from her sweet and wicked lips and liked how she tasted.

"TMI?" she asked with a raised brow.

Too much information. Luke grinned. "Nope. Trust me, I can handle sweet and wicked."

Her eyes left his, but not before Luke caught an odd expression cross her features. "I figured as much."

Luke took a last glance at Trib in the paddock. The horse continued to watch them with a ready-to-bolt stance. "He's sizing us up."

"Together, we're too intimidating for him," Audrey said.

"He'll have to get used to it. From now on, it's him and you and me."

She sighed, and the warmth of her delicious breath wafted by his nostrils. He had a bad feeling that Sweet and Wicked would haunt his dreams tonight. But he kept that thought to himself as he laid a hand to the small of her back and led Audrey out of the barn.

After spending time with Luke, Audrey needed to calm her nerves. She lay down beside Jewel on the bed and the cat immediately started purring loud enough to wake the dead.

"You're happy to see me, aren't you?" she cooed. "Well, I'm happy to see you, too."

She stroked the back of Jewel's head, just under the ears. The cat's coat was soft and smooth under her fingertips. When she had enough, Jewel stretched her neck so that Audrey could scratch her under the chin and the cat's noisy purring settled into a soft hum.

The lull made Audrey's eyes grow heavy and she relaxed on the bed. Rather than fight it, she gave in to her fatigue by closing her eyes and then drifting off to sleep.

Later, the sound of a woman's voice outside her bedroom door startled her. "Audrey?"

Disoriented, Audrey lifted her head from the pillow.

Next came a soft knocking. The cat jumped down from the bed and padded to the door, listening. "Audrey? It's Sophia, Logan's fiancée. Are you okay in there?"

Audrey shook out the cobwebs from her head and glanced at the clock. It was after seven! She scrambled off the bed and strode to open the door. Audrey faced a stunning woman dressed in a summery, soft peach, spaghetti-strapped dress. She had long flowing dark hair, amber eyes and skin that could have been kissed by a Mediterranean sun. "Oh, hi."

"Hello. I'm sorry if I interrupted your sleep."

Audrey's hand flew to her disheveled hair that had come loose from the rubber band. Some people had hat hair. Audrey had bed hair and she could only imagine what the tangled mess sitting atop her head looked like right now. She wasn't brave enough to glance in the mirror. She straightened out a few wrinkles in her clothes for what it was worth. "I usually never sleep in the afternoon."

The woman smiled. "I'm Sophia."

"Audrey Faith Thomas. But everyone calls me Audrey." She stuck out her hand and instead of a shake, Sophia wrapped both hands over hers and gave a little squeeze.

"It's nice to meet you."

"Did I miss dinner?"

"Not at all," Sophia said. "Luke got a little worried when you didn't come down so I offered to check on you."

"I'm fine, just a little more tired than usual. Sorry to delay the meal." Audrey opened the door wider. "Come in. I just want to put a brush to this mop."

Sophia stepped into the room and Audrey rummaged around until she came up with her hairbrush. "I didn't bring too many clothes with me. My friend's sending my things from Reno, but unfortunately, for now, what you see is what you get."

"There's nothing wrong with the way you look," Sophia said. "Dinner is pretty casual at the Slades' these days."

She immediately liked Logan's fiancée. She was honest and didn't try to convince Audrey that she looked perfect or wonderful or beautiful, although Sophia was every single one of those things. "Congratulations on your engagement."

"Thank you. Logan's a pretty great guy." Sophia's lips curved into a mischievous smile. "Except when he wasn't."

Audrey laughed. "I hear you. Luke told me that you once hated each other."

"Hate's a strong word. And it was mostly him being stubborn, but we've gotten past that now. We're very much in love."

"Sounds nice. Like you two were meant for each other."

"I think we were. We've worked through our difficulties and now we're getting married. Honestly, I never thought this day would come."

Audrey sighed as she combed through her hair, battling with a knot here and there. She and Luke didn't have any difficulties. He didn't regard her as anything but a longtime friend. There was no great passion, no love/hate relationship. He'd kissed her today, just a peck on the lips, but it had still been glorious, and Audrey was ready for more. Yet his only reaction had been to apologize.

He didn't remember he'd made love to her. The memory constantly bounced in and out of her brain. It hurt like hell. And reminded her daily what a hopeless case she was.

Starting at the top of her head, she pushed both hands through her hair and roped the mane at the nape of her neck with a rubber band. Her mass of blond curls tapered into a ponytail that reached the middle of her back. "There."

"You have beautiful hair," Sophia said.

"Thanks, but it's a bit long. I've been thinking of having it cut."

"I know of a good hair salon in town when you decide."

"That would be great."

They walked to the kitchen together, and Audrey's steps lightened as she spoke with Sophia Montrose. She was genuinely nice and put Audrey at ease. She shared a little bit about how she'd come to Sunset Ranch in the first place. Sophia had led a very intriguing life before she settled here with Logan. Audrey was eager to hear more, but when they reached the kitchen, the conversation ended. Two gorgeous Slade men sitting at the kitchen table rose from their seats when they walked in. It was a sweet gesture women didn't see very often anymore.

Her gaze locked onto Luke and she met with his bluer than blue eyes. Heart hammering, her breaths came quick. She cursed silently and struggled to quell her jittery nerves.

"There they are," Logan said as he walked over to her. "Good to see you again, Audrey." He gave her a hug and then flashed a brilliant smile. He was a dark-haired, dark-eyed version of Luke, and just as devilishly handsome.

"It's good to see you, too."

"Pip-squeak's going on twenty-five. Can you believe it?" Luke intervened.

"Tell me he doesn't call you that," Logan said.

Audrey would have been mortified if she didn't know Luke was just poking fun. Luke had never called her that. When Casey would, Luke would tell him to show some respect. She sent Luke her fiercest glare. "Not if he wants to live to tell about it."

Luke busted out laughing. "She means it, too." He winked at her, just like he did when she was a kid.

Logan took Sophia by the hand and drew her into his arms. "I see you met my soon-to-be wife." He kissed her cheek. "You two get acquainted?"

"We did, a little." Sophia glanced at her with warmth in her eyes.

Audrey smiled back.

"Are you ready to sit down to eat?" Sophia asked. "I made paella Valenciana. I hope you like it, Audrey. It's my mother's recipe and Logan loves it."

"It's one of my favorites, too," Luke said. "I can't wait to dig in."

"It smells delicious," Audrey said. The flavorful scent of saffron and spices rose up to tickle her senses. She peeked at the concoction on the stove. A mixture of vegetables, rice, tomatoes and what looked like pork pieces filled a cast-iron skillet. "Can I help?"

"Sure," Sophia said. "Why don't you help me dish it into the plates and serve?"

"I'd love to do that." Audrey was glad to work beside Sophia in the kitchen. It made her feel like part of a family, like she belonged.

Audrey filled the plates for Luke and herself and set them onto the table while Sophia portioned out enough for her and Logan. "Audrey, if you could toss the salad, I'll put the bread on the table."

"I'd be happy to." Audrey took hold of the teak salad bowl and used the utensils to give the ingredients several good tosses. Once it was ready, she brought the salad over to the table set with earthen stoneware and very simple stainless-steel cutlery.

Luke opened a bottle of red wine. "Paella goes down easy with merlot." He poured wine into all four goblets and everyone took their seats. Sophia sat next to Logan, which left Audrey to sit beside Luke.

It wasn't a hardship being close to Luke. Somewhere between the paella and a half a glass of wine during the meal, her heartbeats had slowed to normal. The conversation was lively as she became better acquainted with the Slades and Sophia. She'd learned about Sophia and Luke's tight friendship as children and how Logan had felt left out and jealous about it. Sophia didn't go much further into detail but it was something Audrey was curious about. She planned on finding out more one day if Sophia was willing to share the information.

What a sucker she was. Or was she a glutton for punishment? Everything about Luke's life outside the rodeo fascinated her.

"Luke's still my best friend," Sophia said. Logan gave her a nod of approval. "And I hear he was like a big brother to you, too, Audrey."

Audrey gulped the last drop of her wine. Not the brother thing again. Mercy, she was tired of it, but Sophia was just making polite conversation and couldn't possibly know how much Audrey hated the subject, so she answered her with equal politeness. "Yes, when Casey wasn't around, Luke watched out for me."

She glanced at Luke and found him staring, his gaze focused and piercing. Was he remembering that night when he'd rescued her by the bonfire? The night he'd nearly flattened Judd Calhoon on her behalf. Was he remembering all the other times he'd been there for her? His eyes stayed on hers for a few long moments and then swept down to her mouth. Heat curled in her belly and a memory flashed of that nothing-yet-everything kiss from this afternoon.

"My brother is the Goody Two-shoes in the family," Logan said. "In this case, I'm glad he watched out for you two ladies."

"Hey," Luke said. "If a beautiful woman needs my help, I'm there."

A moment ticked by. Then it hit Audrey. Luke had called her beautiful.

Good gracious. She had to stop banking on his every word. It wasn't the first time he'd paid her a compliment. He was Mr. Nice Guy, she reminded herself.

After dinner, they had a second glass of wine, and though the men offered to help with the cleanup , Sophia shooed them into the family room to watch the baseball game.

"The paella was delicious," Audrey said, bringing the empty dishes to the counter next to the sink.

"Thank you. I'll share the recipe with you if you'd like."

"I would love that. I just don't know when I'd have time to try it out. Once my job is done here, I'll be starting veterinarian school again."

"Luke told us what you did for your brother when he broke his back. You dropped out of school to care for him."

"Casey needed me. I wouldn't have it any other way. He's done so much for me and it was the least I could do for him. Of course, I'd hate for him to hear me say that…he and I butt heads a lot."

Sophia rinsed the plates and nodded. "That's what family is all about." A hint of longing touched her voice. "I never had a brother or sister to butt heads with. Maybe that's why Luke and I became such good friends." Sophia was thoughtful for a few seconds, her gaze going somewhere distant. "My mother and I were very close, too. I miss her terribly."

Audrey understood great loss, yet she didn't know her folks enough to miss them with the kind of intensity she saw in Sophia's eyes. More like, Audrey missed the idea of her parents. She missed big Sunday dinners and Christmas mornings and having a mother to come home to after school, offering snacks and hugs. She missed having a father to teach her to ride a bike and kiss her forehead when she did her chores properly.

"I'm sorry to hear about your mother, Sophia. I didn't know my mom. She died when I was a baby, and shortly after, my father married Casey's mom. But we lost both of them in a horrible tornado that passed through our town in Oklahoma just a few years later. It touched down and swept away everything in its path over one square mile."

"Oh, that's awful," Sophia said, her eyes widening with horror.

It was the same incredulous reaction Audrey got when she

explained the circumstances of the tragedy to others. Usually she didn't like talking about it.

"How did you escape?"

"Casey and I were playing with friends on the other side of town. The tornado missed us. It's weird, you know. One side of a street could be completely destroyed, and the other could be eerily untouched."

Sympathy touched Sophia's eyes. "I've seen it on the news and always wondered how that could be."

"It was really hard and nightmarish on us, but we managed. We had no choice." Audrey shrugged then. Life had been tough after that, but Casey had always provided for them. He had uncanny talent as a bronc buster and had made more than enough money on the rodeo circuit to keep a roof over their heads and plenty of food on the table. Audrey didn't dwell on the past. She refused to spend her life feeling sorry for herself. "It's been Casey and me ever since."

Sophia smiled as she loaded the last of the dishes into the dishwasher. "I think we have a lot in common, Audrey. It'll be nice having another female living on the ranch again."

"I'm looking forward to it." Audrey really meant it. She'd been unnerved coming here to face Luke. She'd lost her courage in confronting him, but she'd gained something, too. A job and a chance to matter, doing something she loved to do. She was looking forward to working with Trib and the other horses, spending time on the ranch and getting to know Sophia better. "And who knows, we might just diffuse the toxic levels of testosterone around here."

Sophia laughed lightly. "We can certainly try. I think you and I are going to be great friends."

Her heart panged with warmth. She could use a new friend. "Me, too."

"Hey, everyone, I'd like you to meet Katherine Grady. She goes by Kat."

At the sound of Luke's voice, Audrey whirled toward the

kitchen door. A Marilyn Monroe look-alike with platinum-blond hair stood beside him, her wide green eyes fashionably made-up to match her pretty emerald-and-blue outfit. She held on to Luke's arm and darn if Audrey didn't hone right in on that. A flashback of rodeo groupies—pouty pink lips and all—came to mind. Her heart sank. She struggled to keep her expression from taking a nosedive in front of everybody.

"Nice to meet you," Kat said, her voice soft as butter.

Suddenly, Audrey's head clouded up and spun. It was like the time she'd climbed onto the mechanical bull at Dusty's Dancehall in Texas. She'd been sixteen and trying to prove to the guys she wasn't a child. As soon as the bull started bucking, everything in that honky-tonk got blurry real fast. Only this was worse.

The world around her began to fade. Her legs went numb. She reached forward to grip the kitchen counter and missed, scraping her fingernails on the sharp edges. Desperate to hold on, her arms flailed. She needed support. But it was too late.

Blackness surrounded her.

Right before all the lights went out.

Three

Audrey woke to Luke hovering over her. Her body was flattened out on the Slade kitchen floor and her head ached like crazy. She blinked and stared into his concerned eyes as the palm of his hand rested on her hot face. Her cheeks stung, so she figured she'd been slapped a time or two. Relief filled his voice when he spoke to her. "Audrey Faith, you gave us a scare."

She tried to lift her head up. Two Lukes appeared in her line of vision. She blinked one of them away and as she eased back down, Luke's other hand cushioned her head. "How long was I out?" she asked quietly.

"Not long. Does this happen often?" he asked.

"This was the first time," she said, feeling a little bit ridiculous. Four pairs of eyes—including the blonde woman's—ogled her.

"You fainted." Sophia spoke softly, holding a bottle of smelling salt in her hand. "Luke rushed over to you. He got to you before we had to use this. It was just a few seconds."

A few seconds too many, she thought.

"What happened, honey?" Luke asked.

"I'm not sure. I got light-headed. Then everything went black."

"Logan's calling the doctor," Sophia said.

"Oh, no. I don't need a doctor." Audrey made a move to sit up again and when twin Lukes didn't appear, she figured she was good to go. His hand to her back, he helped hinge her forward slowly. "My head's not spinning anymore. I think… it's just…"

What was it? She didn't know why she'd fainted. It couldn't have been because Kat showed up attached to Luke at the hip. She'd seen Luke with other women before. No amount of nose twitching would make them disappear, though. And as a smitten teen, she'd daydream of trading places with the females on his arm. Audrey knew that this time it wasn't Kat's presence that made her see stars.

She'd been overly tired today and a little stressed. A reasonable excuse came to mind. "I might've caught a bug or something."

"Now I'm sorry I woke you up for dinner," Sophia said, her expression grim. "You probably needed your sleep."

Logan entered the room with the phone to his ear. "I can't get hold of the doctor. Maybe we should take her to emergency."

Luke nodded. "Good idea."

"No, it's not necessary." Audrey summoned all of her strength, planted her feet and rose to full height, refusing Luke's extended arm for support. There. She wasn't dizzy anymore. Whatever happened had been freakish, but it had passed. "I feel better already. I think all I need is a good night's sleep. It's a bug and I need to rest. Honestly." She glanced at Logan first, then at Luke, giving him a pointed look. No way was she going to disrupt their evening by going to the hospital. Besides, she really did feel better.

The men darted glances at each other. "What do you think?" Luke said to Logan.

"I'm fine," she said a little more firmly.

Logan shrugged. "She looks fine, Luke."

Sophia added, "You can check on her during the night, Luke."

Kat, who had been quiet throughout this exchange, raised a perfectly arched brow at that.

"You sure you're feeling okay?" Luke asked, his genuine concern touching something deep and lasting in her heart. As if she needed another reason to worship him.

She nodded, did a pirouette right in the middle of the kitchen—ending with a flourish a gymnast would be proud of—and gave him a big smile. "I promise I'm okay."

"As long as I've got your promise, we're good. I'll walk you to your room."

She wanted to protest. She could walk to her own room, for heaven's sake, but the envious look in Kat Whoever-she-was's eyes made her accept his invitation. "Sure."

She turned to Sophia and Logan, giving them each a big hug. And then, magnanimously, she put out her hand to Kat. "So good to meet you," she said, as if she hadn't just made a spectacle of herself by fainting.

"I hope you're feeling better soon." Kat cupped her hand and gave a little squeeze.

Audrey's gaze shifted to her white knight. "If Luke has anything to say about it, I will."

The comment flew over the men's heads, but Sophia had a glint in her eye as Luke walked Audrey out of the kitchen.

Once they reached her bedroom, Luke turned the knob and opened the door. "I'll check in on you later."

"Not necessary, really."

"I'm gonna insist, Audrey."

She didn't like the idea of Luke coming to her room during the night. Well, okay, she would like the idea if his motives were different. Regardless of his friendship with Casey, she wasn't his obligation. She could fend for herself. He didn't need to lose sleep over her.

When she paused for a moment he added, "Your welfare is my responsibility as long as you're under my roof. You fainted tonight. We don't know why."

"I told you why."

"You're guessing, but you don't know for sure."

He wasn't letting this drop. Mr. Nice Guy was also a Good Samaritan.

An idea popped into her head. "How about if you text me?"

He chuckled from deep in his throat and a boyish gleam lit his eyes. "You're sleeping three doors down."

"It could be fun. And you don't have to be disturbed."

Luke rolled his eyes. "Fine, I'll text you. I've got your number."

"Great. Well then, good night."

"Sleep tight, Audrey."

After closing the door to Luke, her lungs released a whoosh of air, and she slumped against the door as the last bit of her energy seeped out. She was more tired than she'd let on to the Slades. She'd never fainted before. What was that all about? She chalked it up to emotional angst seeing Luke again. By all rights she should feel exhausted after the highs and lows she experienced today. The lowest was finding out that Luke had no memory of their night together. That had been a crushing blow, and she hadn't been allowed time to absorb the implications and heal her wounded heart and deflated ego.

Audrey undressed with deliberately slow moves, carefully peeling off her clothes. No sense tempting fate. A sudden move here or there and she might find herself on the floor again without a dashing prince to awaken her.

She hung up her blouse in a double-wide closet and folded her jeans in half, putting them across a captain's chair in the corner of the room. She washed her face and brushed her teeth, then climbed into bed, giving Jewel a little nudge. "Why aren't you a curl-up kind of cat?"

The cat was stretched out, taking up most of the width of the bed, and the prod moved her only enough to give Audrey room to climb in. She sank into the comfort awarded her in that small space. She picked up the remote control and clicked on the television. Mindless babbling might just comfort her to sleep tonight. She settled on a reality show that Susanna constantly raved about. Her friend, the reality-show junkie, watched them all and had recommended this one specifically for Audrey.

"Wannabes and Wranglers," Audrey mumbled, sinking into the pillow.

The first ten minutes entertained her enough to keep watching the city slickers trying to replicate life in a mock-up Western town. Poor John Wannabe was having trouble saddling up his horse. He got the cinch all wrong and the saddle might have slipped off if it weren't for Wrangler Beth, who'd come to the rescue. They were teamed up for a series of challenges and it was Beth's job to turn John into a horseman in less than two months. John was halfway into his on-camera, heartfelt confession explaining how Beth made him nervous because she was so beautiful when Audrey's cell phone barked. The *ruff-ruff* ringtone had Jewel lifting her head sharply to listen. "It's just a text," she explained to her cat.

She picked up her phone from the nightstand and read Luke's message.

Are you sleeping yet?

She punched in an answer.

Obviously not.

What are you doing?

Watching *Wannabes and Wranglers*. I'm fine.

A few seconds later, another text came through.

Glad you're fine. I'm watching that, too.

Really? Luke watched reality shows? She found that hard to believe.

Because Beth is so hot?

It only took a few seconds for Luke to respond.

Yes.

Then a few moments later:

But I like the concept, too.

What do you think of John?

she texted, closing her eyes briefly after typing in the question.
His next text came instantly.

Not a fast learner.

Audrey smiled as she punched in her reply.

He's distracted by Beth.

So am I. She knows her way around a stallion.

Hardy, har-har. Look, John finally got the horse saddled right. Beth's teaching him how to mount.

That should come naturally to a man.

Was he teasing? She immediately wrote back,

A woman, too, if the stallion's worthy.

An image flashed through her mind of her mounting Luke
and taking them both for a sweet ride. His hips had arched
and he'd bucked from underneath, meeting her every stride
with a fierceness that penetrated her body and soul. The notion layered through her belly in warm waves.

His next text came through.

Mounting a horse, I meant.

Right. You don't fool me, Luke.

I never did. You almost ready to turn in?

Yes. Go to sleep. I'm fine.

Lights out.

I've already done that once tonight.

Funny. Wake me if you need me, Audrey.

That was a loaded comment and a dozen *needs* regarding
Luke flitted through her mind.

Night, Luke.

Night.

Well, it wasn't text sex or anything close, but Audrey
turned off the television and fell fast asleep with a big smile
on her face.

* * *

At seven o'clock the next morning, Audrey was greeted with another text from Luke.

Are you up yet?

She was never one to sleep late.

Up and dressed,

she keyed into the phone and then added,

Feeling fine.

Not five seconds later, Luke was knocking on her bedroom door. "That was fast," she muttered, tossing her phone down on the bed to pull the door open.

He leaned against the door frame, eyeing her from top to bottom, doing a clean sweep and making her wish she'd had something to wear besides her faded jeans and oversize shirt. At least she'd managed to put a comb through her hair and pull it back into a ponytail.

Luke came to her freshly shaven, with that same hint of lime wafting in the air, his longish clean hair curling at the ends. One strand slashed across his forehead to rest on his brow. Audrey mentally sighed. The crisp tight fit of his jeans and snug hug of a dark blue canvas shirt were enough to still her heart. "Mornin'."

"Hi."

"Sleep well?"

"Very well." It was no lie.

"No fainting spells today?"

"None, and I feel great."

Luke's lips twisted downward. "Do me a favor and don't do that again."

"You don't have to keep checking on me."

"I came to deliver a message. Breakfast is ready. Cereal and toast. *Unless...*"

"Unless...I cook up something better?"

"You *can* stir a pot and I'm hungry."

"When are you not? How does bacon and eggs over easy sound?"

"Throw in half a dozen buttermilk pancakes and we've got a deal."

"Okay, but only if you admit you opened my door last night to peek in on me."

He crossed his arms over his chest and planted his feet firmly. "I'm admitting nothing."

"What kind of cereal do you want?"

Luke's shoulders drooped and he sighed. "Okay, fine. I peeked in on you."

Food blackmail always worked.

"I slept better knowing Casey's little sister was sleeping soundly."

She did a mental eye roll. How old did she have to be before Luke stopped thinking of her as Casey's younger sister? "You make the coffee...I'm assuming you know how...and I'll get to work on the rest."

"It's a deal."

The cat jumped down from the bed, took a long stretch and strode over to Luke. She rubbed her body along his legs and bowed her back like a rainbow, purring loudly. Audrey could take a lesson or two in flirting from her cat.

Luke bent to scratch her under the chin. "I think it's time Miss Jewel got out of this room."

"I agree. I was going to ask if it's okay if she roams around the ranch today."

"Yeah, no problem. She's probably smart enough to stay out of trouble."

"She's only used up one of her nine lives. She's got eight more to go."

With that, they headed to the kitchen. During breakfast, Luke mentioned Kat again and Audrey asked him about her. "She's just a friend" was all he said with a shrug of the shoulder.

Audrey figured the woman would never forget her, though. She'd made a lasting impression. How many people fainted the second they were introduced?

After breakfast, Luke gave her a grand tour of the ranch and explained her duties as wrangler. She was to groom and exercise the horses, make sure they were fed properly and assist the head wrangler, Ward Halliday. They wouldn't be working with Trib today, and that was fine with her because she had some shopping to do in town when she finished up her duties.

Luke left her in the barn with Hunter Halliday, Ward's son, who was leaving for college in a few weeks. The big, strapping boy with a friendly smile showed her around the barn and introduced her to each one of the ranch hands during the course of the day. They were nice men who spoke politely and had nothing but respect for the horses on the property.

"We don't sell a horse every day," Hunter said. "Sometimes, only one or two a week, but once they go, you miss them. It's best if you ride them and train them and try not to get close to them. The Slades take care with who they sell a horse to. You gotta tell yourself they're going to a good home."

Hunter used a currycomb on the mare he was grooming while Audrey stood up on a footstool and braided a thoroughbred's mane, something she'd learned to do when she was thirteen. "I volunteer at a horse rescue at home. I know it's not easy saying goodbye."

Hunter nodded.

They worked together on the horses into the morning. Jewel pretty much stayed by her side in the barn, sitting up regally and taking swipes at the flies buzzing around her head. It seemed to keep her entertained. And for the remainder of the morning, they took horses out that hadn't been exercised yesterday. Hunter showed her different paths to follow and made sure the horses got a good workout before they switched them out. More grooming followed and by midafternoon their work was done.

Audrey's clothes stuck to her body and the skin exposed to the hot sun was layered with a fine coating of trail dust. Her mouth could spit cotton, as Casey would say, and her bones ached a little, but she'd never been happier.

She was in her element.

After her work was done, she hummed her way back to the house with Jewel in her arms. "You earned your keep today," she said. "Those dang flies didn't stand a chance."

The shower she took was quick and efficient, cleansing her body of barn grime, and within minutes, Audrey was clean and ready to go.

She had a shopping date with Sophia this afternoon.

"Sophia, I can't possibly wear all of these things." Draped over Audrey's arms and threatening to topple her were two pairs of slacks, three pairs of designer jeans, four blouses, a stylish leather jacket and, so that all was not lost, a skimpy cherry-red thong swimsuit that Audrey wouldn't think of ever wearing out in public.

"Nonsense," Sophia said, eyeing another item from the rack in Sunset Lodge's gift shop. "You can't have too many clothes." Sophia added a pair of white studded jeans to the pile dangling from her arms. "They're a gift from Logan, Luke and me."

"Do they know about this?"

Sophia's chuckle came out warm and friendly. "They give me carte blanche with the gift shop. Neither one of them has ever had anything to do with it."

Audrey understood why. The place was a virtual one-stop shop with classic designer items like sequined evening bags, ladies apparel and jewelry that fit with the Western theme of Sunset Ranch. Over in the corner was one small shelf stacked with men's shirts that were manly enough for any cowboy to wear. Everything was tastefully displayed and organized to appeal to the eye. In short, Sophia's stamp of approval was written all over it.

"This is very sweet of you," Audrey said, humbled by her generosity.

"It's my pleasure. I think you've got some things that'll dazzle."

"Yeah, the horses at the barn are gonna love me in them."

Sophia smiled and began searching the shop further. What could she possibly add to this wardrobe?

"No, I wasn't thinking about the horses," Sophia said. "Here, let me take those from you." She scooped her arms under the pile weighing Audrey down and carried the clothes to the counter by the cash register. "I'll put them aside and have them wrapped for you. After I take you on a tour of the lodge, we can swing by here and pick them up."

"Thank you." Audrey didn't have words enough to express her gratitude.

Sophia spoke to a young girl assisting behind the counter and then they exited the shop. Sophia guided her into the lobby, past the massive stone fireplace that greeted every guest who entered the lodge. Wood beams overhead and sandstone floors and comfortable sitting areas were set off by big windows and a natural elegantly rustic setting.

"I don't remember ever coming here. I've only been to the ranch a few times when I was younger but we never stopped by the lodge. This is a beautiful spot. It's got a rural feel, but it's up-to-date, too. I like the combination of old and new."

"I know what you mean. My mother used to manage the lodge when I was a kid. She was proud to work here."

"I can see why."

"I'm glad I came back. A part of me never left," Sophia said, her eyes darkening with memories.

It was the opening Audrey needed to ask a question that had been burning inside. It was none of her beeswax, but that didn't stop her. She had a compelling desire to learn about the Slades, Luke in particular.

"And Logan wasn't happy about it initially?"

"No, he wasn't thrilled when I showed up here. He and I had prior history going back to our childhood and he resented me inheriting half ownership of the lodge from the Slades. His father…well, Randall Slade was more than generous with me. It's no secret," she said as they stopped by a large picture window that overlooked the grounds, "that I loved living at Sunset Ranch. I grew up here, but things got complicated for my mom and we moved away. It wasn't until I came back that I was forced to confront Logan and my feelings for him. After fighting with each other and holding back our feelings, we finally saw that we were meant to be together. We put the past behind us and it's stayed there. And through it all, Luke and I remained good friends."

"Were you and Luke…ever, uh—"

Audrey was dying to know. Had there been a heated love triangle among the Slade brothers and Sophia?

Sophia's head tilted with a negative shake. "Never. We don't think of each other that way. He's my friend. I'm his friend. It's never been anything more."

It was hard to believe. How could anyone be that close to Luke and not fall madly in love with him? Was she the only hopeless case around here?

They walked to the kitchen and Sophia introduced her to Constance, young Edward's grandmother, who was the head chef. She and the rest of the staff were busy preparing for the dinner meal. "I've met your grandson. He's a nice boy," she said.

"Thank you. I think so, too." Constance's warm smile told

Audrey that Edward was the apple of her eye. "Here, give this a try. I'm not sure it's quite right." She handed each one of them a pastry glazed with chocolate. "Tell me what you think. There's mocha crème filling inside."

Audrey took a bite and chocolate cream squirted into her mouth, hitting all the right sensory points. Her reaction was immediate and honest. "Yummy."

Sophia nodded, too, as she chewed. They were in agreement.

"That's what I was hoping to hear," Constance said.

After chatting and testing two more samples, they left the kitchen to head toward the stables. "These horses are for the guests," Sophia explained. "Hunter and Ward oversee their care as well as the horses at the ranch. We give guided tours and have hayrides and horseback-riding lessons. Most people who come here want to ride in some way or another."

Audrey had a chance to meet the horses that weren't already out with guests and bond a little with each one. A softly spoken word, a pat on the head or an affectionate nuzzle went a long way with animals.

"You're welcome anytime to hang out with them. I'm sure Ward would welcome it," Sophia said. "As you can see, they're gentle and sweet. We worry that sometimes they don't get enough attention."

"I'll visit them as often as I can." She stroked a palomino on the side of her face, looking into her warm brown eyes, and knew they would be fast friends.

A few minutes later, they returned for the clothes at the gift shop. Audrey was ready to put the packages in her pickup truck and give her thanks once again. Before she got the words out, Sophia tilted her head thoughtfully with a smile on her lips. "Logan and I are having a little engagement party next week. We'd love it if you joined us."

"You're inviting me to your engagement party?"

"Yes, it's for family and close friends. Please say you'll come."

Touched by the invitation, Audrey's heart warmed. "Oh, I... Of course. Thank you for including me. Just tell me where and when and I'll be there."

"I'll be sure to do that. I'll call you tonight."

"Okay." Audrey was almost out the door with the packages when Sophia called out. "Wait! I forgot this. I have one more thing for you."

Audrey's eyes grew wide when she saw what Sophia had in her hand. "You... I can't... What am I going to do with that?"

"Isn't it beautiful?" she asked, her voice sweetly determined.

"It's gorgeous, but I sleep in an old T-shirt."

Sophia's eyes lit with amusement. "When you're alone, yes. But this is for that someone special."

The black negligee spoke of hot, raw, wicked sex. It wasn't your grandmother's negligee, she thought, and then laughed at the notion of grandmothers and hot sex. Where had her mind drifted? This nightie was cut low on the bosom, high on the thigh and was woven with intricate, peek-a-boo lace. It said *do me* in a hundred different languages. "I don't have someone special."

Sophia ignored her and boxed the negligee herself, giving it a light tap with the flat of her hands. "I think there's someone special for you on this ranch. I've seen the way you look at Luke."

"Luke?" She gulped air. Was she busted? "Luke and I aren't...anything. I mean...sure, he's been my brother's friend for ages, but—"

But what? She wasn't ready to divulge her secret to anyone, much less Luke's best friend. Oddly, Sophia didn't pry. She didn't try to get any further explanation out of her. She listened and nodded and then placed the box in her arms.

She had an uncanny feeling that Sophia Montrose was

wiser than her years. The alternative was that Audrey wasn't fooling anyone about her feelings for Luke. She preferred to think Sophia had especially sharp perception. "Please accept this as my personal gift to you."

"It's very kind of you."

"Wear it well and knock his socks off."

"I'm not knocking anyone's socks off," she said mildly, but her throat caught with the comment as an image of making love to Luke in that negligee popped into her head.

Sophia shrugged. "Then someone like Kat Grady might just turn Luke's head."

"I—I wouldn't know," she said, feeling glum. "I've only been upright about ten seconds in her presence."

Sophia's gaze stayed on her and a little smile emerged. "Luke was worried about you all evening."

"He feels responsible for me."

"He likes you."

"He thinks of me as a younger sister."

"Men can change their minds in the blink of an eye."

She was speaking of her experience with Logan. He'd hated Sophia and hadn't wanted her at the ranch. The irony wasn't lost on Audrey. She had the opposite problem. Luke had always liked her and had made her feel welcome here, giving her a job and offering his friendship. In a weird and crazy way, she had just as high a mountain to climb to make Luke look at her differently as Sophia had with Logan. "Who is Kat, anyway?"

Sophia shrugged one shoulder. "I don't know much about her. She's new to the county and settled in the next town, Silver Springs."

"She's very pretty, in a flashy sort of way," Audrey said.

"Luke's seen her a few times, but he won't get serious about her. She's got a little baby."

"That doesn't sound like Luke. I thought he liked kids."

"He loves kids. You see how he is with Edward. But he

doesn't want to start up something he can't finish, and getting involved with a single mother could hurt her little boy when it ended."

"How is he so sure it would end?"

"That you'd have to ask Luke about. But I will tell you that he's got this thing about long-term relationships. He says he'll know pretty quickly when it's right, and so far, that hasn't happened. He's usually the first one to walk away."

Audrey didn't want to read too much into it, because hope that faltered and died was worse than no hope at all. And Luke had topped her No Hope list for a long time. If she dared to hope, she could come out scarred for life, but then, wasn't that the whole reason she took the job here? To have some sort of chance with Luke? Sophia knew Luke better than anyone. Didn't she? And she seemed to be encouraging Audrey to muster up, dig in her heels and make a stand.

Yet, deep down she didn't think Luke would ever see her as anything but a friend. Maybe he thought of her in the same way he thought of Sophia. There was a line he wouldn't cross with their friendship. Just like the line he refused to cross with the Grady woman.

Oh, who was she kidding?

Audrey, you are making excuses for your cowardice.

It was true. She was a coward.

She hadn't fessed up to Luke about seducing him and then running off like a frightened juvenile. She hadn't spilled the truth to him when she'd first arrived at the ranch. She hadn't been brave enough to look into Luke's trusting blue eyes and tell him what she'd done or why she'd done it. There'd been a few really good opportunities to bring up the subject, like when Luke had accidentally kissed her or when he'd come to her bedroom door this morning to check on her.

"And you think I'm right for Luke?"

Sophia gave her shoulder a lift and Audrey held her breath waiting for her reply. What would be worse, if Sophia said no or if she said yes? "You could be. But if you don't give it a chance, you'll never know."

Sort of like, if you don't try, you can't fail, but then you're left with years of wondering what if. "Thank you for the beautiful negligee." And for the nudge that had her convinced she may lose her chance with Luke if she didn't act fast. Luke was eligible, handsome and a great guy. He was like a marked target and another Kat might come along and hit the bull's-eye if she wasn't careful. Audrey made a silent, determined vow to speak with Luke soon. Her cowardly days were numbered. "I, uh…I owe you."

Sophia laid a hand on her arm. Audrey valued the comfort and friendship offered. "I'm happy to do it. And you don't owe me a thing." Then a delicious twinkle brightened Sophia's eyes and she added, "But Luke might, one day."

Four

Luke watched Audrey from a short distance away from Trib's paddock. As long as she stayed on her side of the half door, she'd be safe.

"He sees you, Luke. Back up a bit."

Luke leaned against the shaded, wide double door of the barn. If he stepped any farther back, beams of sunlight flowing inside would get in his eyes and not allow him to see a thing. "This is as far as I'm going, Audrey. Deal with it."

Audrey turned to him. Honey-gold strands of hair bunched under her felt hat escaped their confinement and streaked across cheeks reddened by frustration. She kept her tone light, but hissed the words through barely parted lips. "You're not helping. He's wary. Two of us here is hard for him to take right now."

He answered her by crossing his arms over his chest.

Jutting her lower lip out, she blew the strands of hair off her face and whirled back around, giving him a pretty spectacular view of her backside. He grinned at the sequins forming twin diamond shapes on the pockets covering the firm mounds of her butt. She'd grumbled about the designer jeans all the way out here, but Luke thought they looked great on her. So did the tank top tucked inside, with the words *Cowgirls Know How to Ride* printed in hot pink on the front.

A strange fleeting jab affected him. His mind took a journey in search of something…something teetering on the edge of his memory. Something he couldn't put his finger on. But at odd moments like this, while focused on Audrey's sweet derriere, bizarre met with bewilderment in his head.

The same thing had happened when he'd kissed her the other day and he'd plagued his mind for the answer to a question he couldn't even fathom.

Weird.

Audrey used sweet, soothing words on the stallion. Her voice took on the tone of a lulling siren trying to coax Trib away from the back wall of his stable. Luke could easily fall victim to that melodic sweet tone. He absorbed the sound that calmed his own jittery nerves. Audrey was the best at patience and consistency. She earned trust. But it took time. She was hoping for a sign from the stallion. One step toward her would mean progress. Yet, the horse remained rooted to the spot, unyielding. His snorts were pensive and muted, like the quiet before the storm. Luke had been fooled by Trib once. He wouldn't let Audrey suffer the consequences of Trib's explosive temper.

"Luke, he won't come over to me with you standing there."

"You're losing your touch, Audrey." Such a lie.

"You're being unreasonable. Go away."

"I'll think about it tomorrow, Audrey. We should get going now."

"We just got here. You go. I'll stay."

Luke walked over to her. "He's in a mood today. You're not getting anywhere with him."

"Let me be the judge of that. If you leave, I promise I'll be right behind you in five minutes."

He shook his head.

"Five minutes, Luke." Her pretty eyes beseeched him.

He considered it for all of twenty seconds. Audrey's unfaltering gaze stayed homed in on his and it was all he could to do to stick to his guns.

"Not today. Don't rush it."

"I'm not rushing it. But I won't make progress unless you give me some leeway."

"Not at the expense of your safety."

"The stable is sturdy, right? The walls are intact. I'm not planning on going inside the stall."

"Damn straight you're not." In a second he'd lose his cool. He didn't have the patience of a saint and he was used to his employees obeying his orders. He glanced at his watch. "Crap. I'm running late. I've gotta go."

"Got a hot date or something?" Her face flamed with indignation. "Is that why you won't let me do my job?"

"Yes, I have a date." And he wasn't looking forward to it. Kat had pretty much insisted he come over for dinner tonight as a thank-you for helping sort through old stable gear, reins, bits and saddles at Matilda Applegate's run-down little homestead in Silver Springs. Kat had moved in to care for the older woman, who was recovering from a heart attack, and had made it her mission to straighten out the place.

The first time Luke met Kat, she'd been loaded down with grocery bags, hanging onto a sweet-looking little baby boy named Connor and all of his diaper gear. Luke had offered his help and they got to talking afterward. He learned that the boy's father was a marine who'd died overseas, and the man's aunt, Matilda Applegate, was Connor's only living relative. Kat didn't like talking about her loss and he hadn't pried, figuring the subject was taboo and probably extremely painful. Luke should have steered clear then, because the last thing Kat needed was another heartache in her life, so now he had some hard thinking to do. She was beautiful and nice, but there were no sparks.

An image flashed of the blonde mystery woman riding atop him, sucking every last drop of juice from his body. He should have forgotten about her by now, but memories of that night kept playing over and over in his mind.

Audrey's stomping brought him back to the moment. She marched away from the paddock, into the late-afternoon sunshine and kept on going, breezing by him like he wasn't even there. "Fine, Luke. Just fine."

"Don't go getting your spurs in a tangle," he said, following behind.

Her hands flew up and waved in the air and the hat on her head released a few more golden tendrils of hair as she pounded the earth to get away from him. "Just go on your date, Luke. Have fun," she spat out.

She was pissed. She felt that he wouldn't let her do her job. On some level he got that. But he had to watch out for her. There was no sense trying to reason with her right now. Audrey's mind was made up. He was beginning to sympathize with Casey a little bit more. It wasn't easy being responsible for someone else.

Audrey threw up in the toilet bowl. The queasiness came on suddenly when she walked into her bedroom. She had just enough time to make it to the bathroom. "Mercy." She leaned against the wall afterward, holding her pulsating stomach and waiting for it to settle. Thankfully, the slight tremors ebbed after a few minutes and she tossed off her clothes to step into the shower.

She wasn't prone to upsets like this. She'd always had a cast-iron stomach. Casey said she took after their dad. He could eat ice cream and pizza in the morning without any rebellion.

The warming rain of the water eased her agitated nerves. Her body had shaken so badly after her fight with Luke that she'd felt the effects way down in her belly. It had throbbed with anger and frustration. He'd treated her like a child today. He didn't give her the trust she'd needed. He'd been stubborn and bossy, just like Casey. She didn't want to trade one demanding overseer for another. What was the point in that?

And then he'd thrown the final punch to her gut. Katherine.

The thought of Luke with Kat Grady had made her stomach ache. She couldn't hide it, so she'd made a mad dash out of the barn. Thankfully, he'd let her go and hadn't questioned her.

Her stomach seemed fine now, but her heart was another matter. She couldn't bank her jealousy. It was crazy. She hadn't seen Luke for years. He'd probably had dozens of girlfriends, gone on hundreds of dates since his rodeo days.

But you're here now...and have to witness it.

Audrey threw herself into unpacking the boxes from Susanna that had arrived today.

As she lifted one item after another, her tummy was soothed at seeing her familiar things. She put away a few pairs of delicately worn jeans, some blouses, her favorite white cotton undies and bra, a framed picture of Susanna and her in high school and another of Casey and Luke with her as a very young girl standing between them. Then she came to the only photo she had of her mother and father, which was laminated and wrapped in a plastic bag for protection. It was wallet-size and tearing at the edges. The picture always made Audrey long for something that was long since gone—a true family. She hugged the photo to her chest and closed her eyes. The pain of their loss was never far from her mind.

She put that picture in her underwear drawer, on the top and to the side, to keep it from getting crumpled, and then set the other frames atop the dresser, one on each end.

Susanna was a good friend. She knew what Audrey needed.

She'd also sent along Jewel's favorite water bowl and feeding dish along with kitty treats and cat toys. "You are good to go now," she said, tossing Jewel a mouse squeak toy that was three-quarters demolished. The cat gave it a swat and then took a chew, fully occupied and purring.

Audrey wouldn't dwell on where Luke was tonight. She skipped her own dinner entirely. Her stomach needed a rest and she didn't trust herself to eat. But her mouth felt dry and her body needed hydration so she took a stroll to the kitchen.

The house was eerily quiet and dark. She flipped on the lights and poured herself a glass of lemonade. And as she sipped the drink, she wandered over to the oak double French doors and gazed out. The moon was in full force, round and shining like a night beacon, streaming light onto the Slade pool. The glistening waters, so still, so tranquil, reflected back with a twinkle of invitation.

"Not tonight," she mumbled. She finished her drink and padded back to her room. Slipping easily into her T-shirt, she sank into the cozy comfort of the bed. She stroked Jewel behind the ear with one hand and clicked on the TV remote control with the other. This was what her life had turned out to be. In bed early, sitting next to her cat and watching TV.

Her phone barked. "Ruff, ruff." Incoming text. It was probably Susanna wanting to know if the box had arrived safely. Grateful for the interruption, she grabbed her phone and read the text message slicing across the screen.

Are you awake?

It was Luke. She glanced at the clock. Nine-thirty. Her heart sped. Was he home this early? She hadn't heard him come in.

Yes. Hot date over already?

There was a long pause before the next message came through.

Nothing hot about it.

You have my sympathy.

Not really. Inside, she was doing backflips.

Are you home?

Sitting out back. Beautiful night.

I know.

Want to join me?

Yes. Yes. Yes. She held her breath and typed.

I'm still mad at you.

I have beer.

Her stomach couldn't handle alcohol.

Will I get an apology?

Another long pause. Audrey may have pushed her luck. She wanted to see Luke, but it couldn't always be on his terms. She had to stand her ground. She was hired to do a job here and Luke was being bullheaded.

Maybe. Could use some company.

The *maybe* was promising, but it was the last part of the text that broke down her anger and ripped into her heart.

Luke needed a friend. He might have had a tough night to-night, for all she knew. After all, he'd come home early. He needed someone to talk to. How could she refuse him that?

She jumped from the bed and donned her clothes, typing in the words that secured her a seat next to him.

I'll be right there.

She sat on a pool chair facing the water and the great pas-tures beyond. Luke sat next to her, sipping beer. For a while, they just sat there quietly, Luke deep in his own thoughts. It was nice knowing he felt comfortable enough with her not to have to make small talk. There was a connection between them that felt right.

After a while, Luke toyed with the bottle he'd just drained, palming it from one hand to the other. "You know," he began, "I've been thinking that I've been a little hard on you."

Audrey sat still, her breath stuck in her throat.

"You know your way around horses and I have to trust in that. It's just that I'm used to worrying over you, and Casey would hang my hide if anything happened to you on my watch. Trib is a perplexing case. He's hard to break and he doesn't trust anyone. I found that out the hard way and I don't want a repeat of my mistake happening to you."

Audrey put resolution in her quiet words. "I understand your concern. But, if anything happened to me, it wouldn't be your fault. I take full responsibility for my actions. You don't have to protect me."

His eyes narrowed and he ran a hand back and forth over his forehead. "I know that, I guess."

"Are you sorry you hired me?"

He gave her a quick, guilty look and took a long time to answer. "No."

She didn't quite believe him. "Then let me do my job."

He began nodding slowly. "Okay, okay. But I want a daily report about your progress."

"Meaning you want to check up on me."

He grinned and then defended his reasoning. "You're like my kid sister."

"I'm not a *kid*. And I'm not your *sister*."

There was force behind her words, and Luke blinked at her tone and then stared at her. "I guess I'm striking out with females today."

Audrey let her frustration drop. She was curious about his date and took that as an opening to bring up the subject. "You had a lukewarm date with good old Katherine?"

Luke focused his gaze on the pasture. He wouldn't look at her. "I broke it off."

She'd been ready to do more mental backflips, but Luke sounded too miserable for her to start celebrating. "What happened?"

He shrugged. "It was never much of anything. We're friendly. We talked tonight and I figured it was best to lay it on the line. It's not in me to pretend something I don't feel. She's nice and all, but something is off.... Can't figure out what that is. And it's serious stuff when a baby is involved. I think mostly she's lonely and a little worried. She's caring for the baby's great-aunt and her health isn't so good."

"How did she take you breaking it off?"

"She said she understood, but I feel like a heel."

"You did the right thing, Luke."

He gave his head a shake. "I couldn't walk in there and pretend to feel something for her I didn't feel. I don't plan on making the same mistakes my folks made."

"Your parents didn't love each other?"

"They did in their own way. But it wasn't the kind of love you build on. There were business reasons for the marriage and then Logan came along and they stuck it out. But my father wasn't happy and when he found the woman who could make him happy, he had to let her go. I think he died regretting it."

Audrey's heart ached for both of his parents. It wasn't the way a woman wanted to be loved. And it wasn't the way a man wanted to love. Halfway. Audrey had enough halves in her own life to know she wanted it all.

This was the first time Luke had confided anything so personal to her. He was feeling low and had wanted her company. As a friend.

She could be that to him any day of the week. She took his hand in hers. They sat there quietly together, comfortable in the silence. "I forgive you, by the way."

Luke smiled. "I didn't apologize."

"Yes, you did. You just don't know it yet."

Audrey had promised Luke she'd be extremely careful working with Trib today. He was off for an day-long business trip to Vegas this morning and she'd seen the concern on his face and question in his eyes before he left. Giving her the freedom she needed troubled him. He felt such responsibility. That was the reason that she hadn't spilled the truth last night. They'd been alone and sharing confidences by the pool. It would have been the perfect time, if Luke hadn't been feeling down. But her news would have sent him over the edge.

At least that's what she told herself.

Dressed and ready for a full day, Audrey waved to Hunter as she made her way into the barn. "Good morning," she said.

"Hi, Audrey. I've got Felicia, Starlight and Melody already turned out in the corral. You want to exercise Belle and Buck and I'll get the others?"

"Sure. I'll do it before it gets too hot for them. You want to ride together this morning?"

"We could do that, surely."

Audrey liked Hunter. He was genuine and good-natured if not a little bit shy. During their rides she got a chance to know him a little better. They had one thing in common, their love of horses. He'd been practically raised on Sunset Ranch; Ward Halliday, his father, had been the head wrangler here for over twenty years. Ward had been a good friend to Randall Slade and every so often Hunter would recite a story from back in the day. The Slade boys weren't angels in their youth and Audrey loved hearing tales of their antics.

After the morning ride, she spent the better part of the day washing down and grooming the horses. Every few hours, she would pay a visit to Trib. She let him see her. She wanted him to know she was there and would be returning time and again. She wanted him to become familiar with her.

"I'm here and I'm coming back soon. Don't you worry," she'd say.

The horse didn't respond, except to look at her with cautious eyes.

Other than Luke, Ward was the only hand allowed to turn him out to his special corral. One day soon, Audrey would do that. She would also ride him.

For now, each time she was about to exit the paddock, she would leave something special for the stallion on the ground. A few sugar cubes. A scoop of oats. A carrot.

She'd walk out of the barn and into the hot Nevada sunshine, putting her ear to the barn door. She'd listen and, after a few minutes, hear Trib wander over and gobble up his treat.

At the end of the day, Audrey entered the Slade home feeling a sense of accomplishment. She hummed through her shower and dressed in her new clothes, leaving her long blond hair down for a change.

Sophia had invited her to the cottage when she found out Luke would be gone for the day. But Audrey suspected Luke had something to do with that invitation. She didn't mind. She liked spending time with Sophia and Logan. The two were a testament to true love.

Dinner was lovely. Sophia was a gracious host. Logan

grilled steaks outside and Sophia and Audrey made side dishes to complement the meal. Afterward, Logan took a rare long-distance phone call from his brother Justin, who was on his last tour of duty in Afghanistan and due to come home soon. The phone call gave her some private time to spend with Sophia.

Sophia was easy to be around. She didn't judge. She was a good listener and Audrey opened up to her about her life on the road with Casey. About her dreams of becoming a veterinarian and how Casey's injury had slowed that down. Sophia encouraged her to pursue her dreams, as long as she was sure of what she truly wanted.

Audrey left the cottage at nine o'clock after thanking the Slades for a wonderful evening. She parked her truck and headed toward the house. The ranch was quietly settled for the night, the sky starless and black, the air heavy with the day's lingering heat. Not even an owl hooted. The horses were sleeping. Only Jewel greeted her at the door, rubbing against her leg and purring as Audrey walked inside. She wasn't entirely alone; the cat was here. As much as she loved Jewel, somehow that wasn't enough. Seeing Logan and Sophia tonight being so much in love and truly in tune with each other left her feeling a little lost.

It was strange. She was happy for them, but pangs of sadness hit her as she walked into the home of the man she loved. Luke wasn't here. She wanted to talk to him. She'd promised to give him a daily update of her work with Trib. She wanted to share with him the little progress she'd made. But more so, she wanted his company. She missed him and didn't want to waste another second of her time here at Sunset Ranch. Sensations of loneliness rippled over her that far outweighed being physically alone in this big house. She felt it deep in her bones and an unwelcome shiver crept up her spine. Sleep wasn't going to happen right now. And she was too darn edgy for mindless television. She needed a lift, a boost to get her out of this peculiar mood.

An idea struck and her lips curled up.

A skinny-dip was out of the question.

But she did have one other option.

Luke texted Audrey on his way home from the airport. She didn't answer. He glanced at his watch. It was after ten. By all rights she should be in bed by now. Everyone who worked the ranch woke at dawn, put in their hours and it was lights-out by nine usually. She must be asleep after having had dinner at the cottage. But he hadn't heard from her today. He knew darn well she'd jump at the chance to work with Trib. It was a hard call for him to make, giving her that freedom, especially when he wasn't going to be around. He'd worried over it at odd times today but gave Audrey credit for being smart with animals. She'd pretty much insisted on it. He hoped like hell nothing had gone wrong.

His mind flashed to the jet-black stallion rearing up on hind legs and stomping down on his body.

He scrubbed his jaw with his free hand and blew out a deep breath as he drove his truck past the ranch gates. He'd never forget the chest-crushing agony he'd endured when the two hooves beat down on him. Luckily, his body had curled up in a defensive position and rolled partway away. The brunt of Trib's horsepower hadn't hit him, or he probably wouldn't be here today.

He bounded from the truck and strode into the house. Nothing stirred. The house was empty but for one wisp of a girl sleeping in her room. Luke strode to the parlor and poured himself a shot of Jim Beam. He sipped his drink and headed to the kitchen to grab a late-night snack. Maybe Sophia had sent Audrey home with leftovers. He could only hope.

A distant sound filtered through an opened inch of the kitchen window. Luke gathered his brows. It sounded like a splash. He strode to the sliding door and gazed out. Only a slice of the moon appeared, not enough to brighten the sky, but lamps by the water's edge illuminated a female figure in the pool. Luke opened the door without making a sound and stepped outside.

His eyes adjusted to the dim light. The figure of a woman in a red thong bikini emerged clearly now. Her back was to him, her feet skimming the shallow steps of the pool. He zeroed in on her derriere and the sliver of cherry material pressed between twin cheeks of firm melon-shaped eye-popping perfection.

A fast flash of recollection jolted through his system, a dropkick of reality. That murky mystifying night at the cabin was beginning to clear. *He knew that body.*

He swallowed silently and shifted his gaze, hoping to find he'd been mistaken. Hoping to hell it was a wicked trick of the eyes. His gaze locked onto coltish and beautifully sculpted legs, glistening with droplets of water.

He shook his head in denial. *It couldn't be.*

But dread knocked into his gut.

He forced his gaze to travel upward, to the flowing blond waves cascading down the woman's back in layers of un-restrained freedom. His body seized up in a viselike grip. Choked with the truth, he couldn't breathe. Flashes of mem-ory brightened, shining revealing light on the mystery.

Those golden locks of hair had tickled his chin.

Those smooth shapely legs had straddled his body.

Those arousing perfect cheeks had caressed his thighs.

His boots ate up the distance to the pool's edge.

She sensed his presence and whirled around to face him.

"It was you." He heard the disbelief rolling off his tongue.

Her eyes widened with fear. She must've thought he was a stranger, but the second she recognized him coming out of the shadows, her expression quickly changed to guilt.

He caught her red-handed and there was no denying it.

"Luke, I…"

"It was you all along," he repeated. "That night in the cabin."

Luke had never really been aware of the grown-up, feminine version of Audrey before. But now, he couldn't help noticing. She was a stunner in that strip-of-nothing swimsuit. There wasn't much more material on the front side of her suit than there was on the back. Her breasts filled and then spilled out of the top. She was every man's fantasy, a freaking advertisement for sexy and untouchable. Except that he had touched her. He'd touched every inch of her body.

The shock of it bore down on him like a two-thousand-pound steer. He was torn between anger at her deception and raw, unequalled lust. How the hell hadn't he figured this out before now? Was it that her work clothes had concealed an hourglass figure that could send a man straight to heaven… or hell, in his case? Or was it that the idea of making love to Audrey would've never crossed his mind? Or was it that he'd shoved the memory of the seduction to the hidden recesses of his mind because *she* wasn't an option?

All three reasons held merit.

"I'm glad you remember now." The bravado in her soft voice stilled his heart.

"That night, you came into my room—"

"My room," she corrected.

"You came to me without hesitation."

She'd climbed into the bed with bold intentions. Luke had taken what she'd offered—a woman who hadn't been shy about what she wanted.

Audrey took one step up from the shallow end of the pool. The scent of Sweet and Wicked drifted to his nose. Beads of water caressed her body. Lamps beat down and glowed over her beautiful, soft skin. He itched to touch her, to untie the top of her suit and fill his hands with the spillage. A tremor of need ran through him.

"You called me over to the bed."

"I didn't know it was you, darlin'."

"I didn't know that," she whispered. "I thought you knew who I was." The softness of her words traveled over his skin.

From what he did remember, she'd pretty much rocked his world that night. In the morning, he'd woken up sated and smiling and ready for round two, but his mystery woman was gone. He was left to wonder who she was. She'd plagued his thoughts ever since.

The whole thing was beyond wrong.

"It was a mistake. It shouldn't have happened," he told her.

"It wasn't a mistake." Her quiet defiance lifted her chin. "It wasn't planned, but it wasn't a mistake."

"Audrey Faith. Look, I know you had a bad breakup and that you weren't yourself that nigh—"

"I'm not Audrey Faith anymore, Luke. I'm Audrey. I'm an adult and I knew exactly what I was doing when I climbed into your bed and made love to you."

Luke squeezed his eyes shut and drew oxygen into his lungs. Hearing her admit to seducing him got his juices flowing. He was turned on, big-time. Not his proudest moment, but he couldn't force his memory to shut down. For weeks he hoped to hell he'd remember. Now, those flashbacks wouldn't go away. She'd been stark naked and straddling him in the dark, her hair whipping about her face in a frenzy, the scent on her lips and her soft skin driving him wild.

She stood on the second step of the pool, a mass of long, golden hair tumbling past her shoulders, her soft dewy skin moist and glimmering under the lamplight. Her eyes were big and round, the expression on her face fragile enough for him to choose his words carefully. "Audrey—"

"Do you know what it does to a woman not to have a man remember her?"

His throat worked and he swallowed hard, recognizing the injury in her voice. He did remember the act, just not the woman performing the act. He knew that wouldn't make her feel any better. Luke stumbled through his next thoughts. The whole Audrey package made him a little dizzy. And a whole lot of nervous.

He should be angry at her for showing up on the ranch and not telling him the truth immediately. He should be scolding her for letting it go this long, for having sex with him without protection. How the hell did she know that he hadn't been sleeping around? And why had she run off in the morning without a word? Now that was an argument he could sink his teeth into.

But he didn't want to fight with her. He didn't want to scold her like a child. Clearly, she wasn't one. That had become obvious the second he spotted her in the pool. She'd hidden her beauty under scratchy straw hats and youthful ponytails and baggy clothes.

Luke viewed her differently now. But that wouldn't serve him too well. He was mentally knocking himself upside the head. Because she tempted him like no other woman had. She was clearly off-limits, but he couldn't stop the memories from bouncing around his feverish mind. Or put a halt to nerves that were stretched thin by his physical reaction to her.

Now he had the correct face to go with the memory of that night.

And the newfound recollection was worse than the mystery.

The hell of it was, he would never forget making love to Casey's sister, a woman he had always tried to protect.

"I was drugged up and not thinking clear. But you," he began, pointing his finger, looking deep into her wide, expectant eyes, "you should've…" But he couldn't follow through on his reprimand. He dropped his hand suddenly. Hell, he wasn't her teacher or her brother. He took another gulp of air before admitting…he was her lover.

"I should've what?" she asked with a hushed breath.

Luke flicked his gaze over her curvy body. That red thong was messing with his head. He was a man first and foremost and Audrey was killing him in small doses.

He shook his head. "Nothing."

Audrey stepped out of the water, coming up from the last step to plant her feet on solid ground. Even her toes were pretty and now the physical barrier between them was gone. "Nothing?"

Luke didn't respond. Anything he said would either hurt her or get him into trouble. It was the rock *and* the hard place.

"I'm going to bed," he said. It was a good way of settling the matter. In the morning, they'd see things more clearly and could have a serious conversation about it over breakfast.

He had every intention of pivoting on his boot heels and hightailing it inside the house, but his legs weren't moving. He stood rooted to the spot, just a few feet away from the woman clad in a smoking-hot bikini. He needed perspective. He needed to get away, but his brain worked in conjunction with his feet now and nothing budged.

Except Audrey.

She took a step closer and faced him from inches away, the lamps shining a golden halolike glow around her head. His reluctance to move parted her sweet lips and her eyes darkened to a seductive shade. "You don't want to leave."

Slowly, she reached behind herself and grabbed the ties of her halter top at the back of her neck. Fascinated and overwrought with desire, Luke couldn't utter a word. He couldn't tell her to stop. He couldn't tell her this was crazy. She was his mystery woman and he'd secretly hoped to have a thrilling repeat of the night they'd shared.

He could only watch, his body singing a lusty tune, as she gave a slight tug. The material fell away and two beautifully round breasts bounced free on her chest. Shadowy light touched upon ripe pink-hued nipples that lifted toward the sky. His groin tightened at her perfection and the memory of weighing her in his hands, tasting her with his tongue.

"I ran away from you once, Luke. That won't happen again."

Five

Luke wasn't a weak man but he wasn't a damn saint, either. And Audrey was a temptation he couldn't resist tonight. She was naked but for the strip of material below her navel. One flick of his finger and she'd be fully bared to him. Being with the blonde mystery woman again was his fantasy come true.

On impulse, Luke reached for Audrey, wrapping his arms around her slender waist. He gave a sharp tug and she landed up against him, soaking his shirt with her wet skin, her breasts pressed to his chest. Her arms automatically circled his neck and he breathed in Sweet and Wicked again. With his thumb, he shoved her chin up. He bent his head and crushed her mouth with a kiss. A long, deep whimper rose from her throat and he groaned from the depths of his chest, drowning out her sexy sounds of passion.

The kiss wasn't sweet or patient. He demanded that she meet him on his turf. Audrey had no trouble keeping up. Not even when his tongue shoved through her lips and found hers. He swept inside the hollows of her mouth, drawing her out with full strokes that had her body rocking against his in a rhythm that seized his soul and wouldn't let go.

There was no end in sight. He couldn't fathom putting a halt to this. He was consumed now with Audrey's heady, willing and pliant body. She was his for the taking and Luke blocked out any thoughts that said otherwise.

He ran his hands through her hair, weaving his fingers through the silky strands as he kissed her. Leaning her back, he left her mouth to drizzle kisses on the tip of her chin and along her neck, then went farther south to nip at the base of her throat. One hand left her hair to cup her breast. He squeezed gently and filled his palm with a different kind of softness, rounded and silky smooth. His thumb flicked her nipple back and forth.

She moaned and Luke's erection battled against the constraints of his pants. "So beautiful," he muttered, barely able to breathe.

He rubbed his chin over her other breast, teasing the nipple right before he drew it deep into his mouth. He suckled her and stroked the nub with his tongue, until her breathing came in short, labored bursts. "Luke."

Her plea tore at his willpower. He was lost. He'd had her once before, but this time was different. This time they both knew the score. There might be hell to pay later, but Luke was in the now and nothing was going to stop him from taking his mystery woman the way he'd dreamed so many times in the past. "I'm not gonna slow down, honey."

"I...don't...want you to," she eeked out.

Audrey's hands threaded through his hair and she hung on as he worked her into a frenzied state. He wasn't far behind. His blood pulsed through his veins.

He gave her a short, quick kiss then cupped her bottom in both of his palms and lifted her. He loved how she responded to him, without question or qualm. Her legs wrapped around his waist easily and he moved her to the cushioned lounge chair. Her butt was firm and silky smooth and before he lowered her down, he gave her a squeeze, filling his hands. His manhood responded and he almost lost it then. Somehow he managed to regain control and lowered her down.

She gazed up at him, her eyes bright and glazed with passion. In the lamplight, she was amazing and all his. Luke threw caution to the wind, no matter the warning bells going off in the furthest reaches of his mind.

"Take off your shirt, Luke." Her plea, and the picture she made on that cushiony lounge, made his mouth go dry. Her lips were swollen. Golden hair curled around and framed her beautiful breasts. Her legs were long and sleek. Every inch of her body was poised and ready for him. "I want to touch you."

His shirt was gone in an instant and he sat on the edge of the lounge, letting Audrey's hands roam over his chest. His skin flamed from her touch. She rose up and kissed him on the mouth, then lowered her head to kiss the parts of his body exposed to her.

He could only take so much. He kissed her while gently shoving her back against the lounge and then did the thing he'd imagined doing when he'd first seen her wading in the pool. He hooked his finger into her bikini bottom and slowly, carefully eased it down her legs.

Even then, Audrey wasn't shy with him. She gave him a satisfied smile and reached for him again. White-hot heat swamped his body. But this time he was in control. This time, he would bring her pleasure.

They were alone in the dark. The night was silent. Neighboring ranches were miles away and Luke's pool area was private and fenced off in the backyard. Barn scents on the property blew by on occasional breezes, a familiar and welcome smell of horses and leather.

He ran his fingers along the inner smoothness of her thighs until he came to the apex of her legs. She lifted her hips up, parted her lips and closed her eyes, ready for whatever he

would do to her. She trusted him without pause. Luke valued
that trust and began to stroke her, slow and easy, teasing her
with light touches. "Do you like that?"

She swallowed and nodded. "Yes."

"I thought you would. Tell me when you want more."

"I want more," she whispered, and Luke grinned.

He slid two fingers over her again, slipping them inside
this time and gliding them back and forth, inside and out.
"Oh," she moaned.

The throaty sounds she made burned clear through him.
He stretched out beside her on the lounge and kissed her in
keeping with his fingers' steady cadence. She squirmed with
need and Luke sped up his pace, touching her in ways that
would only give her the most satisfaction.

When her release came, Luke wasn't ready for the long,
drawn-out sighs of contentment that whispered from her lips.

Wrapped in his shirt, Audrey reclined on Luke's bed after
he deposited her there with utmost care. No words had been
spoken on the way to his room. With eyes locked on each
other and refusing to break the connection, they were in silent
agreement. Luke had just made her world spin out of control.
She was happier than she'd ever been in her life.

"Are you sure about this?" Luke came down on the bed
beside her, trailing kisses along her jawline.

She nodded, too overwhelmed to speak at the moment.

She wove her hands in his hair as he continued to kiss her.
She felt his need breaking through the restraint he'd managed
as he'd scooped her up into his arms from the lounge chair
to bring her inside.

Just a glimmer of light came through the walnut-wood
shutters. The bed was big and comfortable, and she didn't
care where she ended up, as long as Luke was beside her.

He took his time with her, kissing her gently, stroking her

body tenderly and speaking soft words in her ear. The evidence of his desire pressed the side of her body.

She slid her hand onto his chest, feeling hot, firm skin and powerful muscles underneath her fingertips. Fanning her fingers across washboard abs, she let go a sigh. How many times had she dreamed of this? How many times had she wished she would once again have the freedom to touch Luke and feel his body come alive with hers?

She reached for his belt buckle, helping him unfasten it. Boots flew and pants were tossed aside quickly after that. Audrey got a glimpse of Luke approaching her and her breath caught in her throat. His hair was pushed back and sandy tendrils curled at his shoulders. His chest was big and broad and when she darted a glance lower, her memory was jolted back to weeks before, and how she'd enjoyed every fulfilling second of their lovemaking.

"Come closer, Luke," she said, repeating the words he'd whispered in the cabin.

He stood tall by the side of the bed like a Greek god, tanned and mighty.

She watched him sheath his manhood and then slide a lingering glance over her entire body. Warm waves of expectation zinged through her belly. Before he climbed onto the bed, he cupped her womanhood and stroked her with the heel of his hand several times, making her mind go fuzzy and her heartbeats speed up. Everything inside turned to hot jelly.

He took her thighs in his hands and spread them, then lowered himself over her. Her eyes were wide with wonder. She didn't want to miss any part of this. She needed Luke and wanted to see him take pleasure from her body, in much the same way he had given to her. With a potent thrust, he filled her and closed his eyes. "So tight," he said with a deep rasp. "So good."

He moved on her slowly and she followed his lead, her heart swelling with love. She gave back to him thrust for thrust, and when he increased the pressure and rose above her, she bowed her body back to accommodate him. He took her hips in his hands and drove harder, faster, bending her back even more. Then she closed her eyes and her body burst into flames when he pressed his thumb where they were joined. It was only seconds later that everything spun crazily out of control. Her breaths were short, quick puffs and her body seized up just as Luke let out a long satisfied groan from the depths of his chest. Their cries mingled in the still night and echoed against the walls in a chorus of sweeping sensual sounds.

Every drop of strength oozed from her limbs. She couldn't move, yet she was floating. And Luke, the maker of dreams, was slow to remove himself from her body. He held on and watched her come gracefully down to earth. He took a swallow and bent to kiss her on the lips before he slid to the side of the bed.

He entwined their fingers and set them on his chest. "Are you okay?" he asked, staring at the ceiling.

She was in heaven. "I'm fine."

His gaze roamed over her naked body, taking a leisurely tour. "I'll be agreeing with you there. You're fine."

She smiled at his compliment. After all the years of yearning, wanting and loving Luke, she could finally savor and enjoy this moment. Beams of happiness set her heart aglow. She was where she'd always wanted to be.

"Are you cold?" Gripping the sheet, he was ready to cover her.

"Not at all."

He let the sheet drop and kissed her shoulder, and another wave of warmth coursed through her body. She'd never be cold with Luke nearby. He was beautiful, a perfectly muscled man of the earth. A modern-day cowboy who loved the same things she did.

He leaned back against the bed, staring up at the ceiling

again. He seemed to go someplace that put a frown on his face and then his jaw twitched as if in pain. It only took a minute for his demeanor to change. A long sigh, heavy with regret, rose from his chest.

Audrey prayed she was imagining his change in mood. She wasn't ready for a lecture right now. She wanted to bask in the glory of their lovemaking.

"Why'd you do it, Audrey?" he asked.

She squeezed her eyes closed. "Do what?" But she knew.

"Why'd you come to me that night in the cabin?"

Because I've loved you for the past ten years. Dare she tell him? What if he had the same feelings for her and was only just discovering them now? "I was ready to be impulsive."

"So it was payback. You caught your boyfriend cheating and wanted to get back at him?"

"More like, I didn't care that I'd caught him cheating. It bummed me out to know that I'd invested that much time in a guy I didn't care about."

"Wow. That's deep but I get it."

"You do?" Now that was a revelation. Usually when a girl went philosophical on a guy, he shut down completely. But this was classic Luke. He was easy to talk to and he understood her.

"Yeah, I do. And I get why you ran off that night. You realized your lapse in judgment and couldn't face me in the morning. We're friends, Audrey. But I hadn't seen you in years."

Audrey covered herself with the sheet and hinged up into a sitting position. "It wasn't a lapse of any kind, Luke. That's not why I ran off."

"Then why? Was it because of Casey? Were you afraid of his reaction?"

Luke's expression grew grim. His brows lifted and his eyes widened as if he'd just remembered that Casey was her brother. "Ah, hell. *Casey.*" He winced. "Your brother trusted me to watch out for you and twice now I've betrayed that trust."

"That's not true. You didn't betray anyone."

"Casey warned me you were vulnerable and hurt. And what do I do? The first chance I get, I sleep with his sister."

"I'm not just Casey's sister, Luke. I'm a grown woman capable of making my own decisions."

"I take one look at you in that pool and I can't resist. What does that say about me?"

"You're a man? And maybe you like me a little?"

He twisted his face and blew air out of his lungs.

"Casey had no right interfering in this or telling you about my personal problems," Audrey said. "He surely didn't know I was coming here."

"Yeah, about that…" Luke bounded off the bed and looked around the floor for his boxers. Once found, he put them on and moved to turn on a dimmer light switch. The room was suddenly bathed in a soft glow. He stood by the bed with his hands on his hips now. She'd seen that dubious expression on his face before. He was in interrogation mode. Still gorgeous, still hunky, but with a rigid set to his jaw. "If you weren't coming here for a job, then why'd you show up on the ranch? I want the truth this time."

"I always tell you the truth, Luke."

"I had no idea we slept together, Audrey. You ran off and left me to wonder about a mystery woman."

"Do you always go to bed with women you don't know?" That question had kept her up at night. If he hadn't known it was her, who did he think he was making love to?

His head jerked back. Surprise registered on his face. She'd turned the tables on him and he didn't much like it. "I thought I knew who it was. *Obviously.*"

"Obviously. So who?"

"A woman I'd seen that night at the party. A blonde."

Jealousy burned in her heart. "But not someone you knew very well."

Luke looked away, unable to meet her gaze. "I wasn't… thinking clearly."

"But you were tonight."

He turned to face her, his eyes filled with guilt and regret. That anguished look seared into her every pore.

Don't, Luke. Don't you dare regret this.

Mentally, Audrey spun the Worst-Case Scenario game wheel and wondered where it would land. Was it worse that Luke didn't know he'd made love to her the first time, or that he regretted it down to his toes the second time? Either way, she came out the loser.

He nodded, looking none too happy with himself.

She wanted to go back to ten minutes ago, when life was beautiful.

Now, looking at the pain on Luke's face, all she felt was heartache.

"Answer my question, Audrey. Why did you show up here?"

"I came to own up to running out on you. I felt bad. I didn't know if you were mad at me, or relieved that I had disappeared from your life. I came to Sunset Ranch to discuss that night with you. But when I realized you didn't know it was me in that bedroom, I lost my nerve. It's a pretty low blow to have a man not know he made love to you. Especially since it meant so much to me."

"It meant so much to…" Luke didn't finish the sentence. He was too busy twisting his lips and squeezing his eyes closed in disbelief. He began shaking his head. "Don't go there, Audrey."

He found his jeans and put them on, zipping them up with a quick pull. "We had a good time tonight." He tempered his voice as if afraid to bruise her ego. As if he was speaking to a child. "But don't go reading anything else into this. If you hadn't seduced me in the first place we wouldn't be in this mess."

"You're blaming me for seducing you after what we just shared in this bedroom?"

He continued to shake his head. "When I saw you in the pool, everything clicked into place. I was surprised by you and the temptation to re-create something that's been haunting me took over."

"We did re-create it. It was even better than the first time."

Another heavy sigh escaped. "I'm going to my grave regretting what just happened."

His words slapped across her face. Her cheeks burned with pain. She'd given herself to him again, this time in the hopes of starting something new between them. Something more than friendship, but Luke didn't see it that way. He saw it as a *mess.* He couldn't see beyond the girl she used to be to the woman she was today. And Mr. Nice Guy had guilt because of a promise he'd made to Casey. It hurt like hell and wasn't fair.

Audrey couldn't stay in his room tonight. She couldn't stand to see Luke try to make amends for making love to her or speak about his regret again. That would be the last straw.

She yanked the sheet from the bed and wrapped it around her body then stood up to face him. Her pride bruised, she hid her injury and the pain his words inflicted. "You don't have to regret anything, Luke. Consider it forgotten. A mistake, like you said. A big fat lapse in judgment. You don't have to tell me more than once. I get it."

She held her grief inside, hoisted her chin and marched to the door. Then she whirled around, opened her hand and let the expensive Egyptian cotton sheet fall gracefully to the floor. Buck naked, she had Luke's full attention. His eyes flickered over her body. A few seconds ticked by. Then she turned her back on him. "I'll see you at breakfast," she tossed over her shoulder as she walked out the door.

* * *

The next five breakfasts were quiet affairs. For the most part, Audrey wasn't speaking to Luke except for matters that regarded the ranch. She was invested here now with the animals, especially Trib, and she'd vowed to never again run away because things got tough, so thoughts of leaving the ranch—and Luke—skipped right out of her head.

She spent her days with Hunter and Ward and met with Sophia for lunch several times. She poured herself into the work, adding additional chores to her regimen to keep her mind busy and her heart from sinking into the bowels of the earth. Luke didn't seem all that concerned that their friendship was on stilted terms. He was probably relieved he didn't have to deal with her. He didn't have to pretend to feel something for her that he didn't feel.

It was harder on her. She hadn't breathed a word about what had happened between them to anyone. But every so often, Sophia would bring up Luke's name in conversation and Audrey would shrug a shoulder or give a clipped response. Sophia was smart enough to be a little suspicious, but Audrey managed to change the subject without fanfare or being too obvious.

For the past three afternoons, she'd worked with Trib at the barn. She wouldn't allow her personal feelings to interfere with the job she was hired to do. Luke had come by to watch her progress, keeping a big distance away as she'd asked. But his eagle eyes were on her and she resented that his presence there was solely to make sure she wasn't in danger.

He was always protecting her.

Any other female would've loved the attention. Was she a fool? She ached inside knowing she'd lost Luke as a friend. Though she wanted him as a lover. No, that wasn't true. She wanted to be more than his lover. She wanted a real relationship with him. But she'd have gladly taken more nights like the one they'd shared, hoping it would lead to a richer relationship.

Now Audrey had nothing. No friendship. No lover. No Luke.

Yet, she couldn't bring herself to leave the ranch. She couldn't quit another thing. She was through doing things halfway. She had a job to do; the ranch depended on her, and she felt the challenge of Trib deep down in her bones. Leaving Luke and the ranch would be the easy way out in one respect. She wouldn't have the constant reminder of what she couldn't have. But she would have satisfaction knowing she accomplished something and didn't run at the first sign of trouble.

Luke's painful words rang in her ears; it was a sharp dagger to her heart as she recalled the last thing he'd said to her that night.

I'm going to my grave regretting what just happened.

She didn't want to be anyone's last regret.

Newly fueled anger surged through her system.

The anger did nothing to quell her constant fatigue. Instead, she felt lifeless, her arms and legs weak and her body limping along. She blamed it on Luke. She blamed everything on Luke these days.

After another long day of working with the horses, she came back to the house, peeled off her work clothes and stepped into the shower. A soothing stream of water rained down to refresh her body and her mind. *Wash Luke away from my thoughts tonight,* she implored the water gods. *Heal my heartache and soothe my soul.* Was it too much to ask of a water god? She didn't know but when she wrapped herself into a towel and dried off, she felt a little better.

She was ready for mindless television and a good night's sleep.

She climbed into bed and gave Jewel a big, body-squeezing hug. The cat purred immediately and rubbed her face against her leg. Then she did a belly roll, content in the outpouring of attention she was receiving lately. Audrey accommodated her, petting her under the chin. When the cat rolled over, having had enough undivided attention, Audrey got comfy and picked up the remote control and clicked the TV on.

"Looks like *Wannabes and Wranglers* is on tonight."

It was nice having a cat around to pretend you weren't talking to yourself.

Audrey watched, noting John Wannabe's progress. He rode tall in the saddle now. He actually looked good, but he hadn't mastered the reins just yet…uh-oh. The horse took off at a run. John's hat flew off his head and it was all he could do to stay on the runaway horse…

A dog's bark came from her phone.

Jewel lifted her head again. "It's a text," she said to the cat. Audrey peeked at the screen. It was from Luke.

Are you watching?

Yes,

she messaged back, even though she didn't want to have a conversation with him tonight.

John should hang it up now before he gets seriously hurt.

Maybe John's not a quitter.

It was her anger speaking. She didn't care if Luke read between the lines. One way or another, Audrey would get her point across.

She didn't hear back from Luke until five minutes before the reality show ended.

John got voted off. Probably saved his skin and his neck.

She wrote back,

He was willing to take the hard knocks to achieve his goals. Too bad the others didn't have faith in him. I'm turning in. Good night, Luke.

Audrey shut off the television and sank into the cushy bed. She'd made her point loud and clear and somehow, she didn't feel much like celebrating the slight win. She didn't feel good, period. And the last thing she wanted was to think about Luke right before she fell asleep. She'd probably dream about him.

A soft knock at her bedroom door came thirty seconds after she'd closed her eyes.

It could only be one person.

She could pretend to be asleep. That wouldn't be too far-fetched, would it? But when the second soft knock came, she sighed and tossed off the covers. On bare feet and in her ugly T-shirt that read Cats and Women Know How to Land on Their Feet, she padded to the door.

She wasn't ready for the sight of Luke in faded jeans and a white wifebeater with his arms spread wide, bracing himself against the doorjambs. He leaned in, scruffy day-old beard and all, and she caught the scent of bourbon on his breath. His eyes raked over her legs and followed a path that finally rested on her face. Then his lips tightened to a fine line. "You're in a mood tonight."

She'd been in a mood for several nights. But it was hard concentrating on any of that, with Luke looking like pure sin standing in her bedroom doorway. "Sorry if I disappoint you."

He showed his displeasure by deepening his scowl.

"What do you want?" she asked.

"No argument."

"About what?" Geesh, it was past her bedtime and he was speaking in riddles.

"I'm taking you to Logan and Sophia's engagement party."

A dubious laugh escaped her throat. "Oh, no, you're not."

"Afraid so. Logan asked me specifically and Sophia seconded the notion. And you know what that means…there's no arguing that request."

"I can get there on my own, thank you very much."

"Don't be a child, Audrey."

She rolled her shoulders back and stiffened up, which inadvertently jutted her breasts out. Luke's gaze ventured to her chest and a gleam he couldn't hide shined in his eyes.

She rasped, "I think we've already established that I am not a child."

Luke glanced at her hair, which she'd been leaving down lately. Tonight it was wild about her head. Then his gaze lowered to her mouth in a soft caress. If he chose to speak about mistakes or regrets now, the door would fly in his face. "That's been established," he agreed. "But it'll look real suspicious if you and I drive separately. Logan's restaurant, The Hideaway, is up in the hills. It's a windy road and a difficult drive. There's no reason not to carpool."

"Make up an excuse."

"I've already thought of a few. Nothing makes much sense."

She didn't know why that bruised her feelings, since she was the one trying to weasel out of going with him, but it did. He didn't want to take her as much as she didn't want to go with him. But her reason went beyond her anger at him. Going with Luke to a special party for his brother would seem too much like a real dress-up-in-your-fancy-duds kind of date. And for a big part of her life, she had hoped to go on a date with Luke.

"I'll go with Hunter."

"Hunter is driving up with his folks in Ward's truck. There's no room for you. Face it, Audrey. You're stuck with me."

Sort of like being *stuck* with a rock star for the night. Or a prince.

"Fine." She made it clear with that one word that she wasn't too happy about it.

He nodded.

They stared at each other.

Time ticked by.

"You know," he said softly, "it doesn't have to be like this between us."

Yes. It did. She glanced away for a second to compose herself, before turning to look him dead in the eyes. "What did you have in mind?"

She watched his Adam's apple dip down to the base of his throat when he took a swallow. "We can still be friends."

The old let's-be-friends-because-I really-don't-want-to-feel-guilty-anymore ploy. A dozen reasons why she couldn't be Luke's friend right now streamed into her mind. "Sorry, that's not an option."

"Fine." His voice sharp, he didn't conceal his annoyance.

"Fine."

"We'll leave at five on Saturday night."

"I'll be ready. Good night, Luke."

"Uh-huh." He took her in from head to toe one last time, before drawing a deep breath and turning away. She closed the door, slumping her shoulders as righteous anger slowly ebbed from her body. Tears welled in her eyes. Her heart broke a little bit more as she climbed into bed and hugged Jewel tight to her chest, determined not to dream about Luke Slade tonight.

Six

"That dress is made for you," Kat Grady said. The platinum blonde strode from behind the boutique counter to give Audrey a smile. "It's nice to see you again."

"Same here, Kat."

Audrey didn't know what else to do but to give the dress she'd pulled from the rack a studious glance. She'd been flummoxed when she entered the shop to find Kat working here. Apparently, Sophia was just as surprised. Silver Springs was a small town twenty miles west of the ranch, and Sophia had driven her here this afternoon to find a dress appropriate for the engagement party. The boutique was smack in the center of town and from what Audrey gathered, had stylish clothes that she could barely afford. "I promise to stay on my feet this time."

Kat's eyes softened. "Well, I hope you're feeling better."

"Thank you. It was just a little bug," she explained. "I'm fine now." Although lately, she'd been experiencing occasional bouts of fatigue and melancholy.

"I'm glad to hear that. What do you think about the dress?"

Audrey held the sapphire-blue dress an arm's length away from her to admire the Empire waist and silvery jewels that formed a four-inch band underneath the bodice. "It's nice."

"I think it's perfect for you," Sophia said, coming to stand beside her. "The color will draw out your soft complexion. It's a good complement to your skin and blond hair."

"Would you like to try it on?" Kat asked.

"I… Uh, sure."

"Right this way."

"If you don't like the fit, there's a few others I think would be stunning. But let's see how this one looks on you first."

Audrey followed Kat to a good-size dressing room with a three-way mirror. The other woman gently took the dress from her hand to place it on a satin hook. "I hope you like it. Let me know—"

A child's whimpering cry stopped her from finishing the sentence. "Oh, excuse me. That's my son." Kat rushed to the back room that was only steps away from the dressing area.

Audrey watched her go, noting how the woman's entire demeanor changed from cool professional to a woman with worry lines around her mouth.

Audrey slipped out of her clothes and tried on the dress, peering at the fit from all angles in the mirror. Soft material crisscrossed her breasts and draped in pretty folds from the bodice down to her toes. The Empire style suited her body, and seeing herself in such a pretty gown gave her ego the boost it needed. Sophia had been right—the striking sapphire color did bring out the honey-blond of her hair. "Sold," she said to the mirror.

When she redressed in her own clothes and walked back to the sales floor, Kat stood by the counter with a dark-haired baby in her arms. "Shush now, baby. It's okay." She rocked him and the little boy was comforted. "I'm sorry. My son got a little fussy. He woke up from his nap early. Usually he sleeps for two hours in the afternoon."

The little boy, wrapped tight around his mother like a life preserver, and bobbing up and down in her arms, focused his eyes on Audrey. Jet-black hair curled at his nape and chubby cheeks, ruddy now from crying, pressed into his mother's shoulder.

"He's beautiful," Audrey said. "How old?"

Kat continued cradling his head and rocking him. "Connor is nine months. I apologize about this. I'm only filling in for the owner who's having minor surgery today. I promised to keep the shop open, unless Connor prevented it. He's been good for most of the day."

"That's very nice of you." Sophia smiled at the boy. "Do you work here often?"

"Not really. I'd love to, but Connor needs me at home with him."

Audrey's heart warmed. Kat wasn't the blonde bombshell type she'd originally thought her to be. The woman had certainly looked the part though. With highfalutin hair, deep rose-colored lips and stunning clothes, she left an impression. But looks deceived. Seeing her with her child convinced Audrey that she'd been wrong about her. The bond between mother and baby was strong. She beamed when she looked at him. Her voice held motherly pride when she spoke his name. She was a single mother raising a young son all alone.

Audrey understood Luke's reluctance to get involved with Kat now. That adorable baby had to be considered in the mix. Audrey respected Luke for his decision. The man had honor. He wouldn't deliberately hurt anyone for his own selfish needs. Though she wasn't thrilled with Luke lately, she had to give credit where it was due.

Luke had done the right thing with Kat.

With her, he'd been wrong.

"Well, we won't keep you another minute. I love the dress. I'll take it." *And you can close up shop and take your sweet baby home.*

On the way back to the ranch, Audrey stared out of the windshield of Sophia's car. "I guess you can't judge a book by its cover."

"You're talking about Kat?"

Audrey nodded. "Yes, I misjudged her."

"Maybe I did, too."

Audrey tilted her head toward Sophia. "All I saw was a beautiful woman, dressed to the hilt, hanging on Luke's arm, and I assumed I knew the kind of woman she was."

"Don't be so hard on yourself. You let your emotions rule your head. It happens when you're in love," Sophia said softly.

Audrey stiffened in the seat. "I'm not in love." Even to her own ears, her emphatic tone sounded unbelievable. Her shoulders slumped and she lost all of her fight. "Oh...am I that obvious?"

"No, you're not. Except to me. I recognize the signs. It wasn't that long ago that I felt those same love/hate feelings for Logan. There were times I really despised him."

"Luke's such a good guy. Sometimes, I feel guilty for giving him a hard time. But damn it, all of my life, decisions have been taken out of my hands. Luke's still treating me like a kid, telling me what's best for me. Pushing me away for my own good."

"Does he know how you feel about him?"

She shook her head. "No. I mean, I haven't told him. But we've...we've had a night...or two."

Sophia took her eyes off the road to give her a long look. "A night or two? Are you saying...?"

Audrey nodded. She was tired of holding everything inside. Sophia was her friend and she trusted her. She spent the rest of the drive home confessing to Sophia what had happened between her and Luke these past few weeks. Most of it rushed out of her mouth, unpracticed and brutally honest. Sophia asked a few questions here and there but by the time they'd driven through the gates of Sunset Ranch, her friend had gotten the whole picture.

"Wow. That's an amazing story," Sophia said. "Now it's all beginning to make sense."

"I know. I should have told Luke the second I saw him that it was me in the cabin."

"Luke does like honesty."

"He wasn't thrilled with me. We had an argument about it. So do you think I should tell him how I feel?"

Sophia wrinkled her nose and thought about it a second. "Yes, but only when you know the time is right."

"How am I supposed to know that?"

"Well, if he tells you first, that would be a good time." She grinned.

Audrey rolled her eyes. "Like that'll ever happen."

"Don't be so certain it won't. Luke might surprise you."

"I've loved him for so long and now that I'm here living under his roof, I'm no closer to getting what I want than when I was a kid, except I've got a few great memories to take to my grave."

Sophia's eyes warmed with sympathy. She set her hand on her arm. "I'm going to stop by the cottage. I have something you might need, Audrey. I hope you don't think I'm meddling."

"I'd never think that. You've been so good to me since I've been here and I really value your friendship. So what is it? A magic love potion? The key to Luke's heart?"

Sophia's shook her head and didn't laugh at her attempt at levity. "Nothing like that. Luke's my good friend, too, and we're family now. And well, just remember I want what's best for both of you. And again, I hope I'm not out of line here."

"Okay. I'll remember that." Sophia's serious tone made her clamp her mouth shut and wait.

Sophia parked the car in front of the cottage, which was now under renovation to add on several rooms to enlarge the house. "Logan's not home. I'll only be a moment."

When Sophia returned with a small white bag in her hand, she sat in the driver's seat and handed it over to her. "I hope this is…whatever you want it to be." There was joy in her eyes and caution, too. "Open it in the privacy of your bedroom, Audrey."

A shiver rode up and down her spine.

Audrey looked down at the drugstore bag in her lap and knew what it was. The shape of the rectangular box inside removed any doubt she'd had. "I take it this isn't lubricating jelly."

Sophia cracked a smile. "No."

Denial had been her constant companion and now Sophia was making her face the music. Audrey didn't want to think about the possibilities, but the signs—or should she say, symptoms—were all there and Audrey, coward that she was, had done a good job of ignoring them.

"I keep a few on hand. Logan and I have been trying. No one knows that but you now."

Audrey lifted her eyes to Sophia. "Thanks for trusting me with that. I hope it happens."

"It will," Sophia said, a confident glow in her eyes.

She nodded. "You're right, of course. I should find out." She grasped the edges of the bag, rolling them up tight and taking a swallow. "Luke deserves to know the truth."

Sophia leaned over and wrapped her arms around her. She spoke with sincerity. "My concern is for you, Audrey. You need to know the truth. But only when you're ready."

Tears burned behind her eyes. Emotions overwhelmed her. With a lump in her throat and her belly churning, she couldn't get the words out she wanted to say. Finally, she managed, "You're…a…good friend, Sophia."

* * *

That night, Audrey tossed and turned in her bed. The home pregnancy test sat on the bathroom counter, still unopened, still in the bag. She wasn't ready. She didn't know when she'd ever be ready. Her life was one screwed-up mess right now.

Her restless movements annoyed Jewel so much that the cat gave her a sour look, jumped down from the bed and curled up on the captain's chair by the window. "Sorry, Jewel," she said. "You can have the bed back. I'm leaving for a while."

Audrey slipped out of her bed and dressed, tucking her T-shirt into her jeans, putting her boots on and striding out the bedroom door. It was well past midnight and she'd pay for her twitchy sleeplessness in the morning, but right now, she needed to walk and clear her head.

She tiptoed past Luke's room and out of the house, heading for the stables. Where else would she go when she needed comfort? She stopped at the barn that held the prized animals that made up the bulk of Sunset Ranch. Some horses were awake, shuffling around in their stalls. She whispered hellos to them and smiled at the others that were asleep in the prone position, lying on the soft hay and looking so peaceful.

That peace eluded her tonight.

"How's it going, Rusty?" She peered at a reddish-brown gelding making his approach. "You can't sleep, either?" When he hung his head over the stall's door, she gave his silky coat a pat and threaded her fingers through his coarse mane. The textures, smooth against rough, brought a smile to her face. The scent of straw and dung, of earth and dust, comforted her in ways that warmed her heart. "Yeah, we both had a long day, didn't we?" She rubbed her face along his and was awarded with an affectionate nuzzle.

As she passed by the stalls and other horses approached, she gave each one of them attention, but her restlessness didn't fully subside. She was still antsy. Still unsettled. Her feet moved and she kept on walking. Out of that barn, into the dark

and even farther, until she came upon the special building—
the barn where she'd been unconsciously heading all along.

You're tempting fate, Audrey.

Yet she kept taking the strides, kept digging her boot heels
in and moving forward until she reached her final destination
and stared into the coal-black, dangerous eyes of the stallion.

"Hello, Trib."

Beams of sunlight brightened the darkness behind her eyes
and she lifted her lids. Morning dawned and a groan from
deep in her belly emerged to greet the day. She'd only gotten a few hours of sleep. But as tired as she was, her nerves
tingled with excitement when her first thoughts to emerge
were of the stallion she'd visited last night. Trib hadn't been
such a hard case after all. In the solitude of the night, with
darkness surrounding them, Audrey had made headway with
the stallion. It was only slight, but it was headway she could
bank on. The horse had been at loose ends. She could relate.
She'd felt the same way. And in a weird sort of way, she'd
bonded with Trib. He'd come halfway. They'd talked. Well,
she'd talked and the horse had patiently listened. They were
two lost souls, more lonely than anything else. Trib had been
isolated from the animals. He didn't like that, and although he
didn't play well with others among the horse population, how
else would he learn to get along? Audrey had to work with
him, privately and at night, when it was just the two of them.

She would build his trust.

Jewel scratched at the door. The cat was eager to start her
day. She liked the ranch, had free rein to wander the grounds,
annoy the penned-up animals and catch creepy-crawly bugs.

"Okay. I'll let you out."

Audrey tossed her covers off and sat up. Her head spun.
Waves of dizziness hit her. Oh, no. Fainting again wasn't an
option. When it didn't happen, she thanked her lucky stars.
She'd open that drugstore bag soon, but right now, the room

and her head merged onto one axis and she was grateful. She brought deep breaths into her lungs and rose. Steady on her feet now, she took cautious steps to the door to let Jewel out. "Don't get into trouble."

Audrey moved slowly about the room. Just in case. When she was sure she'd remain upright, she showered and dressed. She had a full day of work ahead of her. Weekends knew no free time on a working ranch. Chores still needed doing.

She plopped a hat on her head and hurried down the hallway. Her tummy tender, she opted to bypass the kitchen and skip breakfast this morning. She strode out the front door and headed straight for the barn. She had horses to exercise and groom and she'd promised Ward to look over the feed order, to make sure he hadn't forgotten anything.

She waved at Boyd and Jimmy, two of the hands working in the corral, and bounded inside the barn. She stopped short when she saw Luke in the middle of the barn. He held a besotted Jewel in his arms and was spoiling the cat by scratching her under the chin. Jewel purred loudly. Audrey could swear the cat's mouth curved up into a smile.

"Mornin'," Luke said, walking over.

Heavens. She'd hoped to avoid him today.

"Morning, Luke."

"You missed breakfast. Ellie made bacon, eggs and biscuits."

Her empty stomach jerked at the mention of food. The Slade housekeeper was back. She'd heard she was a great cook. And now her stomach rumbled. "I wasn't hungry." She'd been queasy.

Luke glanced at her old jeans, sloppy blouse and straw hat. She'd been wearing clothes from Sunset Lodge's gift shop but today she'd opted for ultimate comfort rather than style.

"You don't have to work 24/7, Audrey. You already put in your five days."

"I don't consider it work. I enjoy caring for the animals."
She shrugged. "Besides, what else would I do?"

Luke stared at her. His throat worked as his Adam's apple
bobbed up and down. A moment passed between them. Then
he sighed. "Whatever it is women do with their spare time."

"I'm not like most women."

Luke bent to put Jewel down and when he came up, he
was inches from her face. His voice dropped an octave. "I
know, Audrey."

She held her breath. Being near Luke did things to her
equilibrium and she'd already had one bout of dizziness today.
"Then you know I'd rather be with them than anything else."

"Okay," he said, nodding. "But I'm giving the weekend
staff time off in honor of Logan and Sophia's engagement
party. Most of the hands are invited and they could use the
time."

Darn. She'd almost forgotten about the party. She wished
it was any day but today, though. She hadn't started the day
off on a chipper note.

"I haven't gotten daily reports from you about Trib," he
said.

"That's because you've been right there, watching me."

"I can't see a darn thing from where I'm standing and you
know it, Audrey Faith. And if I'm in the area and see you
over there, there's no harm in me being nearby. The horse
doesn't know I'm there."

Audrey wouldn't argue the point. "He's coming around.
I see some progress. He's lonely in there, Luke. I think he
needs company."

"Female company?"

Audrey blushed down to her toes. She wasn't usually prone
to turning five shades of red at the mention of sex, but with
Luke's expression of surprise as if he should've been the
one to think of it, Audrey couldn't keep the color from her
cheeks. "It's not his time, Luke. I meant that he's isolated in

there. We need to give him some freedom. He needs to be around other horses."

"He'll try to lord over them. The horses here are all high-strung. They're pretty good one-on-one and they manage to get along, but I don't know if Trib's ego could take it. I'm afraid of what he'd do."

"We have to trust him sometime."

Luke spoke through thinned lips. "You're big on trust, aren't you?"

Jewel rubbed against her legs and Audrey bent to pick her up. She rocked her like a baby and the cat purred quietly this time. "Yes. I'm big on trust."

Unfortunately, Luke wasn't. Not when it came to Trib and not when it came to her. He didn't have much trust in himself, either. He always did the honorable thing; that was Luke. But he didn't trust enough to free up his feelings. He wasn't a man who would let down his guard when it mattered most. He didn't trust his own instincts.

"I'll give it some thought."

She nodded and there wasn't anything more to say at the moment.

They stood facing each other in awkward silence. Audrey kept her eyes focused on him. If he wanted to turn away, he could do so, but she held firm.

Luke's eyes narrowed until they were only slivers of blue. His lips tightened and he huffed out on a breath, "I guess I'll see you later on tonight. About five o'clock?"

His enthusiasm wasn't ego-boosting. He sounded like he was going to his own hanging. Her chin went up and she couldn't hold her irritation back. "I'll be ready...*I guess.*"

Luke raised his brows at her retort and then walked away.

It was clear Luke wasn't looking forward to being her escort for the evening. Pain cut through her gut at the notion. Pangs of pride withered away as she thought about how he'd tried to get out of it, to think up another solution. But in the end, Luke had done the honorable thing. He wouldn't let Sophia or Logan down. He would see her to the party, be polite all night and then make sure she arrived home safely.

She could fake an excuse and not go. But then, Sophia would be disappointed that she wasn't there. And she valued their budding friendship too much to do that.

Audrey was stuck. She had to admit she wasn't too keen on being with Luke, either, tonight. It hurt too much to be his date in name only, to know they shared earth-shattering memories in bed, and Luke wanted to forget it had ever happened. The *grave* comment wore on her nerves. He had regrets.

Well, so did she. And they burned through her. She feared she'd lost something precious with Luke, something that could never be restored. The friendship she'd always relied on was ripping away, the wound growing into a scar that would never heal. From the depths of her soul she faced a brutal and hard fact.

She couldn't be Luke's good buddy anymore.

They couldn't go back to being casual friends.

Their friendship was over.

How sad was that?

Well, at least it wasn't a monkey suit, Luke mused as he put his black jacket on over a brocade vest. He adjusted his Resistol hat on his head, straightened out his bolo tie and took a glance in the mirror.

A deep breath steadied his wrought nerves as he stared at his reflection.

He was happy for his brother. He'd found Sophia, and they would probably live out the rest of their lives blissful and content. Luke wanted to enjoy the celebration of their love and upcoming marriage. But he'd rather do that celebrating without Audrey Faith Thomas on his arm tonight.

Lord in heaven, the woman got under his skin.

For years, he'd thought of her as the kid sister he'd never

had. He'd intervened when Casey went off on her, demanding that she obey overly strict, hard-to-abide-by rules. While Casey had assumed the role of father, Luke had befriended her in a brotherly way. It was odd that all of his life, women had been his good friends. First Sophia and then Audrey.

There'd never been any sparks with Sophia, so his friendship with her wasn't difficult to maintain.

But Audrey?

Now that had come out of the blue.

It was hell for him to think of her as a woman, capable of making him act like a hormonal teenager again. Capable of making him forget who the hell she was and why he shouldn't be kissing her, touching her, making love to her.

A wince pulled his mouth down.

Enough already, Luke.

He had to stop beating himself up over it. He reminded himself that she hadn't been completely innocent. She'd brought a lot of this on herself. She'd seduced him and then turned tail and run out on him. For weeks now, she'd been living on the ranch and deceiving him.

He couldn't forget that.

With that notion firm in his mind, he headed out of his room and walked down the hallway. He braced himself and knocked on her door.

She took her sweet time opening it.

But when she finally did, his staunch resolve caved a little. She wore sapphire blue like nobody's business.

"Hello, Luke."

He swallowed. The night was looking grim. "Wow. You look gorgeous, Audrey." He had to say it. It was the truth. Her eyes were prettier than he'd ever seen them. Blond hair framed her face in wisps of softness and then flowed down her back in long luxurious waves. The dress was made for Grecian goddesses.

She smiled and ushered him inside. "You look nice, too."

She turned away to pick up a small beaded purse from the dresser. "I'm ready. We can go now."

Luke gestured for her to lead the way. He followed behind and was grateful once they were out of the empty house and on their way. At least behind the wheel, he could concentrate on the drive and not on her. Except that she wore some sexy erotic perfume that appealed to his base instincts. Images of Audrey's wet body in the pool popped in and out of his head. He didn't want to think about the Sweet and Wicked shine on her lips, either.

He wasn't planning to get close enough to pick up that scent.

He focused his attention on the road, driving toward Tahoe and then along the scenic road up the mountain. Luke hadn't been to The Hideaway too many times. Logan had recently purchased the restaurant and if romantic and dramatic were on the agenda, then the château overlooking the hills with a view of Lake Tahoe was the place.

When they arrived, the car doors were opened by uniformed valets. One of them helped Audrey out of the car, giving her a second look. Luke couldn't blame the guy for admiring a pretty woman. Once the car was driven away, Luke escorted Audrey up the steps of the quaint château, with one hand to the small of her back. That was all the touching he'd planned on doing with her during the entire night.

She stopped and whirled around when they reached the veranda by the front doors. The sun was setting over the tips of the sugar pines and off in the distance, beams of burnished light gleamed on the lake. The Hideaway had a magnificent view of all that was glorious about Nevada.

"It's beautiful," she whispered, totally captivated by the surroundings.

"I won't be disagreeing." It was about all they hadn't disagreed upon lately. But Luke kept his tone light. He wanted Audrey to have fun tonight. She'd worked hard on Sunset

Ranch and he still considered her his friend, even if she was sorely angry at him lately.

Both of them could use a break from the tension at the ranch.

He watched her view the scenery until she'd had her fill and then escorted her into the restaurant. A gasp of pure awe escaped her throat. The place was lit with a hundred candles that gave the restaurant a warm, appealing touch. White lilies, greenery and pinecones adorned tabletops. Tall pillar candles and a gardenia centerpiece decked out the carved fireplace mantel. A three-piece band was set up off to the side. Barkeeps at a carved wood bar were serving drinks, and waiters were offering appetizers to the guests.

"Amazing," Audrey said.

Two of the younger ranch hands huddled in the corner, noticed her and gave her a wave. She returned their greeting with a genuine smile.

"The party is in full swing," he said, then spotted Logan and Sophia finishing a discussion with the caterer. "Let's say hello."

Audrey walked beside him as they made their way over to offer them congratulations.

"We should have a private toast," Luke said. He grabbed a tray of champagne flutes, giving the waitress a smile, then returned to his brother's side. "Here you go," he said, offering everyone a glass. He raised his flute high in the air. "To my brother, for finally waking up and realizing how great Sophia is for him. Something I'd known all along." He gave Sophia a wink.

"I should have realized you'd be an ass about this," Logan said, his tone light and good-natured. "But when you're right, you're right."

Everyone laughed. "Don't worry. I've got a better speech for when the time comes. This is only my warm-up," Luke joked.

"I can hardly wait."

They touched glasses with a clink and Sophia and Logan shared a special look as they sipped their drinks.

It was those special looks, those shared moments that Luke had never experienced before with a woman. He'd been burned ages ago. Yet lately he'd come to realize that those memories had faded into the woodwork of his mind. They no longer hurt. But he had begun to think he was immune to love. There was something missing in his life. Or was he being too careful, overthinking things that should come naturally?

Audrey held the flute to her mouth, ready to take a sip, when she was bumped from behind. "Oh!" Teetering on high heels, the glass dropped from her hand as she flung out her arms. Glass crashed on the floor, champagne spilling all over as she was propelled forward.

On instinct, Luke reached out, catching her fall. It was like some fancy dance move he'd seen on television with Audrey falling into his arms. Except Luke wasn't skilled with the grace of a dancer. He'd simply become her human safety net.

He brought her up tight. Her face inches from his, she looked astonished. The scent of Sweet and Wicked filled his senses, but he didn't care about that now. "Are you okay?"

She gave him a brave nod then winced in pain. "I…I think so."

Luke's teeth ground together. He balled his fists and glanced over Audrey's shoulder at the two men from the catering staff who were responsible for nearly knocking her to the ground. They were clearly oblivious and had no clue what they'd done. Luke gave her a quick kiss behind her ear and whispered, "Hang on a sec." Then he set Audrey aside gently before he approached the men.

"You boys just knocked into my date." His blood pressure pulsed when they gave him blank stares. They'd been moving tables and speaking loudly, ignorant of the guests, and as Luke got closer, he smelled alcohol on their breath. "You don't even know you hurt her. Now, before I ask you to leave, you owe her an apology."

He led the men to Audrey, who appeared pale at the moment. They hung their heads and mumbled an apology. "Okay, now move out. Do your job and be mindful of the guests."

When he turned around, Sophia was beside Audrey, holding her hand. Logan approached. "I'll go talk to them."

"They've been drinking," he said.

Logan glanced at Sophia and she nodded her approval. "They're off this job, then."

Luke was satisfied with that. He didn't have the authority to fire them, but Logan would. They had no call being drunk on the job.

"Are you hurt?" he asked Audrey. She'd really taken a hard rap to the back.

"Not really."

He wasn't sure if he believed her.

"I've been bumped by the best of them, Luke. Horses nudge me to the ground all the time."

Sophia said, "That's because they love you so much."

"And because you let them," Luke added. A smile strained his tight lips as he remembered the silly games she'd play with the horses. They would often whinny and show their affection by nuzzling her neck until she dropped to the ground in giggles. "I'll get you another drink," Luke said.

"No!" She glanced at Sophia and then at him. "I mean, not right now. I think I need some fresh air."

"Okay, fine. I'll take you outside."

"That's not necessary," she told him. "Thank you for catching me. But I think…I think I want to be alone right now."

A crew rushed over to clean up the mess while Sophia dabbed champagne from Audrey's neck and shoulders. "You're lucky. It didn't get on your dress. You look too stunning to have it ruined. Are you sure you're all right?"

"Yes, just a little shaken up."

Luke's mouth twisted. "Then let me help you—"

"Luke," she said, "please don't feel responsible for me to-night. Go, have fun. I plan to do the same in a few minutes. The band is starting up. Three couples have already beat you to the dance floor. Ask Sophia to dance while Logan is busy."

"Yes," Sophia said, angling a knowing smile at Audrey. "I feel like dancing."

Bamboozled, Luke got the message. He let Audrey go, watching her make her way to the outside deck.

"She'll be fine. You've got to stop babying her."

"Is that what you think I'm doing?" Luke asked as they walked into the middle of the room. He took his friend into his arms and they began to move as the band played a rendi-tion of "I've Got You Under My Skin." "I'm not babying her."

"No? Then why do you look so concerned?"

"She got hurt."

"Not that much. Not enough for good-natured Luke to want to rip the heads off those guys who shoved her."

Luke narrowed his gaze and stared at Sophia. "What are you saying, exactly? And remember we're friends, so no bull."

"No bull? All right, then, but you may not want to hear this."

Luke was sorry he asked. Sophia was a straight shooter. She told it like it was. And this time, Luke wasn't sure he was ready for her honesty.

"You're attracted to Audrey. You're just realizing she's not a kid anymore and it's sort of blowing your mind a little bit. She loves the same things you love. She's pretty. Especially tonight. But because of your friendship with Casey and a code of honor you keep hidden in your back pocket somewhere, you're wired to keep your distance from her. But it's harder than you ever thought it would be."

"You're right."

Surprise lifted Sophia's brows. "I am?"

"I didn't want to hear that."

"I thought so. So, how close am I?"

"Audrey is a grown woman. Any man can see that. Casey would tear me a new one if—"

But Luke couldn't finish his thought. He'd already done things with Audrey that would give Casey a stroke—after he beat the stuffing out of him.

"If what? I know you're really not afraid of Casey."

Damn Sophia for being so astute. For knowing him so well. He sighed and twirled Sophia around, and when she came face-to-face with him again, he shrugged. "Do you blame me for not wanting to hurt her?"

Because Luke knew that he would. He'd already let things go too far between them. At one point or another, he'd be the one to walk away from her, when he found that something was missing between them. It had happened too often with too many women in his past. He didn't want to do that to Audrey. Getting further involved with her would just lead to heartache.

"No, I don't blame you, Luke. I'm your friend. I can see this is troubling you."

Sophia let him off the hook and changed the conversation to her upcoming wedding, a subject that had her bending his ear. He was grateful when Logan cut in to retrieve his fiancée.

He headed straight for the bar and ordered bourbon straight up. He spent his time chewing the fat with Hunter, Ward and a few friends from Sunset Lodge. He spoke with little Edward and his grandmother Constance shook hands with a few longtime employees, all the while keeping a vigilant eye on Audrey. She'd pretty much ignored him the whole evening, kicking it up on the dance floor with seven different partners. When she wasn't dancing, she was the center of male attention, like she was the football quarterback in a huddle. The boys seemed to hang on her every word.

When dinner was served, she sashayed her way over to the table and they made small talk throughout the meal.

"Having fun?" he asked.

"Yes, it's a nice party. I'm glad I was invited."

He glanced at her plate. She'd taken two measly bites of her prime rib and picked at her carrot soufflé and potatoes. "You didn't eat much."

"I, uh, no, I'm not too hungry tonight."

"You'd think with all the dancing you were doing, you'd have worked up an appetite."

Her gaze lowered to her plate. She picked up her fork. "I'd be a wallflower if I had to rely on you for a dance." Dainty as could be, she took a bite of food.

Luke studied her. "You're saying you want to dance with me?"

She lifted her chin defiantly. "No."

But her eyes flashed something different. The band had taken a break. Lucky thing. He didn't want to hold her in his arms tonight. Sophia had been right. He was attracted to her. More than he would admit to another living soul.

After dinner, Audrey excused herself to go to the ladies' room. Ten minutes later, when she didn't return for dessert, Luke went searching. He found her on the outside terrace, standing alone.

He sidled up next to her and braced his arms on the railing. He sipped bourbon from a highball glass. She didn't look at him, but remained quietly peering at the stars.

After a minute of silence, she spoke quietly. "I'm ready to leave. Dusty offered to take me home."

"Dusty can go to hell."

Audrey whipped her head around to stare at him with accusation in her eyes. "That was uncalled for. He was polite to offer."

Dusty had been eyeing Audrey all night. They'd danced together a few times. He worked for Sophia at the lodge and from what Luke had gathered, the guy was all right. Which bugged him ten ways to Sunday. He should let her go home and be done with it, but something inside wasn't ready to allow that to happen. "I brought you here. I'm taking you home."

"Your brother's party isn't over. I don't want to drag you away before it ends. This is an important evening for Sophia and Logan."

"So why do you want to leave so soon? Do you want to be alone with Dusty?"

Audrey's face flamed. Her eyeballs were ready to pop out of her skull. She hissed, deep and low from her throat. "How could you ask me that?"

Luke stated a fact. "He's been flirting with you all night."

"How would you know? You haven't… Oh, never mind." Audrey turned to brush past him and right on cue, the band started up again. This time it was a rendition of Elvis Presley's "Are You Lonesome Tonight."

Hell, yeah, he was.

Luke grabbed Audrey's arm before she could get away. "Dance with me."

"I don't need a pity dance, Luke."

His brows rose. He'd always admired her spunk. They stood frozen as the lyrics of loneliness and missing your sweetheart filtered through the speakers. "Then take pity on me. I want to dance with you."

Luke didn't wait for a rejection. He took her small waist in his hands and tugged her closer, then looped her arms around his neck. She gazed at him, her body a little less rigid, her eyes softening. "Luke."

His brain told him this was dangerous and stupid, but he didn't heed the warning. He'd been itching to touch her all night, despite his mental claims otherwise.

They were alone, but for a starry sky and the sound of music and muted laughter coming from inside the château. The air was crisp. The leaves of sugar pines whispered in the breeze. And Luke whispered above them into Audrey's ear, "One dance and I'll take you home."

She trembled as he brought her closer, brushing his lips over her earlobes, breathing in the scent of her hair. She was delicate now in his arms, and he took care with that. She wasn't a wallflower but a woman who had bloomed right before his eyes.

They moved then, back and forth, the soft harmony filling their senses. Audrey laid her head on his shoulder and they danced on. There was something sweet and poignant in the moment, something that Luke didn't want to end. So when the music stopped, they kept dancing, tight in an embrace, clinging to each other until sometime later their feet stopped moving and their eyes locked. Luke lifted her chin with his thumb and used it to outline the shape of her lips. Then he dipped his head and kissed her long and deep and passionately. When the kiss ended, Audrey whimpered in protest. The sound seared into his soul. He felt the same gut-wrenching sense of loss and wanted to go on kissing her. But not here, where curious onlookers might see, where any second now, his brother or Sophia might wander outside to find them together, lip-locked.

"Let's go home," he whispered with quiet urgency.

Reflecting the soft moonlight, Audrey's eyes shined with desire. "I'm ready."

Luke took her hand. He was heading for trouble, but at the moment, he didn't give a damn.

Seven

On the drive home, Audrey sat beside Luke in his car in wild anticipation of what the night would bring. They were halfway home when Audrey got a text message. "It's from Casey," she said, reading the lit-up screen.

"Oh, yeah? What's he got to say?" Luke asked quietly, giving her a smile.

Mercy. She melted into a puddle, and later she would blame his smile for her stupidity in reading the text aloud. "'I'll be coming by for a visit soon. Gotta make sure Luke's taking good care of my…uh, little sis.'" She spoke the last two words with dire dread. She was well aware of the impact that statement could make.

Luke dropped his easy smile.

"He's teasing," Audrey said softly.

But it was too late. Luke completely shut down. It was like she'd splashed ice-cold water on his face. He turned three shades of red before guilt and recrimination set in. He refused to hear her out. He refused to listen to any arguments contrary to his own thoughts on the matter. His mind was made up.

When they arrived at Sunset Ranch, he deposited her at her bedroom door. His face tight, his stance rigid, his words were strained as if he forced them out. "If you think it's easy for me to walk away from you tonight, you're sorely mistaken."

And then he did exactly that.

He closed the door and walked away.

Audrey cursed at the closed door in three different languages. The English words were the most obscene, but she managed to sputter a few choice words in Spanish and French, too.

Luke hadn't been her date tonight. Except for the last ten minutes when they'd danced and kissed out on the veranda under the stars. She'd seen a bright new world opening up to her, and hope had sprung into her heart again until Luke had decided what was best for both of them.

Now she peered at her reflection in the mirror. Her face was pale, drained of any expectation or hope. Her body sagged and her stomach ached. She wouldn't allow Luke and his stubborn ways to dictate her life anymore. If he wanted it this way, he would have it.

She glanced at the unopened pregnancy test sitting on her counter. "Not tonight," she said. She didn't want to know the outcome. She didn't want to have to face the reality of what that test would reveal. But just in case, she hadn't sipped any alcohol tonight. She'd planned on having only one drop of champagne before she'd almost been knocked to the ground.

The spill could've been a premonition, a warning not to imbibe.

She was too mentally exhausted to ponder that. She changed out of her gown and into her jeans. She pulled her hair back in a ponytail and plopped her hat on her head. "Come on, Jewel." She lifted her lazy cat up and tiptoed out of her bedroom, past Luke's room, where she heard the shower going. She hoped he needed three cold showers to-night. She continued on and walked out of the house. When she reached the barn with the cat snuggled tight to her chest, she whispered, "Just behave, Jewel."

The cat mewled softly as they approached Trib's paddock. Quietly, Audrey opened the split door. She found Trib asleep on the ground, looking innocent and gentle.

"Hi, lonely boy," she whispered.

He lifted his head.

"I brought a friend to visit you."

Bringing Jewel to the paddock had a profound effect on the horse. Not that Audrey trusted Trib enough to allow Jewel inside the stall. Heavens, both animals were too unpredict-able for that, but she held Jewel in her arms and spoke sweet words of encouragement until the curious horse wandered over. The two animals stared at each other. When Jewel made a playful swat at the horse's snout, Trib didn't react, except to blink his eyes.

For the next three nights, Jewel was Audrey's accomplice. They would wait until the ranch was tucked in for the night to visit Tribute. On some animal level, Trib began to bond with Jewel. Enough so that on the fourth night, Audrey placed Jewel on the eight-inch ledge of the split door, keeping one hand on the cat. Jewel sat there in a regal pose, watching the horse. And Trib, just like all the other times, wandered over to stare at Jewel. Each night they visited, Audrey noticed Trib taking less and less time to decide to make his approach.

Progress. A bond of trust was developing. During the day, she'd visit the paddock without Jewel, and Trib would respond to her, taking treats from her hand now. Audrey felt she was moving ahead, succeeding in her attempt to tame the wildness out of the horse, yet her own personal life was at a standstill. She'd avoided Luke whenever she could and any *I might be pregnant* notions were shuffled out of her brain.

But on the fifth day that week, she took a hard fall off a stepladder, landing smack on her butt in the barn.

"Oh, no!" A jarring jolt reverberated through her body. But the pain was secondary. Fear engulfed her. What if she was pregnant and she'd injured the baby? The wake-up call rang loud in her head like the shrill alarm of a police siren. *Find out, coward. What are you waiting for? You don't want to endanger the baby,* if *there is a baby. You need to protect that child and keep it safe.*

That night, after work, she opened the home pregnancy test box, read the instructions and then peed on the stick.

And immediately, Audrey's life changed forever.

She was going to be a mother.

Luke, the man she'd barely spoken to for the entire week except for ranch matters, was going to be the father of her child.

A shudder worked through her system. She gripped her stomach as cautious joy swelled in her heart. She stood there, motionless and quiet. Blood pulsed through her veins rapidly, her heartbeats going a little wild. She shouldn't be surprised. She'd fooled herself into believing it wasn't so. But she'd had all the symptoms. She'd been more tired than ever lately. She couldn't explain her slight bouts of dizziness, that one ill-timed fainting spell or the nausea that seemed to come and go. Then there was the teensy-weensy little fact that she'd been late. By at least a week.

"Goodness," she whispered.

She closed her eyes and images appeared of Luke in those early rodeo days. The flashbacks played in her head like a moving picture. Luke sending her a big smile after a nine-second ride. Luke taking her side when Casey was too hard on her. Luke giving her a sweet kiss on the cheek on her birthday. Images played on and on until her legs became wobbly and weak. She made her way over to the bed to lie down. There was no sense fighting her exhaustion. She placed a protective hand over her belly and sank farther into the bed.

A text alert barked from her phone. Audrey stilled and squeezed her eyes tight. She knew it was Luke, texting her good-night. She wouldn't answer. Why change now? She'd let him think she was already asleep, like she had for the past five nights in a row.

The shock of it all overwhelmed her. She had a baby growing and thriving in her belly. She already loved the little thing.

Too bad the baby's father was the last man on earth she wanted to speak to right now.

Instead of heading back to the Slade house after work the next day, Audrey waved goodbye to Hunter and Ward at the corral and strode in the opposite direction. A walk would help clear her mind. Her nerves frazzled, her bones weary, she needed to speak to a friend more than anything else. She moved with determined steps toward the cottage that Sophia shared with Logan. Maybe, if she got lucky, she'd catch Sophia alone so that they could talk.

She wasn't five yards away from the barn when Jewel appeared and trotted in step beside her. "You feel like taking a walk with me?"

Jewel kept up with her strides, and she figured that was a resounding yes in cat talk. Jewel was astute. She knew something was up. Cats had that sixth sense about them.

When Audrey reached the cottage, she knocked on the door. The door opened slowly and little Edward appeared. Blackie jogged over amiably to rub against Edward's legs but the second the dog spotted Jewel, his big chocolate eyes rounded and then it was commotion gone wild. Blackie put his nose to the ground, sticking his rear end up, his tail whipping furiously, and took off after the cat. Jewel's back arched; poised like a big orange rainbow, she sent the dog a scathing hiss. She leaped in midair, jabbed at him with a combo of swats for all she was worth and then ran as fast as Audrey had ever seen her go.

Blackie seemed unfazed by her method of defense. He darted off after her and the merry chase was on.

Edward shouted at the dog, "Blackie, stop!"

The dog ignored him. Jewel raced over a neatly groomed bed of pansies and under hibiscus bushes. Blackie was no slacker. He followed her, barking enthusiastically until Jewel spotted an old oak tree. She climbed it in three seconds flat and by the time the dog reached the tree, it was game over. Blackie lifted up on hind legs, balancing his front paws against the base of the tree and *ruff, ruff, ruffed* his frustration.

Audrey had been betting on Jewel the entire time. The cat wouldn't let a Border collie get the best of her. Jewel sat calmly on a branch ten feet in the air, looking down her nose at the outdistanced dog.

"S-sorry," Edward said. "He's not t-trying to hurt her. He's only p-playing."

"I know," she replied to the apologetic boy. "I doubt Jewel likes his game, but she'll get over it."

After a few moments, Blackie walked off in defeat, glancing every so often at Jewel's perch on the tree as he trotted away. No doubt, the dog wanted another crack at her. When the drama was over, Audrey turned back to the boy. "How are you, Edward?"

The boy shrugged. "I'm o-kay."

"Are you having a good summer?"

He nodded. "I'm w-working."

"You are?"

"I watch Blackie and t-today I'm watering S-Sophia's plants. I brought in her m-mail, too."

"Oh, that's nice. So Sophia isn't home, then?"

"Nope. Mr. Slade t-took her on a little trip. It was a s-surprise and he asked me to w-watch the house so Sophia wouldn't worry about her plants. He g-gave me the key and everything. My grandma's coming h-here to pick me up s-soon."

Disappointment curled in her belly. Her shoulders slumped as the weight of her secret bore down on her. All the way over here, she'd thought about what she'd say to Sophia and how great it would be to unburden herself by telling her the truth. Sophia probably would've taken one look at her and guessed the truth. Oh, who was she kidding? Sophia *had* known. She'd given her the pregnancy test, recognizing the symptoms before Audrey had.

Now, Audrey longed for a pep talk and the moral support that Sophia would've given her. She needed a friend to lean on, a sympathetic ear and someone to convince her that her life wasn't a total wreck.

"I'm sure you're doing a good job," she told Edward.

His eyes lit up, and it made her feel a little bit better seeing how her encouragement gave the boy a sense of accomplishment. He'd had a rough childhood, too. Thankfully, his grandmother had intervened and the boy seemed to be thriving. Audrey had been told his speech was improving every day.

"Do you know when they'll be home?"

"T-tomorrow, I think."

"Okay. Well then, I'll just wait until then to speak with them. Oh, um, Edward. Would you mind calling Blackie? He needs to go back in the house or else Jewel will be sleeping among the oaks tonight."

The boy laughed and after Blackie cooperated, Audrey bid them farewell.

She returned to the Slade home on weak legs and with a touchy stomach, but her worst symptom wasn't physical. Her emotions were piling up, one on top of the other like a cheerleader pyramid. Any slight shift to the balance would have them all crashing down.

She entered the house with cautious steps, walking softly

and hoping to avoid Luke. A sideways glance into the parlor
had her doing a quick double take.

"Hey, sis."

Her brother's familiar voice rang in her ears. His face, so
strong, so caring, filled her heart with love. Forgetting her
sluggishness, she raced over to where he stood in the middle
of the room and flung her arms around him. "Casey!"

Sure he could be a bullheaded pain at times, but he was
her bullheaded pain and right now her heart sang at the sight
of him. His arms, tucking her in close, felt strong and com-
forting. "It's good to see you," she whispered.

"Same here, squirt."

Casey could call her squirt all day long for all she cared.
She clung to his neck and hung on. And when she didn't
protest at the nickname that usually gave her fits, he pulled
her away to gaze at her curiously. "What did I do to deserve
such a welcome?"

You're my big bro and I need a friend now. "What? Can't
I hug my big brother?"

Casey stared at her and then blinked while taking a full
step back to give her a good once-over. Her arms dropped to
her sides and Audrey felt a keen sense of loss without him
hugging her.

His eyes touched on her pale complexion and then his
gaze shifted to scrutinize her body. She tried to lift her sag-
ging shoulders and hide the shakiness of her wobbly legs. A
scowl formed on his face and his loving expression immediately transformed to concern. "You don't look good, sis.
What's the matter, honey?"

The cheerleader toppled from the top of the heap. All balance was gone. Her pent-up emotions unraveled and tears
sprung from her eyes. "Oh, Casey."

She fell into his chest and unleashed her sobs.

Slowly, he brought her into the circle of his arms again.
"It's…okay," he said as if he didn't know how to soothe the

grown-up version of his little sister. He patted her back and hushed her quietly. "Why are you crying, sweetheart?"

She continued to sob, her unbanked tears coming as a surprise to her, as well. She wasn't sure what or how to tell him.

His booming voice shook. "Are you...ill? Did you come here to hide it from me? Tell me, Audrey Faith. You're scaring the life out of me."

She began shaking her head. Casey feared for her life. Oh, heavens. He'd gotten it all wrong. Her brother always looked out for her. She didn't always appreciate it but now she realized how much he'd sacrificed for her. How much he worried over her. She caught her breath between sobs. "No...I'm not ill. I'm fine. It's just that...I'm, I'm...*pregnant*."

It was the first time she'd said the words aloud. They felt strange to her ears and the gravity of her situation and Casey's reaction—a shift in his body temperature from warm to ice-cold—made her feel it all the more. The news paralyzed him a moment.

He didn't move a muscle.

After long, drawn-out moments, he spoke through clenched teeth. "I'll crush that Toby Watson."

"It's not Toby's," she said in a rush.

Out of the corner of her eye, she saw movement at the parlor doorway. A figure, tall and lean and good-looking as sin, strode into the room to stand beside Casey.

Luke's gaze bore down on her. He rasped, "Audrey, you're having my baby?"

Audrey faced him. "Oh, Luke."

Casey's mouth dropped open. He didn't miss the implication. He swiveled his head to glare at the man standing next to him. "You're asking my sister if she's having your kid?"

Luke ignored Casey. His full attention was on her. "Answer me."

Audrey opened her mouth, but before she could utter her reply, Casey's fist met with Luke's face. "You son of a bitch."

Eight

The punch surprised Luke, and he staggered back. He rebounded quickly and came at Casey with his fists clenched and ready, but at the last minute, he backed off.

"Come on," Casey said, waving both hands, egging him on and inviting a fight. "Take a punch so I can knock you to Carson City."

Luke glared at Casey and rubbed his face where he'd been hit. His cheek was swollen. There would be a nasty bruise. "Back off, Casey. I'm not going to fight you."

Casey bellowed, "The hell you're not."

Audrey's tears stopped flowing. She'd made a big mess of everything and she didn't know how to fix it, but she certainly didn't want the two men she loved most in the world to have a barroom brawl in the middle of the parlor. "Stop it. Casey, you're still recovering from a broken back."

He granted her a sideways glance. "Hell, Audrey, I'm fine. Now be quiet."

"I won't be quiet. You're not fine, and you're not going to beat Luke up."

"Like he could," Luke said, puffing his chest out.

The two men sized each other up. Both of them were acting like juveniles.

Casey got in Luke's face. "You're a bastard, Luke."

"No, he's not." Audrey was angry about Luke's stubborn and far-reaching code of honor, but she wouldn't stand here and allow Casey to make assumptions about Luke that weren't true. "None of this is Luke's fault. It was all my doing."

Casey snorted as if she'd handed him a load of manure. "It's always the guy's fault, Audrey Faith. No matter what you did, he did worse. I doubt you forced him into it."

Oh, but she had. Almost. She'd seduced him. "He didn't even know it was—"

"I don't want to hear details, for pity's sake." Casey cut her off, his face pinched tight.

Luke stepped in between her and Casey and spoke directly to her brother. "You're right. I'm a bastard. You trusted me and I blew that trust to hell."

"Luke!" Audrey couldn't believe her ears. Luke was being Luke and manning up for her sake. Luke wouldn't let her lose face with her brother. But the truth was, he wasn't at fault, and his friendship with Casey hung in the balance. "Let me explain it to him. Let me tell him how it all happened the first time. You see, Casey, I was coming—"

Luke turned to her and put up a hand, a warning in his voice. "Don't, Audrey. He doesn't want the details."

"I surely don't."

Luke's cheek was turning a shade of purple. He kept his voice calm, trying to diffuse the situation. His eyes softened on her. "Are you carrying my baby?"

She nodded. "I haven't seen a doctor yet, but the pregnancy test is positive. I have all the symptoms."

Luke swallowed.

Casey muttered a curse under his breath.

A beat ticked by and then the two men spoke in unison.

"You're marrying me," Luke said.

"You're marrying him," Casey said.

The two of them looked at each other, none too friendly, but nodded in agreement.

"Damn right you're marrying her," Casey muttered.

"You just heard me ask her, didn't you?"

"Then it's settled," Casey said.

Both of them turned to her. She faced two stubborn-set jaws on men who had no clue how much they'd just hurt her. She didn't think it possible, but her heart broke even more. Casey loved her and cared about her, but he'd been dictating the terms of her life for too long. She didn't want or need his approval on her decisions. Though if she had his blessing, she'd be grateful and happy about it. But she certainly wasn't going to allow him to make the biggest decision of her life for her.

Luke, on the other hand, didn't love her. That said it all, didn't it? In Audrey's fantasy world, Luke loved her and wanted to marry her and live out his life with her. But that wasn't the case. She couldn't let him demand that she enter into a marriage based on his noble sense of morality. She loved him too much for that. A lopsided marriage for the baby's sake wouldn't make anyone happy. The last thing Luke wanted was a loveless marriage. And the last thing she wanted was to live her life without his love.

Finally, it dawned on her. She deserved better. No more halves in her life. She'd had half a family, living without the love of a mother and father all these years. She'd had half a school life, too—tagging behind Casey on the rodeo circuit while her high school friends were having fun, getting into trouble and learning how to deal with impending adulthood. She'd had half an education, her studies being cut short by Casey's back injury.

She'd sacrificed for him and wanted to help him recover, in much the same the way he'd sacrificed his life to raise her. Neither of them had had a choice.

But this time, finally, Audrey did have a choice. This time she was old enough to make a stand for what she wanted out of life. This time, she had something to say about it.

She didn't want Luke if he didn't love her. She'd never deny him his child. They would work something out later on. But for now, Audrey's decision was seared in her mind as the way it had to be.

"Casey," she said firmly, her sobs from five minutes ago well forgotten, "nothing is settled. I'm almost twenty-five years old. I love you, but you're not my keeper. I make my own decisions."

She turned away from Casey to look straight into Luke's eyes. "Luke, that was hardly a proposal. You didn't ask. But my answer would've been the same. No, I will not marry you."

Never in her life would she have dreamed of turning down Lucas Slade's offer of marriage.

Both men's mouths moved. They started flapping their gums, jawing at her, but this time, Audrey didn't listen. Her decision was final and nothing either of them could say at this point would change her mind. "I'm exhausted. I'm going to bed. I don't want to be disturbed." She held her head high, regally—a lesson learned from Jewel—and pointed a finger at both of them. "Don't argue after I'm gone. For heaven's sake, you two are friends. Promise me you'll get along."

Casey grumbled.

Luke muttered something.

The two of them wouldn't look at each other.

"Okay, I have your promise," she said, darting each one a purposeful glance before she walked out of the room.

Luke and Casey sat on the front steps of the porch, a half-empty bottle of Scotch whiskey between them. A pinkish blaze of light lowered on the horizon. Dusk's long fingers touched the earth and settled around the ranch.

Branches fluttered from a bird's flight. Horses whinnied, and off in the distance an owl hooted. Ranch sounds carried to Luke's ears as the land whispered good-night, but Luke wasn't ready to turn in. Hell, he had the other half of the bottle to polish off.

Casey refused to budge. He sat still as a stone, mumbling as he imbibed the good stuff.

"I'm never gonna forgive you for this." Casey poured an inch of whiskey down his throat and then reached for the bottle to fill up his glass again.

"I know."

"She's a good kid." Casey's gravelly voice rose an octave. "Damn you, Luke," he said for the tenth time.

Luke should be burning in hell from all the damning Casey was doing.

"You were the good one," he said. "I'd be breaking all the rules and you'd be right there, Mr. Clean, always picking up the pieces. Always doing the right thing. Why the hell didn't you do the right thing with my sister? Why the hell did you knock her up?"

Luke sipped his whiskey, looking down at the amber liquor in his glass. "Wasn't intentional."

Hell, no, it wasn't. He hadn't set out to touch Audrey much less get her pregnant. The concept of fatherhood was still foreign to him. He struggled with it. He was going to have a baby. With Audrey. Everything inside him said he had to do the right thing, so he'd demanded marriage of her. But a loveless marriage was the last thing he'd wanted. All of his life he'd planned on something more than his father had with his mother. He'd waited for that zing, for that missing piece of the puzzle, for that extra bounce in his step when he thought about a woman. When it didn't happen, he just figured he needed to wait some more. But now, the baby changed everything.

"I should've knocked you out."

Luke drew breath into his lungs and spoke quietly. "You couldn't if you tried."

"Landed a pretty dang mean right hook, though."

"You sucker punched me."

"I'm not sorry."

"I got that the first three times you told me."

"First thing tomorrow, I'm gonna pack up and go. And I'm taking my kid sister with me."

That was not going to happen. Luke wasn't going to let Casey badger Audrey into leaving. She was pregnant with his child. They had things to work out. Luke's fist balled up. He spoke with menace in his voice. "You can go anytime you want. But Audrey's not leaving until I talk to her."

"She told you she's not marrying you."

"And you think you're gonna bully Audrey into leaving with you?"

"I don't bully her."

"You've been bullying her since the day I met you. She was too young and dependent on you to fight back. But, man, you were clueless when it came to her. Audrey's not a kid. She's all grown-up. Somehow your radar missed that, Case. She's old enough to make up her own mind about things. She's old enough to decide about her life and her future. I slept with her, yes. It was a mistake on my part, but believe me when I say this—she made her decision to be with me. She wasn't forced or bullied. So you may think I'm a bastard, and I may very well be, but don't think for a minute I'm going to let you ramrod her into going home with you."

Luke rose then. The world tipped a little. His head spun, but Luke knew his limits and this wasn't it. He wasn't hammered enough not to see the truth. He had to stand his ground now. He pointed his finger right down the nose of his friend.

"You let Audrey decide what she wants to do." He turned and grabbed the door handle. Right before he walked inside, he added, "And don't you even think about getting behind the wheel of your car tonight."

Casey poured the last drop of Scotch into his glass and muttered, "Hell, Luke. What do you take me for? I'm not that dang stupid."

Luke grinned, satisfied, although he didn't know why he was feeling so darn good. He had a reluctant bride on his hands and a baby on the way.

In the morning, Audrey walked into the kitchen at the usual time. Luke was at the table, sipping coffee, the food on his plate untouched. He gazed up with bloodshot eyes. The bruise on his face had faded some, but it hadn't gone away. There was a round blotch of color just under his right eye. She wondered what Ellie had said about it or if she'd asked at all.

Luke looked sorely hungover. He'd taken the news of her pregnancy like a man, demanding marriage and then drinking himself into oblivion when she'd refused his nonproposal.

"Ellie made breakfast," he said.

A dish of French toast, scrambled eggs and honey-smoked bacon greeted her. Well…thank goodness the sugary and savory scents mingling in the air didn't make her queasy. She might actually be able to handle a bit of breakfast this morning.

"Would you like some coffee?" the plump, white-haired woman asked, coming toward the table with a steaming pot in her hand.

"No, thanks, Ellie. I'll have juice today. Everything looks delicious."

The housekeeper nodded and turned on her heel. A few seconds later, a glass of orange juice appeared in front of her. "There you go. And for you, Luke?"

"I'll stick with coffee this morning. If you're through here, I'd like to speak with Audrey privately."

"Surely," Ellie said, pouring more coffee into his cup. "I'll be back later to straighten up the kitchen."

"I've got it, Ellie," Audrey said. The housekeeper was a one-woman dynamo. Every pot and pan she'd used to cook the meal was already cleaned and put away. Just the tabletop dishes remained. "There's just a few things here. I'll load the dishwasher."

"Well, thank you," Ellie said, wiping her hands on a dish towel, giving her a smile. "You're a dear."

The housekeeper left the room and they sat silently. That was fine with Audrey. She took a few bites of crisp bacon and forked her way through half a piece of one-inch-thick cinnamon-and-pecan French toast. Her stomach didn't rebel and she considered it a good way to start off the morning.

"Casey leave?"

She nodded. "I said goodbye to him this morning."

"He try to get you to go with him?"

"We talked," she said. Her brother hadn't pressed the issue. They'd actually had a civilized adult conversation this morning. She hadn't gone into a lot of detail, but she explained to him about what happened at the cabin and owned up to the blame. Casey didn't fully buy it. Her brother didn't want to let Luke off the hook, yet he hadn't argued with her. She'd asked him to leave the ranch and let her finish the job she came here to do. It was clear Casey didn't want to do that, leaving her in the hands of Evil Luke and all, but he finally nodded in agreement. It surprised the hell out of her when he kissed her cheek, got in his car and drove off without giving her a lecture.

"And you're still here."

"Casey doesn't decide my life, Luke. I think I made myself clear yesterday." She pushed her plate away. Her stomach couldn't handle any more. "I've got a job to do. I plan on finishing what I started."

He nodded and sipped coffee. "I'm glad you're not leaving. I want you to stay."

Endorphins sprang free and she was struck with impossible hope and joy. She fought the warm feeling for all she was worth. Luke was only saying that because of the baby, she reminded herself. A short time ago, he regretted her being on Sunset Ranch.

"I plan to stay."

"Well, then, it's settled."

Luke could be an ass at times, she decided. "Only because *I'm* settling it."

His eyes narrowed on her. They looked patriotic—*red,* white and blue. "Touchy."

"Yeah, well…that's what happens to pregnant women. We get touchy."

"I'll remember that. Are you an expert now?"

"I've been reading up." On the internet. There was an abundance of knowledge there, but some of it was scary stuff. She made a decision to look up the facts only and not get sucked into the thousands of pregnancy blogs and nightmare stories or else she wouldn't sleep nights. It was a classic case of TMI. "I made an appointment with a doctor."

"A local doctor?"

"Yes." She nodded. "For now."

Relief registered on his face. "I'd like to go with you."

At least it wasn't a demand. "I figured you would. Okay, we'll go together. The appointment is late tomorrow morning."

"Thanks."

"I'm not going to keep you away from the baby, Luke."

For all her misgivings, Luke was a good man, and he'd be a wonderful father. She hadn't any doubts about it. "But you won't marry me?"

The breath whooshed out of her. Tears stung behind her eyes. How many times would she have to refuse the very thing she'd been dreaming about her entire life? How many times would she have to hold her head up high and fight for the one thing she wanted, above all else, for her and her baby...a life filled with true love. "I...can't."

"Why not, Audrey? We're having a baby. That changes everything."

"Your parents had a loveless marriage, Luke. And you never wanted that for yourself. They married for the child's sake."

"They lived a decent life. They raised a family. What they had wasn't terrible."

A sigh climbed up from the depth of her heart. "Did you just hear yourself?" The sting behind her eyes burned now and she struggled not to break down in tears. Audrey couldn't resign herself to being a wife to Luke that way. "Do you want something that only isn't *terrible?*"

Luke stared at her. He heaved a heavy sigh. His shoulders rose and fell. "We'll both love the baby."

Audrey stood up and leaned over the table. Sophia told her she'd know when the time was right. She'd know when she had to tell Luke the ultimate truth. And the time had come. Audrey couldn't put it off anymore. She'd lived with this for ten years. It was finally time to come clean. Luke was beginning to soften her resolve. She was beginning to think about how easy it would be to marry him. To live in this big house and see him every day, raise their child together and get along with him the same way they always had, as friends.

She warred with it in her head for long, drawn out moments. It was the hardest decision she ever had to make. And it was breaking her heart a thousand times over. But she couldn't go through with it. Luke had been her dream, one she would completely sully by going halfway. It had to be all or nothing with Luke. No halves when it came to Lucas Slade.

"You don't love me, Luke."

Luke's breath caught in his throat. Her bluntness surprised him. He rose to face her from across the table.

She was glad he stood. Glad she could look him straight in the eyes and give him the truth. "But you see…I love you. I have for ten years. It wasn't just a childhood crush. It wasn't just a fascination with my big brother's buddy. I have loved you for so long, and so hard, for so many years, it's killing me to pretend I don't. You're the only man I've ever wanted. I didn't set out for any of this to happen. I surely didn't intend to get pregnant, Luke. But that night at the cabin, when I walked into the room and saw you there, I realized that if I walked away, I might blow the only chance I had with you. I might've walked away from something I had dreamed about for years. It was important for me to be with you that night. It was my chance to show you how much I cared for you.

"Did you ever ask yourself why I climbed into bed with you that night? Did you think I'd lay with any man sleeping in that bed? Did you think I was a slut? You never once considered that I might have true feelings for you, Luke. You never once looked at me as anything other than a friend, your buddy's little sister. I have strong feelings for you. I love you with all my heart. And I'm having your baby."

Audrey set her hand on the new life growing inside her even as tears wet her cheeks. "We will not go into this halfway. We want one hundred percent of you. We want all-in. We want to be your pot of gold."

Luke swallowed and blinked his eyes. "Audrey."

Audrey's voice began to crack. "I will n-never keep you from your child, Luke. And I wish to heaven that you l-loved me, but you don't, so I won't m-marry you. I hope you can understand that. Now, I h-have work to do. I'll s-see you later."

She turned to leave, wiping tears with the sleeve of her blouse as she headed out the door.

"Audrey, wait!"

Luke's plea only stopped her for a second. She squeezed her eyes closed and stood waiting for Luke to say what she needed to hear.

When he offered nothing else, Audrey turned to face his blank stare. "I have waited, Luke. For ten years."

Then she exited the room.

Nine

Luke canceled his meetings for the morning and changed into a pair of washed-out jeans and a T-shirt. He slipped his hat on his head and walked to the barn. He found Ward there, saddling up the dapple-gray Andalusian gelding that would be leaving the ranch in three days. He'd been sold to a Frenchman who wanted the good-natured horse for his twelve-year-old daughter.

"Hey, Luke, I'm just about ready to exercise him. You need me for something?"

Luke stared at the horse that he'd admired for a long time. "How about I take this one out this morning?"

Ward gave him a quizzical stare. "You want to take Caliber out? Well, sure thing. I'll take one of the Arabians. You want company on the ride?"

Luke didn't blame Ward for questioning him. He rarely rode the horses he intended to sell. Usually Luke rode his own mare, a fast yet gentle bay mare of fine breeding named Nutmeg. "Not this time, Ward. Appreciate the offer, though. I just want to take him out by myself. Say goodbye, you know?"

Ward gave the animal a firm, affectionate pat. "Yeah, I know. Gonna miss him. He's got spirit, this one, but he's a pushover with kids. Edward comes by to see him and the horse has such a tender way with him. That little girl's gonna be real happy on her twelfth birthday."

Luke nodded. He mounted the horse and rode off without saying any more. He wasn't much in a mood for small talk.

He'd tried to small talk his way with Audrey last night with a text message.

Just making sure you're feeling well.

After the bombshell she'd dropped about having his baby, Luke had been at his wits' end. Yet, he'd had to give Audrey the time and space she needed. It wasn't as if he didn't need time, too. This whole thing had been a weird twist of fate and now an innocent child's future was at stake.

I'm feeling okay. Going to bed now.

was her curt reply, and Luke had gotten the hint.

This morning, Audrey had dropped her second bombshell. Apparently, one wasn't enough for her. He didn't know which one had shocked him more. Now, not only did he have an unborn child to deal with, he had Audrey's vow of love plaguing his thoughts.

Summer heat drew down on him. Luke lowered the brim of his hat and clucked his tongue. The Andalusian took off at a run. Caliber's long legs ate up ground and Luke's hat nearly blew off his head as the animal flew across the acreage. Out beyond the pasture, with the house long forgotten in the distance, Luke thought his head would clear. He thought everything would become as transparent as glass or at least as clear as a murky, old barn window.

Solutions didn't magically appear.

One thing kept coming back to his mind. One thing knocked him upside the head over and over again and continued to plague him.

Audrey loved him.

He hadn't seen it coming.

He was a damn fool for being so dense.

Her heartbreaking confession this morning left him dumbfounded. And numb. He'd hurt Audrey in the worst possible way and the sad thing about it was he would continue to hurt her. Because he didn't feel the same way about her.

He brought Caliber to a trot along a path that led to a cropping of apple trees. The fruit wasn't edible yet, the balls were hard and green and the size of a walnut. He dismounted, his boots hitting the earth as hard as his heart was heavy. He ground-tethered the horse and stared out on Slade land from under the shade of a tree.

Why was it that grown-up Luke Slade had never loved a woman?

The horse snorted, his breaths labored and deep from the long run. Luke stared at him for a minute, sorry to see the gelding go. He was a beautiful animal and a good addition to the Slade ranch. Every single one of the ranch hands, the wranglers especially, remarked on the horse's good nature. Even Audrey had called him a sweetheart.

Which was a lot more than she'd called him lately.

Luke took a big swallow. In that moment, he realized something. He'd seen it first in Ward's puzzled expression when he'd offered to take Caliber out. Now, it was as if someone had taken a rag and wiped that old barn window clean. There was clarity that Luke had never seen before. And the news wasn't good.

He had a flaw.

Well, damn, he had many. He didn't think he was all that, but this blemish in his character got his spurs to jingling, as his father would say.

Luke thought back to when he was a boy of six and a sleek, beautiful colt named Smoke was born on the ranch. It had been love at first sight as far as Luke was concerned. He'd eaten, slept and breathed for love of that colt. His dad had warned him not to get too attached because Smoke was bred of champions and he would be sold off. He'd go to a good home, Randall Slade had said. Luke pretended he'd understood, but that hadn't stopped his fascination with the horse. In his young heart, he'd never believed Smoke—the colt he'd loved since the moment the foal was brought into the world—would really be leaving the ranch.

Then one day six months later, Luke's heart had nearly broken in two when he saw Smoke being loaded into a trailer. He remembered running as fast as his little legs would take him, chasing after that trailer, crying and calling Smoke's name. His father had looked at him with regret in his eyes. As if to say, *I'm sorry, son, but I warned you.*

Luke had cried himself to sleep for one entire month, learning a life lesson that was probably way too hard for a six-year-old boy to fully comprehend. But he'd understood the heartache. And the pain inflicted.

After that, Luke had admired the horses on the ranch from afar. As a boy, he would feed them, ride them when necessary, groom and muck their stalls, all chores his rigid old man required. But he would never allow himself to get close to them. To make a lasting bond. He'd come to realize the hard facts of life on a horse farm. It was the family business. Those gorgeous bays and palominos and black stallions… they would be all be leaving eventually. They'd be sold outright and Luke would never see them again.

The only exception was Tribute. Somehow, that stallion had gotten under his skin. Luke had tried to tame him and had been persistent in that pursuit. The why of it wasn't clear in his mind, but he'd felt a kinship with the spirited animal and looked upon him as a challenge.

Luke focused back on the present, his mind racing, thinking befuddled and crazy thoughts. He squeezed his eyes closed and then muttered a curse.

You're a coward, Luke.

A big, freaking coward.

Thoughts whirled in his head and truths came to light.

He feared getting hurt. He'd never made lasting bonds. He'd protected himself from future pain at all costs. It was a pattern in his life and not a truth he liked facing. But it was there, underneath all the other garbage in his mind.

Luke was always the first one to walk away from a woman. Images popped into his head of the women in his past and the relationships he'd refused to work on. His noncommittal attitude and his willingness to call it a day when things got rough or when things looked like they were getting too serious played over in his mind.

He'd done the same with Audrey. And she'd come with an additional warning tag—she was Casey's sister. Yet of all the women Luke had been with, the only one he'd want to carry his child and spend his future with was...Audrey. That was a good thing, wasn't it? Marriage and parenthood with her were doable. He liked Audrey. She was a good friend. She was pretty. Beautiful, he would say. And she came from the same background as he did. She was a country girl and loved ranch life. The notion of life with her *wasn't terrible*.

Crap.

Dang it if Audrey wasn't right about him. It was a sad state of affairs. He shook his head and muttered, "You are sorely jaded, Luke Slade."

He mounted Caliber and rode the horse back to the ranch at a slow, easy trot. When he arrived at the stables, he decided to groom Caliber himself, wash him down and currycomb him. He checked his legs and picked out a pebble from his shoe and then let the horse feed from a bucket of oats. He slipped the gelding a few sugar cubes, too. His efforts raised eyebrows among the ranch hands and he also caught Audrey, mother of his child and woman who refused to marry him, staring at him a time or two.

Audrey tiptoed out of the house just after midnight with Jewel at her heels. Her work with Trib was paying off. It seemed the horse looked upon Jewel as an equal and somewhat of a friend. What choice did the stallion have? Jewel was the only game in town. Hopefully, it was more than that. Hopefully, Trib's temperament was mellowing and he was beginning to trust the both of them. That's all she wanted. Some trust from the horse.

Quiet as a church mouse, she entered the barn and opened the top half of the paddock door. Immediately, Jewel jumped up on the ledge with the grace of, well…a cat, to take her regal pose and greet her new friend.

Meow.

The second Trib spotted her, he wandered over. He settled right by the paddock door and stood nose to nose with the cat. Audrey whispered, "Hi, boy. That's right. Come closer. We won't hurt you."

The horse shifted his gaze to her for a moment, then back to the cat.

Carefully, Audrey dug into her pocket and came up with half a dozen sugar cubes in her palm. She arranged them carefully and slowly brought her hand toward the horse's mouth. "A treat for you."

Trib craned his neck and turned his head toward her hand. Out came his long pink tongue to lick her palm and gobble up the sugar cubes. Audrey released a breath. Success. "You are lonely," she whispered. "Well, don't you worry. We're here now."

Maybe it was her imagination, but the wariness that she'd come to expect from Trib was gone. At least for right now. She wanted so badly to let this horse know he had nothing to fear from her and that he didn't need to guard himself quite so carefully when she was around.

Making progress with Trib helped ease her heartache about Lucas Slade. At least she had these nights to look forward to. At least she felt needed and wanted by the very horse that had severely injured her baby's father.

How strange was that?

That night, Audrey fell into an exhausted sleep. In the morning, she rose and dressed, readying for her first appointment with the obstetrician who would be treating her while she lived on Sunset Ranch.

She walked into the kitchen and found Luke there, seated at the table. He lifted his beautiful face, his blue eyes brightening the second they landed on her. Emotion rocked and rolled inside her belly, which wasn't at all fair, since she'd just gotten over her morning sickness. She'd never get through these next few weeks if Luke continued to look at her like that.

"Morning," he said.

"Good morning."

She distracted herself by looking at the big breakfast Ellie had whipped up. Flapjacks and eggs sat waiting for her along with a bowl of fresh late-summer fruit. She turned to Ellie, who was wiping a dish at the sink. "Looks great, Ellie."

"I hope so. I've got more coming, if you're inclined."

Ellie liked to feed people. "Oh, no, I'm sure this is plenty."

She took a seat at the table.

"You sleep well?" Luke asked, always the gentleman. Though Audrey figured she looked like heck since her secret work with Trib kept her awake half the night. Afternoon naps were not overrated and she'd managed to slip a few in this week to make up for the loss of sleep.

"Yes, I did. Thank you."

He nodded.

Lime-scented aftershave wafted in the air and teased her nostrils. Luke always smelled so good. He wore a crisp black-and-white-checked shirt tucked into the waistband of brand-new Wrangler jeans.

They ate in silence, both aware of Ellie's presence. Audrey hadn't told anyone but Casey, Sophia and Luke about her pregnancy. She was certain Ellie didn't know and she wanted to keep the news close at hand for a little while longer. Luke would want to tell his brothers, she was sure, but when he thought it best.

When Ellie excused herself from the kitchen, Luke lifted his eyes to her. "I put aside my work for the morning, so I can drive you into town for the appointment. I'm…uh, well, I want to support you and let you know you're not in this alone."

Tears stung behind Audrey's eyes. It was a beautiful thing to say, yet somehow those words spoken from Luke, the man she loved, made her ache inside. "I know. You're too decent to abandon me."

He straightened in his seat as if she'd insulted him. "I'd never do that. I asked you to marry me."

Audrey glanced away. Luke just didn't get it.

And later that morning, after driving into Silver Springs, they met with Dr. Amanda Ayers. After an examination that Luke insisted on attending, the fine doctor confirmed the pregnancy, giving them both insights as to what to expect in the coming months, along with a list of instructions to follow. The reality of her motherhood sank in like a sledgehammer pounding wood.

"I guess there's no getting around it," Audrey said, as Luke took her hand and guided her out of the doctor's office.

Luke smiled. "The pregnancy? Only way I know happens nine months from now."

Gladness filled her heart. At least Luke was taking it like a man. He'd fully participated in the discussion with Dr. Ayers and now he seemed to be adjusting well to becoming a father. She wouldn't go so far as to say he was happy about it. The situation wasn't ideal. The details of her life were murky at best. If she decided to move back to Reno, the baby would have two homes and parents who weren't together, but it pleased Audrey to see Luke's gradual acceptance. "That's seven months and one week from now, buster."

Luke gave her hand a little squeeze and chuckled as he opened the car door for her. He had no idea what his touch did to her or the loss she felt when he let go.

"Yeah. You gotta forgive my math skills."

She slid into her seat and strapped her seat belt on, glancing up at him. "Hopefully, the baby will have my brains."

Luke didn't miss a beat. "As long as he has my good looks, we're golden." He winked and closed the door before she could think of a witty retort.

They left Silver Springs in the dust. And once out of town and onto the open road, Luke reached over to take her hand in his. Bone-melting warmth spread through her system. Did he know what he was doing to her? Was it a deliberate attempt to soften her and get her to change her mind about marrying him?

He gazed into her eyes then and for several magical moments she saw something new, something different in the way he looked at her. She wasn't imagining it. There was a connection now, fragile as it was, and the hope in her heart was becoming a tangible thing.

Mercy.

He paid attention to the road for the next ten minutes and then turned to face her again. "I'm pretty darn hungry." The caress in his eyes was still there. "Would you have lunch with me? I know this little place just off the road that I think you'd like."

She didn't have to think twice. Her appetite for food and for Luke had returned. "Would love to."

Content, he made a right turn onto a single-lane highway and parked in front of the Chipmunk Café.

She reread the sign above the cabin-esque building and gave a slight shake of the head.

"What is this place?"

"You'll see."

He helped her out of the car and held her hand as they strode into the wood cabin diner. Audrey took a look around and her mouth dropped open. Her gaze roamed over tables and bench seats made of molded plastic that resembled split-wood logs. The walls were decorated with oversize walnuts, woodsy foliage and greenery. Off in one corner was a children-only section where little ones crawled into a simulated underground chipmunk burrow and sat on stools that stood less than one foot high to eat their meals. Other game areas were strategically placed throughout the large dining hall that kept kids racing from one to the other with big smiles beaming on their faces.

"I heard Dr. Ayers say that protein is good for the baby," Luke said. "I hope you like nuts and seeds, because every dish here is made with them. Either in the recipe or crushed and sprinkled on top as a coating. My favorite is the peanut-crusted hamburger."

Audrey felt her smile widen. She already loved this place. "How long have you been coming here?"

"Ever since I was a kid. Wasn't often enough for me back then. It was a special treat if Mom and Dad agreed to bring us here. Dad hated the noise and Mom was allergic to nuts."

"Oh, wow, Luke. I don't remember you ever talking about this place."

Luke looked around. "There's an empty booth. Wanna try it?"

"Of course." She wouldn't think of disappointing him.

Luke put his hand to her waist and guided her across the room, fending off three small children racing toward the burrow. Luke smiled like a little boy when a waitress dressed in a furry russet-colored chipmunk costume came to take their order. Audrey opted for the candied-walnut chicken salad and Luke ordered his favorite burger.

During the entire meal Luke rattled on and on about the baby and the things he wanted to do with him or her. Audrey found herself caught up in the enthusiasm and they both agreed, once the baby got old enough, they would put the Chipmunk Café on their radar.

That warm light in Luke's eyes didn't diminish throughout the meal or on the drive home. Something was definitely different with Luke today. He kept finding ways to touch her. To slip her hand into his or to spread his palm across her back as they walked along. But she didn't place much faith in it. He was getting excited about the baby. Not her. Never her. She'd pretty much convinced herself of that.

They entered the house together, Luke closing the door behind them. She took a step toward the hallway that led to her room and felt a gentle pull on her arm. A strong hand slipped down to her wrist and she turned to look into Luke's incredibly handsome face.

"Thank you," he said, "for letting me come today."

His grasp on her wrist tightened as he drew her closer. She drifted to him as if on a windswept cloud. "It's important that you be there. You're, uh, the baby's father."

Sincerity touched his eyes and he gave a slight nod.

"Thanks for the Chipmunk Café," she whispered, her ridiculous heart beating like mad.

"I had fun."

"So did I. It's a wild place for kids."

"For some grown-ups, too," he said with a cocky grin that brought out all of his boyish charm.

"Well, I'd...uh, I'd better get changed. I have wor—"

Luke glanced at her mouth. Then a smile broadened his lips and he bent his head. She didn't move. She didn't step back. Fool that she was, she wanted this. The second his lips touched hers, all the warning bells ringing in her head went on mute. A tiny whimper rose from her throat. Luke deepened the kiss until her breaths came fast and heavy. Thoughts of pushing him away entered, then fled her mind. She couldn't breathe, much less think.

She curled her arms around his neck. He pulled her closer. His hand cupped the back of her head and strands of her hair flowed over his arm. The kiss went on a good, long time.

Finally, Luke allowed her to come up for air.

The impact of his passionate kiss pleasantly stung her lips. She stared at him, trembling. "Wh-what was that all about?"

"Sweetheart," Luke said, his brows gathering and a question in his expression, "I wish I knew."

"Good news," Logan said, walking into Sophia's office at Sunset Lodge and interrupting Luke's conversation with his good friend. Sophia not only managed the place but was now a full partner. "Justin will be home in time for our wedding. He'll be here in a few weeks."

Luke was glad to hear it. Justin had been gone for too long. Luke and everyone else at Sunset Ranch missed him. "Don't you knock?"

"Why should I knock on my fiancée's door?" Logan asked with a wry smirk. "I didn't expect to find you here wasting her time."

Luke caught Sophia grinning at Logan. The two of them were ridiculously happy. "She was my best friend before she was your fiancée."

"Old news, bro. I'm so tickled about our little brother coming home, I won't even let you rile me," Logan said.

"You mean the little brother who could probably whoop both our butts without breaking a sweat?"

"That's the one. Just don't let him hear you admit that."

"You think I'm crazy?" Luke asked.

Logan strode over to where Sophia was sitting behind her desk to give her a kiss.

"Looks like there's good news for all three of the Slade brothers," Sophia said. She shot a quick look at Luke, giving him the opening he needed. "Luke was just about to tell me something important."

He sat in a comfy leather seat at an angle to her, his legs stretched out, his arm braced on the edge of the desk as he toyed with a ballpoint pen. *Click, click, click.*

"Oh, yeah?" Logan took a seat beside him and shifted his gaze to him. "Our wedding, Justin's homecoming and what else?"

Luke had to face his brother with the truth and it pained him to admit that doing the right thing by Audrey wasn't in his hands. She held all the cards. "Audrey and I are having a baby."

Logan's mouth dropped open. He blinked a few times, absorbing the shocking news, and Luke couldn't fault Logan his reaction. Audrey had always been off-limits. It was an unspoken rule, a code of honor between friends. At least in the Slade world it was. "You and Audrey? I'll be damned. Does Casey know?" Logan examined his face. "Oh, wait a minute, is that what happened to your cheek?"

Luke's mouth twisted. The bruise was barely visible anymore but his brother was as sharp as a tack. "He wasn't too happy about it. But it's not his concern. This is between me and Audrey. I've asked her to marry me."

A smile formed on Logan's face, and he put out his hand. "Well, congratulations."

Luke didn't make a move to shake his brother's hand. His fingers gripped the pen tighter. *Click. Click. Click.* "She turned me down."

Logan's hand dropped to his side. "Why would she do that? Anyone with eyes in their head could see she's crazy about you."

"Logan," Sophia said, her voice sweet with warning. "It's a little more complicated than that."

"How complicated can it be?" he asked.

Luke tossed the pen down. "You'd be surprised."

Without going into the intimate details, Luke painted a picture for Logan and Sophia, explaining the situation between Audrey and him. Logan could be an ass at times, but not today. Today, both he and Sophia listened and gave their support.

"Well, you gotta give her time," Logan said. "You can't blow this. There's a baby involved."

"Not too much time, though," Sophia said. She appeared thoughtful. "Women need reassurances."

"Go after what you want," Logan said. He'd been persistent with Sophia and it had paid off.

"Be genuine," Sophia said.

"Got it," Luke said. Maybe getting Audrey to agree to marry him wasn't as impossible as it seemed. Maybe he hadn't tried hard enough.

Or maybe you don't want to hurt her anymore.

Luke gave his head a quick shake. He'd been reeling from Audrey's rejection and stressed out about how to change her mind. He couldn't lie to her and tell her what she wanted to hear. That would be cruel. And she'd see right through it.

Sophia walked around the desk to give him a hug, her embrace tight with affection. Logan congratulated him about the baby if not an upcoming wedding. Luke strode out of the lodge, grateful to both for their advice. A sense of relief curled in his belly that at least his family knew the situation now. Audrey would be the mother of his child.

All day long, Luke had been thinking about her. There was something sexy and beautiful about a woman carrying your child. The notion had settled in his gut and clung there, making him smile at times, making him look at Audrey Faith Thomas differently.

Later that night, Luke sat in his bed thinking about going

after what he wanted, about being genuine and about giving Audrey reassurances. He didn't know if he could do the last thing, but two out of three wasn't bad and he had to try something.

He picked up his phone and hoped to heaven Audrey wouldn't ignore his text messages the way she had for the past few nights.

R u asleep?

Her reply came quickly.

No. I should be but I'm not tired.

Not tired, either. Keep thinking about today.

She wrote back.

Meeting the doctor and realizing we're going to be parents?

That, too. But thinking about what happened after.

Chipmunk Café?

Kissing you, Audrey.

There was a minute delay in her response.

It was a good kiss, Luke.

He had to keep her talking. He was glad she responded. Glad she hadn't shut him down.

I bought a *What To Expect When You're Going to Be a Daddy* book the other day.

R u reading it?

No, I'm texting with you. Want to read it together?

Now?

Yes.

R u really asking me to come to your room to read a baby book?

He went for broke. *Be genuine. Go after what you want.*

That would be my second choice when you got here. It's up to you, darlin'.

She was chilly from every part of her body the do-me black negligee didn't cover. That had to be why she was shivering. Any second now, things could get really hot, though. Gosh, she hoped so. Audrey squeezed her eyes shut, stood at Luke's door and knocked.

A few minutes ago, she'd nearly dropped the phone from her hands reading Luke's message. And the rebellious, wild, sadistic part of her told her to put on the skimpy black nightie, march into Luke's room and spend one last glorious night with him, reason be damned. Oddly—or maybe rightly so—she'd followed her gut instincts. Now, here she stood, trembling like a kid watching her first horror flick, her blood pulsing and her heart zipping along.

She heard footsteps approach from behind the door. Her breath caught and she choked with fear as all semblances of bravado and courage abandoned her.

The door opened to Luke, barefoot, wearing unsnapped faded jeans and nothing else.

Mercy.

The moment his eyes landed on her, they flickered and blinked and turned warm as honey as he pored over every ounce of her body. A slow, sexy smile gradually eased the corners of Luke's mouth up, making this devastatingly good-looking man even more beautiful.

How was that possible?

To think she was having a child with this man.

The notion warmed her heart.

She would love Luke until the end of time.

"I came to, to, uh—"

"Read?"

She moved her head to nod, but Luke was too fast for her. Before she could complete the gesture, he pulled her through the doorway and backed her up against the wall. He pressed his body so close she could feel the steam radiating off his broad, bare chest. "Some say reading is overrated." He cupped her shoulders, tucking his index finger underneath the spaghetti straps that held her negligee in place. He teased the straps to and fro. "I don't agree," he whispered. "You can learn a lot from the written word."

Tenderly, he slid the straps down her arms.

Her breasts popped free.

As she absorbed the impact of Luke's quick intake of breath, her eyes gently closed.

"Some books are page-turners."

He kissed her shoulders, taking little nips.

Her skin sizzled like hot oil from his touch.

"Some books you want to keep on reading."

He weighed her bosom in his hands at the same time as his mouth covered hers. A groan of pleasure and satisfaction rose from his throat and for the first time since she'd knocked on his door, she was certain she'd made the right decision coming to him tonight.

He looped her arms around his neck and continued to kiss her, giving her the sliver of heaven she'd needed tonight.

"You're beautiful, Audrey Faith."

"So are you," she whispered.

The room was cast in shades of light and dark. The silence

of the empty house surrounded them. She loved him with all her heart. He didn't love her back. She wished he would. She wished it wasn't lust but love spurring his desire for her.

"I don't know what I am doing here," she breathed through tenderly bruised lips.

Luke didn't offer platitudes but seemed to speak straight from his heart. "I'm just glad you decided to come, sweetheart."

It was enough for her. For now.

He picked her up and carried her to his bed. Laying her down carefully, he peered at her with an expression of tenderness and began to peel her nightie off. His fingers were gentle on her skin as he pulled the garment past her waist and down the legs. "I like this."

She didn't say he could thank Sophia for the do-me outfit. She only smiled.

He set the nightie at the foot of the bed and then lowered down next to her. "The doctor said lovemaking won't hurt the baby."

Audrey gave a nod. At the doctor's office, she'd blushed down to her toes when she'd heard that comment.

"I want you, Audrey." He cradled her face in his hands and kissed her again. There would be no guilt and repercussions on Luke's part. He couldn't claim foul or use his code of honor to back away. He'd invited her here tonight.

"In case you didn't notice, Luke, I'm naked on your bed. That's got to tell you something."

He chuckled and covered her with his body.

It felt right. It felt so very good.

Making love to Luke was better than ever.

And afterward as they lay together, arms and legs entwined, Luke kissed her good-night and she sighed inwardly, wishing Luke had whispered in her ear, "Some books you never want to end."

Ten

Audrey woke to an empty bed. Well, not entirely empty. She glanced to her side and picked up a lavender shoot with light purple buds lying across the sheets. She brought the pretty flower to her nose. The scent was fragrant and sweet and flavored the air in Luke's bedroom. Then she lifted the note he'd left beneath the stalk and read it silently.

> *Sorry to leave you. I have an early appointment in Carson City. See you tonight at dinner.*
> *Luke*

"You've got a date," she breathed softly. Pain squeezed her heart. She wished he'd declared his love for her and asked her out on a real date. Last night, she'd ignored her internal warnings to stay clear of him, to protect herself at all costs. And today, she'd pay the price for her one night of indulgence. Nothing had changed.

She rose, her bare feet hitting the hardwood floor from

the tall four-poster bed. On impulse, she turned to run her hand along the smooth Egyptian cotton sheets where Luke had made love to her. A sigh of longing escaped her throat. His hot kisses, his sensual caresses and their joined bodies totally in sync with each other meshed in her mind. She savored the heady memory.

The rest of the morning flew by. At the barn, she saddled up three horses and led each one of them up into the hilly country for long, brisk walks. Then she took time to wash down and groom each one. Audrey was in her element among the animals and the ranch hands. Today, especially, was a productive day.

Ward Halliday approached her as she was putting away tack. "Hey, Audrey."

"Good afternoon, Ward. How're you doing today?"

She turned to face him across the length of the tack room. The friendly smile that brightened his leathery face was gone. The usual spark in his eyes was gone, too. "I'm doing fine."

"Really? Because you're looking a little frazzled around the collar."

He shrugged a shoulder, his lips tight with regret. "My boy has to leave for college a week early. They moved up orientation and it's no point him going all the way to Texas and back. He's gonna stay put once he gets there."

"Oh, no! When's he leaving?"

"On the red-eye tonight. My wife, Molly, is fixing him a big farewell supper, all his favorites."

"So what are you doing here?"

"Well, I'm working. Gonna finish out the day."

She began shaking her head. There was no way Ward was going to miss being with Hunter on his last day home. "Ward, please let me finish up the few chores that are left. You should go home and be with your family. The boys can help me with anything else that needs doing."

"I appreciate that but—"

"Please, let me do this for you. Go home and spend time with Hunter today. He's probably excited and nervous and can use you around to settle him down."

Ward lifted the rim of his hat and gave her a sheepish look. "Who's gonna settle me down?"

"Molly."

Ward chuckled.

"I've got this, really. I'll make sure the horses are fed and stabled for the night."

He looked at her like a child opening an early Christmas present. "Thank you, Audrey. I'll be sure to stop by the house on our way to the airport so Hunter can say a proper good-bye to you all."

"Darn right you will. I've gotta give Hunter a big hug and some tips on college life."

Audrey walked with Ward arm in arm outside the barn doors. She watched him get into his truck, start the engine and drive along the road that led to the main highway.

Jewel brushed against her legs and she glanced down at her cat, who had pretty much taken over the Slade house perimeter. "What are you up to, Jewel?"

Meow.

"Same as usual, I see."

Audrey finished up her chores and then strode over to the other barn to see Trib. It was her daily outing, and she was thrilled to see the horse really beginning to relate to her. He no longer shied away when she opened the half door of the paddock and Jewel jumped up. The horse was turning the corner in the trust department and Audrey couldn't be more pleased.

Jewel took her seat on the ledge of the half door and looked for her new friend. Then the cat meowed and glanced at Audrey curiously. Audrey scanned the paddock. Tribute wasn't in his stall.

In her haste to convince Ward to head home, she'd forgotten about Trib and apparently so had the foreman. Now, as she walked outside and peeked around the corner of the barn, she saw Trib standing on the far end of the corral, blending into the shadows under an oak tree.

"There you are," she said congenially.

Trib spotted her and snorted. He could make this hard for her, or he could make this easy. "Come here, boy," she called to him. "Gotta get you settled for the night."

The horse gave her a stubborn stare and didn't budge. "Are you kidding me," she muttered under her breath. Apparently Trib was going to live up to his nickname of Tribulation today.

Jewel's nose nudged her leg. "Would you look at our friend over there," she said to her cat. "I think he wants me to come get him."

The horse whinnied softly and took a few steps forward, toward them. Audrey smiled. "He does. He's telling me to come get him."

Audrey knew he was ready. He was giving her his trust. Over the past few days, she'd made incredible progress with him. She had to thank Jewel for some of that; the two had become cautious, but endearing friends.

She didn't waste another second. This was an opportunity to really earn her keep around here. She was being paid to do a job, and with Ward gone, and no one else close enough to the stallion to bring him in, she knew she could do it.

Trib would cooperate.

She felt it in her bones.

The horse took another step closer, then stopped and watched her. "I'll be right there, I'm coming to get you, Trib."

She quickly walked into the barn, grabbed a handful of sugar cubes and gathered up a bridle and lead rope.

Jewel seemed bored with it all and began swatting at flies buzzing around the feed bags in the barn. Audrey left her there and walked back outside.

Taking measured steps, she kept her eyes on the horse as

she made her approach with the rope and halter in one hand and a fistful of sugar in the other.

Now out in broad sunlight, away from the dark and light shadows Trib appeared friendly and amiable. She walked within a few feet of him and put out her hand. "Here you go, boy."

He craned his neck forward and brought his mouth to her hand, nibbling away at the sugar until it was all gone.

"I've got to get you home," she said softly. Steadily, she fit the rope halter over his head and adjusted it under his chin. Trib stood still and allowed her to fasten the five-foot lead rope to the harness.

She gave his mane a soft pat. "Okay, we're almost ready. You're doing fine."

With great care, she led him forward toward the barn, all the while talking quietly and calmly to him.

Midway to the barn, she caught a glimpse of a cowboy at the fence post.

Uh-oh.

"Audrey. What in hell are you doing?" Luke spoke quietly enough not to spook the horse. But his angry tone was unmistakable.

Refusing to be distracted, she stared at the horse. "I've been working with Trib and he's ready."

"Audrey, get out of there, *right now,*" he rasped with menace in his voice.

"You're paying me to do a job." Eyes still trained on Trib, she spoke softly. "And we're doing just fine."

"You're fired. I don't want you to—"

And suddenly, out of nowhere, an orange blur appeared, racing at top speed toward her, Blackie, the Slades' Border collie, chasing Jewel and barking like crazy. Luke cursed. He bounded over the corral fence just as Trib jerked his head back and yanked on the lead rope. Audrey held on tight, as long as she could. But Trib was more powerful. The rope jerked free of her hands. She stumbled forward and managed at the last second to turn her body. She landed with a thud on her butt.

Jewel whizzed by with Blackie at her heels. It all happened so fast. Trib whinnied loudly enough for the next county to hear. He reared up, his front legs coming eight feet off the ground. Audrey froze. Seconds ticked by in slow motion as she watched the horse balance himself on his hind legs as if trying to keep from crashing down on her.

"Watch out!" Luke shouted, running toward her.

He fell to his knees and pressed her close, cosseting her with his body and creating a shield of protection around her. She thought for a split second everything would be okay.

And then the force of Trib's frustration landed on Luke with a crushing sound.

She felt a thump.

Luke bellowed in pain. And then slumped over her like a rag doll, lifeless and limp.

"Luke! Luke!"

"Don't move him!" one of the ranch hands shouted from a distance.

"We're calling for help," another one said.

Audrey held her breath, bearing Luke's weight and sending up prayers for his life.

Audrey's tears stained her shirt as she unpacked her bags with Jewel looking on. They were home. Finally back in Reno. Finally back where she belonged.

She hated herself, hated the pain and anguish she'd caused Luke. She couldn't stay on at the ranch, though everyone tried like crazy to convince her not to go. How on earth could she stay? How could she face Luke after what had happened? She had a hard enough time facing herself in the mirror.

She'd almost caused his death.

She hadn't listened to his warnings.

She wanted so badly to prove to Luke he'd been wrong about Trib.

But she was the one who'd been wrong about everything.

More tears spilled from her eyes. It wasn't good for the baby for her to cry like this, so she forced herself to stop. It was hard and she didn't deserve to give herself a break. She didn't deserve much of anything right now.

Poor Jewel. Even her cat knew something was off. Jewel glanced around her surroundings with dismay. Her sheep-skin kitty bed and three-tier cat house seemed to have lost their appeal. Jewel moped. The cat had gotten accustomed to being on Slade land. She'd grown out of her separation anxiety. Living at the ranch had been like therapy.

Audrey steadied her breathing. She couldn't seem to keep a dry face. She had the feeling she would have cried just as hard even if she weren't pregnant. No, her tears couldn't be blamed on hormones. Her tears would've been shed regardless.

Inside, she bled for the big mess she'd made of things, but she couldn't think about that at the moment. She couldn't wallow in self-pity. Luke was the important one. He would survive. Though he'd be spending the next week in the hospital, he would make a full recovery.

He'd been lucky, the doctor said. The horse hooves hadn't made a direct hit. The thick-lined leather jacket Luke was wearing had lessened the impact of the force. But one hoof had knocked into the back of his head.

Luke had gotten another concussion.

Strike one for Audrey.

His body took a hard pounding.

Strike two for Audrey.

His spine wasn't injured, but all of his organs were badly bruised.

Three strikes and you're out.

As soon as she'd gotten the news that Luke would make a full recovery, she'd left the ranch. It hadn't been easy to leave, but guilt and remorse had a way of convincing her that she wasn't worthy. That sticking around would just make matters worse. She'd already caused Luke a world of grief and pain. She would've been the last person he'd want to see when he woke up in the hospital. At some point, she would have to face him, because of the baby. He'd want to know the baby was all right. She wouldn't deny him anything regarding their child, but she also didn't want to burden his life with her presence. He had every right to blame her for all the trouble she'd caused him.

Oh, he probably would never forgive her.

She couldn't fault him that; she'd never forgive herself.

Fresh tears burned behind her eyes. She squeezed them shut to prevent another flood. She would be eternally thankful to Luke for protecting the new life thriving inside her belly. The baby wasn't injured. If Luke hadn't come along when he did, who knows what would have happened?

A chill ran up and down her arms.

Our baby is safe. Thank you, Luke.

The phone rang. Audrey walked over to look at the digital number blinking on the screen.

Casey.

Like a mother hen, her brother had been calling her every day since he'd found out about the baby. Audrey didn't pick up. She let the machine get it.

"If you're there, please pick up. I need to talk to you."

Please?

Since when did her brother say please?

Audrey plucked a tissue from the box and wiped her eyes. She took another one to blow her nose. Then before the machine clicked off, she grabbed the phone.

"Hello."

"Well, you sound like death warmed over," he said.

"I love you, too."

Casey's voice was full of concern. "How are you doing, sis?"

"At the moment, I'm not putting anyone's life at risk, so I suppose it's a good day."

Her brother took an exasperated breath. "Audrey Faith."

"I'm sorry, Case. But Luke was almost killed by that horse."

"I'm gonna go out on a limb here and tell you it wasn't your fault. None of it. The horse was spooked by the confusion in the corral. If he hadn't been so darn isolated all that time, he wouldn't have gotten jittery about seeing a dog chase a cat."

"So now it's Luke's fault for keeping the horse in the paddock after he nearly trampled him the first time?"

"I'm saying it's no one's fault. It was a freakish accident."

"Luke warned me about him, Casey. And I didn't listen. I just went right ahead and did what I pleased. My gosh. Do you realize what might have happened?"

She shuddered in fear and wrapped her arm around her middle where the smallest baby bump had appeared just this week.

She was grateful to Luke for his fathering instincts. He'd rushed over to protect their child.

"And you pay him back for saving you and the baby by running out on him?"

"He fired me."

Casey sighed. "To get you outta that corral safely."

"I will work something out with Luke later on about the baby. He knows I won't keep the baby from him. He knows—"

"You won't marry him. That's what he knows."

"He doesn't love me, Casey. What kind of marriage would it be?"

If he had loved her, he would've said something to her on their last night together. He would've known by then, wouldn't he? But it wasn't in Luke to lie to get what he wanted. He was too honest. Too good a man to do that. And sadly, Audrey had to face the reality that her child wouldn't have an ideal life. He wouldn't live in a home where his parents loved each other and harmony abounded. More than likely, their child would be shuffled back and forth between two homes.

"You should go back. Luke deserves better than this," her brother said. "You both do."

"You're saying that *now?* You wanted to knock Luke on his ass the last I heard."

"He has been knocked on his ass. And you leaving when you did was like kicking him when he was down."

Her heart squeezed tight and she whispered, "That's a low blow, Casey."

"It's the truth, honey."

Audrey paused for a second. Had she made a mistake in leaving the ranch so abruptly? Casey sure thought so. She glanced at the languid cat sleeping on the bed. Jewel thought so, too. She was depressed. "The truth is, he's glad to get rid of me. I caused him nothing but trouble."

Casey cursed under his breath. "You're being stubborn."

"I take after you."

"Think about what I'm telling you. Go back to Sunset Ranch."

Audrey couldn't face Luke. Her guilt was a tangible thing that dragged her down and made her ache inside. She couldn't bear to see him hurt, bandaged up and immobile, knowing she was the cause of his agony. If that made her a coward, so be it. In her heart she knew she was saving Luke in her own way. With her gone, he could recover with no reminders of Casey's troublemaking little sister.

"Casey, I…can't. I just can't."

Luke was determined to get out of bed and have dinner tonight in the dining room. Logan and Sophia were coming and Ellie had prepared his favorite meal. Not that he had much of an appetite lately, but after five days in the hospital and three days in his own bed, it was time to get a move on. Since he'd come home, he'd refused to take pain meds other than simple ibuprofen for his lingering aches and pains. Every day he saw improvement in his mobility.

At least nothing was broken this time. His breathing was normal and his head no longer ached. As for his pride—now, that had suffered the greatest injury.

Not only had Audrey run out on him that night in the cabin, but she'd deceived him and disobeyed his instructions about Trib. Then the woman up and ran out on him again. Emptiness stole through his body and it befuddled him why anger wasn't the strongest emotion he felt.

Luke sat on the bed and took his time putting his legs into his jeans, one foot then the other. He moved slowly, testing his muscles as he bent to pull up his pants.

Okay. That wasn't so bad.

He zipped his jeans and then carefully slid his arms into a light-gray-and-black-plaid shirt. The snaps were easy. Then he frowned when he glanced at his boots. Pulling them on would be a chore, so he opted to go downstairs barefoot.

He walked down the hallway to where a batch of bright sunflowers wrapped in raffia sat in a vase on the foyer table. The card read, "I'm so sorry. Love, Audrey."

She'd sent them to him the day after he'd been hospitalized. He thought they'd die long before this and he wouldn't have the reminder every day of how badly things had spiraled out of control between them. But they'd survived and looked as if they had no intention of wilting anytime soon.

Luke felt much the same way.

"There he is," Logan said, glancing up once Luke walked into the dining room.

He and Sophia walked over to him. Sophia gave him a kiss on the cheek. Logan patted his back once as if he was afraid of injuring him.

"Sorry if I'm late," he said.

"Right on time," Logan said.

"You're looking good, Luke." Sophia smiled.

At least Luke didn't feel like a pile of crap anymore, so progress was being made.

"Ellie's in the kitchen fixing all your favorites."

Luke raised his brows. "Smells delicious. Pot roast with all the fixin's?"

His brother nodded. "That's right." The two took their seats at the table while Luke leaned against the wall and glanced out a tall window that overlooked Sunset Ranch. "It feels good to be up and dressed and walking on my own power."

"It's great to see you that way, bro."

Luke stared out the window for a few more seconds then gingerly took a seat. "You have that talk with Ward?" he asked Logan. Ward had felt guilty about Luke's injury, thinking it was his fault for abandoning his duties and leaving early that day. Two days ago, he'd offered Luke his resignation.

"Yep, we talked. Between you and me, I think we got him convinced he wasn't at fault. Can't imagine a day when I'd accept his resignation, and I told him so. I'm still waiting on your decision about Trib. I can unload him for a song, anytime you say."

Luke pursed his lips and contemplated. He didn't know if he wanted to unload the stallion right now. He was trouble, but the stallion had come a long way. And there was something about that horse that clung on and wouldn't let go.

"He's a menace," Logan said firmly.

"I can't argue with that. But Audrey's work with him did pay off." He hated to admit that, but it was true. And that day, as much as he'd wanted Audrey out of that corral and away from that horse, he'd been impressed to see the horse respond to her. To see how far Trib had come in the short time she'd been working with him. For all the trouble the horse caused him, he shouldn't blink an eye in getting rid of him. Yet he couldn't quite do it.

"Are you thinking about keeping him?" Sophia asked.

Logan gave him a dubious look. "That damn animal put you in the hospital *twice*."

Luke nodded. "I know. I know. But I've got more important things on my mind right now. Are you forgetting I've got a baby on the way?"

Sophia's voice was sympathetic. "Have you spoken with Audrey?"

Luke didn't know if he wanted to delve too far into the subject. Audrey had been on his mind a lot lately. "No, just Casey. He tells me she's doing fine."

Sophia sipped from a glass of sparkling water. "You know, when we were at the hospital waiting for you to wake up from your concussion, you kept calling out her name."

"Did I?"

Luke remembered waking up in a daze and how the first words out of his mouth were for Audrey. He'd asked the doctor if she was injured. He remembered the relief he felt to find out she wasn't harmed. Funny thing, at the time and with his mind so foggy from being knocked unconscious, he hadn't remembered about the baby. All of his concern had been for Audrey.

Logan and Sophia peered at each other and then nodded at him. "You must've asked for her a dozen times," Logan informed him.

"Once Audrey found out you were going to make a full recovery, she excused herself and walked out of the hospital," Sophia said quietly. "She was beside herself, Luke. I've never seen someone cry so hard. She feels responsible and so terrible about this. She really cares for you."

Luke took a sip of water and swallowed hard. He couldn't figure out why he wasn't angrier with her. She'd gone against his wishes deliberately and endangered herself. All he wanted now was to see her. To make sure she was all right. But she'd taken off again.

"An injured man doesn't have a woman's name on his lips for no reason," Logan said.

His brother had a point.

"Here you go, Luke," Ellie said, coming in with a large platter of pot roast, carrots and potatoes. The savory scent whetted his waning appetite. "I hope this makes you feel better." She set the dish down in the center of the table.

"Looks delicious, Ellie. I'll do my best at putting this away."

The elderly woman gave him an affectionate pat on the shoulder. "You just eat what you can. Build your strength. The biscuits and gravy are coming."

"I'll get them," Logan said. "Luke, you go on and dig in."

Logan got up to help Ellie, and Luke filled his plate. It pleased Ellie to see him take that much food, and she walked out of the room with a satisfied expression on her face.

Luke forced smiles and conversed with his family during the meal, grateful to them for being here, for worrying over him. Yet he was struck with a bitter sense of loss. Now that he was beginning to recover, he realized something was terribly wrong. And he knew exactly what that was.

That night, Luke sat up in his bed, picked up his iPhone and sent a text message to the one person who could make him feel better.

How r u?

Audrey's reply came immediately.

I'm fine. How r u?

Doing ok. How's the baby?

Healthy. I have a little bump now.

Luke choked up. He wished to heaven he could see her swell with his child.

What r u doing?

Getting ready for bed.

Luke smiled and a wave of warmth roared through his body.

What r u wearing?

The question was audacious and he knew he was playing with fire

Luke? Is your head right? R u feeling okay?

Answer my question and I'll feel a whole lot better.

Anything to make you feel better. Just my old T-shirt.

The one that says, Cowgirls Do it With Their Boots On?

Yes.

R u wearing boots now?

Of course not. I'm going to bed. Luke, I'm so, so sorry.

Apology accepted.

So, u r not mad at me?

He wouldn't lie.

Pissed beyond belief.

There was a long pause.

What can I do? I feel awful about it.

Put your boots on. The tan ones that ride up to your knees.

Why?

R u really asking why?

Another long pause.

Ok, they're on. Now what?

He missed her like crazy. She loved him and he'd thrown that love back in her face.

Now, I'm gonna imagine u on my bed, curled up next to me, boots and all. Sleep tight, sweetheart.

Luke clicked off his phone.

He lay back against his pillow and shut off the light. Closing his eyes, he imagined Audrey beside him on the bed, beside him on the ranch, beside him as they raised their children together. He imagined Audrey Faith Thomas in his life forever.

Something had always been wrong in his past relationships with women. He'd never let himself get too close. He'd never allowed himself to create a bond. The pieces of the puzzle never quite fit right.

Now he knew what was missing.

Her.

Audrey had been missing in his life.

He loved her.

The emotion knocked him upside the head and spiraled down his body, touching every ounce of his being, absorbing into his bones. He'd always had affection for Audrey, but the intense sense of loss and emptiness without her was keen and sharp. That part surprised him most. What he felt for her was real. It wasn't anything he wanted to run from. With or without a baby, he wanted a future with Audrey. Up until now, true love had been absent in his life and now he welcomed it with an open heart.

The best healing happened during the wee hours of the night when the body and soul were at rest. Luke knew that for fact now. He slept his best sleep ever, finally at peace with his emotions.

And along with the healing, came great clarity.

"Jewel, please get off Susanna's couch," Audrey said, staring her feline down. Jewel felt entitled and refused to budge off the arm of the outdated flower-print sofa. She lay there with a blank look on her face, but Audrey knew the real reason for Jewel's disobedience.

"It's okay, Audrey," Susanna said. "She won't do it any harm. It's hanging on by a thread. I'm almost ashamed to have you sitting on it."

"Don't be silly. The couch has at least another good year left in it."

"Bite your tongue."

Audrey smiled. "I have fond memories of sitting around this room with your family, Suse. The couch is part of that." Whenever there was an important event at school, or a test Audrey couldn't miss, the Harts would invite her to stay overnight. Sometimes she'd stayed for an entire weekend while Casey was gone. "Jewel's separation anxiety came back when we returned home. She won't leave my side now. I think she's punishing me for taking her away from Sunset Ranch. She loved it there."

"I think you did, too," Susanna said.

"I did, Suse, but I couldn't stay. Now with the baby com-

ing and all, I'm going to have to make some tough decisions.
I have to postpone veterinarian school for another year. Dr.
Arroyo offered me a full-time job in the vet clinic. It means
long hours, but doing something I love to do."

"And your hunky Luke's okay with the whole situation?"

Audrey wished he *was* her hunky Luke. Unshielded guilt
consumed her. She'd been nothing but trouble for Lucas
Slade. Still, she looked forward to the nightly text messages
she'd been getting from him lately. They made her whole day
worthwhile. She found herself anxiously awaiting the evening
hours to hear from him. But it was Luke being Luke. Checking up on her. Making sure the baby was okay. She was certain any day now he'd bring up the subject of custody. How
would they work out the details?

"It's early yet. I'm only nine weeks along. I think we're just
getting used to the idea of becoming parents so we haven't
discussed it yet. But…but I'm sure we will. Luke wants to be
a big part of the baby's life."

Just not a part of hers.

He offered to marry you and you turned him down.

"I hope you have a good time at Casey's tomorrow," Susanna said. "I'm glad you decided to visit him. Maybe being
at the lake will help clear your mind."

She hoped a trip to the cabin would help her get a handle
on her chaotic emotions. There were too many variables in
her life now—joy about the baby but heartache over Luke.
She had indecision about the job offer and worried about what
her future would hold. All of it made her queasy with anxiety.

"I hope so, too. So long as Casey doesn't dwell on my piti-
ful life, I think I'll be fine. My brother is convinced he knows
what's best for me."

Susanna smiled. "Casey misses you. I think you'll have a
good time together."

"You're right. Gosh, I'm sorry I'm such a downer lately."

"Hey, you've been there for me, too. That's what friends are for."

They said good-night with an embrace and Audrey went home to pack a few things.

In the morning, she made the drive to the north shore of Lake Tahoe with Jewel beside her in the travel carrier. Fall was beginning to show signs in the crispness of the air and the fresh scent of pine. Early sunlight cast the lake in shades of indigo that gleamed off the water and brightened her entire outlook.

Casey came out to greet her and they hugged tight. He was full of questions about the baby, and as they headed inside the cabin, she laughed at some of the silly notions he had in his head about pregnancy. Not that she was an expert, but she was pretty sure that no, the shape of the woman's belly did not determine the baby's sex. And yes, it was true that she would probably develop a dark hormone line that would run from the top of her torso to below her navel that would divide her body almost in half. No, she wouldn't need to drink the two half gallons of milk in his refrigerator to build up her milk supply. "Goodness, Casey. I'm only staying two days. You've got enough milk in here for an entire kindergarten class."

"Well, just making sure you have what you need."

She kissed his cheek and they spent the entire afternoon being lazy on the deck, stretched out on cushioned chaise longes and watching a few local sunbathers trying to catch the last rays of warmth for the season.

"Pretty soon, snow will top the mountains," she said.

"Not soon enough for the skiers," Casey said. "They can't wait for the cold weather to hit." He tilted his head and gave her a tentative look. "I've got reservations at Emeralds for tonight. We never had a chance to celebrate you having a baby. You up for it?"

Audrey reached over to touch his hand. "That's sweet, Casey. Yes, I'm up for it."

"No pets allowed. Think Jewel here will let you go?"

Jewel's head perked up from her prone position on the patio deck at the mention of her name.

"Knowing Jewel, after she eats she'll probably pass out in front of the fireplace. She won't know I'm gone."

Casey gave her a nod of approval. "Smart cat."

Audrey chuckled. "Thanks, Casey for…well, for not being so, so…"

"I'm trying, honey. You'll always be my little sis, and I'll always watch out for you, but I get that you're all grown-up now. You don't need me anymore."

"I need you, Casey. Just not your interference in my life. I'm ready to make my own decisions," she said softly.

He swallowed and stared out at the lake.

That evening they had dinner at an exclusive restaurant with a spectacular view of Emerald Bay. The crescent-shaped alcove cradled shallow, pale emerald-green waters. Fanette Island reached out of the center of the bay with a Hershey Kiss–topped peak. The food was delicious and Audrey's mood lightened being with her brother.

By the time they returned to the cabin, Audrey was beat. "I'm going to bed," she said to Casey. "Thanks for a wonderful dinner. I'll see you in the morning." She reached up on tiptoes and gave Casey a peck on the cheek.

"Good night, Sis."

Audrey showered and dressed in an old T-shirt. Some people had comfort food, but Audrey had comfort wear. She was cozy in worn-out, old bed clothes that felt soft against her skin. The baby seemed to love it, too. She snuggled into the bed and when the ringtone barked, she picked up her phone and read the text. It was Luke.

How r u?

Fair. How r u?

Fair. But now that I'm talking to you, I'm better.

Audrey squeezed her eyes closed. A viselike grip tightened on her heart. More and more now, Luke would say something sweet like this, or make an innuendo that begged an invitation from her. She didn't have the courage to act upon it. She couldn't face another rejection. And then, there was the guilt she harbored that reminded her daily of the injuries she'd caused him.

I'm glad you're feeling better.

R u in bed?

Yes.

In a T-shirt?

Yes.

Well?

It says *Cowgirls Party in the Paddock*.

Luke didn't waste a second to answer.

Sounds like a party I'd want to attend.

Mercy. Audrey nibbled on her lower lip.

I'm not a party girl.

Could've fooled me a few months ago.

Are you still pissed?

That you seduced me then ran away? That you lied to me? That you disobeyed my orders with Trib?

Her hopes faded.

I guess I have my answer.

I'm mellowing.

Doesn't sound like it.

Do you still love me?

Audrey couldn't believe he was asking her that. A person didn't fall out of love that easily. It just showed how little Luke knew about love. And about her. She'd loved him for ten years. She couldn't just forget about that because things didn't work out. Life was messy and she'd certainly stepped in it this time. If anything, her love for him had grown stronger after he'd saved her and the baby.

It doesn't matter.

You don't love me.

I take that as a yes. There's going to be a knock at your door any second.

What? Panicked, she glanced at the bedroom door before she remembered she was at the cabin. She typed,

I'm not home.

I know.

Then the door opened and Luke strode in, cell phone in hand.

She jumped and hit her head against the backboard of the bed. "Luke!"

He tucked the phone into his pocket. "I gave you warning."

"You...you didn't knock."

"Didn't I?" He grinned and moved farther into the room. "Seems to me you didn't knock a few months back when you crept in here and destroyed my sleep."

"Wh-what are you doing here?"

This whole thing reeked of Casey *not interfering*. Her brother must've set this up.

But oh, how she'd missed Luke. His devastating smile and the light in his eyes were enough to floor any female, much less one who was already crazy about him. She tossed the covers off and was about to get out of bed when Luke's piercing gaze froze her in place. He sat down next to her. The scent of leather and musk put her mind in a tizzy.

Jewel woke from solid sleep, got up and rubbed at the back of his legs. He bent to scratch her behind the ears and she purred so loudly, it echoed off the walls. Traitorous cat. "Did Casey put you up to this? I'm going to—"

"I did some fast talking with Case to get him to allow me to come here. This was all my idea." He glanced around the room and then his reverent gaze touched on her. "This room is where our baby was conceived."

"I...I know."

Her mind was muddled. It was late. She was tired. She couldn't think straight with him sitting on her bed, so near. If he wanted to talk custody in legal terms, she couldn't do it. "I can't think right now, Luke. Can we talk another time? Maybe, if you came back in the morning."

He gave his head a shake. "You're a flight risk, Audrey. I'm not giving you a chance to take off again. Seems that's what you do to me. Leave."

"That's only because—"

"I love you, Audrey."

"Wh-what?"

"I said, I love you. I need you in my life. I'm not leaving here until I convince you of that."

The words were foreign to her ears. Luke didn't love her. How could he? She'd done horrible things to him. She'd nearly caused his death, for heaven's sake. "You love the baby."

"True. I love the baby. It's a part of you, sweetheart. That baby is the best part of both of us. If I didn't love you, why on earth would I forgive you for everything you've done? Why would I call out your name when I was unconscious? Yes, I did that, they tell me. And as soon as I woke up, your name was the first on my lips. I called for you, Audrey. And you weren't there. It was an awful feeling. It hurt more than my injuries."

"Oh, Luke. I'm so sorry about that. I hated to leave you, but I thought I'd be the last person you'd want to see when you woke up."

"You left Sunset Ranch without saying goodbye."

Her guilt was as sharp as the tip of a knife.

Luke reached for her hands. He applied gentle pressure that shot straight to her heart and made her hope for the first time in a long time. Then he looked her square in the eyes. "I've never lied to you, Audrey. I think you know that about me. I asked you to marry me, but I didn't tell you I loved you. I didn't know it then, but I know it now."

Audrey's hope register shot up. "Wh-why do you know it now?"

Luke looked past her, as if trying to find a way to explain it. "I thought I wasn't capable of love or allowing myself to get close to anyone for anything other than friendship. It has to do with my roots and my love of a horse that was taken away when I was very young. It didn't help to see the kind of marriage my folks had. I guess I put up barriers and wouldn't let anyone breach them. Until Trib came along."

"Trib? I don't understand."

"For some reason that horse got under my skin. Even after all the trials and tribulations and the trouble he caused, I can't seem to part with him. I see his spirit and know he'll be mine one day. I don't ever intend on letting him go. Now don't take this the wrong way, but that's exactly how I feel about you. You and Trib have a lot in common."

Audrey's brows knitted together as she tried to make sense of it.

Luke continued, "I never let myself get close to any of the animals on the ranch after that one devastating incident when I was a boy. It scarred me for life. So I steered clear and when I felt like I was feeling more than I should, I would back off and detach myself for fear of being hurt. Just recently, I realized I did that very same thing with women. Until you came back into my life. That's how I know I love you. After all the deception and lies you told, Audrey, I couldn't dismiss you. I wouldn't even consider firing you."

"You did fire me."

"That was bogus. I was desperate to get you away from Trib. I was falling in love with you and didn't realize it."

Audrey's heart was ready to burst. Still, she droned, "Because I reminded you of a horse?"

His eyes grew serious, as if this next question meant a great deal. "But you get it, right?"

His honest plea had her convinced. She nodded. "I think so."

He continued, "I told myself I had a physical attraction to you and I'd get over it. But I didn't get over it. I couldn't write you off like I had all the others. Because as much trouble as you've caused me, I didn't give up on you. I didn't back off. Then when I learned you were pregnant, I wanted to marry you because it was the right thing to do. And you were right to refuse me. I see that now. When I lay hurt in that hospital bed, I began to see my future without you. And it was a killer. I never want to feel that way again. I don't want to live my life without you, Audrey. To me, you're perfect just the way you are."

"Oh, Luke." Tears welled in her eyes.

He smiled and kissed her fingertips. "You're amazing and talented and smart. You're pretty and sexy and you make me laugh. This isn't about the baby, Audrey. I swear, I really do love you."

Audrey's hope soared. Luke never lied. He would stretch the truth at times to keep his dashing knight status, but he never flat-out lied. "I love you, too."

Luke grinned. "Thank God. I was worried."

He was worrying about her love for him? Not a chance in hell that would ever change. But she did have one tidbit that she needed to come clean about. She held her breath, vowing to strive to be Miss Goody Two-shoes, if only he could forgive her this one last thing. "I, uh, I do have to fill you in on something that might make you angry."

Luke squinted as if he was afraid to hear what she had to say. "Lay it on me."

"It's not really a lie, exactly, just an omission of truth. When you were being so bullheaded about Trib, I sort of went behind your back to work with him late at night. After you went to bed."

Luke ground his teeth together and she could tell how hard he was trying to keep his cool, but the vein popping out of his neck was a dead giveaway. "So you're saying after I fell asleep, you'd head out to the barn in secret?"

"Yes, with Jewel. Trib took a shine to the cat and it helped me make a breakthrough."

He was silent for thirty seconds.

"Are you angry?" she finally squeaked.

"That depends on whether you'll marry me or not?"

"That's a heck of a proposal, Luke."

"Don't push it, sweetheart. I'm envisioning all the things that could've happened to you out there. And it's not sending endorphins racing through my body."

Shoot, she hoped she hadn't just ruined the moment.

She thought back to the time when she was sixteen and Luke had come to her rescue with those two boys. He'd made her a deal and asked one thing of her. Audrey would honor that vow now. She put her heart on the line and gave him her answer. "I promise you, Lucas Slade, I won't do anything reckless or dangerous after we're married."

"So you'll marry me?" A smile spread across his face, and he seemed to forget about her confession.

Audrey couldn't hide her relief. Her words rushed out, "Yes, of course I'll marry you, Luke." She looped her arms around his neck. "I love you with all of my heart. Our baby thinks he's getting a pretty good dad, too."

Luke put his hand over her belly and felt the little bump developing. The blue in his eyes deepened with love. "We're going to be a great family."

"I think so, too," Audrey said. Her dreams, her fantasies were all coming true. She was over-the-moon happy.

Luke brought his lips to hers and took her in a lingering kiss that knocked out any iota of doubt she had about his love for her.

"I missed you," he said, drawing her up tight, his gaze scorching right through her T-shirt. "I want to party with my cowgirl."

"Oh, I want that, too, but Casey—"

"Is gone. I told him he'd better get out of Dodge if he wanted me to make a legitimate woman out of you."

Audrey's laugh came out throaty and pure, her heart filled with joy.

Luke laid her down on the bed and spread his body next to hers. She shuddered in anticipation.

"I owe you a seduction," he rasped. "Payback is usually a bitch, but this time, I'm going to make sure it takes us straight to heaven. Hang on to the bedpost, sweetheart. We're going for a long, sweet ride."

Audrey closed her eyes.

She hung on.

She loved Lucas Slade inside and out.

And her knight in shining armor, Mr. Nice Guy and Good Samaritan all rolled up into one, gave her a night she would remember for all their sunsets to come.

* * * * *

Brody turned on his heel, ready to return to his office.

"Mr Eden?"

"Yes?" He stopped.

Samantha rounded her desk and approached him. His body tensed involuntarily as she came closer. She reached up to the scarred side of his face, causing his lungs to seize in his chest. What was she doing?

"Your shirt…" Her voice drifted to a stop.

He felt her fingertips gently brush the puckered skin along his neck before straightening his shirt collar. The innocent touch sent a jolt of heat through his body. It was so simple, so unplanned, and yet it was the first time a woman had touched his scars.

Without thinking, he brought his hand up to grasp hers. Sam gasped softly at his sudden movement, but she didn't pull away when his fingers wrapped around her own. He was glad. He wasn't ready to let go.

His every nerve lit up with awareness, and he was pretty certain she felt it, too. Her dark brown eyes were wide as she looked at him, her moist lips parted seductively and begging for his kiss.

A BEAUTY
UNCOVERED

BY
ANDREA LAURENCE

Published in Great Britain 2013
by Mills & Boon, an imprint of Harlequin (UK) Limited,
Eton House, 18-24 Paradise Road, Richmond, Surrey TW9 1SR

© Andrea Laurence 2013

ISBN: 978 0 263 90488 8
ebook ISBN: 978 1 472 00643 1

51-1013

Harlequin (UK) policy is to use papers that are natural, renewable and recyclable products and made from wood grown in sustainable forests. The logging and manufacturing processes conform to the legal environmental regulations of the country of origin.

Printed and bound in Spain
by Blackprint CPI, Barcelona

Andrea Laurence is an award-winning contemporary romance author who has been a lover of books and writing stories since she learned to read. She always dreamed of seeing her work in print and is thrilled to be able to share her books with the world. A dedicated West Coast girl transplanted into the Deep South, she's working on her own "happily ever after" with her boyfriend and five fur-babies. You can contact Andrea at her website: www.andrealaurence.com.

To the Victims
of the Sandy Hook Elementary School Shooting—

This book is dedicated to the children who were lost,
the teachers and faculty who died to protect them,
and the families and students who will live with
this senseless tragedy for their whole lives.
My thoughts and prayers are with you.

One

"Confidentiality agreement?"

Samantha Davis frowned at her godmother. Agnes had been there for Sam her entire life. She trusted the older woman, who had stepped in as a mother figure when Sam was still in elementary school. And she was helping her get a job when Sam needed it the most. But even then, she didn't like the sound of this.

Getting up to Agnes's office had been a feat of its own. Sam was pretty certain there were fewer security measures at CIA headquarters.

What was she getting herself into?

Agnes shook her head and pushed the form across the desk to her. "It's nothing to really worry about, honey. Mr. Eden is very particular about his privacy. That's why there are so many restrictive measures to get up to this floor. No one in the building has access except me, Mr. Eden and the head of security. I'm the

only one at the company that ever has any personal in-
teraction with him. If you're going to fill in while I'm
on vacation, you will interact with him as well, so you'll
have to sign the agreement."

An uneasy prickle ran up the length of Sam's neck.
Although she and Agnes were the only people in the
room, she felt like she was being watched. Looking curiously around the modern, yet comfortably decorated
office, she spied a tiny video camera watching her from
the corner. There was a second camera on the opposite
wall to capture another angle of the room. Who needed
surveillance equipment to monitor their secretary?

If it was anyone but her godmother telling her to
take this job, she'd walk right out the door. But Agnes
wouldn't rope her into a bad situation just so she could
go on vacation for her fortieth anniversary. It must seem
worse than it was.

And yet, she couldn't put her finger on what was really going on here. She scanned over the confidentiality paperwork with distrust. Brody Eden owned Eden
Software Systems. Office solutions and communications. Nothing classified. Nothing that might threaten
national security if it was leaked. And yet if she failed
to follow the terms of the agreement, she would be ob-
ligated to pay a five-million-dollar settlement.

"I don't know about this. Five million dollars? I don't
have that kind of money."

"You think I do?" Agnes laughed. "It's deliberately
high to ensure no one breaks the agreement, that's
all. As long as you do your job and don't talk about
Mr. Eden to anyone but me, you'll be fine."

"I don't understand. Talk about what?" As far as Sam
knew, Brody Eden was some kind of wizard behind the
curtain. He was like Bill Gates without a face. Reporters

had tried and failed to find information on him, raising even more questions, mystery and interest. He simply didn't exist before launching his software empire. If people found out she had access to him, she supposed they might come to her for details, but what was so important that she couldn't tell? How he liked his coffee?

Sam didn't understand all the mystery. She'd always assumed it was only to stir up buzz about the company, but the cameras and the contract made her wonder if there wasn't more to it.

Agnes sighed. "Sign the agreement and I'll tell you. It's not a big deal. Definitely not worth blowing this opportunity and this salary while I'm gone. You need the money. Sign." She pushed a pen to her and nodded. "Do it."

Sam did need the money. And the pay was very good. Too good. Suspiciously good. There had to be a reason why, but apparently she wouldn't know until she'd already signed her deal with the devil. Well, in the end, it really didn't matter. Her rent was due and she had fifteen dollars in her checking account. She picked up the pen, signing and dating the agreement at the bottom of the page.

"Excellent," Agnes said with a smile. "Mediterranean cruise, here I come." She got up from the chair and slipped all the paperwork in a folder. She carried it over to a small, silver door mounted in the wall that turned out to be some kind of drawer. Agnes placed the file inside and then slid it shut.

"What is that?"

"I was giving Mr. Eden your paperwork."

"You don't just walk into his office and hand it to him?"

Agnes chuckled. "No. I very rarely go in there."

Sam turned to look at the massive oak doors that separated them from the secret lair of Brody Eden. They looked like they would hold up to a battering ram and were likely wired with sophisticated locks and security like every other door she'd gone through. They were intimidating. Damn near unapproachable. And she was itching to find out what was on the other side.

"And he won't come out here to get it?"

"He does, but only when he feels like it. He communicates mostly through the speakerphone or the computer. He tends to email and instant message a lot throughout the day. The drawer works best for anything else. That's how you'll give him his mail and exchange paperwork with him. When he's done with something, he'll slide the drawer back to you."

"Like Hannibal Lecter?"

"Something like that," Agnes said. She sat back down at her desk, where Sam would be working for the next month, and folded her hands. "Okay, now that the legalities are handled, we have to have a chat."

Sam took a deep breath. The last half hour's discussion had built up a nervous tension that drew all her muscles tight. Now that she'd signed on the dotted line, she wasn't sure if she really wanted to know what was so closely guarded. And yet her curiosity was burning at her. "What have you gotten me into, Agnes?"

"Do you think I would've worked here for as long as I have if the job was terrible? I have had horrible bosses and he isn't one of them. I adore Brody like he's my own son. You've just got to learn how to handle him. He'll be less…prickly…if you do."

Prickly. Sam didn't like that word. She preferred her bosses to be without sharp, biting barbs. Of course, having a sexy, charismatic boss had only led her to heartache and unemployment. Maybe a prickly, distant one would be better. If she was rarely in the same room with him, she couldn't possibly have an affair and get fired.

Sam turned to one of the video cameras. She was uncomfortable having this discussion knowing he might be listening in. "Is he watching us on those?"

Agnes looked at the camera and shrugged. "Probably, but there's no sound. He can only hear us on the speakerphone unless you yell through the door. Right now, we're able to speak candidly, so I'll tell you the big secret. Mr. Eden was disfigured in an accident a long time ago. Part of his face was damaged very badly. He's very self-conscious about it and doesn't like anyone to see him. He also doesn't want anyone to know about his injury. That's the main reason for all the mystery. No one can know he's scarred like he is. When and if you do see him face-to-face, it's best if you go on like you don't even notice it. Keep the surprise, the disgust, the pity inside. It might be hard at first, but you'll get used to it."

She wasn't supposed to, but Sam couldn't help the pang of sympathy she felt for her new boss. How lonely it must be to live like that. It sounded horrible. It made her want to help him somehow. It was just her nature.

Her father had always called her "Daddy's Little Fixer." Sam's mother had died when she was in second grade, but being only seven hadn't stopped Sam from stepping up to be the lady of the house. She was never much of a nurturer, but she got things done. Socks with holes? Mended. No money for groceries? Macaroni Surprise for dinner.

If someone had a problem, going to Sam would guarantee it would get dealt with quickly and efficiently. Even if they didn't think they had a problem, she would fix it. That's why her two younger brothers referred to her as "The Meddler," instead.

But how could she help Mr. Eden if he kept himself hidden away? "Will I even see him? It sounds like he doesn't come out."

"Eventually, he will. Grumpy, like a hibernating bear. But his bark is worse than his bite. He's mostly harmless. Mostly."

Sam could only nod while she tried to absorb all of this. Agnes continued on, telling her about the various tasks she was responsible for. Aside from the basic secretarial stuff, she was also expected to run errands for him.

"I pick up his dry cleaning? Doesn't he have a wife or something to do that?" she asked as she looked over the list Agnes had typed up for her.

"No. He's single. When I say you and I are the only ones to see him, I mean it. You'll pick up coffee for him in the morning. Sometimes I get his lunch, but most times he will bring his own or have something delivered to the lobby, which you'll have to go get."

The man really didn't go out in public. It was mind-boggling. "How can someone live their life without going outside? Without going to the store or the movies or to dinner with friends?"

"Mr. Eden lives his life through his computer. Whatever he can do from there, he will. What he can't do, you do for him. You're more of a personal assistant than a secretary. He doesn't pay a premium salary for you to sit around filing your nails and answering the phone."

Apparently not. But Sam could deal with this. Now that all the secrets were out in the open, the nervous butterflies had faded. This might not be so bad. "When do I start?"

"Tomorrow. You'll shadow me tomorrow and Friday, and then you'll be on your own for the next four weeks."

"Okay. Any particular office dress?"

Agnes shrugged. "Most of the employees here are fairly casual dressers. Mr. Eden wears suits every day, although I've never been able to figure out why given no one sees him but me. You have such a flair for fashion, so I'm sure you'll be fine."

Sam tried not to laugh at her godmother's mention of her "flair for fashion." That was one way to put it. Another way was that she was obsessed with clothes and shoes. The more girly and feminine the better. She loved sparkles and glitter, pinks and purples. The right pair of platform heels or leather handbag could nearly send her into a climax.

Sadly, her past two months of unemployment had been devastating for her wardrobe. She'd gotten so discouraged from how everything ended at her last job that she'd slipped into wearing sweats and T-shirts all the time. Heels seemed like overkill for watching Lifetime movie marathons.

But that was in the past. She had a job, she was out in the world and her fashionable ways would reign once again. So yes, Mr. Eden would be getting a trendsetting eyeful from his little video cameras.

"Let's go get your badge and codes setup. They'll scan your fingerprint to get you access to this floor while we're there, too."

Sam got up from her seat and started following her godmother to the exit. Feeling brave, she stopped for a moment and looked back up at the video camera that was tracking her movements across the room.

Looking directly into the lens, she flipped her long blond curls over her shoulder and straightened her posture defiantly. "If you're going to spend the next month watching me from that little lens," she said, knowing he couldn't hear her, "I hope you like what you see."

"Like" was an understatement. Samantha Davis was distracting.

Brody had watched his new assistant train with Agnes for the past two days as though he were watching a fascinating new film. The two large screens that were connected to the surveillance cameras had captured his attention the moment Samantha came up for her interview. He'd ignored most of his work. Missed a conference call. He was just intrigued by her and the way she would turn to the cameras as though she were watching him as he was watching her.

He supposed it might be because he wasn't exposed to many people—women in particular—but even if he were, he couldn't help but think that Samantha would catch his eye. He liked the thick golden-blond curls that spilled over her shoulders and down her back. Her skin had a kiss of sun like she enjoyed jogging or swimming outside. He was drawn to her large brown eyes and bright smile. She wasn't particularly tall, but she made up for it with sky-high heels that made her legs look fantastic when she paired them with short pencil skirts.

She was really quite striking. Certainly a change of scenery from fifty-nine-year-old Agnes.

He loved Agnes like a mother. She was hardworking, efficient, if not a touch crotchety, but he liked her that way. Agnes was an office dynamo. It made Brody wonder how he was going to get through the next month without her.

Agnes had mentioned this anniversary trip months ago. He had had plenty of time to prepare. And yet, he still wasn't ready to deal with the actuality of her leaving for that long.

When Agnes suggested hiring her goddaughter to fill in while she was away, it seemed like a sensible suggestion. But he hadn't thought to ask if her goddaughter was attractive. He supposed most people wouldn't think that mattered either way, but it did to him. Brody avoided most people, but he avoided beautiful women the most diligently.

It didn't make much sense to anyone, especially his foster brothers, who were constantly riding him to get out and date. But they didn't understand what it was like. When they approached a beautiful girl, they only had to worry about rejection. And considering his three foster brothers were all handsome, successful and rich, they didn't get rejected very often.

When Brody approached a beautiful woman, he knew rejection was a given. But that wasn't the worst of it. It was the look on a woman's face when she saw him. That first reaction. That flicker of fear and disgust that even the most sensitive and polite person couldn't suppress. In Brody's world, that always came first, even if followed by a quick recovery and an attempt at indifference.

But what was even worse than that was the expression of pity that inevitably came. Brody knew there were people with worse injuries than his. Soldiers came home from the Middle East every day with burns that covered over half their bodies. They didn't hide away. Some were even outspoken advocates, role models for other victims. People were inspired by their strength to look beyond their scars.

That was a noble choice, but it didn't suit Brody. He hadn't been injured serving his country, and he wasn't interested in being the public face for acid burn victims. Being pitied one person at a time was bad enough. He couldn't take the massive public wave of sympathy all at once. He supposed that was why he'd gained a reputation of being not just a recluse, but a real bastard. He didn't like being that way, but it was a necessity. People didn't pity the villain, even if he was disfigured. They just figured he got what he deserved.

Turning back to the monitor that showed Samantha and Agnes going over some files, Brody sighed.

Looking at a beautiful woman, then having her look at you like you're some kind of sideshow freak... Brody didn't want to deal with that any more than he absolutely had to. And that was why he'd opted not to go out and introduce himself yet. Let her think he was rude. Everyone else did.

He was enjoying watching her from afar and not knowing what she looked like when she was horrified by his twisted and scarred face. She would be here for nearly a month, so Brody would probably go out eventually. But no matter how long he waited, she would still be beautiful and he would still be...what he was.

A loud ping from one of his computers distracted him from his dark thoughts. Spinning in his chair, he rolled over to one of the six machines that surrounded his desk.

The alert chimed after his web crawler software finished running one of its queries. He'd designed a system that scoured the internet daily for any searches or mentions of several things, including his given name, Brody Butler. The results were filtered to exclude any duplicates or mentions of the various Brody Butlers that he'd established as someone else.

From there, he'd review the results for anything ques-

tionable. Anything that might cause him or his foster
family any grief. If someone, somewhere, was looking
for him, Brody would be the first to know. He was a
very private man, and he didn't want his past interfering with his present. It was the reason he'd taken his
foster parents' name after high school. He wanted to
put his childhood behind him. He wanted to start fresh
and be a success because he was smart and savvy, not
because people felt bad for him.

And for some reason, he worried that if someone
connected Brody Butler and Brody Eden, it would lead
to more questions about the past than he wanted to answer.

Blame it on his childhood, but Brody never let his
guard down. If something could go wrong, he was fairly
certain it would. His brothers accused him of being pes-
simistic, but he preferred to be prepared for the worst.
He hadn't been able to stop his biological father from
beating him, but he had always been mentally and physically ready when it came.

So, like he had as a child, he slept with one eye open,
so to speak. His eye was on the internet. If someone was
looking for him, the internet was the smartest place to
start. And he would be watching and waiting for them.

"So what have we here?" Brody scanned over the
report and breathed a sigh of relief. Someone named
Brody Butler had driven his truck through a conve-
nience store window in Wisconsin. False alarm. No
one was looking for him today. Or yesterday. Or the
past five years Brody had been watching. Perhaps no
one ever would.

His former identity had vanished after he'd gradu-
ated from high school. He was simply another kid lost in
the foster system. Not even his real parents had looked

for him. His father had limited access in prison, but his mother had never tried to contact him, either. Given that she had chosen to side with her abusive husband over her scarred son, that was just as well.

Brody wasn't sure he would ever understand women. He was smart, caring and successful, but most women didn't see anything but the scars. And at the same time, his mother was attending every parole hearing, waiting for the day his abusive father was released from jail and they could be together again.

It was better he stay in seclusion, he decided. Women, beautiful or otherwise, meant nothing but trouble and pain. He was certain that his new assistant was no different. She was a novelty, a shiny new toy. It wouldn't take long before the shine would wear off and he could put his focus back on his work.

Dating the secretary was not only passé, it was a bad idea. Even fantasizing about it was certain to cause problems down the road. He'd be wise to keep his distance until Agnes returned.

Brody turned back to the surveillance monitors and found Samantha sitting alone at the desk. She looked so lovely with a blond curl falling across her forehead. It made him want to go out there, introduce himself and brush the hair from her face. It was a stupidly unproductive thought. He needed to stay as far from Samantha as he could. That meant working hard to put a sturdy barrier between them.

He pressed the button on the speakerphone. "Where is Agnes?" he asked.

His tone was a little sharp, and he'd deliberately skipped the pleasantries. He could tell she took offense to it by the way she straightened up at the desk and frowned at the phone. She brushed her curls over her shoulder with a sharp flick of her wrist and leaned in. "Good afternoon, Mr. Eden," she said in a pleasant voice, pointedly ignoring his question and emphasizing his lack of manners.

Interesting. Molly, his foster mother, would have his hide for being this rude, but he depended on his unpleasant reputation. It kept people away. Hopefully it would keep Samantha away, too. "Where is Agnes?" he repeated.

"She went downstairs to take a file to accounting and to pick up your lunch from the lobby. She left me here to watch the phones."

Lunch. He'd almost forgotten he'd ordered food from his favorite Thai restaurant. "When she comes back, tell her to bring my lunch in. I want to ask her something."

He watched her on the monitor as she considered her words for a moment before pressing the intercom button again. "You know, she's going to be gone for a month and you're pretty much stuck with me. Might as well start now. How about I bring in your lunch, introduce myself and you can ask me your question? I'm sure if I don't know the answer, I can find it out."

She was certainly a feisty one. Her second day on the job and she was already trying to push her way into his office. He was going to put off speaking to her face-to-face for as long as possible. Maybe even entirely, if he could.

"That won't be necessary, Miss Davis. Just send in Agnes when she returns."

There was very nearly steam coming out of her ears as she leaned in with a chipper "Yes, sir."

Brody watched for a few minutes as she angrily straightened up all the items on her desk. When that was done, she looked up at the camera. The breath caught in his lungs for a moment as he was pinned by her dark glare. He knew she couldn't see him, but it felt as though she really were looking right at him.

Looking at him without fear or pity or revulsion. She was irritated, yes, but he'd take that in a heartbeat to have a beautiful woman look him in the eye and not flinch.

Too bad it wouldn't be the same once there were no cameras between them.

Two

"I need this job. I *need* this job. I need *this* job."

Sam pressed into her temples and repeated the mantra to herself every time Mr. Eden buzzed her desk, but it didn't do much to improve her mood. Frankly, it had given her a miserably pounding headache. It had only been three days without Agnes, but her godmother couldn't come back soon enough. She had the touch for dealing with the beast, but Sam obviously did not.

Agnes had warned her he was "prickly," and there couldn't be a more accurate description of him. He just rubbed her the wrong way. Okay, he was busy. He had an empire to run. But would it kill the guy to be friendly or at the very least, polite? To ask how her day was or to tell her good morning? But no, he only barked commands at her. "Get me this." "Go do that." "Pick up my lunch."

She'd already come to terms with the fact that she

was never getting into his office. He had shut down any suggestion she made that involved that, so the mystery would have to remain buried. But he hadn't come out of his office, either. He was there when she arrived and still working when she left. Why force her to sign a confidentiality agreement when the only gossip she could spread was that he was a jerk? From what she'd heard around the building from other ESS employees, that wasn't exactly a secret.

"I need this job."

Sam glanced at a few new emails and started typing up a letter. As the day wore on, it was getting harder to concentrate on her work. The headache was getting worse and she was starting to feel queasy. She hadn't had a full-blown migraine in a while, but if stress set one off, that's probably where she was headed. Her monitor was too bright. Every sound shot a sharp pain through her skull. She needed to go home, pop one of her migraine pills and take a nap to cut off the worst of it.

"Mr. Eden?" Sam pressed the speakerphone button, as much as she didn't want to.

"Yes?" His response, as usual, was impatient and short.

"I'm not feeling well. Do you mind if I go home?"

"Is it terminal?"

His blunt question startled her. "I don't think so."

"Is it contagious?"

Her new boss certainly had high standards for sick days. If she wasn't on her deathbed or in quarantine, he didn't seem to care. "No, sir. It's a migraine. My pain medicine is at home."

He didn't respond, but a moment later, the silver drawer shot out. Sam rose slowly from her chair and walked over. There was a lone bottle of ibuprofen in it. That wasn't quite going to cut it. Apparently Mr. Eden was not afflicted with migraines. But his answer was clear. No, she couldn't go home. She took the pills out and swallowed a couple. It was better than nothing. Maybe if she caught it before it was full-blown, she could keep it from getting too bad.

"I ordered Italian delivery for lunch," he said as though they hadn't had the previous discussion and the issue was resolved. "They should be in the lobby in about fifteen minutes."

It took everything she had not to reply, "And?" He didn't care that she didn't feel well. He didn't even bother to ask her to go get it for him, much less say "please" or "thank you." It was just implied. He never asked her if she wanted to order, either. If she felt better, she might want to smother her irritation with a layer of mozzarella cheese, but she was never given the option.

Sam couldn't quite figure out if he was some kind of genius who was thoughtless of others or if he just didn't consider her worthy of his attention.

"Put it through the drawer when it arrives," he added as though there were another option. He wasn't going to let her bring it to him, so in the drawer it had to go.

Without responding, Sam reached for her purse, pulled out a couple dollars and picked up the laundry bag he'd left by her desk that morning. If she wasn't going home, she might as well carry on as best she could. While she was downstairs, she'd drop off his dry cleaning and grab a turkey wrap from the deli next door. Maybe some caffeine would help. If she left now, she'd have enough time to run over and get back before the deliveryman arrived.

Her timing was perfect. As she strolled back into the

lobby, she saw the delivery guy at the desk with a sack of food. Sam grabbed it from him and headed through the ridiculous layers of security to get back to her desk. She set both sacks on the desk and then walked over to the minibar where Agnes stored supplies to get a cup for her drink. She was about halfway there when she heard his growling voice over the intercom.

"*Uh*...my lunch, Miss Davis?"

"One damn second," she said as she snatched a cup and slammed the cabinet door. She hadn't spoken through the speakerphone, but unless the walls of his office were made of soundproof material, he certainly heard her. She didn't care. Her head hurt, she was cranky and she'd reached her personal breaking point. There was no reason for him to be this rude.

Back at her desk, she clutched the paper sack with his food in her fist, ready to sling it in the drawer. Then she stopped. This whole thing had gotten old, quickly. He wasn't concerned about her headache, so she wasn't going to be concerned about his empty stomach. If he wanted food on his own timetable, maybe he should come get it. She brought it upstairs. He could come the last ten feet.

Sam slid the sack to the edge of her desk and looked up at the camera with an expectant arch of her brow. A moment later the metal drawer slid out to her. Nope, she thought.

She unplugged the cord from her phone, switched off her monitor and slipped out of her black Michael Kors cardigan. Walking to the closest camera, she whipped the sweater over her head, covering the lens. The other camera couldn't see her desk from its angle, so she returned to her seat and pulled her lunch out of the bag.

She needed this job, but *he* also needed *her*. If he

wanted his lunch, he was going to come out and get it. If he wanted her to do something, he was going to ask nicely. Sam wasn't working here to be abused. If he didn't like it, he could fire her, but she was pretty certain he wouldn't.

He had no one to interview a replacement.

Five minutes passed. She could hear instant messages chiming on her computer, but with the monitor off she couldn't see them. Another five minutes.

Then she heard it. The click of a lock and the turning of a doorknob. She'd roused the beast from its den. She was getting what she wanted.

And suddenly, she was nervous. She tried to go through everything in her mind that Agnes had told her. *Scarred...don't react...ignore it...* She braced herself for his appearance and her non-response.

The door flung open, and her stomach tightened into a knot. She expected him to charge angrily at her, but instead, she only saw his profile as he walked over to the surveillance camera and tugged down her sweater.

It must be the other side of him that was damaged because what she could see was...nice. Really nice. He was tall and strongly built, which was surprising for a computer geek. His expertly tailored navy suit stretched across wide shoulders. He had dark brown, almost black hair that was short but a little shaggy and curling at the collar. And his strong jawline, high cheekbones and sharp nose gave him quite a regal and aristocratic air.

He was actually quite an attractive man. He almost had a movie star quality about him. Sam preferred her men tall, dark and handsome, and he seemed to fit the bill. She didn't understand what he was...

Then he turned to face her. Sam struggled to hold a neutral expression as he walked to her, but it was hard.

The whole left side of his face was horribly scarred. The skin was puckered and twisted from his temple to his jaw and down his neck. It extended back to his ear, warping the cartilage and pushing his hairline back about an inch from where it was on the other side of his face. His eye, nose and mouth were unscathed, but as he reached out to hand her back her sweater, she saw why.

His left hand was scarred, as well. You could almost see the outline on his face where he had reached up to protect himself from something. She didn't know what, but it must have been horrible.

She swallowed hard and accepted her sweater, refusing to break eye contact. That part was easier because he had the most amazing blue eyes. They were dark blue like the most expensive sapphires, and they glittered just as brightly, fringed by thick black lashes. Sam could easily lose herself in those eyes and forget about everything else.

Only the loud click of the phone cord being plugged back in pulled her away. She looked down in time to see him snatch up his lunch. He paused for a moment, narrowing his eyes at her with a mix of irritation and confusion.

Unsure of what else to do, Sam smiled widely. She knew she was probably in trouble, but she'd used her brilliant smile on more than one occasion to smooth over her mistakes.

He didn't smile back. Instead, he turned and stomped back into his office without speaking. He slammed his office door so forcefully that Sam leaped in her seat.

And then…silence.

She kept waiting for a scolding from the speakerphone. An email telling her to pack up her things. Certainly she was due for a tongue-lashing via instant messaging at the very least. But it was silent in the office.

Maybe she did know how to handle him. Agnes certainly wasn't the kind of woman to take orders barked at her. Perhaps he needed to know what his boundaries were with her. His boundaries were abundantly clear and she'd respect them. For now.

Finally she was able to relax and eat her own lunch. Or at least she tried. A few bites into her wrap, the headache and nausea from earlier had faded, but something else seemed to be gnawing at her.

Her mind kept straying back to those beautiful, deep blue eyes.

Given the stern warning from Agnes about his face, Sam had expected him to be...ruined, somehow. But he wasn't. Yes, he was scarred terribly. It made her sick to her stomach to think of what he must've gone through to have scars like that. But that was only a part of him. The other side of his face was strikingly handsome. He was tall and muscular. She could easily imagine running her hands down the hard muscles of his arms and pressing her body against the wall of his chest.

And those eyes...

The tingle of anxiety from earlier had now become a tingle of another variety. Sam twitched uneasily in her seat and took a deep breath to wish away her misplaced desire.

"Enough of that," she said aloud. "We are not doing this again." Picking up her wrap, she took another bite and tried to force her mind onto her lunch and off of her boss.

If the fiasco of her last job taught her nothing else, it was that work relationships were bad. Relationships with your boss were catastrophic. Especially when they were married and conveniently left that fact out of every conversation they'd ever had.

Sam was naive when she had let herself fall for her boss, Luke. She'd let her guard down for the handsome, charming liar. But she'd learned a hard lesson she wasn't about to repeat. Given the circumstances of this job, she never thought it would be a problem. Brody was a grumpy, scarred recluse. Not exactly sexual fantasy material. But now she had seen him and things had changed. Which was frustratingly pointless. Agnes said Brody wasn't married, but he was as off-limits as any other employer.

Disgusted, Sam flopped her lunch back onto its wrapper. She needed to start focusing on work and maybe she'd forget about the whiff of his cologne and the full curve of his lips. Or not.

Maybe she should've just let him stay in his office.

Brody shouldn't have gone out there. He knew it, and yet he did it anyway.

Now he sat at his desk, silently brooding. He hadn't been able to touch his container of baked spaghetti for the past hour. It was his favorite, but he'd lost his appetite the minute he came face-to-face with Samantha Davis.

The surveillance cameras hadn't done her justice. She was absolutely breathtaking in person. She had a glow of confidence—a radiance—that didn't translate through the lens. Neither did her scent. Her sweater had left the smell of her floral perfume on his hands. When he got closer to her, he also picked up a hint of what he assumed was her cherry lip gloss. It had made her full pink lips shiny and alluring.

Brody was suddenly very warm. He kept his office

cool to offset the heat produced by all his computer equipment, but it wasn't enough. He leaned forward and shrugged out of his suit coat, tossing it aside. It barely helped.

He wanted to kiss her and taste those lips more than he had wanted to kiss another woman in his life. His body had quickly reacted to being so close to her. His pulse raced, his groin tightened and his grasp of the English language vanished. It was an instantaneous reaction. One that forced him back into his office before he made a fool of himself.

Samantha would never kiss him. At least not because she thought he was attractive and wanted to kiss him. On the one occasion in the past where a woman had appeared interested, it was his bank account, not his body that drew her in. Once she got what she came for, she was gone.

Truthfully, Brody had enough money for women to overlook the scars. He'd known women to put up with worse for access to the black American Express card. Every billionaire in Forbes magazine had some busty blonde twenty years younger than him clinging affectionately to his arm in photographs. It didn't matter how old or ugly or unpleasant the men were because they were rich. But that's not what Brody wanted.

He wanted more than arm candy or a trophy wife. He wanted more out of a relationship than what he could buy. He might get sex in a dark room. He might get companionship in exchange for expensive gifts. But Brody would never have love and he knew it. It only took one time getting burned to learn that lesson.

But Samantha gave him hope. She hadn't reacted the way he expected her to. There was the initial draw of air into her lungs, but there the reaction stopped. Or changed, he should say. Instead of her gaze running over his scars, it had found its focus in his eyes. There had been a softness there, a comfortable warmth in her dark brown eyes. And then…she had smiled.

No disgust. No pity. No irritation. If he didn't know better, he might think it was actually attraction. He'd seen the same look in a girl's eyes as she admired one of his brothers in high school. Or the way his foster mother, Molly, looked at Ken. But it had never been directed at him.

The problem now was figuring out what to do next. He was tempted to drop the rude act and actually try talking to her. Maybe from there he could consider asking her out. His gut warned him to stay away while his body urged him closer.

Turning back to the monitor, Brody lamented his inexperience with the fairer sex. The past few years with Agnes hadn't helped much. What if he was wrong about Samantha's reaction? He'd feel like a fool when she rejected him. And she would. The work relationship would be even more strained then. So he would keep his mouth shut on the subject.

But at least the worst was over. Samantha had seen him. The veil had been lifted and the awkward moment was behind them.

The chime of his email program turned his attention back to his computer. He had a teleconference with his executive staff in fifteen minutes. Not even his most trusted and senior employees ever spoke to Brody in person or saw his face. Typically his employees spent the entire time talking to a red curtain backdrop while he sat to the side. He could've just called a conference call, but he liked to see their faces during meetings. He could get so much more from their expressions than just their voices.

Before the meeting started, he needed the agenda and financial reports he's asked Samantha to pull together earlier.

Brody reached out to press the speaker button and hesitated. There was absolutely no reason to go out to Samantha's desk aside from the fact that he wanted to see her again. He almost wished she had recoiled in horror so he could return to focusing on his work instead of the sway of her hips as she walked.

Perhaps he'd read her reaction wrong. She might just have a good poker face. If he went out there and she avoided looking at him...if she shied away from his scarred hand...then he could return to his life in progress and know all was right with the world again. Yes, that was why he was going out there.

He pushed away from his desk and walked past the vintage pinball machine to the door. His hand rested on the knob for a few moments before he worked up the nerve to turn it. Earlier, he'd been angry and hadn't thought before he reacted. Now he couldn't shut his brain off long enough to make his wrist rotate. What if he was wrong? He didn't want to be wrong, but what would he do if she *was* attracted to him?

"Coward," he cursed at himself and forced his way into the reception area.

Samantha immediately shot to attention at her desk. She looked at him with wide-eyed surprise as he came out and approached her desk. Under the initial shock was a bit of apprehension. Her delicate brow furrowed as she fought a concerned frown. Was she afraid of him? She wouldn't be the first, although he hated to think so.

"Is s-something wrong, Mr. Eden?" Samantha leaped

up from her chair, nervously straightening her blouse and fidgeting with a ring on her right hand. "I apologize for earlier, sir. That was unprofessional of me. You'll come out of your office when you want to."

That explained it. She thought he was mad over her little stunt. She had probably been stewing at her desk, worrying she was about to get fired while he was thinking of kissing her. That only proved how far off base he was. He hadn't been thrilled at the time, but it was just as well that they got over that first hurdle. She wasn't about to be fired. Nor, sadly, was she about to be kissed. Brody shook his head dismissively. "No apology is necessary, Miss Davis."

She breathed a soft sigh of relief and every tense muscle in her body seemed to uncoil at his words. He couldn't help but notice every detail of her body from the slight movement of her full breasts as she breathed to the curve of her throat.

"Sam, please," she said, distracting him from surveying her body.

Sam. He liked that. There was something sassy and decidedly feminine about the nickname despite its traditionally masculine use. "I should've come out sooner. I'm very busy."

Sam nodded with understanding, but his excuse sounded lame to his own ears, so he figured it had to seem hollow to her, as well. "Of course." She reached down to a file on her desk and handed it to him with a wide smile. "Here's the report for your one o'clock meeting."

Brody froze in place, momentarily entranced by the stunning beauty of her smile. Full, pink lips. Dazzling white teeth. It seemed so sincere, begging him to trust her. It lit up her face, making her even more attractive.

His foster mother had always insisted that he was so handsome when he smiled. He never believed Molly— moms had to say things like that—but it was never a truer statement than with Sam.

He reached out and took the file from her, tucking it under his arm. At this point, he knew he should return to his office, but something kept him anchored to the spot. He wanted to stay. His mind raced for an excuse.

Brody sucked at small talk, so he wouldn't even try. Instead, he thrust his hand into his pants pocket and found his USB flash drive there. The tiny memory stick held most of his important files, and he carried it with him everywhere he went. It was perfect, he realized. Just the thing he needed to help him figure out if his new secretary was sincere or a really good actress.

Grasping the flash drive in his scarred hand, he reached out to her. "I need you to print a file off this drive while I'm in my meeting."

He watched as Sam looked down at the small device on the open palm of his hand. She hesitated for a moment and then reached out for it. Using her shapely, pink glittery fingernails, she plucked it from his hand without touching his skin. He might not have noticed how deliberate the movement was if he hadn't been watching for just such a thing.

Brody tried to swallow his disappointment. She didn't mind looking at him, but she didn't want to touch him. It wasn't surprising, but it was a letdown. She was polite and friendly to him because he was her boss. Nothing more. He should've known better than to let his mind wander to places it didn't need to be. "There's a white paper I've written on there about our latest database management innovations. Please print it out so I can redline changes later this afternoon."

"Yes, sir."

Brody turned on his heel, ready to return to his office and lick his wounds, when he heard her voice call out to him again.

"Mr. Eden?" she asked.

"Yes?" He stopped and turned back to her.

Sam rounded her desk and approached him. His body tensed involuntarily as she came closer. She reached up to the scarred side of his face, causing his lungs to seize in his chest. What was she doing?

"Your shirt…" Her voice drifted off.

He felt her fingertips gently brush the puckered skin along his neck before straightening his shirt collar. It must've flipped up when he took his suit coat off earlier. The innocent touch sent a jolt of heat through his body. It was so simple, so unplanned, and yet it was the first time a woman had touched his scars.

His foster mother had often kissed and patted his cheek, and nurses had applied medicine and bandages after various reconstructive procedures, but this was different. As a shiver ran down his spine, it *felt* different, as well.

Without thinking, he brought his hand up to grasp hers. Sam gasped softly at his sudden movement, but she didn't pull away when his scarred fingers wrapped around her own. He was glad. He wasn't ready to let go. The pleasurable surge that ran up his arm from her touch was electric. His every nerve lit up with awareness, and he was pretty certain she felt it, too. Her dark brown eyes were wide as she looked at him, her moist lips parted seductively and begging for his kiss.

He slowly drew her hand down, his eyes locked on hers. Sam swallowed hard and let her arm fall to her side when he finally let her go. "Much better," she said, gesturing to his collar with a nervous smile. She held up the flash drive in her other hand. "I'll get this printed for you, sir."

"Call me Brody," he said, finding his voice when the air finally moved in his lungs again. He might still be her boss, but suddenly he didn't want any formalities between them. He wanted her to say his name. He wanted to reach out and touch her again. But he wouldn't.

Sam looked away to glance down at the pink and crystal watch on her delicate wrist. Brody couldn't help but notice how every detail about her was so...*sparkly*. Her watch was simply the latest piece. The large cocktail ring on her right hand made her earrings look demure. The stitching on her silk blouse reflected the light as did the glitter that seemed to be embedded in her pink eye shadow. Her heels had a pattern of sequins and stones across the toe shaped like a daisy. Even the buttons on her sweater looked like dime-sized diamonds.

He wasn't used to that. His sister, Julianne, was feminine, but she was also raised in a house full of boys. She could hold her own and very rarely, if ever, sparkled. Most of the time, she was actually covered in sculpting mud from her pottery.

"You're going to be late for your executive meeting, Brody."

His name coming from her lips sounded wonderful to his ears, but he couldn't dwell on it. He looked down at his own watch, which was expensive, painstakingly accurate, but not at all flashy. She was right. He reluctantly took the file out from under his arm and held it up as he backed away. "Thanks."

Returning to the safety of his office, he closed the door and flopped his back against the solid wood. He took his first deep breath in five minutes, the scent of her perfume in his lungs. It made his head swim, the blood rushing from his extremities to fuel his desire with a restless ache he'd grown accustomed to over the years.

No woman, sparkly or otherwise, had ever deliberately touched his scars like that. With every fiber of his being, he wanted her to do it again.

Three

The house was empty. It always was when Brody came home. At least as far as people were concerned. He hung his overcoat on the hook by the garage entrance, tossed his laptop bag onto the kitchen table and whistled loudly.

His answer came in the form of excited clicks of toenails on the hardwood floor and thumps down the stairs. A few moments later, a large golden retriever rounded the corner and bounded straight for him. Brody braced himself as the dog stood up onto her hind legs and placed her paws on his chest. Normally she met him at the door, so she must've been sound asleep on her giant beanbag pillow upstairs.

He leaned down to let her lick him and scratched gently behind her ears. "Hey there, Chris. Did you have a good day with Peggy?"

The dog jumped down and danced around his feet,

her tail wagging enthusiastically. Chris was a very happy dog and a great companion for Brody. It was impossible for him to sulk with her around. His foster sister, Julianne, had gotten the puppy for him as a birthday present three years ago. She decided that he needed a hot blonde in his life, so he named her after sexy pop singer Christina Aguilera as a joke.

Admittedly, she had been a great gift. She kept Brody company in his big empty house. His housekeeper, Peggy, walked and cared for her during the day, and the dog occasionally stayed with Agnes if Brody had to travel. It wasn't much of a burden. Everyone loved Chris.

"Did Peggy feed you dinner yet?"

Chris darted over to her empty bowl and stared up expectantly. Brody looked down into the dog's big brown eyes and knew she'd never admit it, even if she'd already eaten. She was a canine garbage disposal. "Here you go," he said, filling her bowl with her favorite kibble. "I wonder what Peggy left for me to eat?"

He had a good guess. Tonight, the air was filled with the spicy scent of Mexican food.

Peggy arrived after he left for work and was gone before he came home. She kept his place tidy, took care of Chris, handled the laundry that didn't go to the cleaners and did all his grocery shopping and cooking. Peggy was an excellent cook. She made a pot roast so good it could make you cry. It was even better than Molly's, although he wouldn't admit to that even if one of his brothers had him in a headlock.

Peggy had worked for him for five years, but Brody wasn't entirely sure what she looked like. There was a copy of her driver's license photo in her file from her background check, but few people actually looked like their pictures. Agnes had interviewed her, so he'd never met Peggy in person. All he knew was that she could deal with his idiosyncrasies, and that made her perfect.

Brody tossed his suit coat over the stool at the kitchen bar and looked for the note Peggy left him every night. He'd bought her nice stationery with an embossed "P" on the front and she'd opted to use it for her daily communications with him.

He found it sitting beside a plate of freshly baked chocolate chip cookies on the kitchen island. He popped one in his mouth and groaned. That woman deserved a raise. He chewed as he flipped open the card.

There's enchilada casserole in the oven. Picked up your favorite beer at the store today. It's in the fridge. New sheets on the bed. Mail on your desk. Chris has eaten dinner, don't let her fool you. You also got a package from your brother.—Peggy

A package from his brother? Frowning, Brody set down the card, went to the fridge for a bottle of microbrew and snatched up another cookie. He carried both of them down the hallway into his study with Chris quick on his heels. On his desk was a stack of various bills, junk mail and a large brown box. The label said it was from his foster brother Xander.

Brody had gone to live with Ken and Molly Eden when he was eleven, only a few months after his father had attacked him. He grew up on their Christmas tree farm in Connecticut with their daughter, Julianne, and a list of other foster children. He considered the Edens and the three other boys that remained on the farm— Wade, Xander and Heath—his true family. Xander and his younger brother, Heath, had come to the farm after their parents were both killed in a car accident. Xander was in the same grade as Brody, just a few months younger. He was currently a Connecticut congressman living in D.C.

He ignored the mail and went straight to the package. It wasn't his birthday. It was October and far too early for a Christmas present. There was no reason he should be getting a box from Xander, so it was a mystery. Until he ripped the brown paper away to reveal a picture of an inflatable woman.

The torture of brothers never ended. Neither miles nor years would get them off his back about his love life. He knew it would be even worse if they ever learned the truth of it. Brody dropped the box onto his desk and went for his phone.

"This is Langston," Xander answered.

"You know," Brody began, skipping the small talk. "I expect this kind of crap from Heath, but not you. You're supposed to be the sensible, non-controversial one."

"At the office, absolutely. But the rest of the time, I'm your brother and it is fully within my rights to give you grief about your love life, or lack thereof."

"You have no room to talk, Xander. When was the last time you actually went on a date?"

"I took Annabelle Hamilton to a reception last week."

Brody chuckled and sat back on the edge of his desk. "A political fund-raiser?"

"Well, yes, but—"

"Doesn't count. When was the last time you went on a date where you didn't talk about politics, attend a political event or leave your date stranded alone while you talked to some lobbyist that came up to your table?"

There was a long silence before his brother spoke. "I reject the unreasonable boundaries you've placed on my love life. The life of a single congressman is complicated." Xander said the words with his official man-in-power voice, as though he were addressing a congressional committee.

"That's what I thought. You should've kept that doll for yourself."

Xander laughed, turning from his phone to say something to someone else. Despite the late hour, he was still at the office. Xander was always at the office.

"Got someone with you?" Brody asked.

"One of my congressional interns. He's leaving for the night and reminding me about my early appointment tomorrow. I have to give some VIPs from my district a tour of the Capitol building."

Brody settled into the brown leather loveseat in his office. Chris immediately jumped up beside him, curling up to lie down with her head in his lap. His free hand went to rub her ears. "It's awfully late to still be at the office. I'd hate to work for you. You're a mean boss."

"Not as mean as you are. At least I speak face-to-face with my employees instead of barking at them over an intercom."

"I pay them well for the inconvenience of dealing with me," Brody argued.

"That's fair, I suppose. Mine don't get paid. It's the beauty of government internships. I can work their idealistic hearts to death for free so when they graduate college, they will be jaded and fully prepared for a job in public service."

"You sound run down, Xander. Are you sure you're up for a campaign and another term?"

"I've just had a long day. I don't have much free time. And I know that both of us aren't the best at making time to date. Which is why I sent that lovely plastic woman to you. It's secretly an invitation to a fund-raiser my party is having next week. If I sent you a card, I knew you'd ignore it, but that doll got you on the phone."

Of course. There was always something behind it. He would've ignored an invitation. And he'd ignore this one, too, after he hid it away where Peggy wouldn't find it and faint. "I'll mail a check."

"I don't want you to mail a check, Brody. I want you to come."

Oh, yeah, because socializing at a cocktail party with a bunch of strangers was his idea of a good time. He'd jump right on the next train from Boston. Xander knew it, too, so there had to be more to the story than he was telling. "What's her name?"

"Why would you—?"

"You're as transparent as Mom."

Xander sighed heavily into the phone receiver. "Her name is Briana Jessup. *Dr.* Briana Jessup. I met her a few weeks ago. She's a plastic surgeon that specializes in reconstructive surgery. She spends several weeks a year in third world countries helping disfigured children."

Brody listened to his brother talk, but the more words that came out of his mouth, the more irritated he got. "I don't know which is worse. Thinking you're fixing me up on a date again or trying to lure me to another doctor."

"It's just social," Xander corrected. "I thought you might be more comfortable with a woman if you knew she had…" His voice trailed away as though he weren't quite sure how to say it. Xander was always on a mission to find the right way to say things. It made him a great politician. But dealing with him as a brother could be frustrating when everything he said was polished to a point of near insincerity.

"Seen worse?" Brody suggested.

"You know what I mean, man. Don't get offended."

Brody took a sip of his beer. He understood what his brother was doing. It wasn't a bad idea. A woman who had experience with severe injuries like his might not react so negatively to it. She might even touch him, although it might be more for professional curiosity than attraction. It was certainly a better choice than the last woman Xander tried to set him up with. "I'm not offended. I'm just not interested in starting up something with this doctor of yours."

And he wasn't. Maybe if Xander had asked him a week ago. But now, his mind was overrun with thoughts of one particular woman touching him. A sunny blonde with luscious curves and an affinity for pink.

"Then are you still upset about the thing with Laura? It's been three years."

Brody chuckled into the phone. "Why would I still be upset about Laura? Just because you set me up with a woman that pretended to like me long enough to steal my personal information and charge a hundred-thousand dollars on my credit cards…? I mean, after three years that would be petty of me."

Xander sighed. "You know I'm sorry about that. She seemed like she really liked you, and I hate that she stole from you. But this other lady is different. I think you'd really like her."

"I'm too preoccupied for something like that right now. I have my mind on…other things."

"Are you seeing someone?" Xander asked, his voice laced with an edge of incredulity.

"No," Brody said. "Don't be ridiculous."

"But you're *interested* in someone, aren't you?"

That, Brody couldn't argue with. He was interested. He didn't know if that would make any difference in the end, but he was. He couldn't stop thinking about Sam and what it would feel like to touch her.

"I suppose you could say that…."

Sam slammed back another shot of espresso from the coffee shop in the lobby, but she wasn't sure it would help. The first four hadn't. She was still exhausted. She hadn't gotten much sleep last night. Her mind kept spinning with the previous day's developments.

She had started Wednesday irritated with her boss. Brody was demanding, rude and thoughtless of others. By the time she went home, she was intrigued by him. More than that—aroused by him. When she wasn't lying in bed fantasizing about touching him again, she was plagued with questions.

What happened to him? How long had he been like that? How could he live his life separated from other people? Wasn't he lonely? Why was he so unpleasant?

The "fix-it gene" in Sam was alight with the need to get her hands on Brody's life and put it right. It seemed a shame to her that he was hiding. He was a smart, successful and handsome man. He shouldn't let his accident keep him from living a full life.

Sam eyed the door to his office. She wanted to march in there, grab him by the hand and drag him out into the sunlight. It would be good for him, she was certain.

Then she saw it. The door was ever so slightly ajar. It hadn't quite latched earlier. That was odd. Brody was always very meticulous about shutting and locking the door. His mind must be on other things.

Or maybe it was a subtle invitation. A subconscious

slip. Sam wasn't a big believer in accidents. Everything happened for a reason. What if Brody wanted a fuller, more open life, but didn't know where to start? She could help him. Maybe he knew that. Could this be his way of reaching out?

"Sam, could you get me that new distribution proposal?" Brody's voice crackled over the speakerphone.

"Yes, sir."

Sam grabbed the file out of her inbox and let her gaze wander between the silver drawer and the unlatched door. She wasn't sure if Brody left it open on purpose, but she decided to take the opportunity fate, or Brody, had provided.

She quickly reached down for her purse and pulled out her compact. Her makeup was good. Her blond curls were swept back into a messy bun today. Her lip gloss was still shiny. She looked great.

Getting up from her seat, she tucked the file under her arm and gently tugged down at the hem of her sweater dress. She smoothed over her wide, patent leather belt before reaching out and grasping the doorknob. She didn't have to turn it. The light pressure was enough to unlatch it completely and the door swung open.

Sam poked her head into the dark room, expecting Brody to start yelling at her at any moment, but there was nothing. As her eyes adjusted, she noticed a pinball machine to her left. Beside it was a Track and Field arcade game. Both of them flashed and blinked, lighting the corner of the dim room. Beyond that, she spied a seating area with plush, leather couches. A small kitchenette with a sink and a refrigerator.

In the corner were a universal weights machine and a treadmill. That explained those arms. She half expected to see a bed, but that was the only thing missing. He had his own little world behind these doors.

Taking a step inside, she found his desk to the right. It was a large U-shaped configuration with multiple monitors and computers. The first two screens she looked at displayed the feed from the lobby surveillance cameras. He had a good view of her at her desk, despite the grainy black-and-white feed. He was currently facing the other direction or he would've seen her approach his door and come into his office space.

Sam took a deep breath and closed the gap between them in a few steps. The hum of the multiple computers and the constantly running air-conditioning unit disguised the click of her heels across the marble floor.

When she was about a foot behind him, Sam paused, looking down at a large bowl of multicolored jelly beans on his desk, giving a bright pop to an otherwise monochromatic space. Her bravery was waning. But it was too late to turn back. He'd likely notice her making a quick escape. Instead, she decided to wait a moment and see if he finally turned around. Saying his name would probably send him three feet out of his chair.

Sam's gaze drifted past his shoulder to the screen he was staring so intently at. At the top was the name "Tommy Wilder" with a long series of links and descriptions that were too small for her to read. She'd never heard of Tommy Wilder. Then she spied the screen beside it, where her own name was shown just as prominently. Was he doing some kind of background check on her?

She couldn't help the gasp that escaped her lips. She was close enough to Brody now that the small sound caused him to immediately spin in his chair to face her.

His initial look of surprise quickly morphed into

anger as his jaw locked and his eyes narrowed at her. He stood up in one fluid movement and Sam took an instinctive step backward.

"What the hell are you doing?" he asked. "How did you get in here?"

Sam clutched the file to her chest and took another step back as he charged forward. "I brought the file you w-wanted. The door was open and I—"

"What? You thought I left it open for *you?*" he interrupted her shaky explanation.

Apparently her ideas about Brody subconsciously reaching out to her were woefully incorrect. "No, I…" She didn't have a better explanation. She took another two steps back, pausing when she felt the press of cold metal on her back. A quick glance showed her she'd backed herself against the pinball machine. With Brody moving closer, she was pretty much trapped there to take her punishment.

"What did you see?" he asked, pointing to his computers. "Tell me," Brody demanded, his booming voice amplified by the acoustics of the dark room.

Sam was wide-eyed with confusion. He was mad that she was in there, but somehow he seemed more concerned that she was spying on him. What did she see? Nothing important. What did it matter, anyway? She had a confidentiality agreement in place. She could've seen the truth about the Roswell crash site and the JFK assassination and she couldn't tell anyone. "Just some names. My name. Nothing else."

Brody crowded into her space, placing his hands on each side of the pinball machine as though he were playing to prevent her escape. His blue eyes were nearly black in the dim lighting as he leaned into her.

Even with the file between them, Sam could feel the

heat of his body penetrating her clothes. The scent of his cologne crowded her, filling her lungs as she took a deep breath to calm herself.

Goodness, but he was tall. In her four-inch heels, she was almost looking him in the eye, their bodies aligning perfectly. Her heart started racing as she thought about reaching out and touching him. Her touch before had been fleeting, innocent, yet powerful. She craved that connection again. It was a ridiculously counterproductive thought, given the man was in a big enough rage to fire her, not kiss her.

Sam licked her lips, noting his gaze dropped down to watch, then came back up to look into her eyes. She had her share of experience with men, and she knew when a man wanted her. Sam was surprised, given all the barriers Brody had deliberately put between them, but it was clear. He wanted her. Yet he was holding back.

"What was the other name?" His voice was calmer now but still deadly cold.

Sam was so wrapped up in her thoughts about Brody that she could barely remember. "Timmy? Tommy? I don't know. I only saw it for a moment."

At that, Brody nodded and the muscles in his body seemed to uncoil from the pounce he'd been ready to make. But he didn't pull away. He stayed put.

The blinking lights of the pinball machine behind her cast Brody's face in dancing shadows. He was so beautiful, and yet, so damaged. She watched him, knowing she shouldn't linger too long on his injuries, but wanting to understand what he'd been through.

Before she could stop herself, she reached her right hand up and placed it on his damaged cheek. Her palm barely made contact with the wavy surface of his skin before he jerked back. Sam didn't want him to shy away. She wasn't afraid of him or his injury.

Slipping her hand behind his neck instead, she pulled him forward, meeting his lips with her own. His mouth was stiff against hers at first, making her fear she'd made a gross miscalculation in kissing him, but then he relaxed and she felt one of his hands move to her waist.

His lips were soft and slightly sweet, as though he'd been eating some of those jelly beans she'd spied on his desk. Like his office, he seemed to be just as physically closed off. Sam had to coax his mouth open wider, running her tongue along his bottom lip to let her in.

Sam anxiously waited for Brody to take charge of their kiss. To press her back against the pinball machine and dig his fingertips hungrily into her flesh. But he didn't. His every move was hesitant, as though he were thinking about it. You weren't supposed to think about a kiss, you were supposed to feel and give in to it.

The file she'd been holding slipped to the floor. Sam didn't care. With both hands free, she wrapped her arms around his neck, easing closer to him. If he wasn't going to do it, she would.

Her move made him bolder. He pressed into her, snaking his arms around her waist. She could feel every hard inch of him as he leaned in and she arched her body against him. The movement elicited a low groan against her lips.

The sound was a reality check for Sam. Even though she'd been the aggressor, it wasn't until that moment that she really realized what she'd been doing.

Kissing her boss. *Again*. She was determined to let history repeat itself. Last time was a disaster. Why would it be any different now?

Sam placed her hands against Brody's chest and gen-

tly pushed until their lips parted and he eased back.
They stood still, their warm breath lingering in the
space between them. Finally, she crouched down to
gather up the paperwork she dropped and pressed the
mess of the distribution proposal against his chest.

Brody took another step back, clutching the wild
scattering of paper. But his eyes didn't leave hers. There
was a curious expression there as he watched her. His
eyes narrowed, confusion and distrust still evident, but
eventually, that faded into confidence.

And then, for the first time, the corners of Brody's
mouth curled upward and he smiled at her. Her knees
started to quiver beneath her. His smile was so charming it caught her off guard. His whole face lit up, his
eyes twinkling with a touch of mischief. It made him
even more handsome, if she could believe it. His smile
made her want to tell him stories to make him laugh. It
made her want him all the more.

A hot flush swept over her body as the rush of
arousal from their kiss surged through her with no outlet. Her fingertips tingled where she touched him and
ached to reach for him again. Her heart was still racing, although the flash of his smile had caused a mo-
mentary skip in her chest.

This was bad. Very bad. She needed to get out of
here before she completely lost her mind and started
taking her clothes off.

Turning on her heel, Sam rounded the pinball machine and ran from Brody's office, slamming the door
shut behind her.

Four

Sam didn't say good-night when she left. Brody had simply looked up at his surveillance monitor at some point and noticed her desk was empty and her coat was gone. It was just as well. If she'd tried speaking to him, he doubted he would've managed a sensible response.

Even three hours later, the cacophony of thoughts in Brody's head made it hard for him to think. He'd gotten zero work done. There was no way he could focus properly. In a flash, so many things had gone right and wrong at once.

She'd kissed him. Really kissed him. It wasn't some chaste peck or tight-lipped obligation. It had fallen nearly into the "making out" category, by his assessment, such as it was. But she'd also snuck into his office, spied over his shoulder and completely invaded his personal space. It didn't really matter, though. Brody found he couldn't be mad at her while he could still taste that cherry gloss on his lips.

It had been a long time since Brody had been kissed by a girl. The week before his accident, Macy Anderson had kissed him at the bus stop after school. Seventeen years later, the woman Xander set him up with kissed him. Mainly so she could get close enough to steal his credit card. But compared to what just happened in his office, they hardly counted.

Brody didn't like to think about the parts of his life he had missed out on because of his father's temper. It wasn't only depressing, it was embarrassing. The burden of it grew with each passing year, making it harder to bear yet more critical to hide. So much so that not even his brothers knew the full extent of it.

But even as desperate as Brody was, getting what he wanted would require him to open himself up to someone. There was no way he could keep all of his secrets hidden. He would just have to decide what was more important if the moment ever arrived. So far, he hadn't had to choose.

Would Sam have kissed him if she knew he'd never…?

Brody shook his head. He wasn't going to taint the moment any more than it was already was. It was a milestone he wanted to savor, but he couldn't waste his time fantasizing about his secretary. Something more important had happened. It was bad timing that she'd come into his office at the worst possible moment. She'd seen *his* name on the computer screen.

He'd been so engrossed in his work that she could've driven a tractor through his office and he wouldn't have noticed. Between the time that he buzzed for the file and she brought it to him, his world had started to crumble. The day had come. The one he'd been anxiously waiting for. One of his web crawler queries had turned up something. Someone was looking for Tommy Wilder.

Damn it.

Just like the one that searched for Brody Butler, there was another crawler that sought out any interest in Tom, Thomas or Tommy Wilder. If someone, somewhere, was looking for him, Brody wanted to be the first to know. Once he assessed the risk, he and his brothers could determine what action needed to be taken. It was imperative that Tommy not be found and that questions not be asked about his current whereabouts.

That's because his location for the past sixteen years was a makeshift grave on the property where they grew up.

The Eden kids never talked about that day. It was as though they decided as a group that they could pretend it never happened if no one mentioned it ever again. They all went on with their lives, became successful and wealthy. But nothing they did or achieved could erase those memories. You can't forget the sight of that much blood. You just have to focus on other things.

That had worked for a long time. Then about a year ago, everything changed. Julianne had called in a panic last Thanksgiving when she discovered their parents had sold off a large portion of the family property. The part where Tommy was buried. All three plots were being developed and ran the risk of uncovering his remains.

The question was, which plot? Only his older brother Wade knew where Tommy's body was located and even then, after all this time, it was a good guess. They sprang into action and Wade returned to Cornwall to buy back the property. He'd been unsuccessful in his initial attempt, but given he was currently engaged to the woman that owned the land, the Eden children felt fairly secure that they'd retained control of the right plot and Tommy's body wouldn't be found.

All but Brody. And he hated to be proven right about these kinds of things.

Now that Sam had gone home for the day and he had finally quelled the distracting desire she stirred in him, he returned to the report on his machine. According to his records, someone had entered the search query *Tommy Wilder Cornwall Connecticut* with a variety of other keyword combinations including *jail, dead,* and *arrested.* Whoever was looking for Tommy didn't have a lot of faith in what he'd been doing the past sixteen years.

Fortunately, the person running the Google query was logged in under their Gmail account. In addition to the query details and results, it provided the IP address, internet provider, location and email address of the person running the search.

dwilder27. A Hartford, Connecticut, connection.

It would take a little legwork to figure out who this dwilder27 was and what he was after, but it was obvious he was a relative. Tommy had never been very forthcoming about his background. If he had family that might look for him, he kept that to himself. Brody wished he'd kept his hands to himself, too.

Fortunately, dwilder27's query hadn't pulled up any useful results. Mainly because Tommy couldn't get arrested in his current condition and no one knew he was dead. There was only an old, archived Cornwall news article about Tommy when he ran away from his foster home at the Garden of Eden Christmas Tree Farm. Molly and Ken had reported their oldest foster child as missing, but since his eighteenth birthday was the following week, not much effort went into the search. He was an adult and out of the system regardless of his location. End of story. For now.

Brody had queried Tommy periodically to make sure nothing else came up. As far as the internet was concerned, Tommy Wilder had vanished from the face of the earth. He hit the button to send the report to his home network and shut down his machines. He grabbed his coat, scooped up his laptop bag and headed for the elevator.

Passing through the multiple security measures he put in place was like a soothing ritual to him now, the barriers carefully crafted layers of protection. He was happy to be a ghost, an enigma. That was better than the reality.

A swipe of his badge and a scan of his thumbprint opened up the private elevator doors. On the ground floor, he turned away from the exit Sam and Agnes used to a narrow corridor. At the end was another door. A second badge swipe and rotating key code opened up his private entrance and exit to the building. Waiting for him was his car—a black Mercedes sedan with a tint job on the windows that was illegal in some states. He supposed he could've selected something flashier, but he didn't want to draw attention, just to block it out with the darkened glass.

As it was, he got a few looks from people who thought he might be *somebody*. They were wrong. He was nobody.

It was late to be heading home and traffic was easily navigated out of downtown Boston. Most people probably assumed that as an eccentric multimillionaire, he had some big loft apartment in the city, but nothing could be further from the truth. He'd opted for the exclusive and sprawling suburb of Belmont Hill. The lots were large and wooded, backing up to a bird sanctuary. Chris loved running around the backyard barking at the various birds that dared to light on the fence. Aside from that, it was a very quiet, secluded location. It made his home feel like a private retreat. It also helped that the neighbors kept to themselves.

It gave Brody the luxury of going outside from time to time during the day. He wasn't exactly an outdoorsy guy, but shooting hoops in his backyard and digging in his garden made him feel normal and boosted all that vitamin D synthesis. He could have wide-open windows letting light spill in and never worry about someone seeing him. That was something a home in the city could not provide.

The landscaping lights that highlighted the curve of his driveway were already on by the time he arrived. He enjoyed the fall, but the shorter days were hard because with his hours, he wouldn't see the sun at all.

Maybe that was part of what drew him to Sam. She was undoubtedly beautiful, but with her golden hair and bright smile, she was like her own source of sunshine. Simply having her at that desk would be enough to keep the winter blues away. She made him think of his roses.

Attached to the side of his home was a glass greenhouse. He had started growing roses in there a few years back. He didn't like watching his plants shrivel and die in winter. When it was cold and dreary, he needed their color and vibrancy as much as they needed the warmth. He had about twenty different varieties growing there, but his favorite was a dark pink hybrid tea rose called Miss All-American Beauty. Maybe he would take one to her tomorrow.

The click of toenails on the hardwood greeted him

as he came through the door. He wouldn't dare compare Sam to his golden retriever outside of his own mind, but he couldn't help smiling when he saw them both. Chris, of course, inspired Brody to throw a ball and scratch her belly. He had entirely different ideas where Sam was concerned.

On cue, Brody smiled as Chris skidded around the corner into the kitchen and then greeted her with an enthusiastic ear scratch. "How was your day?" he asked, anticipating no reply. "I had a great day and a terrible day all at once."

Chris sat down and cocked her head to one side while he spoke. Finally, she lifted a paw in the air and placed it sympathetically on his pant leg.

"More on that later, though. Let's get some dinner." He went through the routine of feeding the dog, reading his note from Peggy and plating up whatever dinner she'd left for him that night. Today was roasted lemon chicken and mashed potatoes with freshly shelled peas.

That handled, he headed into his office with his plate and his dog, ready to start research into the mysterious dwilder27.

"What is going on with you and this new job? You seem tense."

Sam looked up from her salad and found herself pinned by the knowing gaze of her best friend, Amanda. She'd avoided talking about her work at ESS. She didn't know what fell into the confidentiality agreement and what didn't, but it pained her to keep things from the friend she'd known since junior high. "What do you mean?"

"You've been really quiet lately. You haven't talked

about the new gig at all, which is weird considering how excited you were to finally get a break."

"I've just been busy," she said with a dismissive shake of her head. "My supervisor is very demanding."

"Who exactly are you working for at...?" Amanda paused with a frown. "Have you even told me where you're working?"

Sam didn't remember if she had. "Eden Software Systems." Certainly her working there wouldn't be a secret.

"How could you have not told me that yet?" Amanda's eyes lit up with unexpected excitement. She leaned over her lunch and spoke low. "Have you caught a glimpse of the mysterious CEO?"

This was definitely dangerous territory. "No. I don't have access to his floor," she lied.

"Oh, well," Amanda said with a sigh.

Her friend always kept up with celebrity gossip. Insider information on the most elusive CEO in history would be huge on the blogs. There was probably a bounty for details about Brody, but it wouldn't be enough to pay off the penalty of breaking her agreement.

"So what's got you all wound up?"

Sam bit at her lower lip. Now, more than ever, she needed girl talk. She wanted to confide in her best friend and figure out what to do. Maybe she could stay vague enough to talk but not tell too much. "I think I've done something stupid."

Amanda's fork paused in midair. "At work?" Sam nodded. "Well it can't be as bad as last time. You haven't slept with your new boss, have you?"

Her friend's blunt words might have stung if they

hadn't been so close to the truth. "I haven't slept with him. But I did kiss him yesterday."

Amanda rolled her eyes and shook her head. "This isn't a conversation for lunch. This is meant for Happy Hour with half-price wine." She eyed her iced tea with disdain. "What possessed you to kiss your boss? Did he come on to you?"

"No." And he hadn't. She had gone after him. Aggressively. Since almost the first day of work. "I kissed *him*. Frankly, he seemed a little stunned."

"Why on earth would you do that after that mess you went through before? This is the first job you've been able to land."

"I know. I'm not sure what I was thinking."

One of the perks of this job, however strange, should've been that her boss was a weird recluse who didn't come out of his office. Given she'd been fired for sleeping with her last manager, she should've been thrilled with the arrangement. The distance was a guaranteed buffer to ensure she couldn't make the same mistake twice. And yet she'd done everything she could to breach the barrier and coax the beast from its den. And then she'd kissed him.

Success felt bittersweet. First, she'd found a rose on her desk when she arrived this morning. A single pink rose stood on her desk in a tall silver bud vase. It was a deep fuchsia, her favorite shade of her favorite color, captured in her favorite flower. It was flawless, with silky petals that opened farther as the day went by. Brody didn't leave a note, but given no one else could get to this floor, there was no question from whom it had come. It was a romantic gesture. Not some over-the-top, massive bouquet. One single, perfect rose for one single, perfect kiss.

Then Brody had come out to see her twice this morning. He'd been surprisingly chatty, asking her about her evening and other pleasantries. Oddly enough, they'd both avoided the subjects of the kiss and the rose. Later, he had asked her—politely—to bring his lunch into his office before she went to meet Amanda, so she was able to enter his private space without being harassed.

Somehow, by invading his domain, she had tamed the beast. It was good and bad all at once.

"Is he married?"

"No," Sam said emphatically. She was pretty darn certain this time. He seemed too isolated for that, and Agnes had told her he was single. She would know. "And he's nothing like Luke. It's a completely different situation. But it complicates everything."

"Kissing your boss can do that. Here's a question for you, though—do you want to kiss him again?"

Sam took a deep breath and admitted the truth to herself. She did. It was so unproductive. So complicated. And yet she couldn't help the way he made her feel.

Her affair with her last boss had been purely physical. He was far too involved with himself to contribute any emotion to their relationship, and she was aware of it. It wasn't until later that she realized why. Brody was different. He aroused all the same physical desires, along with a protective instinct and emotional longings she couldn't ignore. Combined, it cranked up the intensity dial of her body to a point where she could barely concentrate when she was around him.

Brody was like an injured tiger. Dangerous, beautiful, fascinating…and yet, she couldn't fight the need to fix the hurt she saw in those blue eyes. Someone needed to be brave enough to go into his cage. Sam wanted to be the one. Even when she knew she could get bitten.

"I do," she finally said aloud.

"So, he's not married. He's not a sleaze. He's got a good job. You're interested in him, or you wouldn't want to kiss him a second time. If he's interested in you, what's the problem? This is a temporary job, after all."

Amanda always had a gift for cutting through the mental clutter to get to the heart of the issue. That's why Sam needed to talk to her so badly. She just wasn't sure it was that simple. Her body seemed to think so, but it had proven on more than one occasion that it couldn't be trusted. "I guess I'm worried it won't end well. I don't want to make the same mistake twice."

"Honey, I saw you go through that mess with Luke. I'm pretty sure you learned your lesson. Don't be so hard on yourself. If this guy really is different, you can't let that cloud your judgment. Take it slow. See what happens. You might be pleasantly surprised."

Sam eyed her watch and nodded. She needed to finish eating and head back to the office. "I will take all that under consideration."

Amanda smiled. "Keep me posted on the hot *seksi* times. I want every detail. I haven't dated anyone in months, and I need to live vicariously through *someone*."

They wrapped up lunch and Sam went back to work. The afternoon was busy, with Brody sending her multiple emails with tasks that kept her mind on work and off their situation. When she finally got the chance to glance at her clock, she realized it was time to go home for the day.

Yesterday after their kiss, she'd slunk away with her tail between her legs, too embarrassed to say goodbye. She wouldn't do that today, but she probably shouldn't initiate a lot of conversation as much as she wanted to.

She slung her magenta peacoat over her arm, scooped

up her brightly colored Dooney & Bourke purse and knocked gently at his door.

"Come in."

Sam turned the doorknob and stuck her head inside. Brody was seated at his main monitor, but he stood up when she entered so she could see more than his eyeballs over the top of it.

"Sam," he said with a smile she was getting rather used to seeing. "Do you have plans tonight?"

Her eyes widened, her jaw falling open. He was asking her out. It was Friday night. *Was* he asking her out? He talked to her, gave her a rose and now he was asking her out.

"Plans?" she repeated, not sure what her answer should be. "Not really. I was going to repaint my toenails and watch a sappy movie on the Hallmark channel. Why?" she added, unable to turn off the flirtatious response that was certain to get her in more trouble. "You got a better offer for me?"

Brody didn't respond right away. Any other man she knew would give her a sly grin and ask to take her out for a drink. He didn't seem to know how to react to her boldness. "Not really," he said with a frown. "I'm going to be working late tonight and I was wondering if you could stay for a while and help me with this briefing I'm presenting next week. I know it's Friday night and probably not your idea of a good time, but I could really use your help."

"Oh," Sam said, not sure if she was relieved or disappointed. "I thought you were asking me to dinner or something." She said the words without thinking, immediately regretting them the moment they left her mouth. Why would she even bring up the idea of them going on a date when he hadn't suggested it? Stupid.

Brody didn't notice her mental chastisement, as he seemed too busy trying to connect the pieces that would make her think such a thing. His eyes widened. "Oh, Sam, I'm sorry. I, uh…don't go out to dinner."

"Forget it," she said, wishing they both could.

"If you can stay tonight, I'll order Chinese for us. How about that?"

It wasn't the most romantic offer she'd ever received, but the overtime she'd be earning made up for it. "Sure." Sam tossed her things back onto her desk and returned to his office with the tablet he provided her to take notes.

About an hour later, the security desk called to let them know the Golden Dragon delivery guy was in the lobby. Sam didn't even know they had ordered yet. Brody hadn't asked her what she wanted. She could feel the heat of irritation at the back of her neck. She hated those arrogant men who ordered for a woman without thought to what she might actually want. "I'll be right back," she told him, leaving the office before she said something smart.

She returned a few minutes later with an increasingly poor attitude and a heavy sack of food. It was a good thing they weren't on a date. "What did you order?" she asked.

Brody had moved over to the living room sitting area so they could eat at the coffee table. He had already poured each of them a drink. "Kung Pao chicken, beef and broccoli, fried rice with no peas, hot and sour soup with extra wontons and vegetable eggrolls. Is that okay?"

Sam had been on the verge of telling him she didn't appreciate a guy choosing her food, but she had no complaints. He'd ordered everything just the way she would want it, down to no peas in the rice. Stunned into silence, she nodded, pulled a few cartons from the bag and set them on the glass table. They settled in and ate for a few minutes before she worked up the nerve to ask.

"How did you know what I wanted?"

"I looked it up," Brody said casually before crunching into an eggroll.

"Looked it up? My Chinese food preferences?"

Brody shrugged. "Everything can be found on the internet if you know where to look."

"Did you get it from that report you were running on me yesterday?" She'd been so flustered by his anger and the passionate kiss that followed that she forgot about seeing her own name on his computer. She wanted to know what that was all about. "Are you running a background check on me?"

Brody laughed. "Not yesterday. I ran a background check on you about a week before you even interviewed. Yesterday was merely a query to soothe my curiosity about you."

Sam stiffened slightly in her seat. How much did he know about her? Would her mistake with Luke show up in his file? It was a little unnerving to think about someone digging up every detail of her life from her credit score to her favorite foods. "You know, normal guys take a woman on a date and then ask her questions if they're curious. Running a background check is creepy."

"Creepy? Really?" He shrugged. "I see it as practical. Your way seems inefficient to me. The information I can find on my own is far more detailed and likely accurate than what I might get in person."

"Accurate? You think I'd lie to you about what kind of Chinese food I liked?"

"That's a bad example, but you could say you liked something you didn't just to be nice."

"But asking someone questions when you're on a date is more fun. And the street runs both directions," she added. "They get to know things about you, too." It would never occur to her to look on Google for information about Brody. Even if she didn't know there was nothing to find.

"As you can imagine, I don't date much. I'm far more comfortable with computers."

Sam set down her plate and leaned into Brody. "Do I make you uncomfortable?"

Brody swallowed hard, the thick cords in his neck moving up and down. He nodded. "A little. I'm not that good with people. Especially face-to-face."

Sam was such a people person, she could hardly imagine living a secluded life like his. By the age of two, she was chatting up strangers in grocery stores and making friends with every kid on the playground. To her, computers were the complicated and unreasonable ones. "Well, the best way to improve is to practice. The more you're around me, the more comfortable you'll be."

His dark blue eyes focused on her for a moment, and then he shook his head. "You say that, but I don't find that to be entirely true. At least, with you."

Sam knew exactly what he meant. The more she was around Brody, the more restless and intrigued she became. He didn't think or react the way most men did. Everything he did was so calculated. Even when they kissed, she could tell he was stuck in his own head. He seemed to overthink everything, hesitating when he wasn't sure of the right course.

In a way, he reminded her of the boys in junior high

who couldn't decide if they wanted to kiss the girls or yank their ponytail. If a girl they liked actually spoke to them, they'd totally freeze up. Only this boy was thirty, in an expensive suit and had shoulders as broad as a Greek statue.

"That's normal," she admitted, "when you're getting to know someone new. Especially if you like them."

Brody diverted his eyes quickly back to his food, silently chewing and pondering her words. Sam did the same. She was nearly finished when he spoke again.

"I do like you, Sam. Would you be interested in having dinner with me tomorrow night, as well?"

Sam looked up from her plate of chicken and rice with surprise. More overtime? Well, she supposed she could put it into the bank in case it took a while to come across another job. Or she could get that new leather bag she'd drooled over in the window display at Saks Fifth Avenue. "Okay. What time do I need to be here?"

"Here?" Brody frowned and then nodded when he understood his mistake. "I'm not asking you to work over the weekend, Sam. I'm asking you to have dinner with me tomorrow night. A real date, like you suggested."

Had she suggested a date? "You said earlier that you don't go out to dinner." It was a stupid response, but it was the first thing that came to her mind.

Brody smiled. "I don't. That's why I'd like you to join me for dinner at my house."

Five

"I should've said no. What was I thinking? I should've told him I had plans."

Sam sat muttering to herself in the back of the town car Brody sent to pick her up. The man behind the wheel paid no attention to her neurotic rambling. He'd hardly even spoken. He'd knocked on her door, introduced himself as her driver, Dave, and escorted her to the car. She told Brody she could drive herself, but he insisted it was difficult to find his house. To be honest, she'd never been in this area, so it was a good call. But that didn't mean she had to like it.

She couldn't change her mind and drive home, she thought with a sigh. If she chickened out in the driveway, it would be a long walk back. It was the right thing to do, wasn't it? As tempting as her handsome, brilliant, millionaire boss was, he was her *boss*. This couldn't end well.

And yet, Brody was nothing like Luke.

Sam had fought this battle with herself since she left the office Friday night. It might be the wrong choice, but the part of Sam that wanted to go on this date won. She wanted to see Brody outside of the office and all his barriers. To know what he was really like. She would be very disappointed to find retinal scanners in his home.

Sam had spent two hours getting ready. Half her closet was lying on the floor of her bedroom from going through her parade of options. She had finally decided on a champagne-colored pencil skirt with a black lace overlay, a black silk tank and lace shrug. She pulled her hair back into a clip to showcase her glittering gold chandelier earrings. Every inch of her body was scrubbed and painted and sparkled. She put on her most expensive perfume and her Sunday-go-to-meeting pant-ies. These weren't the actions of a woman that didn't want to go on this date. She needed to silence the nega-tive voice in her head and enjoy her night.

The car slowed and turned onto a narrow neighbor-hood street. Sam looked out the window at the houses they passed. They were huge. Each one was more of an estate than a home, on a plot of land big enough to fit nearly fifty of her apartments on their lawns. They'd passed about ten homes before they turned into a long, circular driveway. "We're here, ma'am."

This was it. The moment she'd looked forward to and dreaded all day. Her heart started racing in her chest, but she had to get out of the car when the driver opened the door. She took a deep breath, grabbed her clutch and stepped out onto the cobblestone drive. "Thank you," she said.

The driver nodded and pulled away before she could turn back. She faced the sprawling home, admiring the lighting that made the shrubs and trees glow golden. It was multileveled and L-shaped with a three-car garage at the end of the driveway. A covered patio ran along the front, sheltering a few rocking chairs. It wasn't at all like she expected except for the tiny surveillance cameras pointing to the front door and to where she was standing. That was more like the Brody she knew.

She hadn't taken a single step when the front door opened and a big yellow dog charged straight for her. The animal was at least eighty pounds, and Sam had nothing but a beaded purse to defend herself. Running was impossible in the four-inch Stuart Weitzman heels she'd chosen for tonight. She could only close her eyes and brace herself for the mauling.

Instead there was the thump of heavy paws against the lapel of her wool coat and a wet glide along her cheek. The weight sent her stumbling back on her heels. She misstepped on the uneven cobblestones and before she could right herself, she and the dog toppled back into a mulch flower bed.

"Chris!"

Sam opened her eyes to find herself nose-to-nose with a golden retriever. She struggled to push aside the overly affectionate canine and get up, but she was no match for its enthusiasm.

"Chris*tina!*" A man's voice shouted again, this time closer and more sternly.

The dog was jerked away a second later, and Sam looked up to see an apologetic Brody hovering over her. He held out his hand to help her up. "I am so sorry. Chris is harmless. She was more excited to see a new person than I expected."

Sam stood up, dusting the wood chips from her lace

pencil skirt and subtly rubbing her bruised rear. "Chris is apparently not as antisocial as you are."

"Not at all. Are you okay? Did you twist your ankle or anything?"

"No, no," she said dismissively. "The only thing hurt is my pride."

Brody smiled and Sam couldn't help but do the same. It was amazing how quickly she had been able to see past the scars. That charming smile and those soulful blue eyes made the rest just fade into the background.

And then he turned to look down the street. A car was coming toward the house. Sam watched with disappointment as his smile faded in the shine of the oncoming headlights. He was so worried about people seeing him. Sam had seen him. He was growing more comfortable with her by the second, but it appeared that she was a notable exception. Brody was far from strolling through a shopping mall filled with people, or even meeting face-to-face with his own employees.

"Let's get inside," he said, reaching his hand out to her.

She accepted it, a tiny thrill running through her as she walked beside Brody up the stairs to the front door. Sam was stunned the moment she walked in. The outside of his home wasn't nearly as surprising as the inside. It wasn't what she expected at all. The house was bright and open with light oak floors and white trim. The walls were a soft mocha color. The living room furniture was cream with plush rugs and large windows that ran nearly floor to ceiling.

Brody stopped and turned around when her hesitation pulled her hand from his. "Is something wrong?"

Sam immediately felt guilty for thinking he lived in some kind of dark cave. "No, I just…it wasn't what

I was expecting. It's very different from your office, I mean."

He nodded, helped her out of her coat and hung it on a brass hook inside the entryway. "Come with me to the kitchen. Dinner is about ready," he said. "I feel a little more comfortable out here than I do in town. There's no one that can see in."

"No one can get into your office, either. You could paint it purple with pink polka dots and no one would see it. I mean, who even cleans it?"

"I do. I don't trust anyone else to go in there and for good reason. The security measures and tinted windows are there because more than a few journalists have tried to hitch their careers to exposing me. My security team caught one posing as a window washer not long ago. Another tried to apply to housekeeping thinking they could get to me. Keeping my office dark and locked up is the only thing that keeps me from being exposed."

"What about here?"

"No one knows about this place. My home is owned by a shadow holding company with no public tie to me or ESS. I, of course, own the company, but no one knows that. And no one but my immediate family and a few people on my payroll has ever stepped foot on the property, so there's no chance of a leak."

Sam swallowed hard. Somehow she'd managed to not only make it into the beast's secret lair, she'd gotten into his private retreat. And this time by invitation. She didn't know if she should be flattered or terrified. "I'm honored, I think, that you trust me enough to invite me over. I'd never reveal that information, of course."

"You've got five million good reasons not to." He smiled.

Sam shrugged. "I wouldn't tell anyway."

"I know. I wouldn't have asked you on a date and brought you here if I thought otherwise. Come on, dinner should be done any second now."

Sam followed Brody down the hallway, noticing as he walked ahead of her that he was wearing nicely snug jeans and a blue plaid button-down shirt that was left untucked. He was also barefoot. It was the first time she'd seen him in something other than a power suit and she liked it. It was a very sexy look for him. He appeared relaxed and comfortable in a way he never seemed to be at the office.

She rounded a corner and walked into a large, spacious kitchen with cream-colored cabinets and butcher block countertops. It was a chef's dream, or so she imagined. Sam wasn't much of a cook, but she got by. A place this luxurious would be wasted on her limited culinary abilities.

Dinner was in progress with several pots on the six-burner gas stove and bowls scattered around the counters. For some reason, she hadn't expected him to actually cook, even though he'd invited her over for dinner. Given his affection for takeout, she didn't picture him as the kind of man who was very comfortable in the kitchen.

Brody poured a glass of white wine for each of them and held one out for her. She accepted it gratefully. "You're cooking," she said with surprise lacing her words. Sam sniffed delicately at the air. "What are we having? It smells like cheese and…charcoal."

Brody's eyes widened for a moment. He quickly spun on his heel, turned to the set of double ovens mounted in the wall and frowned. A cloud of black smoke rolled out of the top oven as he quickly snatched out a charred cookie sheet with a dark crusty bundle in the center.

He dropped the contents into the trash and tossed the pan into the sink to cool. "Well, it was supposed to be a chicken roulade with goat cheese, sundried tomatoes and spinach."

Sam switched on an overhead fan to disperse the smoke so the smoke detectors didn't go off. "Sounds good."

"Yeah," he said with dismay as he examined the controls and the recipe on the counter beside it. "If I had put the oven on three-fifty instead of four-fifty, it would've been."

Sam drowned her giggles in a sip of wine. "A computer genius that can't set the temperature on a digital stove?"

"Give me some credit," he said with a laugh. "As a kid, I was the only one in the house that could program the VCR." Brody rested his hands on his hips and looked around the kitchen with a frustrated pinch to his brow. Sam could see the CEO in him wanting to start firing off orders to deal with the situation. Unfortunately, tonight he was a corporation of one.

"My housekeeper offered to make us dinner tonight," he admitted, running his fingers through his hair. "I told her no, I wanted to cook for you myself. I guess she didn't have as much faith in my culinary skills as I did, and rightly so."

"Do you cook much?"

Brody shook his head. "Almost never. Peggy leaves dinner for me every night. But I wanted to impress you, and I figured following a recipe would be easy enough. I can't take you to an expensive restaurant, so it seemed like a nice touch. Now we're going to have to order pizza. I don't have enough stuff left over to make it again."

Sam smiled and made her way over to the Sub-Zero refrigerator. They wouldn't be eating pizza if she had anything to say about it. "Don't give up on us quite yet."

Brody was amazed. He knew from working with Sam that she was smart, efficient and innovative. But seeing her at work in his own kitchen was an entirely different matter. She had taken charge of the situation, and he had to admit that it was a huge turn-on. He could only sit back and watch as she kicked off her heels, slipped out of her lace shrug and took his kitchen by storm.

Chris sat down beside him to watch her work, as well. She ran the risk of getting stepped on if she got into Sam's way. Brody patted her head and sipped his wine, answering questions as he was asked where one thing or another was. He enjoyed watching her work. It was much better in person than watching her from his surveillance monitors. She was full of color, moving with a gracefulness and ease. Occasionally she would look over at him with a smile that was so brilliant it would make it hard to breathe.

It was difficult for him to tear his eyes away from the seam of her stockings that lined the back of her shapely legs and disappeared under her fitted lace skirt. He wanted to interrupt her work to press her against the cold steel of the refrigerator. He wanted to know what it would feel like to let his hands glide over those silk stockings. He wasn't that hungry, anyway.

Before he could make a move, Sam turned triumphantly toward him with a second, unburned dinner made. She carried two plates to the oval table in the breakfast nook where he was sitting. There were marinated chicken breasts she'd cooked on the grill set into his range and angel hair pasta tossed with olive oil, garlic, herbs and parmesan cheese. With them, she'd paired the green salad and garlic bread he hadn't ruined from their first menu.

"It looks wonderful," he said, admiring her hard work and the flush of her cheeks from activity. "I feel bad, though. I invited you to dinner and you ended up cooking."

Sam smiled and shook her head. "It was fun."

"You really seemed to be in your element. Do you like to cook?"

At that, Sam laughed. "Actually, no. And to be honest, I'm not really a very good cook, either, so don't put away the takeout menu yet. But I know enough not to go hungry. It was a necessity when I was younger. My dad became a single father overnight. He was so unprepared for everything that came with it, especially handling mischievous twin boys and the girliest little girl on the planet. He had his hands full and I knew it, so I tried to help out where I could. My dad was a horrible cook. My brothers and I would've starved if I hadn't stepped up and shoved Dad away from the stove."

Brody recalled the background investigation he'd done on Sam. It said her mother had died when she was seven. He remembered that now. But he knew better than to mention it. Instead, he cut into his chicken and took a bite. "This is great. My mother wasn't a very good cook. She tried, but it never came out quite right. When she overcooked things my father would get so angry at her."

And him. And the dog. And anyone else who got in his way when he was in a rage.

"My mom was a great cook. At least that's what I remember. I was seven when she died. She had been letting me help around the kitchen with little tasks at dinnertime, but I certainly wasn't prepared to take over. It didn't stop me, of course. Things had to get done. It might not be the best tasting food or the smoothest ironing job, but I tried. That's why my dad always called me 'Daddy's Little Fixer.' From a very young age, I've had this drive to fix everything."

"Sounds like a harmless compulsion."

Sam swallowed her own bite of food and chased it with some wine. He could tell she was trying to cover a frown. He watched as a blond curl came loose from her hair clip and tumbled down along her cheek. Brody wanted to reach out and gently wrap the golden silk around his finger. He imagined it would feel as soft as her lips had.

Sam absentmindedly tugged the loose strand behind her ear and continued talking. "You'd think so, but not always. My brothers weren't always as appreciative of my help. They prefer to call me the Meddler. Apparently, I don't know when to stop or mind my own business. I just get this idea in my head of how things should be and I can't ignore the problem. I have to fix it."

Brody watched the woman he'd allowed to breach his inner sanctum as she continued to eat. This dating thing was going okay so far. He was learning about her and sharing some of himself, like she'd described. They'd worked together to overcome a minor crisis. The boxes on his date checklist were being checked off, one by one. If he managed not to do something stupid to run her off, this might be a really great night. He enjoyed Sam's company, which was something he couldn't say for most people. She was everything he'd always hoped for in a woman. Sam was smart and funny, beautiful and caring. She hadn't seemed very interested in his money, either.

From the monitor in his office he'd watched her eyes light up with delight at receiving that single rose just as if she'd received a hundred roses. Or diamonds. And most importantly, she looked him in the eye with the flame of desire instead of disgust.

What he couldn't put his finger on was what she saw in him if money wasn't the draw. It was one thing to be polite and friendly at work to develop a good rapport. But why had she kissed him? Or agreed to this date? She didn't have to do any of that. Or perhaps she did. Maybe this was it. Was he only a project to her? "Are you going to fix me?" he asked.

She looked at him then, her wide dark eyes searching his face for something. He expected her to blow off the question, lie about it outright or make a joke. He knew that most people in his life disapproved of his lifestyle. If Molly, his foster mother, could tell him what to do again, things would be very different, he was sure. For someone with an itch to help like Sam, he was surprised she hadn't broken into hives restraining herself.

But she didn't dismiss the question. Instead she looked him straight in the eye and said, "Fix what?"

At that, he almost laughed. "Fix what?" he asked, getting up from the table to put his empty plate in the sink. "Come on, now. I'm a grouchy, scarred hermit. You're the first woman to step into this house that isn't related or paid to clean it. Certainly you've come across something about me that you're dying to put right."

Sam followed him through the kitchen and smiled reassuringly when he turned back to her. "All that stuff is on the outside. I'm not worried about that apart from how it impacts you on the inside." Her hand rested gently on his chest, over his heart.

Brody's blood started pumping furiously through his veins at her touch. His heart beat so hard, he was certain she could feel it pounding against her fingertips. Her innocent gesture had lit a fire inside him. The heat of it spread through his body like warm honey and caused every muscle to tense with anticipation.

"You're a brilliant businessman. A computer genius. A strong leader for your company. You have amassed more money and power in a few short years than most people will in a lifetime. You do the work you love. I'm sure your life isn't perfect, but whose is? Everyone has their own tolerance and thresholds of what they can live with. From where I sit, I don't know what I could do to make your life better."

"You could kiss me." Brody said the words before he could lose his courage. She saw him as decisive and bold. He needed to be tonight if he was going to get what he wanted. And whether or not he should, he wanted her. More than he'd wanted any other woman in his life.

He took her hand in his, pulling it away from his chest and wrapping his other arm around her waist. He tugged her against him, sprawling his palm across her lower back.

Sam looked up at him in surprise, and then a coy smile curled her lips. She pressed into him, bringing her hand behind his neck to tease at his collar. "I think I can do that," she said, climbing up onto her toes.

Brody dipped his head down and closed the gap between their heights. Without her heels on, she was more petite than he anticipated. Their lips met in a soft, tender kiss. He relished the feel of her fingertips against the stubble of his jaw and the gentle, probing glide of her tongue along his own. It was an easy movement, one he didn't have to think too much about. But Brody was a strategist, and he was always focusing on his next move instead of enjoying the moment like he should.

He was lost in his own thoughts when Sam thrust her tongue into his mouth. She crushed her breasts against the wall of his chest, cranking up the intensity between them. The movement sent a jolt of electricity down his spine, urging him on. On instinct, he backed her against the kitchen island, pressing his body into hers. His hands planted on the countertop, flanking her waist. It was easier than trying to figure out which part of her he wanted to touch next.

Their kiss was no longer sweet, nor gentle. Sam's hands roamed across his chest, her fingernails scratching the coarse fabric of his shirt and teasing the muscles beneath it. Her touch coaxed an ache of desire that strained against his tight jeans. He pressed himself against her stomach and swallowed a deep groan of pleasure. It came out like a growl vibrating in his throat.

The feeling echoed through Brody's entire body. She felt so amazing against him. His mind started racing again. Was this *it*? Could this really be happening after all this time? He thought he was reading the signals correctly. With every nerve in his body, he prayed for it to be true.

"I want you so badly," he whispered against her lips. "Say yes. Stay with me tonight."

Brody could feel a stiffness settle into Sam's muscles, and then she pulled away from his kiss. The few inches between them brought a rush of cool air that helped him regain some control. She looked at him, her brow gently furrowing into a V. There was a hesitation, a worry there, and he didn't know how to make it go away. He couldn't lose her after getting this close. He wouldn't let her go. If she walked out the door, his chance with her might have passed forever. He wanted Sam more than he'd ever wanted a woman before. No matter what it took, what he had to expose of himself, he would do what he had to do to keep her here with him.

"Please, Samantha."

When she looked away, she shook her head just enough to send his heart sinking into his gut. The hands that had caressed him a moment before were now pushing gently at his chest. He took a step back. Somehow, he'd ruined it.

"I'm sorry, Brody. I can't."

Six

Sam watched the conflicting emotions fly across Brody's face. He tried hard to hide them, but she could see his disappointment. Could he see hers? Would he be able to understand how much she wanted him but feared having him at the same time?

"I should probably go. Dave gave me his card so I could call when I was ready to leave."

"Don't leave, not yet." His voice was low but even. He wasn't demanding or even begging. "Peggy made a cobbler for us, and I have French vanilla ice cream. We can eat it out on the patio."

"I don't know, Brody." Dessert, although it sounded nice, would only be putting off the inevitable. She was either going to go home or sleep with Brody. So she probably should just go ahead and go.

"It's cherry," he added, his blue eyes a little hopeful as he watched her reaction. "I won't touch you again unless you ask me to. I promise."

Sam sighed. Her resistance was wearing down, fast. "It's not that I don't want you to touch me, Brody."

"Then you don't want cobbler?"

"No, I would love some cobbler. I just—"

"Great." Brody turned away, cutting off her excuses and pulling a carton of ice cream from the freezer. On the counter was a deep casserole dish covered in foil. He lifted the top to reveal a golden flaky crust with deep red cherry juices oozing along the edges.

She wanted to grab his arm and insist that she really had to leave. *Right now.* But Sam really loved cherries. And if she was honest with herself, she didn't want to go home. She was having a good time. She was only worried things were moving too quickly.

Brody dished them both out a bowl with a scoop of ice cream on top. The cobbler was still warm enough to start the vanilla immediately melting into a pool over the top. "Here," he said, handing her the dish. "We can talk about whatever it is outside."

It was then that she realized how chilly it had gotten lately. Boston had stayed unseasonably warm for the area until the day before yesterday. With the sun having set an hour or so ago, the night air would have a definite chill. Not exactly the right weather for eating ice cream on the porch. "Isn't it too cold out? It's October."

He shook his head. "I've got it under control."

Sam followed him through the maze of the house, admiring the winding central staircase and the museum-quality artwork on the walls that wrapped around it. They passed an area that looked like his office and then a den with a large television and comfortable chairs. There were French doors leading off to a covered patio.

When she stepped out onto the deck, she was greeted with an unexpected blast of warm air. Perched on each side of the seating area were tall gas torch heaters, and a third flame roared from a massive stone fireplace. It continued on into an outdoor kitchen that wrapped around the deck and down into the yard.

Beyond them was a swimming pool. It shimmered a deep turquoise-blue in the darkness, the steam from the heated water rising up in the cool night. There were massive trees and bushes flanking the yard, some adorned with tiny fairy lights. To the left was a glass enclosure that glowed with a golden light. The heat inside had fogged up the windows, but she could see the dark green foliage and pops of bright colors inside. A greenhouse. Perhaps where he'd grown her rose?

It was all so beautiful. The perfect yard for throwing parties, oddly enough, although it could also be considered the perfect private retreat from the world.

Brody was standing beside the fireplace holding their dessert. "Do you like it? Is it warm enough?"

"It's beautiful. And quite toasty, thank you."

Sam sat down in the outdoor love seat directly across from the fireplace and accepted her dessert. Brody sat beside her. She expected him to start pressing her for answers regarding her abrupt about-face, but he appeared content to eat his cobbler and enjoy her company. Even Chris curled up in front of the fireplace with a rawhide bone and started happily munching on it.

It wasn't until her spoon scraped the bottom of the empty bowl that Brody spoke again. "So, talk to me, Sam. Did I do something?"

"What makes you think you did something wrong?"

Brody settled his bowl on the table and turned so he was facing toward her as he spoke. "This is uncharted territory for me here. I'm not so arrogant as to think I might not misstep."

"You mean you've never seduced one of your employees?" It was a fairly direct and prying question, but she needed to know if this was something he did often. If she'd asked Luke that question, it might've saved her a lot of heartache and time at the unemployment office. If he'd answered honestly.

It was a serious question, but Brody started laughing. And continued to laugh. It went on for so long that Sam began to get irritated.

"Hey!" she said, snapping his attention back to her. "I'm serious."

"I know, and I'm sorry. But you do realize the only two employees I've seen in person since I started this company are Charlie, the head of security, and Agnes, right?"

At that, even Sam had to smother a giggle. Charlie was sixty with a bristly, mostly gray beard and a rapidly expanding beer belly. Civilian life had been a rough adjustment for the former Army intelligence officer. And then, of course, her godmother, Agnes. She was in her fifties, married since near birth and looked more like a stern Sunday school teacher than a romantic outlet for Brody.

"Fair enough," she admitted. It did make her feel better to know he didn't make a habit of this, even if only for a lack of opportunity. But it didn't change things between the two of them.

"Have you ever slept with your supervisor?"

Brody turned the question around on her, and the time for laughing was over. "Yes," Sam said, struggling to swallow the knot in her throat. "And it ruined my career and damn near my whole life."

Brody sighed and leaned back against the cushions of the love seat. She could tell he hadn't expected that serious of an answer from her. At least *that* hadn't shown up in her background check. Everyone at her office knew the truth, but the HR records were squeaky-clean, probably to protect Luke. "Tell me what happened," he said.

Sam didn't want to rehash all of this tonight, but she could see the determination etched into Brody's face. He had a solid dose of "fix-it" in him, too. "I was new to the company, and I was hired as the administrative support to the head of marketing. His name was Luke. I was immediately taken under his spell. He was movie-star handsome. He dressed well and smelled amazing. He was so nice to me, too. When he asked me to accompany him on a business trip, I was thrilled. I didn't expect something to happen between us, but when it did, I was powerless to fight it. Away from the office, he was such a romantic. We spent each day working and each night making love in his suite."

She felt stupid admitting to this out loud. "I would've believed almost anything that man said. And that was a mistake. He was married. To the woman that headed up the finance department, of all people."

"You never suspected he was married?"

Sam shook her head. "I know it sounds ridiculous. But I swear to you he never mentioned her. He didn't have a single photograph of his family in his office or a wedding ring on his hand. I had no reason to think he might be..." Her voice drifted off.

"Anyway, one day we were in his office and he had me pressed against the filing cabinet. We were just messing around—I would never have slept with him at work—but his wife came in and caught us. She blew a gasket. The next thing I knew, people were whispering as I went into the break room and I had become the woman that climbed the career ladder on her knees. I was laid off a few weeks later. Wouldn't you know that the finance department determined that marketing was suddenly overstaffed?"

Brody's jaw tightened as he listened to her tell her story. He seemed angry. Sam hoped it wasn't at her for being so stupid and naive. "Didn't anyone realize what was really going on?"

"If they did, they didn't care. I was a home wrecker, out on my rear end, and couldn't get a reference to save my soul. This job working for you is the first thing I've been able to land. And I only managed that because of Agnes, I'm sure."

Brody leaned into her but didn't reach for her. "What happened to you was terrible. That Luke guy should be strung up by his junk. But let me ask you something… do you really think I'm going to sleep with you and toss you out onto the street like he did?"

Sam felt a flush of embarrassment rise to her cheeks. "No…and yes. It's a hard-learned lesson, Brody. I'm already a temporary employee. Easy to get rid of. And if you sleep with one boss, it's a fluke. Twice…and it's a bad habit. I don't want to make the same mistakes."

Brody's hand came to rest heavily on her shoulder. His touch was warm and the massaging motion of his fingertips made her want to close her eyes and curl up in his lap.

"Sam, let me assure you first that I am not married. Not even close. No serious girlfriends or fiancées tucked away, either. I am very, *very* single. Two, I am not a sleaze. Please don't think for a moment that I'm trying to use my position as your supervisor to pressure you into something you don't want to do. I don't ever want to make you uncomfortable. Here, or at work."

"Thank you." Sam knew what he was saying was

true. She'd been telling herself that since the first buzz of attraction between them. She was just scared to get burned again.

"And finally...I want you to understand that I'm not the kind of guy that casually sleeps around with women. I really like you, Sam. You're beautiful and smart and funny." Brody reached out to caress her cheek. "You look at me—really look at me—when no one else does. I don't think you truly understand how rare that is in my life. I don't need coded doors and thumbprint scanners to keep people away. They stay away on their own.

"Since my accident, no one looks at me the way they did before. It was so hard, living my life every day and dealing with the stares and the reactions of people. I was just a kid, Sam. When I got old enough, I started my company and hid away because I didn't want to deal with it anymore. It's my choice to keep people away now. But in shutting away the bad, I shut away the good, too. It was probably a mistake. It has cost me so much of my personal life, but I did what I thought I had to do to protect myself."

Sam's heart ached listening to his story, but she didn't quite grasp where he was headed with the conversation.

"It might be unheard of in this day and age, Sam, but...I'm still a virgin."

Brody had never spoken those words aloud to another living soul. Not even his brothers knew the truth. They thought he'd lost it to a working girl they'd all chipped in and bought him after high school. And he let them believe it. It was easier than telling them that even their well-paid whore couldn't look him in the eye when she touched him.

He'd walked away from her without regrets. Getting laid would be nice, but he wanted more. Call him a hopeless romantic, but it was true. He wanted companionship. Intimacy. Love. Until now, Brody hadn't met a woman who might be interested in him for anything but his money. He hadn't come across anyone who inspired him to open up and expose his demons to her.

Sam had come so close. He didn't want her to walk away and he'd decided that telling her the truth might be the only thing to convince her he wasn't like other men. But it may have backfired. He was pretty sure by the extended silence between them that he'd driven her away with his blunt confession instead.

Brody held his breath. Sam's mouth had dropped open slightly when he'd spoken, but she hadn't moved since then. She was watching him. Probably thinking about how to gracefully get out of this uncomfortable situation. He was on the verge of giving her an out when she set her cobbler bowl on the table and stood up. His stomach sank. She was leaving.

Him and his big mouth.

But she didn't go. Instead, she reached out to him. He took her hand and she tugged until he stood up. He looked down at her with his brow drawn in confusion as she stepped close to him and wrapped her arms around his waist. She rested her head against his chest and sighed.

The feel of her pressed against him was amazing. He swallowed a groan as every inch of her soft body molded against his own. He hesitated to touch her. If this was just a pity hug and she would be out the door in a moment, he didn't want to let himself fall into it. And if he did, he was afraid that it might send her running again. But he simply couldn't help touching her. He enveloped her in his arms and pressed his lips against the golden curls at the crown of her head.

He didn't want to let her go, yet before he was ready, he could feel Sam pull back.

A sly smile curled her lips as she looked up at him, her body still pressed against his. "I can fix that," she said at last.

For a moment, Brody couldn't quite piece together what she meant by that. Of course, it was hard to think with her breasts pressing against his chest. She couldn't possibly mean…? His mind backed up. He'd said he was a virgin, and she said she could fix that. He swallowed hard and took Sam's face into his hands. "Are you sure?" he asked. "I mean, are you doing this because you want to, or because you have this need to fix—"

Sam didn't respond to his question. Instead, she climbed to her toes, pressed her mouth against his and silenced him. Her lips were soft and warm, and this time, she tasted like cherry cobbler instead of cherry lip gloss. He lost himself in the kiss, his thumbs stroking the smooth skin of her jaw.

When Sam pulled away, she took Brody's hand in hers and started walking back into the house. He followed her inside, and when she paused at the staircase, he nodded. At the top of the winding stairs, he pushed ahead of her and led the way to his master suite.

As he opened the double French doors that led to his bedroom, his heart started pounding so loudly in his ears he was certain Sam could hear it. He kept turning a nervous gaze her way, but she just smiled and followed him without concern.

He paused in the center of the space. His king-size bed was on the right, facing a wall of windows that gave him the perfect view of the sunrise every morning. Past it was a small sitting area with a fireplace and the entrance to the master bathroom.

"So, this is my room," he began as he turned to face Sam, not quite sure of the best approach to take from here. He hated feeling so awkward at this when he was able to confidently take charge in so many other areas of his life.

Sam had no question of how to proceed. Her dark eyes looked into his own as her fingers went to his collar. On reflex, his hand shot to cover hers and halt the movement.

Sam gasped softly at his sudden movement. "What's the matter?" she asked, her dark eyes wide with concern.

Brody closed his eyes and swallowed hard. What would he tell her? That he wanted to leave his shirt on during sex? That he wanted the lights out? It sounded ridiculous in his mind, much less said aloud. Was it worse than admitting the truth? That as badly as he wanted her, he didn't want her or anyone else to see what his bastard of a father had done to him?

Some people might have seen Brody's face, but no one outside of a hospital had ever seen his chest. Even as a kid sharing a room with Wade, he always kept covered. He came out of the bathroom fully dressed after a shower. He never went swimming with the other boys. They probably expected him to have more scars from his accident, but Brody didn't want anyone to know the full extent of what his father had inflicted on him long before that last day.

"Nothing. I just..." His voice trailed off. Brody wanted Sam more than he wanted to hide, but his sense of self-preservation was deeply ingrained in his every response. "I want you so badly. But I don't want you to see—"

"I don't want you hiding from me, Brody. There's nothing that you could show me to make me want you any less."

She seemed to know. Even with his shirt still buttoned, Sam knew what he was hiding. Brody let go of her hand and let her continue. She watched his expression with unmatched intensity as inch by inch of chest was exposed. He tensed, holding his breath as his shirt opened and she pushed it over his shoulders. He watched and waited for the reaction he dreaded. She might think she meant what she said, but she hadn't seen all his scars yet.

Sam paused only a moment in taking in the hard lines of his chest to follow the trail of rippled skin that ran down his shoulder and over the heart that beat like a bass drum in his rib cage. Then her palm went to it. Sam covered his heart with her hand and then traveled the path back up his neck to touch the scarred side of his face.

Brody fought the urge to pull away from her touch. He always pulled away. He didn't like the idea of anyone touching his scars. His injuries were bad enough to look at, even more distressing to feel. Sam didn't seem to agree. She was determined to challenge his every barrier. There wasn't the slightest flinch of disgust as she cupped his cheek and drew his mouth to hers.

He kissed her again, the thoughts of his scars fading away. It was done. She hadn't run. Now he could try to focus on other things. His hands moved to her waist, gliding easily over the slick fabric of her top. His fingers pulled at the material, tugging it out from the waist of her skirt so he could make contact with her bare skin. Unlike Brody with his rough scars, Sam's skin was flawless and silky soft to the touch. She was delicate and feminine and beautiful, so different from himself. He loved the feel of her against his palms as they ran over her back and around her sides to brush the edge of her rib cage.

Sam gasped against his lips and pulled away. Brody froze in his tracks and frowned nervously. "What did I do?"

She shook her head and smiled. "Nothing. Your hands are just a little cold for such a sensitive spot."

"I'm sorry."

"I can take care of it," she said. In one fluid movement, her arms twisted around her torso and pulled her top up and over her head.

Brody's mouth went dry as a desert when he was faced with the sight of her breasts confined in a black lace bra. They were large and full, threatening to spill over the scalloped edge of the cups that were stitched with tiny crystals. She was a buxom pin-up girl come to life in his bedroom. He tried to swallow, but the lump in his throat stayed stubbornly in place.

Sam reached behind herself and unfastened her bra. It dropped to the floor, exposing the very things he'd been admiring. They were lovely. Brody had seen his share of breasts in magazines and movies, but they didn't prepare him for this moment. The full pale globes had tight pink tips. He ached to touch them but couldn't make himself move.

Sam reached out and took both of his wrists in her hands. She brought them up to her mouth and blew hot air across his palms. The feel of her breath on his skin sent a sizzle up his arms, but when she brought the heated palms down to cover each breast, the sizzle turned into a jolt.

He watched as Sam closed her eyes and indulged in the feel of his hands on her. His palms grazed over the tips, his fingertips pressing into her flesh. Sam made a soft hum of pleasure in her throat as he teased and explored her skin. But he wanted to taste them, too. His head dipped to take a nipple into his mouth.

Sam gasped and arched her back, pressing her breasts even harder against his touch. Her skin was both sweet and salty against his tongue. He drank her in, drawing hard at one breast and then the other, lightly flicking his tongue over the swollen pink tips. She squirmed in his arms, lacing her fingers in the curls at the nape of his neck and tugging him closer. Her reaction urged him on, building confidence in him as he tried different ways to make her cry out with pleasure.

Brody only pulled away when he felt the graze of her touch at the fly of his jeans. With sure fingers, Sam unbuttoned and unzipped, slowly backing him toward the bed. When his calves met with the emerald-green brocade comforter, her hand slipped beneath the elastic of his waistband. Her fingers curled around his firm heat, sending a shockwave of sensation through his body.

"Oh, damn," he groaned and reached back to the bed to steady himself.

She pressed against his chest with her other hand, easing him to sit against the edge of the mattress. He braced himself with both arms propped behind him. Sam tugged at the jeans, pulling them and his briefs down his legs. Lying naked with Sam crouched down between his legs was a surreal experience. He'd never felt so exposed in his life. And yet with Sam it was different. It wasn't like going out in public and having people stare. It was exhilarating.

With the last of his clothes tossed to the side, Sam knelt down and reached for him again. She stroked him slowly, running her thumb from the base to the tip. Brody wanted to watch, but he couldn't keep his eyes from closing and savoring the feeling. He wanted to remember every sensation of this night.

Sam caught him by surprise when she took him into her mouth. His lids flew open, a shudder running through his whole body as the hot, wet heat of her mouth moved over him. It took every ounce of control he had to keep from going over the edge when she touched him like that. But damn, it felt amazing.

It was no wonder people seemed to be so obsessed with sex everywhere he turned. Brody had been seriously missing out all these years.

Finally, he had to put a stop to it or this would be over before it truly began. "Sam," he managed in a hoarse whisper. "Stop. I can't…" he said, curling tight wads of the comforter in his fists. "Please."

When she pulled away, he was both relieved and disappointed, but neither feeling lasted for long. He watched her stand up and unzip her skirt. It shimmied over her hips and fell to the floor. Beneath it she wore a pair of matching black lace panties and thigh-high stockings. She put one foot on the edge of the bed, watching his face as she rolled the stocking down her leg. When she switched to take off the other stocking, he caught a flash of pink flesh peeking out from beneath her flimsy panties.

Sam knew it, too. He got the feeling she was doing it on purpose. She smiled as she threw the other stocking aside. She took a step away, allowing him the full view of her body, then turned around. The luscious round curves of her backside were accented by the high cut of her thong panties and the tiny crystal heart stitched at the top. She glanced seductively over her shoulder at him, hooked her thumbs beneath the lace and drew her panties down over her hips. Brody couldn't tear his eyes away as the fabric inched lower, sliding down her shapely legs.

Lastly, she reached up behind her head and unclipped her hair clasp. The mess of blond curls rained down over her shoulders and back as she shook her head. Then she turned around and faced him.

She was the most beautiful thing he'd ever seen in his life. Powerfully seductive, curvaceous, feminine... And she was crawling, naked, over him until she was straddling his waist and looking down at him. His hands went to her hips, stroking the soft skin and steadying their nervous shaking.

Sam leaned down, kissed him and then whispered against his lips. "Protection?" she asked.

"Yes." He did have that. And it wasn't a pathetic box that expired ten years ago, either. He'd ordered a new box of condoms online this week when he was feeling optimistic. He rolled onto his side and moved higher up the bed to reach for the nightstand beside it. He pulled one out and rolled onto his back.

Sam took the foil packet from him and opened it. He gritted his teeth as she sheathed him in latex and crawled back up to him. He could feel his arousal pressing against her inner thigh. She reached between them and aligned their bodies just right. Sam moved his hands back to her hips. And then she nodded.

It was time. He pressed her back, feeling her body slowly expand and envelop him. Inch by inch, he sank into the heat of her until he was fully buried. It was excruciating, balancing the fine line of pleasure as he fought to keep control. He'd waited a long time to finally experience this moment. He wasn't about to let it go by in a flash.

And then Sam started moving her hips. She rocked forward, then back in one long, slow stroke. Brody groaned and pressed his fingertips into the ample flesh of her backside. Sam moved again, this time faster. And again. And again.

She arched her back, giving him a magnificent view of her breasts as she braced herself on his thighs. He moved one hand to slide across her taut stomach and cup a breast. Brody pinched her nipple between his thumb and forefinger, and Sam cried out. She moved faster, thrusting him inside her body at a pace that neither of them could withstand for long.

And then it happened. He felt Sam's inner muscles tighten around him. Her hips continued to move frantically as her cries grew louder. "Brody!" she cried, over and over until Brody could no longer hear her over his own groans of anticipation. As Sam screamed out the last of her orgasm, he let go. The white-hot sensation of pleasure exploded inside, flowing out of him and into Sam in a throbbing, pulsating wave.

"Yes!" was all he could say. Yes, it was really happening. Yes, he was no longer a virgin. Yes, he had the sexiest woman he'd ever seen in his bed. And finally, yes, he would like to do that again very, very soon.

Seven

Sam awoke the next morning to a beam of sunlight stretching across her face. She pried one eye open to find herself facing a gloriously sunny morning. The windows of Brody's bedroom faced the eastern horizon. She wasn't quite sure if he liked the view or needed nature's alarm clock to wake up.

She turned her head and found the bed empty beside her. Apparently he just liked the view. She ran her hand over the mattress. His side of the bed wasn't even warm. He'd been up for a while. Then her fingers brushed over something unexpected and soft.

With a yawn, she sat up, tugging the sheets to her chest. Looking down, she saw one of her pink roses beside her. She picked it up and brought it to her nose. It was lovely.

The whole night had been amazing. Sam never expected it would be like that. She had been attracted to him from the very beginning. A part of her was drawn to his dark, brooding personality. She wanted to understand him. To know what kind of secrets had driven him into this self-imposed exile. Sam had worried herself to death thinking this was going to be just like the scenario with Luke. She couldn't have been more wrong, but she never imagined Brody would tell her that he was still a virgin.

It surprised Sam, although in retrospect, it was the missing piece that made everything about Brody make sense. The hesitation in his touch. The awkwardness of being near to her. The charming innocence…

When he confessed to her that he'd never been with a woman before, it was one of the saddest and sexiest things she'd ever heard in her life. She'd never been a man's first before, and it was an amazing turn-on for her. Even her first time had been with an older, more experienced guy. You never forget your first. And she wanted so badly to be that woman for Brody.

But she also wanted to make love to Brody because it was something she could do for him. She couldn't free him from his prison. She might not be able to make him a happier, more open person. But she could give him her body. Sam could tell how much his confession pained him. No man ever wanted to have to say that to a woman. And if nothing else ever happened between them, she would be happy knowing she shared that part of herself and lifted one burden of the many from his shoulders.

Sam inhaled the rose's perfume again and flopped back against the pillows. Her muscles ached and she'd barely gotten five hours of sleep, but she didn't care. She was too happy and satiated to care.

The first time they made love, Sam had wanted to

make it all about Brody. Every move, from the seductive slide of her panties over her hips to the glide of her tongue along his aching flesh, had been to give him an experience he would always remember. She took control so he didn't have to worry about making a misstep. Sam had been with more experienced men that fumbled with bra clasps and poked around her body like they were lost. She didn't want that on his mind for even a moment, and it had gone perfectly.

As had everything else last night. By the time they finally fell asleep, no part of her was left unadored, no need unfulfilled.

Sam sighed. A week ago, you couldn't have convinced her that she would be where she was right now. Her irritable mystery boss held more surprises than she ever could've imagined when she first sat at her desk and looked up at those surveillance cameras.

"Sam? Are you awake?"

Before she could answer, Chris leaped up onto the bed and gave her a wet morning kiss on the cheek. Brody scolded her and forced her down off the bed.

Sam sat up, clutching the sheets to her chest. "I am."

Brody gave her a crooked smile of concern. "Were you awake before Mauling 2.0?"

She laughed. "I was. Thank you for my rose."

"You're welcome."

Sam couldn't help but notice how handsome Brody looked this morning. He was wearing a pair of khakis with a white, collared shirt that was rolled up over the muscles of his forearms.

It made her realize what a mess she must be herself. She certainly had bed head, last night's makeup smeared around, and clothes in so many different places she might never find them all to go home today. She ran a self-conscious hand over the wild curls of her hair, but there was nothing her hand could do to tame them. On the bright side, she had a toothbrush in her purse. After years of teenage orthodontia, carrying one with her became a habit she hadn't broken.

"I put your clothes on the chair." Brody pointed to an upholstered chair a few feet away. Each piece of her clothing was neatly folded and stacked there, with her heels on the floor beside it.

"Thank you."

"If you would like to take a shower, there's fresh towels on the stand beside it. I'll be downstairs when you're ready. I was thinking of making breakfast if you're hungry."

"Breakfast?" After last night, she doubted he would attempt cooking again anytime soon.

"Bagels," he corrected with a grin. "I can manage bagels." Brody called Chris and the two of them slipped out of the bedroom, shutting the door behind them.

At least there would be no walk of shame. Sam always hated that part. She flipped back the covers and carried her clothes with her into the master bathroom. The shower stall itself was bigger than her whole bathroom with glass tiles and shiny chrome fixtures. It took her five minutes to figure out which knobs controlled what, but once she got it working, she was rewarded with a decadently hot, steamy spray from three different nozzles.

About thirty minutes later Sam came downstairs. She was a little overdressed, but cleaned up pretty well. She found Brody back in the kitchen. He was pouring two mugs of coffee. She watched him add a splash a cream and a teaspoon of raw sugar before stirring and handing it to her.

"Are my coffee preferences online, too?" she asked.

"Not that I'm aware of." Brody laughed. "But the barista writes it on your cup."

"Oh." Sam took a sip and watched him doctor his own coffee. "So you mentioned bagels?"

"Yes. I have whole wheat, cinnamon raisin and everything."

"Cinnamon raisin would be great." She didn't need poppy seeds in her teeth or onion breath.

"An excellent selection, ma'am. I will toast it to perfection and deliver it to you on the patio if you'd care to relax outside."

"Why, thank you. That would be lovely. Come on, Chris." The dog picked up her red ball and trotted down the hallway with Sam.

This time, Sam paid more attention as she walked through the house. A portrait on the wall caught her eye and she stopped to look at it. There were five people in the portrait, four men and one woman. They all looked like they were in their twenties, each with a different look about them. Brody was in the portrait, smiling, with his arm around the blonde woman. There were pine trees and a bright blue sky behind them.

It was interesting to see Brody like that. He looked so comfortable. He didn't even appear to mind having his picture taken. It was a huge departure from the man she was getting to know. It made her wonder who those people were. And although she had no reason to be jealous considering everything that happened last night, it especially made her wonder who the blonde he hugged to his side was.

Chris waited impatiently for her on the patio. She dropped her ball and barked. Sam continued outside as requested. "Sorry, Chris." She bent down and picked up the ball, tossing it out into the yard.

Chris leaped off the patio, dashing through the dewy morning grass. When she returned, Sam was sitting in the chair by the fireplace. They tossed the ball a few times before Brody showed up with bagels and cream cheese.

"That picture in the hallway," Sam said, after smearing her bagel with the fluffy white cheese. "Who's in it with you? Are they friends from college or something?"

Brody glanced through the doorway and shook his head. "No. That's my family."

His family? Only two out of the five in the portrait shared even the slightest resemblance. She expected Brody to elaborate, but he took a bite of his bagel instead. He didn't seem to want to talk about it. Things had gone well enough that she didn't want to push it. But it made her curious. He never mentioned having brothers and a sister before.

"Are you busy tonight?"

Brody's question startled Sam from her thoughts. "Tonight? No. Why?" She'd already spent a large portion of the weekend with him. She didn't mind seeing him again, but she thought he might be ready for some alone time.

"I still feel bad about dinner last night. I promised you a proper dinner date, and if you're available this evening, I'd like to make good on it."

Sam wrinkled her nose. "Are you attempting to cook again?"

"Oh, no," he said. "This time I'm leaving it up to the professionals."

Brody dialed Sam's phone number at exactly seven that evening. He would've liked to pick her up at her door, but since she lived in a large and busy apartment building, he would have to settle for meeting her at the curb in his Mercedes.

Sam slipped into his passenger seat wearing a pale pink iridescent dress. It was one-shouldered, short and gathered at the waist with a belt made of large chunky rhinestones. When she sat beside him, the dress rode high up her thighs and made her legs look like they went on for miles.

He eyed her with a sly smile. "I told you I was taking you out for dinner, and you wear a dress that makes me want to take you home and strip you naked right now."

Sam grinned. "Do you like it? It's one of my favorites."

"It's very sparkly," he noted.

"It is. And as for stripping me naked, it's all part of the anticipation."

"I've had thirty years of anticipation. It's not novel for me. I'm frankly tired of it."

"Too bad. You said you were taking me to dinner and you're not getting out of it."

Brody reluctantly shifted the car into gear and pulled out of the parking lot. "If you insist."

"Where are we going, anyway? You said you don't go out to eat."

"I don't," he said, ignoring her first question. He wanted to surprise her.

A short while later, they stopped outside of a Beacon Hill town house, the home of one of the finest French and Italian fusion restaurants in Boston. Instead of pulling up to the valet, Brody drove around back and entered a private parking lot.

"Are we really going into a restaurant?" Sam asked. "With people in it?"

"Not exactly." Brody had made special arrangements for a private service. He'd done this once before when Wade brought Tori to Boston, and it had worked out well. He opened the back door and she stepped inside ahead of him. "Take the first right," he said.

Sam turned down the first hallway and they went through a door marked "PRIVATE." The room beyond it was small. At most it could seat four people. A crescent-shaped table extended from the wall. It was draped in white linens and lit with several candles. There were two place settings and two chairs waiting for them.

Brody helped her into her chair at the table and took his own seat. The wall they were facing had a small window with what looked like wooden shutters over it. He reached forward and tapped at the blinds. Less than a minute later, the doors opened and someone reached through to place two glasses of white wine on the table.

"What is this place?" Sam asked. "Are there no menus? No waiters?"

"This restaurant does private chef's tastings. Small groups are invited back here to eat some of the best food in the city. They only take one reservation a night. It's as close as you can get to the action without eating in the kitchen itself. I think you'll like it."

"No one is going to come in the room?"

"Not if they want my generous tip. The only person we will see is the chef. The executive chef presents the food and talks with the diners about what he's prepared."

"Can the chef see us?"

"Yes," Brody said. "But I'm not worried about it. The room is dark enough. He's only going to be interested in what he's serving us."

Sam smiled and sipped her wine. "I was wondering how you would pull this off."

"I thought about renting out an entire restaurant, but this seemed more...intimate." Brody took advantage of the dim lighting and private room to lean in and press his lips against Sam's neck.

She sighed and tipped her head to the side to give him better access. "It certainly has its benefits," she said.

The window opened again and Brody pulled away. The executive chef leaned through the opening and presented them both with a salmon plate with dill and caviar, the first of several courses. Each plate included a perfectly paired wine. It took nearly two hours to complete the tasting, but Brody enjoyed every minute of it. Because Sam did.

He liked watching her face light with excitement as each new course came out. There were a few things she'd never had before, but she was brave enough to try everything and enjoyed almost all of it. Brody ran the risk of some people seeing him while he was here, but it was worth it.

Sam deserved a decadent night out and more. She had changed his entire world since he met her. And last night had been one of the most incredible nights of his life. He'd dreamed of that moment since he was fifteen years old, and nothing he'd imagined in all that time could compare with the reality.

She did everything in her power to make that night special for him. There was no way he could ever repay her for that. But he would try. If everything fell into place the way he hoped, he had a special surprise in store for her.

The chef served their last course and thanked them

for joining him. Brody shook his hand and passed him a credit card to cover dinner and gratuity. They were now left alone to enjoy their trio of canneles. He took his first bite, letting the hazelnut cream melt on his tongue. A moment later, he felt Sam's hand on his thigh.

It seemed as though Sam had a special surprise in store for him, too. He had difficulty swallowing his next bite as her fingers kneaded the muscles, inching ever higher. Brody looked over at Sam. To see her sitting there, she was quietly eating her dessert. If anyone were to see them, they would never suspect that her hand had dipped into his lap.

"Mmm..." she said. She turned to him with a smile and licked the last of the ice cream from her spoon. "The brown butter one is really good." Her dark eyes fixed on him, the elegant line of her brow arching up. "So, do you like it, Brody?"

He knew she wasn't talking about ice cream. "Oh, yeah," he said, nearly groaning as she stroked him through the fabric of his pants. "I think this is the best course so far."

"Me, too." Sam leaned over and kissed him.

Brody dropped his spoon and turned toward her to cup her face in his hands. He really enjoyed kissing Sam. There was something about it that made him want to indulge in kissing her for hours. He didn't know if it was the softness of her lips, the sweet taste of her mouth or the soft cries of desire against his skin, but he couldn't get enough of her.

His hand went to her waist, stroking and clutching at the shimmery fabric of her dress and the skin beneath it. He could think of a few other places he would prefer to touch, but since making love to Sam in this tiny room was not a viable option, he needed to leave the naughty antics to her.

His tongue glided along hers and Sam mimicked the stroke with her hand. Despite the layers of clothing between them, she had him balancing on the edge. He groaned aloud this time, unable to suppress it. Brody was certain someone in the kitchen had heard.

Sam pulled away from him with a smug expression. "What's the matter? Aren't you going to finish your dessert?"

Brody shook his head and grasped Sam's roaming hand with his own. He pulled her away, as much as he hated to do it. "I think I'd like my dessert to go."

Eight

Sam didn't regret a moment of her weekend, but at the same time, she dreaded this first day back at the office. Would things be weird between them because they had had sex? Would he act differently around her? Or worse yet, would he find a reason to replace her now that he had got what he wanted?

The thoughts haunted her on her Monday morning commute. Her strategy today was to keep quiet, lie low, make Brody come to her and see how he acted around her. She was probably worried over nothing. Things on Sunday morning had been fine. Their dinner was wonderful and dessert was amazing. It wasn't awkward at all. But that didn't mean something else couldn't happen to ruin it.

Sam quietly crept into the office when she arrived. The lights were on, which meant Brody was already in, but his office door was closed. She wasn't quite sure why she was bothering to sneak around. If Brody wanted to know if she was in, he would watch the cameras for her.

She made her way to her desk and found another fresh pink rose in the silver bud vase. Despite her anxiety, the single rose made her smile. It was romantic and sweet, and knowing now that Brody grew the rose himself made it all the more special. After getting to know Brody better this weekend, it was just the kind of thing she would expect from him.

Sam slid the rose to the corner of her desk and busied herself settling in and catching up, but after an hour with no word from Brody in person or via email, she began to worry again.

Somehow, she thought he'd come out to greet her. Or at least ask her for something. He usually buzzed her phone or sent her an instant message once an hour or so. And he'd made a point to always tell her good morning. But today, silence.

The rose was the only thing keeping her from going crazy with anxiety. She opted to focus on her work and try not to worry. He might be busy. His calendar looked open, but he might need to deal with personal matters. Sam had been to his home and taken his virginity, but she really knew very little about Brody's past or his family. He didn't talk about it aside from a few vague comments during dinner Saturday night. He wouldn't have even brought up his family on Sunday morning if Sam hadn't asked him about the picture. And even then, he immediately clammed up about it.

Even as secretive as Brody was, that struck her as odd. He obviously had family. They helped shape who you are as an adult. It was something that came up in conversation. But not once had she heard him mention something funny a brother had done or tell an interesting story about his family. His mother was a bad cook and his father would get angry about it. That small tidbit was enough to make Sam worry that he didn't have the happiest of childhoods, even without his accident.

He hadn't spoken about that, either. The expression on his face as she slipped off his shirt nearly broke her heart. It was so hard for him to expose himself to her like that. It seemed almost painful. And when she saw how far his scars extended across his chest and back, she was surprised and concerned. It was as though a rain of fire had poured down his body.

In addition to that, there were other scars of different types sprinkled across his chest and arms. Small circles, long gashes, deep welts. She hadn't allowed herself to react to the sight of them because he was so self-conscious, but she was still concerned about the scars. What could've caused all these injuries? She couldn't imagine an accident that could do all of this at once. To her, it looked like the results of years of painful abuse.

How long had it taken him to recover from all those injuries?

Sam looked over at the heavy, closed door to his office. Maybe he hadn't recovered at all. Just physically.

Finally, a chime sounded at Sam's computer. She looked down to see an email in her inbox from Brody. It was a forwarded message. His instructions were for her to print the attachments out on the color printer and bring them to him.

Sam scrolled down to the forwarded email. It was from a man named Mickey who worked at Top Secret Private Investigators. The note was brief in the email.

Hey, Brody. Here's what you asked for. Nothing newsworthy on this one. Didn't I run a background check on a secretary for you a few weeks ago? You're going through them like tissue paper, man. Hope this one works out better for you. Let me know if you need anything else.

Sam's stomach sank. Attached to the email was a background investigation on a woman named Deborah Wilder. From Mickey's message, it sounded like this Deborah woman was her replacement. Because despite what he told her Saturday night, he was going to use her and toss her away like Luke had.

Tears stung Sam's eyes as she opened the file and pressed the button to print the paperwork as requested. The first page had a picture of the woman. She was thirtysomething with dark hair and a round face. A little chubby. Not particularly attractive, but not unattractive, either. DMV photos were never the most flattering.

Sam's hands were shaking as she picked the pages up off the printer. Looking into the brown eyes of her replacement fueled a fire in her stomach that turned her tears into anger. How dare he ask her to print out the information on her replacement! Was that his way of breaking the news to her? He couldn't even tell her face-to-face?

She snatched the last page of the background check off the machine and pivoted on her heel toward his office. She slung the heavy door open, sending it banging against the wall and swinging back.

Brody stood up, startled, when he heard the racket. His smile of greeting immediately faded into a concerned frown when he saw the furious expression on Sam's face.

"What the hell is this?" she asked, holding the pages up. "Is this how you planned to get rid of me? You can't even tell me to my face?"

The lines of confusion in Brody's forehead deepened as she spoke. Then his gaze darted to the papers in her hand and the photograph of Deborah Wilder on top. "Now, hold on," he began, but Sam didn't listen.

"You know, I believed you when you said you wouldn't sleep with me and toss me aside. Ignorant of me, right? Stupid, trusting Samantha always believes what men tell her."

"Just stop!" Brody yelled over her tirade.

Sam quieted down, but she was far from calm. Her heart was pounding, and her cheeks were hot and flush.

Brody turned to his computer and swore at the screen. "I forwarded you the wrong message," he explained. "I wanted you to print out the quarterly financial reports."

That didn't make Sam feel any better. "So you're still replacing me, but you didn't want me to know yet. Nice."

"No," he insisted. "You're not being fired. Or replaced. I don't want you to go anywhere, Sam. Why would you think I would do that to you after everything that happened between us?"

Sam straightened the paperwork in her hand and started reading Mickey's words back to him. *"You're going through them like tissue paper, man. Hope this one works out better for you."*

"I can explain that," he said.

Sam planted her hands on her hips. "Great. I can't wait to hear it."

"Mickey is the guy I use for background investigations. I hired him to check on you. When I needed some information on someone else, it was easier for me to tell him it was for another secretary. I couldn't tell him the truth."

"Why not?"

Brody frowned at her and took a deep breath before he spoke. "I needed to protect my brother."

"Is this one of the brothers from that picture?" she asked.

"Yes. I have three brothers and a sister. All of us were in that photo you saw in the hallway. My brother Xander is a Congressman. He's been seeing that woman for a few weeks. They've kept it quiet, but he's getting fairly serious about her. I wanted to make sure she didn't have anything in her background that could hurt his reputation and chances of reelection next term."

"You're only investigating your brother's girlfriend?" Sam immediately felt sheepish. The anger and hurt that had rushed through her just a moment ago spiraled away, leaving a hollow place in her chest. She had thrown a hissy fit for no reason.

"Yes."

"And you're not replacing me?"

Brody came out from behind his desk. He took the papers from her hand and set them aside before wrapping his arms around her. "How could I possibly do that?" he asked, hugging her tightly against his chest.

Sam sighed and snuggled against him. "I'm sorry," she said. "I overreacted. This weekend was so nice. It was almost too nice."

"You've been burned before, Sam. That's hard to forget. It's difficult to believe people when they tell you they would never hurt you like that. They have to prove themselves, but even then, a part of you just waits for the other shoe to drop. Believe me, I know all about that."

Sam felt the truth in his words. He'd lived that and his scars were more than only physical ones. She should know better than to think he would do that to her. She hugged him tighter, trying to stave off the tears that threatened again for a different reason.

After a few moments, Brody pulled away. He looked down at her with his hands gently rubbing her upper arms through her sweater. "How does my calendar look at the end of this week?"

Sam shrugged. She hadn't looked this morning. "I'm not sure. Last I checked, you were pretty open."

"Good. And what about you? Do you have any personal plans, say, Wednesday through Sunday?"

Sam didn't have many plans. The past few months of unemployment had put a massive dent in her social life. Even Amanda could barely lure her out of her apartment. "Nothing I know of."

"All right. Today, I want you to clear my calendar of anything this week from Wednesday on. If it's important, move it to Tuesday or next week. And Wednesday morning, I want you to be ready with a suitcase packed for a long weekend. I'll come by your place to pick you up at eight."

Sam's eyes widened with surprise. He was taking her somewhere? Her heart started to flutter with excitement for a moment, but reality quickly set in. The logistics of travel with Brody would be complicated. They'd have to drive and stay in a private residence because anything else would require a hotel or an airplane. Someone would see him. Right? "Where are we going?" she asked.

Brody smiled and shook his head. "It's a surprise."

"And how will I know what I should pack?"

"Dress for warm weather. Very casual. Bring a

swimsuit or two. That should be all you need. If I have things my way, you'll be naked most of the time, anyhow."

He leaned down to kiss her. Sam felt a thrill run down her spine when his lips touched hers. A rush of excitement and arousal pumped through her veins as she molded her body against his.

"Okay," he said, finally pulling away. "That's about all I can handle of that right now, or I'm going to bend you over the pinball machine."

Sam smiled and reluctantly stepped back. "If you insist." She eyed the pinball machine for a moment but opted against pushing him. At least for today.

Brody watched Sam walk out of his office, admiring her snug curves in the skirt she'd worn today. She had an excellent collection of fitted skirts. They were modest in length, with only a small slit up the back to hint at the creamy flesh of her thigh. But now that he knew what delights were hidden beneath that fabric, he had a whole new appreciation for the seductive sway of her hips.

But after she shut the door, the smile faded from his face and he returned to his computer.

How had he made such a stupid mistake? To send Sam the wrong email? Now he knew what his brothers joked about when they said they had sex on the brain. It was a total distraction. Before their weekend together, he would fantasize about her, and now his mind kept drifting back to their time together. He'd had Sam four times in the past two days. There were plenty of images seared in his mind and they kept leaping into his thoughts without invitation.

This could've been a major problem. Thank goodness he'd managed to come up with the story about Xander's non-existent girlfriend. Normally, he didn't like talking about his family—biological or foster. Brody Eden was a ghost. Part of that was not having a past or giving anyone a way to trace him back to being Brody Butler. The press was always looking for an angle to dig up information on him. But this was more important. Sam was held by the confidentiality agreement, and he'd rather talk about his family than tell her what the email was really about.

Sam had bought it without asking any questions he couldn't answer. Her only concern was that this person was her replacement, and he was able to quell those fears with his tale. Fortunately, she hadn't looked closely enough at the report to notice Deborah was recently married with a new baby and didn't live anywhere near Washington D.C.

He shook his head and forwarded her the quarterly report he'd intended to send the first time. Then he reached for the paperwork Sam brought in.

The papers were a little crinkled from the angry way she'd clutched them, but they would do. He'd been reading over the digital copy when Sam burst into his office. He'd been so engrossed in the material, he hadn't noticed she had arrived for the morning. He would've stepped out to say hello. Ignoring her had probably dumped fuel on the fire.

But it didn't take long to scan the pages and realize he had bigger problems than an angry, sexy secretary.

Finding out the real name of dwilder27 hadn't been hard. An evening at home had traced the IP address and with a little digging, he had the name and address of the account owner. From there, he opted to have Mickey do the legwork. The guy was pretty trustworthy when it came to these things. He'd done a great job finding information on his brother Wade's fiancée, Tori. He'd been very thorough on Sam. And judging by the papers in his hands, Mickey had done just as good a job on Deborah Wilder.

He knew it would be a relative of Tommy's. Who else would look for him after all this time? Finding out it was his only sister was a bigger problem. Some curious, estranged relative might be prone to look up someone on the internet from time to time. But they would let it go if they didn't find what they were looking for fairly easily. Not a sister. A sister would keep digging until she found her brother.

That was an issue. He hadn't mentioned anything to his brothers yet. He didn't want to alarm them if it was nothing. But this was something. They needed to know in case Deborah started sniffing around Cornwall looking for the trail Tommy had left for her to follow.

It should be a dead end. Everyone in town would tell her the story they knew as the truth—Tommy had run away from his foster home right before his eighteenth birthday and was never seen or heard from again. Good riddance, as far as most of them were concerned. He and his brothers were fortunate in that way. If they had to be involved in someone's death, at least it was someone most people wouldn't miss. Tommy had been arrested several times for assault and theft. His own parents couldn't handle him and the state had taken him away. Tommy Wilder was trouble; a kid no one but the Edens would even take in. If anyone could get through to him, it was Molly and Ken. But even they couldn't work their magic on him.

Once he came to the Garden of Eden, he immediately started problems. He'd stolen from Molly's cash drawer at the gift shop. He refused to do his share of chores. He'd gotten in a fight with Wade over that and blackened his eye. And none of the boys liked the way he looked at Julianne, who was only thirteen at the time.

Tommy was a ticking time bomb. If he had made it to his eighteenth birthday and left the farm, he would've ended up in jail. Someone would've gotten hurt or worse.

That's what Brody told himself when he thought about that night. Tommy's death hadn't been deliberate, but it had protected the future victims he hadn't gotten around to yet.

Brody picked up the phone and dialed his brother Wade. Wade had lived in Manhattan for years but recently moved back to Cornwall when his fiancée, Tori, finished building their home. It had been a long process, but they'd moved into their massive dream house at the end of September.

If Deborah Wilder showed up in Cornwall, Wade would be the first in the family to know it.

"Hey, Brody," Wade answered, sounding chipper as usual. After he proposed to Tori and their worries about the body being discovered were put to bed, his older brother had tried to forget about their past. He wanted to focus on his upcoming marriage and building their life together.

Brody hated to ruin the bliss, but Wade had to know what was going on. "Hi, Wade. Do you have a private minute? I need to talk to you about something important."

"Sure," Wade said, a serious tone creeping into his voice. "Tori's working in her office upstairs. I'll step out onto the deck in case she comes out."

Brody could hear the doors open and the wind

against the speaker as Wade moved to the patio with the panoramic view of the valley below. "I've gotten a hit on my search query for Tommy. I did some research and it turns out that it's Tommy's younger sister, Deborah. She's looking for him, Wade."

There was a moment of silence on the phone. Brody had a bad reputation for being the buzzkill of the family, but this couldn't be dismissed as his paranoia.

"What have you found out?" Wade finally responded.

"I got the first hit about a week ago and started looking into the user's information. Since then, she's tried a couple more times with different search strings, but she hasn't had any luck. I'm worried she might come to town and start asking questions. I wanted you to be prepared since you'll likely hear about it first if she does."

"Okay. I'll put a bug in Skippy's ear."

Skippy was the bartender who worked in the local Cornwall watering hole, the Wet Hen. He was a hundred-and-fifty years old if he was a day, with skin like aged leather and hearing like a dog. "Do you really think you can trust Skippy with something like this?"

"Absolutely. Skippy knows everything that goes on in this town. Hell, I wouldn't be surprised if Skippy already knows about Tommy and what happened. He's a bartender. He's paid to listen and not talk. If he wanted to, he could probably blackmail half the county with the things he knows. He wouldn't tell a soul. Besides, if she shows up, odds are, she'll end up at the Hen. I can count on him to let me know the moment she arrives, even if I don't tell him why it's important."

Wade seemed confident in Skippy. Brody was less so, but he would defer to his older brother on this point. "Her name is Deborah Curtis now, although she might still introduce herself as Deborah Wilder if she's talking to people that might have known her or her brother as children. Curtis is her married name. She lives in Hartford with her husband and six-month-old daughter."

"Do you think she's going to be a problem?"

"I don't know," Brody admitted. "If our story sticks, she won't get anywhere asking questions. Everyone will tell her he ran away and she'll go home disappointed."

"You don't think our story will stick? We did a pretty convincing job. Xander burned all of his things. I told Ken and Molly I heard him sneak out in the night. Until there's a body there's no reason for anyone to question it. He could've crossed into Canada on foot and changed his name. There would be no trace of him."

Brody wished he could be as confident as Wade was. "I hope you're right. But keep an eye out for her, just in case."

"I will. I'll let you know the moment I hear something. I've got a question for you on a different subject, though."

Brody frowned at the phone. He didn't like the subtle teasing tone Wade's voice had taken on. "Yes?"

"I spoke with Xander the other day. He mentioned you had a *lady friend*."

Brody couldn't disguise his heavy sigh. If you told one brother, you might as well tell them all. They were worse than gossiping old women sometimes. "You could say that."

"Is it serious?"

"I'm not sure. It's a little early to speculate."

"Why didn't you tell me about her?" Wade complained. "Who is she? Where did you meet her? You don't go anywhere."

"I didn't tell you because there wasn't much to tell at the time. I only mentioned it to Xander so he'd stop trying to fix me up with a plastic surgeon. Anyway, to make a long story short, it's my administrative assistant."

"Agnes?" Wade asked, his voice strained with incredulity.

"No, not Agnes," Brody snapped in irritation. "I'm not so hard up that I'd chase after my married, retirement-age secretary. She's older than Mom, I think."

"Whatever floats your boat, man. I just want to see you with someone."

"That does *not* float my boat. Her name is Samantha. She's filling in for Agnes who is on vacation."

"I remember you saying something about that, but I wasn't sure when she was leaving town. So, it's going *well?*" There was a naughty lilt to the way he spoke that made his real question very clear. Wade didn't know Brody had been a virgin until a few days ago, but even then, he didn't think Brody got nearly enough action for a man in his prime.

"It's going *extremely* well," Brody replied. He couldn't keep the wide grin on his face from slipping into his voice. "She's amazing. Beautiful. Smart. And so sexy I can barely focus on my work."

"Wow," Wade commented. "You're damn near gushing. I hope we'll get to meet her soon. Maybe you can bring her to the farm for Christmas. In the meantime, congratulations for getting laid in this decade, Bro. I feel like we should throw you a party or something."

Brody shook his head and chuckled at his brother's blunt observation. If he only knew the truth....

Nine

"Are we going to a big city?" Sam attempted to uncover their secret destination for the tenth time today by playing twenty questions. The moment she and Brody loaded up in his car, she'd started in on him. So far, she'd eliminated Dallas, Los Angeles, Orlando and New Orleans. He told her it was someplace she could dress warm and bring a swimsuit. They weren't going to a lake or a river. He hadn't told her to pack her passport, so that eliminated the Caribbean and Mexico.

"No." Brody didn't even look her way when he answered. His eyes were focused on the expressway and the morning traffic.

"Are we going to the beach?"

Brody sighed. "Give it up. I'm not going to tell you."

"We *are* going to the beach," she said. "Otherwise you would've said no. Are we going to the Florida Keys?"

He didn't respond but slowed the car and turned into a private airport outside of the city. They drove past the main terminal to a hangar on the far side of the property. It had a sign on the side that said "Confidential Luxury Private Jets."

Since Brody told her they were taking a trip, she hadn't been able to fathom how they were going to get there when he didn't go out in public. She'd thought perhaps their destination was within driving distance. It never occurred to her that they could take a private jet instead of a regular, commercial airliner. Of course, she couldn't afford a jet in a million years, so she wouldn't have even dreamed of it.

Brody paused outside the hangar and honked his horn in two short bursts and one long one. A moment later, the massive door rolled up to reveal a shiny white jet inside. Brody pulled into the hangar and parked his car in the far corner. He killed the engine but left the keys in the ignition. "Come on," he said with a sly smile. He was enjoying torturing her with this surprise.

They got out of the car and Brody opened the trunk. Instead of pulling out their bags, he took her arm and led her across the empty building to the jet. She expected a place like this to have crew running all over the place. Or at the very least a pilot and someone to direct the plane. "Where are all their employees?" she asked.

"They're hiding inside until we get on the plane."

"Why?"

Brody turned to her with an amused expression. "Because I pay them to, of course."

That made sense. With enough money, Brody could do things however he chose to. It had gotten so easy to look at him and not see the scars any longer. But everyone else still saw them. And Brody was still living a shadow of a life. She started up the stairs of the jet with Brody behind her. The cockpit door to the left was already closed with the pilots inside.

The sign on the building had been right. This was a luxury jet. It didn't look like any plane she'd ever been inside. It had plush gray carpeting and captain's chairs that faced each other with polished mahogany tables between them. A large flat screen television was mounted on the far rear wall with a row of seats that turned to face it. There was a minibar, a sofa, a dining room table and what looked like a full-size bed in a room beyond the television. A bucket of ice with a bottle of champagne was waiting on the table beside them as they entered.

"Wow," was all Sam could say. And to think she thought flying first class was something special.

Brody pulled a thick curtain to separate them from the front of the plane. Sam settled into one of the soft leather seats as the engine of the plane roared to life. Someone she couldn't see came out of the cockpit to close and secure the door and then disappeared back inside.

She looked out the window to see ten employees appear out of nowhere. Several loaded their bags into the cargo hold. Others were using neon batons to guide the plane out of the hangar and toward the runway.

Brody sat down beside her with a flute of champagne in each hand. "Here you go."

Sam accepted one and took a sip. The golden bubbles exploded on her tongue with a seductively smooth, dry flavor. It was really nice champagne. Nothing like the sparkling wine she bought at the grocery store on New Year's Eve.

"Time to buckle up," Brody said with a smile.

The plane slowly taxied down the winding paths of the small airport. Sam could only watch in amazement.

"Good morning, Mr. Eden," a man's voice announced through the overhead speaker. "We'd like to welcome you and Ms. Davis aboard our luxury jet today. I am your Captain, Louis Holmes, and my co-pilot is Rene Lejeune. Please let us know by pressing the call button if there is anything we can do for you. We are currently number two for take-off. Our flight time today will be about four hours, and we have smooth, clear skies ahead of us. As requested, a prepared brunch is waiting for you in the dining area. The seat belt sign will turn off when we've reached cruising altitude and it's safe for you to move about the cabin. Enjoy your flight."

Sam took another sip of her champagne and blinked a few times to see if her amazing surroundings would disappear. "Is this how you usually travel? I can't even imagine this being the norm."

Brody nodded. "If it's too far to drive, yes. I have standing orders with this company and they know exactly how I want things arranged. Normally there would be a flight attendant that would bring us drinks and serve us lunch, but I decline her services on my flights for apparent reasons."

"When was the last time you flew on a regular plane?"

Brody thought hard for a second, narrowing his eyes at her as he tried to remember. "I flew with my dad to Ohio when I was sixteen."

"What was in Ohio? Family?"

"No. We went to see a doctor and facility there that specialized in the latest and greatest burn reconstruction procedures. He was the best in the country at the time. We had high hopes that he could help me."

Sam sat silently waiting for him to continue. When he didn't, she prompted, "What happened?"

Brody looked at her, his brow furrowed. "Obviously nothing could be done or I wouldn't look like this."

Sam opted not to press on that topic. Instead, she reached for his hand and held it as the engines kicked into high gear and they started down the runway. She wasn't afraid of flying, but she still got a little nervous, especially in a small plane like this one.

A few minutes later, she was able to look out her window and see nothing but ocean. "This is amazing."

"I'm glad you think so. But you ain't seen nothing yet."

Sam smiled and sank into the plush leather of her seat, thinking she could fall asleep that instant, it was so comfortable. By the time the plane leveled off and the seat belt light kicked off, she had finished her champagne and was fairly certain life didn't get much better than this. "You're going to spoil me with all this luxury. Ten-course meals, private jets… What am I going to do the next time I have to fly coach and eat fast food?"

"Sadly, you'll have to suffer like the other 99.9 percent of the population. Are you hungry?" Brody asked.

"Yes." Sam had forgotten her protein bar when they left this morning, and her stomach had been rumbling for a while. The champagne went straight to her head on an empty stomach.

"Let's go check out what they left us for brunch."

Sam followed him back to the dining area. On top of the minibar was a platter with all sorts of breads and pastries. In the refrigerator was an assortment of sliced fruits, cheeses and rolled, thin sliced deli meats. There was a plate of canapés like bellinis with caviar and crème fraiche and another with a fresh variety of sushi. Two pitchers were in the bottom of the refrigerator. One held a dark red sangria and the other, a cold strawberry mint soup.

It was more than she could eat in a few days, much less a few hours.

"I hope you skipped breakfast," Brody said, pulling the first platters out to sit on the dining table.

"I guess I'll eat myself into a coma and then go flop onto the bed in the back." Sam scooped up the tray of baked goods and followed him.

"That sounds like an excellent plan." Brody held out a strawberry to Sam and she took a bite of the juicy fruit. "Ever considered joining the Mile High Club?"

Several hours later, they touched down on the small island of Culebra, Puerto Rico. Brody watched Sam gaze out the window at everything as they taxied through the small airport. When they got off the jet, a limo was waiting for them. The driver did not get out of the car to greet them as they usually did. Instead, Brody opened the door for both of them to climb inside. The partition between the front and back of the limo was closed. He could hear the driver's door open once they were in the car. Through the dark-tinted glass, Sam watched the driver collect their bags from the jet and place them in the trunk.

"So, are we staying in Puerto Rico?" she asked.

"Nope." He has having fun playing this game with her. She couldn't stand not knowing what was going on.

"And where are we going from here?"

"To the marina."

"We're going on a boat?"

Brody turned in the plush leather seat to look at her. Sam's cheeks were still a touch flush and her hair a bit disheveled from their private tumble in the back of the plane. Every time he flew down here, he'd eyed the jet's bed and fantasized about using it for more than a nap. Given that he always flew alone, it wasn't really a possibility until now. "You aren't good with surprises, are you?"

She shrugged, a sheepish look drawing down her smile. "No, sorry."

Brody put his arm around her shoulder and sidled up alongside her. He kissed her temple and whispered into her ear. "Why don't you just enjoy the trip and I'll let you know when we're at our final destination?"

The limo started to pull away as she reluctantly agreed. There wasn't long to wait. The car arrived at the marina only a few minutes after leaving the airport property. After the driver moved their luggage to the deck of a small speedboat, they got out. The car pulled away as Brody helped Sam down onto the deck. He'd made enough trips out here and paid enough money that everyone had his requested process down pat.

Brody started up the boat and slowly chartered it out of the marina and into the open water. Sam sat beside him, marveling at the view. The water here was amazing—bright turquoise, clear and sparkling. You could see the schools of fish moving through the water beside them. The sky was a vivid blue without a single cloud to mar it. It was a beautiful day to be in the Caribbean.

After about thirty minutes of plowing into the open water toward his desired coordinates, Brody spied the dark shape of their destination on the horizon. "We're almost there," he said.

Sam watched anxiously as the island came into view. He couldn't tell Sam where they were going because the island technically didn't have a name. He hadn't gone to the trouble of officially naming it yet. When he purchased the island, he was told a few of the locals called it *Joya Verde,* Green Jewel, but it wasn't plotted as such on any maps.

Brody slowed the boat as they reached more shallow waters and pulled up alongside the dock that stretched out into the water from the beach. He tied up the boat, hauled their bags onto the pier and helped Sam out.

The look on her face was priceless. It was half the reason he wanted to bring her here. Her eyes were wide, her mouth open, as she took in every sight. He had reacted the same way when he first saw his green jewel. It was a beautiful little island with smooth golden sand beaches, dark green palms and other lush plants that grew out of the jutting black rock. There was about six acres of the island to explore while they were here. Around the other side was a mangrove lagoon that harbored a surprise he would show Sam later.

"What is this place?" she asked.

"It's my escape. The only place in the whole world where I can walk on the beach or swim in the ocean without the prying eyes of another living soul on me."

Sam had started rolling her suitcase toward the beach but stopped and turned to him. "You own an island? The whole thing?"

"Yes. It seemed like a good investment since I can't travel anywhere else."

Sam shook her head and continued on her path to the shore. "Rich people," she muttered under her breath.

Brody laughed at her and led the way from the beach up a winding path to the house that was made of crushed seashells and small pebbles. He opened the front door of the two-story beach house and gestured her in ahead of him. He hadn't built the home, but he was eternally grateful to the previous owner who had. The house was built on the edge of a rocky incline that rose up from the beach. The entire front of the home facing the ocean was glass, floor to ceiling. It faced west, so he could watch the sunset every night.

The floor plan was open and modern. The first floor had a gourmet kitchen, a great room and a deck with a swimming pool, hot tub and an outdoor shower. Off of the deck were stairs leading down to the beach. The entire second floor was dedicated to the master suite. This was not a vacation home for families. There was only the one bedroom. This was a retreat for lovers, or more appropriately, millionaire recluses.

"Come upstairs and I'll show you the best part."

Sam followed him up a winding open staircase to the master bedroom. Directly over the bed was a massive, square skylight that made you feel like you were sleeping beneath the stars. He'd lain there many nights, counting them until he fell asleep. Last, he led her out onto the second-story balcony. It wrapped around three sides of the house. The breeze was a little cooler up here, especially in the winter, but the view was exquisite.

She walked out to the railing and Brody came up behind her. She leaned back and he wrapped his arms around her waist to pull her tight against him. They looked out together at the vast aqua ocean that sprawled ahead of them. It was a patchwork of various shades of blue and green as the water changed depths and covered coral reefs. In the distance, they could see the faint outline of Culebra, but it was the only thing in sight.

"Not a bad view, eh?"

"It's so beautiful," she breathed. "I've never seen anything like it."

"It's not nearly as beautiful as you are."

Sam turned in his arms until she was facing him. She reached up and pulled the sunglasses from his face. "I want to be able to see those gorgeous baby blues."

Brody tried not to chuckle bitterly at her compliment, but he couldn't help it. He didn't see anything about himself as attractive. He'd never liked his eyes. They were exactly like his father's. When he looked in the mirror, all he could see was his father's dark, angry, blue gaze fixed on him when he did something wrong. And as for the parts of his face he did like, his father had ruined that, as well.

"What's so funny?" Sam asked, wrinkling her nose with irritation.

"Nothing is funny. I just have no idea what it is about me that you're attracted to," he admitted.

"Everyone has flaws. I hate my nose," Sam complained. "I took a soccer ball to the face when I was nine and it's bothered me ever since then. It didn't heal right. I also have troll feet, so I wear cute shoes to disguise them. I won't even get started on my hips."

"You have excellent hips."

"Thank you, but I've never been happy with them. I jog constantly, but there they stay. The point is that you are always going to be your own biggest critic. But everyone has at least one attractive feature. The key is to make the most of your best features. At the wrong angle my nose might make me look like I've lost a boxing match, but when I'm having a good hair day, I feel great about myself. The more confident you are, the more attractive you appear to others."

That was a nice idea. And given that Sam was nitpicking her minor imperfections, that might work for her. But if he had to see beauty in himself for others to see it, he was doomed. He shook his head and looked back at the horizon. He was uncomfortable with the way she was studying him. Even knowing that for some unfathomable reason she was attracted to him, he wanted to squirm under her gaze.

"Look at me, Brody." Her hand rested against his scarred cheek and turned his face back to her. "You don't see anything but the scars, do you?"

He swallowed hard but couldn't avoid her question. "I do. Usually the scars are the last thing I notice. Mostly, I see the drunk, angry face of my father. Sometimes I see my mother's mouth, tight with disapproval and stone-silent when child protective services asked her questions. But the worst is when I see how I used to look before this happened and what I might look like today if I hadn't startled him that day in the garage."

His words were harsher than he intended them to be, but he needed Sam to understand. There was nothing beautiful about him in his opinion. He was broken.

"What happened to you, Brody?"

He didn't want to talk about it. Not here in this magical place where he could escape from his past. He never should've said the words to lead them to the conversation he dreaded. He should've nodded and accepted her compliment. And yet, he knew he needed to tell her. After sharing something as intimate as they had, she deserved to know why he was the way he was. That didn't mean he had to like it.

Brody's hands dropped from Sam's waist and he turned to walk back into the house. He heard her come in behind him and slide the glass door closed.

"Brody, please."

He sank onto the edge of the bed and dropped his head to look down at the polished wood floors between his feet. The bed sagged as Sam sat beside him. She placed a reassuring hand on his knee.

"My father was the best-looking guy in Goshen, Connecticut. He also had a raging temper and was an alcoholic by the time he was twenty-three. My mother was an enabler with no self-esteem. She always thought she wasn't good enough for a man like him. Probably because he told her she was fat and ugly at every opportunity. Why they got married, I'll never know, but at least they bothered to. My mother thought that having his son would be the best way to win him over."

Sam's sharp intake of breath beside him was enough to let him know she knew it was a bad idea. "What she didn't realize was that any child she had would be just as big a disappointment to him as she was. I could never do anything right. Sometimes I think my father only wore a belt so he would always have something handy to hit me with."

Her hand tightened on his knee, but she didn't speak. "I didn't believe it was possible, but he got meaner as he got older. When the belt didn't make me scream loud enough anymore, he switched to fists. Or burning cigarettes. My mother looked the other way and would lecture me about angering him while she bandaged my wounds. By the time I reached fifth grade, I was certain it was coming down to a final fight. Him versus me. I was finally getting big enough and strong enough to fight back.

"One day I came home from school and he wasn't at work like he should've been. His car had a dead battery, so he was in the garage working on it. I don't know why I went out there that day. I should have just gone into my room and hid like I usually did. When I opened the door, it made a loud squeaking noise and startled him. He hit the back of his head on the hood of the car and dropped the car battery he was pulling out. Somehow, it spilled some of the acid on his hand and he started yelling."

The rest of the day was a sketchy composite of memories and things that people told him. "I remember my father screaming and hitting me. I remember slumping against the wall and sliding to the ground, fighting to stay conscious. I opened my eyes at one point and saw him walking toward me with something in his hand. I tried to shield myself, but it was a pointless effort. After that, I only recall hearing someone screaming and realizing it was me. I blacked out and woke up in the hospital a week later."

"Oh, my God," Sam said.

Brody turned to look at her and saw the tears welling in her eyes. "Please don't cry. I don't want to upset you. This was twenty years ago. It's too late to cry now."

"What was it?" she asked, her voice almost too quiet for him to hear her.

"After he beat me, he poured the acid from his battery into an empty quart-size can we'd recently used to paint the bathroom. Then he threw it at me. The neighbors called the cops when they heard me screaming."

"Please tell me that he's in jail."

"He is, at least for now. If he had stuck with beating me as usual, the maximum sentence in Connecticut is a year, but the prosecutor nailed him with first-degree assault against a minor ten and under and he got twenty years, the maximum sentence. I went into foster care after that."

"What about your mother?"

For some reason, this was the part of the story that always bothered him the most. His father was a bastard. He'd come to terms with that long before the accident. But her... "She chose him."

"She *what?*" Sam's voice was sharp and angry. He wished his mother had shown half as much emotion for him.

"She blamed me for my father going to prison. I brought the worst out in him, you see. To this day, she goes to every parole hearing and begs them to let him out. That's the one public place I do go. The judge usually takes one look at me and sends him right back to the prison. She hates me for that, but it's only fair since I hate her for choosing a man over her child. I might not have gone into foster care, but she never came to the hospital to claim me, so social services had no choice."

"What a horrible mother."

"You'd think so, but it turned out to be the best thing she could've done for me. I would've done nothing with my life if I had stayed with her, but my foster home was amazing. My foster family is my real family now. Wade, Xander and Heath are my brothers. Julianne is my sister. Molly and Ken are my parents. They never looked at me like I was different. They gave me the faith and drive to make something of myself. Without them, I wouldn't have built my company and I certainly wouldn't be flying in jets to my private island. My life is so much better because of the Edens. That's why I took their last name when I turned eighteen. If it weren't for these damn scars, I might even forget that my biological parents ever existed."

Sam sat quietly for a moment, absorbing everything he'd told her. "I'm glad you found people who cared about you, Brody. I can't imagine what you've been through, especially so young. But thank you for sharing this with me. I know that was hard for you."

Brody covered Sam's hand with his own and gave it a gentle squeeze. It was done. He'd put everything out there. And now he wouldn't have to talk about it again. Ever.

Hopefully, now, they could start to enjoy their vacation. "Now that all that unpleasantness is out of the way, what do you say to putting on our swimsuits and taking a dip in that fantastic ocean?"

Ten

"Where exactly are we going again?" Sam clutched her flashlight and followed Brody down a dim, gravel and sand path.

"I didn't say."

Sam would normally say that she liked surprises, but Brody seemed full of them. She never knew what they were doing. But considering his last surprise included a luxury jet and a private island, she needed to just go with it. They'd spent two days on the island being decadently lazy. After dinner, he'd eyed the darkening sky and told her to put on her swimsuit. She couldn't fathom what she would do in the dark in her swimsuit, especially when he handed her a flashlight.

Walking through the dark to the far side of the island made her even more nervous. The path they traveled was narrow and went straight through his private rain-forest. There were strange trees and potentially poisonous plants and unseen things living in them. She could hear *something* rustling in the branches, but she couldn't find it with her flashlight. Hopefully it was a bird and not some big scary lizard or snake.

"We're almost there," Brody said, rounding a thick, knotted tree trunk. He was clutching a camping lantern in his hand.

The path curved ahead of them and opened to a small oval lagoon ringed with a dark tangle of trees and vines. It was almost entirely enclosed from the ocean except for a narrow inlet. There were no sandy beaches on this part of the island. At least that she could see. By now the sun had fully set and there was only a touch of purple lighting the night sky. There was no moon tonight, but there was enough light left to see two kayaks and paddles lying along their path.

"We're going kayaking?" That wasn't exactly what she had in mind.

"Yes." Brody hung the lantern on a sturdy branch and bent down to pick up a paddle. "Have you ever done it before?"

"No. I'm not particularly outdoorsy."

"That's okay. It isn't hard. The water is calm tonight. These are open kayaks, so you don't have to worry about rolling it."

Sam swallowed hard and eyed him with renewed concern. She hadn't considered *that* until he mentioned it. "Great. Any particular reason why we're doing this in the dark? No one will see us."

"I know. But we have to go in the dark. You'll see why." He grabbed one of the kayaks and hauled it to the edge of the water. "Come here and step in."

Sam made her way over and kicked off her flip flops. Brody braced the kayak and held it steady as she climbed inside and sat down. It rocked slightly, but she kept her balance.

Brody handed her the two-ended paddle. "I'm going to push you off so I can put mine in the water. Just sit still and don't paddle around until I get out there with you."

She braced herself for the push and glided out into the lagoon. A few minutes later Brody pulled up alongside her. "Let's paddle out into the middle. It's almost dark enough."

Sam dipped her paddle into the water on one side of the kayak, then the other. She was surprised at how easily she moved across the surface. It only took a few moments to reach the center of the lagoon. She let the kayak glide to a stop and held her paddle across her lap. The night was silent and still around them. She looked up to the dark sky and gasped. With no sun, moon or city lights, the stars were like a thick blanket overhead. There were millions scattered across the darkness instead of the fifty she was lucky to see in Boston. Suddenly, the mysterious hike through the dark was worth it.

"It's beautiful," she said.

Brody looked up at the sky and laughed. "Yes, it is. But that's not why we're here."

"It's not?"

"No. I wanted to show this place to you. It's a secret. No one knows this is here. I don't even think the previous owner knew. I found it by accident. There are only a few locations like this in the whole world and mine may be the only privately owned one."

Sam looked around herself, searching for what made it so special. She didn't see anything but some weird trees. And then she saw it. A fish darted through the water beside her. It glowed a bluish-white, leaving a streak behind it like a trail of stardust. After a moment it faded away. "What was that?" she asked. "You have glowing fish."

Brody smiled. "It must be dark enough now. It's not the fish that glow. Watch." He dipped his paddle into the water and agitated it. It stirred up a swirl of glowing white clouds beneath the surface.

Sam did the same with her own paddle. Every movement generated the blue glow in the inky black water. It was eerie and hauntingly beautiful. She'd never seen anything like it before. "What makes it do that?"

"This is a bioluminescent bay. The mangrove lagoon and warm, calm water creates the perfect environment for the tiny little creatures to thrive. They put off a blue-green glow as a defense mechanism when they're agitated by movement."

"Is it safe to put my hand in the water?"

"As long as you don't have on any bug repellant. It will kill them."

"I don't." Sam let her fingers comb through the water, making squiggly green designs like she was drawing in the air with sparklers on the Fourth of July. When she pulled her hand out of the water, it glowed for a moment. "Wow. This is really incredible."

"I thought you'd like it. Do you want to get in?"

Sam smiled. "Can we?"

"Yeah." Brody laid his paddle inside the kayak and threw his legs over the side into the water.

Sam watched him slip beneath the surface of the water in a haze of blue-green clouds. She could follow his every movement through the dark water. He swam under her kayak coming up on the opposite side. When he surfaced, his whole body was dripping with iridescent green water.

"Come on," he said, holding his hand out to her.

She was nervous about swimming in the ocean at night, but she couldn't pass up this opportunity. She'd try to forget there might be sharks or other creepy creatures nearby.

Sam took his hand and followed his lead, throwing her legs over the side and slipping into the water. She was too nervous to stay under for long and immediately reached for the surface. When she reopened her eyes, she was amazed by the glow of her every movement as she treaded water.

Brody watched her with a soft smile curling his lips. It was a curious expression considering their circumstances. "What?" she finally asked as she pushed a wet strand of hair out of her face.

"You're even beautiful when you're green."

Sam chuckled and shook her head. If she looked anything like Brody did, it was more likely that she looked like a human glow stick or space alien. Of course, Brody looked handsome even as the drops of luminescent water dripped down his cheeks. The glow of the water around them was bright enough for her to see his face clearly in the darkness. Nothing about him had physically changed, and yet he looked like a completely different person here on his island. It had taken until today for her to really notice the change, but it was definitely there. He was relaxed. Open. She dared say he even looked happy. He didn't have the same countenance in Boston. Not even at his home, which should've been a place he could relax and be himself.

It was as though a massive burden had been lifted from his shoulders coming here. Maybe telling her about his past and his parents had helped, too. That was a huge secret to carry around. He had his foster family, which was wonderful, but who else could he talk to? Confide in? Not Agnes. But he could tell Sam. And she was glad to be that for him.

As she watched him here, in this beautiful, magical moment, she realized she wanted to be more to him than a confidante. More than just his secretary. Sam wanted to be with Brody. And not only physically. The shy, mysterious charmer had stolen her heart away.

Temporarily stunned by the turn of her thoughts, she stopped swimming and her head slipped under the water again. It was too deep in this part of the lagoon. She pushed herself back up, turned and started swimming closer to the shore where they'd come in. She stopped when she could feel sand and stones scraping against her toes. It made her feel more stable physically, if nothing else. "That's better."

"Was the water too deep?" Brody asked, coming up behind her.

Sam turned to him and smiled. She didn't want him to know she was having thoughts about her feelings for him. "Not usually. But it's so amazing and romantic out here, and I want to kiss you so badly. I'm afraid I'll get distracted touching you and drown."

Brody chuckled, wrapping his arms around her and pulling her against him. She moved easily through the water, colliding with his chest. "I'll keep your head above water, don't worry."

She was sure he would. His hands glided over her bare back. He'd grown so much more confident since that first night. He was a quick learner, she was pleased to discover. Like a true left-brainer, he had set his mind to learning every inch of her body, memorizing every

response. She'd never had a man figure out so quickly
how she liked to be touched.

When his lips met hers, she felt a chill of excitement
run down her spine. With a little hop and a luminescent
cloud following her movement, she wrapped her legs
around his waist and pressed her body into his. Brody
groaned against her mouth as her center made contact
with the firm heat of his arousal. The thin fabric of her
bikini bottoms and his swimming trunks did little to
disguise how badly he wanted her.

Sam was intrigued about the idea of making love
to him right here. The blanket of stars and eerie glow
of their movements was so romantic. But there were
no smooth sandy beaches here. Or protection. It was
an interesting but impractical idea. They needed to go
back to the house.

"Take me to bed," she whispered.

Brody complied, walking them out of the water and
onto the beach. She expected him to put her down once
they reached the trail back to the house, but he didn't.
He continued walking, carrying her as though she were
no heavier than a small child. She clung to him, bury-
ing her face in his neck. She couldn't resist tasting his
skin with him so close. Her lips and tongue moved over
him. He tasted salty from the ocean.

Seeing the lights of the house shining on the land-
scape around them made her bolder. She let her tongue
swirl up the side of his neck to the sensitive skin just
below his earlobe. She flicked it and then gently bit at
him. She could feel Brody shiver and tighten his grip
on her.

They climbed the steps to the deck with the pool and
walked through the open sliding glass door. Brody continued up the stairs to the master loft without putting her

down, but she could feel the gentle tug of his fingertips at the tie of her bikini top. Easing back from her grip on him, she let the tiny white fabric slide down and fall to the ground, exposing her breasts and the tight pink tips.

Brody allowed his gaze to dip down for a moment, then tore it away so he didn't trip on the stairs. Sam pressed her breasts into his bare chest, eliciting a sharp hiss in her ear.

At the top of the stairs, he went directly to the bed, dropping her onto the mattress and immediately covering her body with his own. Sam was grateful for the heat of him over her. The cooler air of the house combined with her still damp hair and skin drew goose bumps across her flesh and made her nipples even more painfully tight. Brody captured one in his mouth, and the sharp pleasure of it sent her head flying back with a gasp.

It was then that she saw that they'd brought the blanket of stars back to the house with them. The skylight over the bed showed a perfect snapshot of the inky black night with its shimmering sea of twinkling stars overhead. It was awe-inspiring, and combined with the pleasure of Brody's hands gliding over her skin, she was very nearly overwhelmed by the moment.

Everything about the past few days had been perfect. Like a dream she never even dared to imagine. Even Brody's confession about his childhood, while tragic, had breached one of the last barriers between them. She'd never felt closer to another man in her life. He was amazing in so many different ways and he didn't even know it.

She wished she knew of a way to tell him that he would believe. Words were easily brushed off. She would have to show him how much he meant to her. How much she…loved him.

Sam tried to take a deep breath and focus on the stars overhead as tears started to form in the corners of her eyes. Her chest was painfully tight, even as her stomach fluttered with excitement and nerves.

"Sam, is something wrong?"

She shifted her gaze from the skylight to Brody's concerned face. He was hovering over her, his strong arms pressed into the mattress beside her. His damp hair was curling slightly as it dried, and his eyes were black in the dim light but still just as penetrating. He was worried that he'd done something wrong, when in fact, he'd done everything right.

At that exact moment, the first tear rolled down the side of her face. With a slight shake of her head and a soft smile, she reached out and pulled him back down to her. She closed her eyes as their lips met and another tear escaped. She wasn't certain if most men understood tears of emotions other than pain and sadness. Sam could cry through any number of emotions, including joy and contentedness. And she was anything but sad right now. Being with Brody here on this beautiful island felt so perfectly right.

When he eased forward and filled her, she could only cling to him and bite her bottom lip to keep from telling him how she felt. It would be so easy to whisper it into his ear or to cry it out to the night when she came undone. But she was afraid to. There was no way to know how he would react, and she didn't dare ruin this moment. There would be time later, and maybe then, she might get the response she wanted to hear.

Instead, she turned off her thoughts and tried to focus on loving him. It wasn't long before she was swept up in the pleasure he coaxed from her, drunk on the warm musk of his skin. When her powerful climax came, she didn't cry out. She buried her face in his neck, gasping his name as he filled her again and again.

Brody was tossing the last of his things in his suitcase when his cell phone rang. It was Wade's ringtone, "Opportunities" by the Pet Shop Boys. The song was upbeat, but for some reason, it made his stomach ache with dread. Wade knew he was at the island with Sam. He would only call if it was really important.

Deborah Wilder.

He checked to make sure Sam was still in the shower before he answered the phone. "Hello?"

"I'm sorry to interrupt your trip," Wade began, but Brody could tell exactly where this was going. "You told me to call the minute I heard something."

Brody sank down onto the bed and let Wade talk without interruption.

"Deborah is in Cornwall. She was at the Wet Hen last night asking around for anyone that knew her brother."

The Wet Hen was the center for a lot of activity in their home town. If you wanted to have a beer with the mayor and the sheriff, that was the place to go. It was also the place to start trouble quickly because everyone in town would know about it as certainly as they were sitting there.

"Skippy called, but by the time I got down to the bar, she was gone. I hung around and chatted with a few folks for a while. It didn't take much to find out what happened before she left."

"Did she learn anything?"

"No," Wade said. "It's been a long time and most people have forgotten Tommy Wilder even existed. Those that remembered told her what she already knew—he ran away from his foster home and was never seen in Cornwall again."

Brody nodded. Maybe that would be enough to convince her that Cornwall was a dead end and send her packing. "Is she still in town?"

"Yes. And apparently she went to the farm first to talk to Mom and Dad."

"What?" Brody nearly shouted into the phone. This was way too close for comfort.

"I didn't find out until later. Mom mentioned it when I went by this morning. Nothing came of it, but Mom is a little upset to know that Tommy has been missing since the night he vanished. I don't think she's ever forgiven herself for 'failing' that one."

Even knowing that she'd raised three millionaire CEOs, a U.S. congressman and a world-acclaimed artist, Molly would focus on the one that got away. "Not even Mom could have saved Tommy. I hate that she upset Mom like that. Where is Deborah staying?"

"She's staying at the Cornwall Inn. I gave Carol a call at the desk, and she said Deborah hadn't checked out yet. She had a reservation through tomorrow. For now, I think things are okay. I don't know who she could possibly talk to that might cause us trouble."

"Her presence in town causes us trouble, Wade. It starts to raise questions. People forgot about Tommy, but knowing he hasn't been seen since then will make people wonder what happened. The sheriff is new. If Deborah pressures him enough, it might make him curious. Hell, Mom might even encourage the sheriff out of some misguided feeling of disappointing Tommy. He might start looking at the old case file and start his own search for him. The farm was the last place he was ever seen. Tell me that won't bring questions into our lap."

"Then we tell him the same story we've always told. Why would we know what happened to him after he ran off?"

"He's dead, Wade. We killed him. Eventually people are going to wonder why he completely disappeared off the face of the earth."

A soft gasp over Brody's shoulder set ice running through his veins. He turned to find Sam standing in the doorway to the bathroom, wrapped in a towel. Her eyes were wide with surprise and fear, her lips parted to speak but silenced by shock.

"I've gotta go, Wade. Call me if you hear anything." He hit the button, ending the call before his brother could respond. Brody dropped the phone to the bed and slowly got up to face her.

Sam watched him warily as he moved, her whole body tense.

He didn't go any closer. She looked like she would spook too easily, and there was nowhere for her to run. She could scream bloody murder on the beach and no one would hear her, but he didn't want her to be afraid of him. Brody hated to see that expression in her eyes. She'd always looked at him with interest and openness, even early on. Now the fortress walls had slammed down. It made his chest ache with disappointment. He couldn't let her slip away over this.

"Sam, I know that sounded bad, but it isn't what you think."

"You didn't kill someone?" Her voice was icy cold.

"No. I didn't kill anyone," he said, and that was true. Heath had been the one to actually kill Tommy, although that was splitting hairs. "Please relax. I'm not some serial killer about to slaughter you in the basement because you've uncovered my horrible secret. I've got enough problems right now without you, of all people, turning on me."

Sam took a deep breath, relaxing slightly but not making a move toward him. "So tell me what's going on, then."

"I can't talk about it." Brody wished he could. He would love to have someone he could confess his darkest secrets to, but the brothers had a rule—protect the family above all else. He sat back down on the bed, defeat hunching his shoulders. "I wish I could."

Sam watched him for a moment before crossing the room and sitting beside him. She wasn't shoulder to shoulder with him like usual, but it was an improvement. "Yes, you can. I know of five million reasons why you can tell me anything you want and know that I would never tell another living soul."

"The confidentiality agreement won't cover this." And even if it did, he didn't want to burden her with it. He'd already dumped enough crap on her this weekend. He looked down at the floor, unable to meet her eyes as he spoke. "You're…important to me, Sam. Even if I knew I could trust you enough to keep this secret, it's only a partial consolation. You'll still know. I don't ever want to tell you something that changes the way you look at me. You're one of the only people in the world that looks at me with something other than shock and disgust. I can't risk losing that."

A hand rested gently against his scarred cheek. He turned to Sam, hoping to see the fear gone. It was. In its place was a drawn brow of concern and a slight frown. He wasn't sure that was much better.

"You won't lose it, Brody. You can trust me with this. I want you to tell me."

Her dark brown eyes were penetrating as she spoke. She meant every word. He had to have faith she meant what she said. Rejecting her promise and walking away without telling her would likely do more damage to their relationship than the truth. He would still speak carefully, though. Some details didn't need to be shared to help her understand his situation.

"Do you remember the first day you came into my office?"

She nodded, a smile faintly curling her lips. "Our first kiss."

Brody was glad that's what she remembered instead of his angry rant. "Before that, when I was so angry… I thought you'd seen my computer and what was on it. It was information on a man, a child really, I knew when I was younger. Tommy. When we were teenagers, we were all living as foster children with the Edens. He was trouble from the start, nothing like the rest of us. I worried about him and what he might do, but the others told me I was just paranoid because of my accident."

"You were right." It was a statement, not a question. She had come to know him so well, so quickly.

Brody nodded. "He did something terrible one day while we were all out working on the farm. Our dad had the flu and was in bed, so we were out there doing our chores alone. Tommy took advantage of that. One of my brothers tried to stop him, and when it was over, Tommy was dead. We were kids. We didn't know what to do."

"Of course not. Most adults wouldn't know what to do, either."

"I was afraid that they would take us away from the Edens if someone found out about what happened. None of us wanted that to happen. It was our home. So we panicked. It was an accident and we should've called the cops, but we were too scared to risk it. We hid the body, cleaned up and pretended like it never happened. When our parents asked where Tommy was, we told them he left in the night. He was treated as a runaway and since he was almost eighteen, they didn't spend much energy looking for him."

"That's a long time for you to carry a secret that big."

"It is. We try not to think about it, but it's hard to forget. I always keep an eye on the internet for people that might look for him. The day you came into my office, I had gotten a report that his sister was searching for him. We'd hoped that everyone would forget. My brother called and told me she's in Cornwall asking questions about him."

"Do you think she will find out the truth?"

"I don't know. Only the five of us kids know the real story, aside from you, and even then, we each only know our piece of what happened that night. We didn't talk about it with each other, much less anyone else. I don't know of any way his sister could find out unless one of us tells her. Or the body turns up."

Sam's eyes widened. "Is that a possibility?"

Brody shrugged. "I hope not. But we were kids, not master criminals. We didn't have a clue how to dispose of a body and keep anyone from ever identifying the remains. We've been lucky so far. Without a body, there's no reason to doubt that he ran away."

"And if someone finds him?"

Brody swallowed hard. "I try not to think about that."

Eleven

It felt strange to be back in Boston. It was an odd thought for Sam to have considering she was born and raised in Boston and loved it. She had never even entertained the idea of moving, even when her job prospects in town were weak.

She was cold. It was overcast and sleeting. It wouldn't be long before the snow and ice started in earnest and didn't let up until April. The only bright spot in the day was the fuchsia rose that was on her desk again this morning.

Sam looked through her office window and dreaded going out to lunch today. Even to see Amanda. She really just wanted to go back to the island. Everything was different there. Including Brody.

The open, happy, carefree man from the island was gone. He returned to being wary, guarded Brody the moment their jet landed back in Boston. He was still affectionate with her, that hadn't changed, but there was something in his sapphire eyes. A worry. A tension that hadn't followed him to his tropical retreat. She missed that Brody, and she had no idea how to coax that side out of him. At least not at work.

The alarm sounded on her computer, reminding her to go meet Amanda. With another glance out the window, she grabbed her lined, turquoise raincoat, slung her scarf around her neck and grabbed her Coach bag. She paused at Brody's door, knocking gently until he called for her to enter.

"I'm going to meet a friend for lunch at the deli on the corner. Do you want me to bring you a sandwich back?"

Brody nodded, his eyes darting to his monitor several times as she spoke. He was distracted by his work. Another thing she hadn't missed about Boston. He'd barely scrolled through his emails in Puerto Rico.

"That would be great." He scribbled an order on a yellow sticky note and handed it to her. "Thank you."

"I'll be back in about an hour."

Brody gave a quick wave and returned to his computers. With a sigh, Sam shut the door behind her and headed through the various security hoops she needed to get outside. On their island, they hadn't even closed the doors, much less needed fingerprint scans to open them.

She got a text from Amanda as she crossed the street. She had a table in the back of the deli with her food. Sam ordered quickly and joined her, setting her phone on the table beside them.

"You have a tan," Amanda remarked. "I hate you."

Sam smiled sheepishly. She did get a nice tan. And no tan lines at that. It had been indulgent and naughty to sunbathe nude on the beach, but she took the chance while she had it. "Sorry."

"What brought on this impromptu vacation? You didn't mention it the last time we had lunch."

"I didn't know I was going then. My boss wanted to surprise me with a long weekend away. It was spur-of-the-moment."

Amanda's eyes widened. "Wow. This romance is progressing quite nicely."

Sam nodded and opted to take a bite of her sandwich to avoid elaborating. Amanda had no idea of the truth of her statement. But Sam couldn't even tell her best friend that she had feelings for Brody. It was all too fast, and she had to leave so many details of their relationship out of the conversation. Declaring her love for her nameless supervisor would send up a red flag, and she didn't want Amanda to be more concerned than excited for her budding romance.

"Well, while you were cavorting on the beach, I had my own development in the man department."

Sam immediately felt guilty. She should've noticed how much her friend was beaming, but she'd been distracted by her own thoughts. Amanda was wearing one of her nicest outfits, her hair and makeup done with more attention to detail than usual. "What? Do tell."

"His name is Matt. I met him at a bar downtown on Thursday night. They had a band in that I wanted to go see. And since you were out of town, I had to go it alone. Matt was there alone to see the band, too. We started chatting and he bought me a drink. It blossomed from there. We went out Friday night and Saturday night. Then we had breakfast Sunday morning," she added with a sly grin.

"Very nice. Sounds like you two have really hit it off. Tell me more about him."

"He's an investment banker, but he's not stuffy. Thirty-four. He's divorced, but no kids. He's got a really nice place in town. And there's a dragon tattoo on his shoulder that was so damn sexy I almost climaxed the first time I saw it."

Sam and Amanda giggled over her exploits as they ate their lunch. She was glad that her friend had found someone. It had been a long time since Amanda had dated a guy with much promise.

"What are you doing Friday?" Amanda asked.

"I have no idea. Why?"

"Maybe we could all go out. Like a double date. It would be fun. I want to introduce you to Matt, and I'm dying to meet your guy. You haven't even told me his name. What's up with that?"

Sam let Amanda talk, but the moment the first words fell from her lips, she knew the answer. She tried not to feel disappointed about it, but double dating was out of the question. So was going out to a nice dinner at the hot new restaurant in town. Or seeing a movie on opening weekend. Or going to her friend Kelly's annual New Year's Eve party. Sam never had a date for that party, and when it finally looked like she might not be single for New Year's, she knew her date would decline the invitation.

Would Brody even be willing to meet her dad and her brothers? She didn't know. The thoughts had brought down her spirits faster than finding out Brody had committed a crime. Being in love with him on a private island was easy. Loving Brody in Boston, surrounded by six-hundred thousand other people, was another matter.

How exactly did she imagine their relationship to work in the real world? She had no idea.

"Sam?"

She looked up from her sandwich and tried to remember what Amanda had asked her. She opted to ignore the question about Brody's name. "I think he's busy Friday. Maybe another time," she said, knowing full well there wouldn't be another time.

"Okay," Amanda said, looking a touch disappointed. "Let me know when he's available."

"Sure." Sam took a deep breath, relieved that Amanda hadn't pressed the issue. She didn't want to lie to her friend, but it wasn't like there were a hundred Brodys working at ESS. She tried to focus the rest of their conversation on Amanda's romance, which was easy to do. She was all too excited to fill the time talking about Matt.

When they were finished, she ordered Brody's food and headed back to the office. Despite the cold, she took her time walking down the sidewalk to her building. She couldn't make herself move any faster even as the icy sleet pelted her face. The lightness in her heart from the past few days had deflated, and all it took was the suggestion of a double date jabbing it like a sharp pin.

Brody had been an enigma to her. A puzzle she wanted to put together. The more she learned, the more she was determined to learn. Ever the meddler, she not only wanted to know Brody but to help him. He didn't seem very happy locked away in his tower. She had done her best to help where that was concerned. But now what? Had she thought her love would change him? Give him the courage to step into the light?

As she stood dripping onto the rug in the lobby, she realized she simply hadn't thought that far ahead. When

Sam had held Brody's lunch hostage and forced him from his office, she had never expected things to go this far. She never dreamed she would kiss him, much less sleep with him or go away on a romantic vacation. And she certainly never imagined she would fall in love with him.

But now that she had…what was she going to do? If Brody wouldn't live his life in public, was she willing to live her life in the shadows with him?

Sam watched the numbers climb on the elevator as it spirited her up to the top floor. By the time the doors opened, she knew she had her answer. Yes, she would. *If*—and that was a very emphatic *if*—he was happy. And she really didn't think he was happy hiding from the world. Even with her in his life. So now what?

At her desk, Sam slipped out of her coat and hung it on the rack. She didn't even bother to knock on Brody's door. Instead, she slid his lunch through the silver drawer she'd ignored since nearly her first day on the job. Slamming it shut, she slumped into her chair and started reading her new email.

When Brody's door opened and his head peeked around the heavy wood, she immediately felt guilty. His eyes were wary as he watched her from a distance. Apparently thrusting his lunch at him through the drawer after all this time had set off alarm bells in his mind. "Everything okay?"

"Yes," she said, pasting a smile on her face that she hoped looked authentic.

He didn't seem convinced but came out from behind the door. He was looking very handsome today in a gray pinstripe suit and smoky blue tie. Sam still didn't understand why he dressed so nicely when no one would ever see him. She preferred him in jeans and barefoot.

"Lunch go all right?"

"Yes," she repeated, then shook her head. She might as well be honest about how she was feeling. "No, not really. My friend Amanda asked if you and I wanted to double date with her and her new guy on Friday."

His brows shot up. "Your friend knows about me?"

Was that enough to cost her five million? She hoped not. "Not much. Not your name or who you are. She just knows that I've been seeing someone at work. And that I've been very happy."

"You don't look happy," he noted.

"At the moment I'm not."

"Why?"

Sam sighed. "Because you were too distracted by what I might've told Amanda to hear the rest of the sentence. She wants us to go out with her, but we can't. And we can't go out to dinner or a play. Or go Christmas shopping together. *Ever*. Because you don't go out in public."

Brody's face went neutral and stony. If there was a hint of emotion in his eyes over her being upset, he hid it away. "I'm sorry that upsets you. You know that I—"

"I know," she interrupted. "You're the Great and Powerful Oz. The man behind the curtain that no one ever sees. Except me. And it doesn't matter that I see a man who is beautiful both inside and out. That I see a man who is caring and funny. The world will forever be deprived of him."

Brody pursed his lips but didn't respond to the compliments or the complaints. With a sigh, he shook his head and turned back to the subject he was more comfortable with—work. "I have a virtual meeting with the marketing director at one-thirty. Hold my calls until after the meeting is over."

Sam nodded and he went back into his office. She was so frustrated with him, she wanted to shake his shoulders and scream. Not because he was afraid of people's reactions in public. Not because he wasn't willing to do it for her. But because he continued to hide himself away despite how unhappy it made him. That's what really made her crazy.

Those damn scars were a prison all their own. The security measures were a backup plan in case someone was brave enough to try to get close. If Sam could get close enough to Brody's father, she would throttle him with her bare hands for what he had done.

There had to be a way to make Brody more comfortable in his own skin. He'd mentioned how he'd traveled as a teenager to see a specialist about reconstructing his face. That was fifteen years ago. Certainly there had been enough medical advances in the past few years to make a difference. It's not like he needed insurance approval for treatment. He had enough money to do what needed to be done.

She opened an internet window and started searching for skin reconstruction treatments. She scanned through one article after another, site after site. After a few dead ends, she found a fairly promising site for a plastic surgeon in New York City. He was using cutting edge laser technology and other methods. The before and after pictures in his photo gallery were stunning. The results weren't flawless, but they were far better than she had ever imagined. It made her wonder if Brody even knew these kinds of advances had been made in reconstruction technology.

She glanced briefly at the doctor's phone number on the computer screen and a shot of panic rushed through her. Her cell phone. Sam dashed over to her purse and searched through it, but it wasn't there. She checked the pockets of her jacket, but they were empty. She'd left it at the deli. Hopefully it was still there and someone hadn't stolen it.

Sam pressed the intercom button. "I have to run back to the deli. I left my cell phone." She didn't wait for his reply, leaping out of her chair and rushing down to the lobby.

Brody had spent the past hour sitting in his office and feeling like crap. He hadn't said anything to Sam, but he could see the pain and disappointment in her face when they spoke about her friend. She wanted him to be like any other man. To do things most couples did. But that wasn't a possibility. She knew that from the beginning. And yet, she'd hoped for more.

So did he.

He reached out to grab the gift-wrapped box he'd left sitting on the edge of his desk. It was a gold necklace with a sun pendant. The rays of the sun were multiple hues of yellow, white and rose-colored gold. The center was a yellow diamond. Sam was his personal sunshine, and the necklace was the perfect way to thank her for it. He'd ordered it before they left for the trip and Peggy had left it in his home office when he returned.

He'd wanted to give it to Sam several times today, but the timing hadn't been right. He didn't want to give it to her when she was upset. But maybe now was a good time. He could leave it on her desk while she was across the street.

Brody rounded her desk and left the box just to the side of her keyboard. His hand brushed the mouse as he moved away and the screensaver turned off, revealing her web browser.

He felt sick to his stomach when he saw the pictures on her screen. Instead of email or briefing charts, it was page after page of burn reconstruction photos. He clicked back through her search history at a variety of sites, all focused on the latest methods of "fixing" him.

Brody felt the anger of betrayal begin to swirl in his gut. He didn't know why he was so surprised to find this. She was Daddy's Little Fixer, right? She fixed everything else, why wouldn't she want to fix Brody? She'd only played to his ego that night at dinner when she told him she didn't see anything about him that needed fixing.

He was a fool. Stupid for believing that she might be the one woman who would love him just the way he was. Frustrated, he grabbed the pink rose from the vase and crushed the petals in his hand. A thorn stabbed him, muddying his skin with a smear of blood, but he didn't care. It didn't hurt nearly as much as the truth.

A moment later, Sam came through the door with her cell phone in her hand. She stopped in her tracks the moment Brody looked up from her screen. He wasn't sure if it was the expression on his face or her own guilty conscience, but her eyes widened with fear.

"Beautiful inside and *out,* you said. What a load of crap." Brody threw the rose against the wall where it left a wet, bloodstained smear on the wallpaper.

Sam jumped at the violent slam of the flower on the wall, but she didn't move. Or defend herself. How could she? They both knew she was guilty.

"I really thought you were the one. The one woman who could see past my scars and love me anyway. One who would want me for more than my money. I must've been blinded by your beauty. It was hard to see the truth when you were naked and seducing me."

"Hold on right there," she said, sudden anger flushing her cheeks red. "What the hell are you talking about?"

Brody looked down at the screen and read aloud. "'Doctor Jensen's groundbreaking treatments can provide patients with significant improvements to their cosmetic appearance and functional activities of everyday life.' Is that what you want, Sam? You want to fix me so I'll go to your parties and your dinners?"

Her bottom lip quivered as she fought to hold back tears. "Yes, but that's not why I was—"

"You're fired."

"What? Brody, please. It's not what you think."

"I think it is, Sam. I would've given you everything. I would've treated you like a cherished treasure for your entire life. All you had to do was accept me. I thought you had."

"I do accept you! You just don't accept yourself!" Sam slammed her phone down onto her desk. "You are a miserable hermit. You have spent your whole life hiding from the world because you're too afraid to face your fears. I looked on those web pages because I was hoping that one of those doctors might be able to help you. Not because *I* thought you needed fixing, but because *you* do."

Sam's words were like a slap in the face. He nearly flinched from the sting of it. "You're calling me a coward? After everything I've faced in my life you have the nerve to tell me I'm hiding away because I'm scared? There's nothing any person on the street could do to me, Sam, that would be more horrible than what has already been done."

"Then why don't you come outside with me and prove it." Sam marched over to the office door and held it open for him. "Go down into your own damn lobby and say hello to your front desk security for the first time."

How dare she challenge him? Who the hell did she think she was? If he wanted to go to the lobby he would. He didn't want to. And he certainly wasn't going to do it only to prove something to her. She didn't know anything about him. She was his secretary and a temporary one at that. His hands curled into tight fists at his sides.

Finally, he turned away from her. He grabbed her coat, phone and purse and followed her to the door. He threw both of them through the doorway into the elevator lobby, following it with the gift box he'd put on her desk. He didn't want it around to remind him of her. Her purse opened and the contents scattered across the marble floor. "I said you're fired, Miss Davis."

When Sam turned away from him to lunge for her things, he snatched her ID card off of her shirt collar. The door shut as she bent down to scoop up her purse, and she realized too late that now she was trapped. Without her ID, she couldn't come through the door or go down the elevator.

Her face flushed a flaming red as she clutched her coat and purse to her chest. She pounded on the glass with her fist. "You can't just leave me in here!"

Her words were muffled, but he could still hear the angry edge of desperation in her voice. "I won't," he said confidently. "I'll have the head of security come escort you out of the building momentarily."

"And is he going to make your copies? Or bring you your lunch? Or pick up your dry cleaning? Agnes won't be back for another week. You're helpless without an assistant."

"I'd rather have no assistant than have you in this office another minute."

Sam flinched but stood her ground. With a sad shake of her head, she said, "Good luck finding another woman like me."

He nearly snorted with contempt. "Secretaries aren't that hard to come by."

She narrowed her dark eyes at him. "I meant in your bed, Brody. It took over thirty years to get a woman into it. Let me know how long the next one takes!"

That was a low blow and she knew it. She could tell the moment the words crossed her lips and Brody's expression crumbled from angry to just plain hurt. A part of her was glad. She was hurt, too. It was only fair that he feel the same. But then he regrouped and she dreaded what might come next.

"It shouldn't be difficult," he said, his lips curling into an angry sneer. "You aren't the only woman in this town willing to sleep her way to the top. Of course, you must not be very good in bed. Every boss you sleep with fires you."

Brody had gutted her with words. Sam could only stumble back against the wall to brace herself from the impact of his insult. He had reduced their love affair to something sleazy that she'd engineered to further her ambitions and called her a lousy lay in one breath.

There was nothing she could say to that. She closed her eyes and prayed she could keep the tears back a few more seconds. When she opened her eyes, he had turned away. She caught only a second's glimpse of him before he stormed into his office and slammed the door.

The moment he was gone, her bravado crumbled. She slumped back against the wall and slid to the floor. The tears poured out of her almost faster than her body could manufacture them. She could only hold her things to her chest and sob into them.

How had this happened? Why wouldn't he listen to her when she tried to explain herself? She'd sat patiently waiting for him to explain about Tommy's death. She deserved equal consideration for a far lesser crime.

Yes, she wanted Brody to see the doctor in New York. But not for the reasons he claimed. His self-esteem was so low he couldn't even fathom that she would want him the way he was. At the slightest evidence to the contrary, his fears were realized and he pushed her away. Why couldn't he understand that the person who wanted him fixed the most was him?

This morning, she'd been saddened thinking she might never be able to introduce the man she loved to her friends and family. Now, she was heartbroken and none of that mattered because she'd lost the man she loved for good.

Sam looked around, feeling lost. That was when she noticed the box on the floor. It wasn't hers, but he'd tossed it out with her things. She reached for it and opened the box. She gasped when she saw the golden sun necklace inside. It was stunning with a center stone so perfectly cut, it shimmered even in the dim florescent lighting of the lobby.

He'd bought it for her, she realized sadly. What could've been a beautiful moment between them was ruined. She grasped the chain and clutched it against her chest with fresh tears falling.

The chime of the elevator sounded and Charlie, the head of security, stepped out onto the landing. The older man looked at her with concern and then bent down to pick up a tube of lipstick that had rolled across the room when her purse dumped out.

"Come on, Samantha. Let's get you out of here." He held out a strong arm to help her off the ground and slowly walked her back to the elevator.

"I'm sorry about all this, Charlie."

"Don't be. It's the most excitement I've had around here in a while. Despite all the fancy locks and alarms, this isn't exactly like the covert ops I'm used to. I almost never get to walk people out. Especially not pretty young ladies with broken hearts."

How could Charlie see what Brody couldn't? "He wouldn't listen to me. I mean I…I love him. I want him to be happy."

Charlie frowned at her and put a reassuring arm around her shoulder. "I know, kiddo. But have some faith. He'll come around soon. And if he doesn't, Agnes will knock some sense into him the moment she comes back from her trip."

Twelve

"What, in the name of all that is holy, has happened here while I was away?"

Agnes's sharp words penetrated Brody's near sound-proof walls. He didn't even need to look up at the surveillance cameras to know she was back from her vacation and fit to be tied.

Brody stumbled out of his office to greet her and knew immediately why she was upset. Things had not gone to plan over the past week. Being without an assistant had been harder than he thought. The janitorial staff wasn't allowed on his floor, so he had days of trash piled up outside his door with more than a few stinky food cartons in it. Charlie had graciously picked up his lunch deliveries and brought them upstairs, but that was all the assistance he'd received.

The printer had run out of both toner and paper over the past few days. When he finally found the replacements in the credenza, he'd only had a brief moment of glory before the machine started to jam. The printer was currently in about twenty-three different pieces, scattered across the floor. He'd stayed at work until after midnight, certain he could fix it. Until he realized he couldn't. And he wasn't able to put it back together, either.

He was as big of a mess as the rest of the place. Despite not having a drop of coffee, he hadn't slept more than three hours at a time in the week since Sam left. He hadn't shaved. Instead of his immaculately pressed suits, he was wearing a T-shirt and jeans. It was all he had clean without asking someone to drop off and pick up his dry cleaning. Peggy only handled his everyday clothes, and he'd been too stubborn to ask for help.

Agnes could only stare at him with her arms overflowing with office mail he couldn't pick up. In a huff, she dumped the mail at her feet and planted her hands on her hips. "Brody Eden, is that a bloodstain I see on the wall? What is going on here? What happened to Samantha?"

This was the moment Brody had been dreading. From the second he'd called security and slammed down the phone, he'd regretted every word he said to Sam in anger. He'd lifted weights for nearly an hour to burn off his emotional maelstrom, and when he was calm again, he knew for certain that he was a first-class jerk. Agnes would no doubt confirm his suspicions and not mince words to do it.

"She's...gone."

"Why? Did she quit? I told you to be nice to her, Brody. No one appreciates being barked at all the time."

"No, she didn't quit. I fired her."

Agnes's fingers twitched. He could tell she was itching to grab him by the ear and drag him to a chair where he would spill his guts. He would save her, and his ear, the trouble. "We had a disagreement."

"About?" Her brows rose expectantly. "Don't make me drag every word out of you, Brody. What did you fight about?"

Brody sighed. "She wanted me to go see a doctor in New York that does facial reconstructions. He specializes in burn treatment."

"And this made you angry because…?"

Agnes was going to make him say the words that he dreaded out loud. There was no way around it. If he lied, she would know. "Because I am in love with her, and I thought she was happy with me the way I am."

Agnes's expression softened at his use of the *L* word. "It sounds as though you two had an eventful month while I was away." She looked around the room with a resigned sigh. "Give me an hour to deal with this mess. I'll go get us some breakfast, stop by the dry cleaner and then we'll sit down and finish this conversation, okay?"

"Okay." Brody was a successful, powerful man, but he knew when to step back and let Agnes run the show. Right now, he'd proven he couldn't do it without her.

"While I'm gone, why don't you clean up in the bathroom, shave and perk yourself up?"

Brody's office had its own bathroom, complete with a shower stall that he used after his workouts. He nodded at Agnes like an obedient child and disappeared into his office. By the time he stepped out of his bathroom, there was a black suit and red dress shirt hanging on the door, still in the bag from the cleaners. Slipping into his usual clothes made him feel more normal and confident again. As did the scent of warm coffee.

The aroma lured him out to Agnes's area. She truly

was a miracle worker. The trash was gone, the mail was sorted and there was a new, fully assembled printer on the credenza.

She was sitting in the guest area that had never actually been used. Brody had put the couch, chairs and coffee table there because the space was big enough and it seemed like the thing to do. But since no one came to this floor, it was more like a museum piece.

On the glass coffee table were two steaming cups of coffee and two breakfast croissants wrapped in deli paper.

Agnes patted the chair beside her. "You're looking much better."

"Thank you for dealing with the mess, Agnes."

She opened a packet of sugar, dumped it into her cup and took a tentative sip. "From the sounds of it, there's still more to clean up. What exactly happened between you and Sam?"

Brody slumped into his seat and reached for the coffee. It was hot, scalding his mouth, but he didn't care. He needed it desperately to think straight. "She's the most amazing woman I've ever met. She is beautiful and stubborn and gentle. She wasn't afraid of me at all. At least, she didn't back down if she was. She looked me in the eye without the slightest hint of revulsion." He shook his head and took another sip. "For some reason she thought I was handsome."

"You *are* handsome, Brody."

"You saying it is like my mom saying it. But I can hardly believe any of you, especially Sam. If it wasn't for the fact that she backed her words with actions, I might never have thought she was serious. She touched me, Agnes. She touched my scars. I didn't know what to think."

"She saw in you what I see. There's a lot more to you than your scars, Brody."

"It all happened so quickly. She kissed me one day. I invited her to my house for dinner, and the next thing I knew, I flew her to *Joya Verde*. Sam was everything I'd hoped for and feared I would never have. I guess I was so afraid to lose her that I pushed her away."

"Did she tell you why she wanted you to see that doctor?"

"She tried to. She said something about wanting me to be happy and accused me of being a miserable hermit. I was too angry to listen at the time. All my brain could process was that I wasn't good enough for her the way I am. Despite everything she said and did, she wanted me to be fixed."

"You know, she might be on to something there." Agnes reached out and took Brody's hand. "You're not happy. And don't tell me that you are. I've worked for you for years, and I can't ever say that I saw you content. You're very successful and comfortable with the way you've structured your life. But what kind of life can you have living all alone?"

"I thought Sam would be enough to make me happy."

"And?"

"She was. To a point. But then I realized that having her in my life only solved part of the problem. She got upset that day because she couldn't introduce me to her friends. I realized later that this relationship was awesome for me but horribly unfair to her. I was asking her to live her life hidden away, but I refused to make even one step toward living my life with her in the open."

"She probably thought that the doctor could help you feel more comfortable with yourself. Sure, maybe she had some selfish reasons for wanting you to be normal, but can you blame her? How many things would she miss out on in her life because you couldn't be there with her? Would you guys elope alone instead of having the big wedding she always dreamed of? Or would she give birth to your children by herself because you wouldn't go to the hospital with her?"

Brody had been so shortsighted. He'd spent so much time alone that he never really considered how his life and his future would play out with someone else in it. Sam had every right to ask more of him, and yet she hadn't. She'd only wanted him to be as confident in himself as she was in him.

"My knee-jerk reaction is to say 'of course not,' but when I really think about it, I know you're right. How did I expect to continue on this way? This life I've lived was okay for me, but I can't subject someone else to it. I know that now. But by the time I put everything together it was too late. I said terrible things to her. I literally threw her out of the office, Agnes. She's never going to forgive me for that."

"Do you think she loves you?"

Brody thought back to the painful tears he'd seen in Sam's eyes as he walked away from her. It looked like her heart was breaking, but he couldn't know for sure. "I'm not certain how she felt. She never told me that she loved me."

"Did you tell her that you were in love with her?"

"No," he admitted. "But I hadn't really figured it out yet. I haven't done this before, Agnes."

The older woman smiled sympathetically. "I know, honey. This kind of thing is never easy, whether it's a first love or your fifth. But you've realized you made a mistake and you love her. So now there's only one question left to ask."

Brody thought he knew what she was going to say, but he let her say it first. He had to figure out what the answer was going to be. It wasn't going to be easy.

"What are you going to do about it?"

Sam was grateful for her new job. Amanda had helped her find a position at Matt's investment firm. She was currently supporting the accounting department. It was a temp-to-hire position, but that was fine with her. She didn't intend to do anything that might jeopardize this job, so she would be a permanent employee before too long. And since her new boss was a plump woman in her fifties who did nothing but talk about her grandchildren, there was no temptation. It was perfect.

Her first day had gone as well as could be expected. She had been worried at first. Not about the job, but about her ability to keep herself together. Normally that wouldn't be a problem, but the past week hadn't been a particularly good one for her.

She had only thought the fallout from the mess with Luke was bad. Sam hadn't loved Luke the way she loved Brody. This time, she couldn't even bear to watch movies on the Hallmark Channel. The big upswept happy endings where the hero did the right thing and won the love of the heroine only made her cry, and not with happy tears. She wanted her own big upswept happy ending. But without a single word from Brody in a week, the odds were that she was out of luck. She wasn't even the leading lady of her own life. From the looks of Amanda and Matt's fast-moving romance, it seemed that Sam was playing the role of the supportive best friend.

The only hiccup in her day so far had been the call

Sam received from Agnes. Her godmother was back in the office. She didn't mention Brody at all but asked how Sam was and what she was doing. Sam was happy to tell her she'd found a new job and the people she worked with were all great. She hoped Agnes would relay the information to Brody so he could stew about it.

Several times as they'd spoken, Sam had wanted to ask about him. But she wouldn't. She really didn't want to know if he was doing fine without her. In her fantasies, he was a mess and she liked it that way. It made her feel better when she lay alone in bed and wished she could see the stars overhead like she could on *Joya Verde*.

Sam's fingers sought out the golden sun pendant at her throat. She should've given the necklace back. Knowing Brody, she guessed it cost more than a year of her salary, but she couldn't make herself do it. It was all she had left of him, and she needed that near to her heart if she was going to make it through this breakup.

"Hey, Sam?"

She turned to find one of the women in the department heading toward her desk. She wasn't certain, but she thought her name was Kristi. "Yes?"

"Do you know where the human resources office is?"

"I think so. I had an in-processing there this morning, so hopefully I can find my way back." It might take her three tries, but she was confident she could do it.

"Great. Could you take this file down to them?"

"Sure." Sam was glad to get up from her desk and move around for a while. If this was going to be her new workplace, she wanted to get familiar with the layout and meet the people. She was always quick to make friends with her coworkers, so hopefully she could fill up her social circle and be too busy to think about Brody.

Luckily, the HR office was right where she left it. She dropped the file off with their assistant and grabbed a bottle of water from the break room before heading back to her desk. She was about to sit back down when something caught her eye and sent the water in her mouth sputtering into her lungs.

There was a bright pink rose on her desk in a silver bud vase.

Sam coughed violently, the water stinging her lungs and drawing pain-filled tears to her eyes. She tried to look around her for the person who had left the rose there, but she could barely see two feet in front of her, much less down the hallway.

When she had finally soothed her lungs and the blood rushed back out of her face, Sam wiped her eyes. The rose was still sitting on her desk. She hadn't imagined it. She walked up to examine it more closely. It was the same vase. She'd left it behind in her hasty departure from ESS.

"You know, the employees that work at the front desk of my building are very nice people."

Sam spun on her heels at the sound of a man's voice behind her. Brody was standing a few feet away, another single fuchsia rose in his hand. She blinked her eyes a few times to make sure she wasn't seeing things.

Brody was still there and looking as handsome as ever in a black suit and a flaming red shirt. But it couldn't be real. Brody didn't go out in public. Ever.

"I feel bad that I didn't meet them sooner. Of course, I gave them quite a shock when I marched through the lobby and introduced myself."

Not only was she seeing things, but her imaginary

Brody was talking crazy. She could not afford to have a nervous breakdown on her first day here. She needed this job too much. Sam squeezed her eyes shut and took a deep breath.

"Aren't you going to say something, Sam?"

At the sound of his voice, she opened one eye and found he was still there. "It's one thing to have delusions. It's another to interact with them."

Her imaginary Brody strode across the room until he was standing right in front of her. She could smell the warm scent of his cologne and feel the heat of his body so close to her. This was a really nice delusion. It was a shame she couldn't have it at home, at night.

And then he touched her. Sam gasped as Brody's palms cupped the back of her upper arms. Her eyes flew open wide, and she found herself gazing into the sapphire depths she'd fantasized about since the first day they met.

She placed one tentative hand on his lapel, then another. "You're really here."

He nodded. "I know. Your new job is so close I was able to walk over here from my office."

Brody walked? Through a public space? "Who are you and what have you done with Brody Eden?"

"I smacked him around until he came to his senses and realized that he was in love with you. And then I knew that I would do anything to hold you again, including walking through several public places to find you."

Sam didn't know what to say. Her jaw dropped open, the words escaping her. There were so many things packed into his last statement she could barely process them. But the word *love* was blinking in her mind like a neon sign.

Brody glanced down at her throat and smiled. "You're wearing the necklace I bought you."

She nodded. "I wanted a piece of you with me. This was all I had left."

"I'm sorry for the things I said to you. I lashed out because you were right about everything. I've been hiding from my life because I was afraid. I punished you because of my own insecurities. Deep down, I could never really believe that you wanted to be with me."

"Why?" she managed.

"Because you are everything I wish I could be and never dared to hope for in a lover. You're confident in yourself. You're comfortable in your own skin. You know your own worth. I envy that about you. I couldn't understand why a woman like that would even look at me twice."

"Brody..."

"But I've realized," he interrupted, "that that's my problem, not yours. I've got an appointment after Thanksgiving with that doctor in New York. I know a lot has changed since I last saw a specialist, but I've been too afraid to go and find out that I'm still a lost cause. We'll see if they can do something to help me feel better about myself. But if not, that's okay, too. I need to learn to accept myself and see value in who I am either way. Like you said at the beach house, I need to find something I like about myself and be more confident in knowing I have good qualities, inside and out. And I think you can help me with that."

So much had happened in the week they were apart. She was stunned by his honest words. "How?"

"First, you can tell me that you love me, because I love you and there's nothing more I want to hear than those words coming from your sweet lips."

Sam's heart was racing double-time in her chest. The blood was rushing to her ears making it difficult to hear anything else. But she heard that he loved her and that was the most important thing. "I do love you, Brody."

He smiled and Sam nearly melted into his arms. He had the most amazing smile. She didn't know how anyone could see any flaws in him when he looked at her that way. He handed her the rose he had in his hand. "This is for you. And so is this."

Brody reached into his pocket and pulled out a small, velvet box. "I told the woman at the jewelry store that I wanted a ring sparkly enough to satisfy a woman with pink glitter running through her veins. This is what she showed me."

He slipped down to one knee in front of Sam and opened up the hinged lid. Inside was the most beautiful ring she'd ever seen in her life. It was a large cushion-cut diamond surrounded by a double circle of bead-set diamonds. The platinum band had diamonds set into it, as well. And he was right. It was sparkly enough even for her.

"Samantha Davis, I was living in the darkness before you came into my life. You're like my own personal ray of sunshine. That's why I bought you that necklace. You make me want to step out into the light and stop being afraid. If you will do me the honor of being my wife, I promise you a wedding with five hundred people there if you want it. I'm done hiding, and I'm ready to start living the rest of my life with you. Will you marry me?"

Sam could only nod yes. The tears flowed over as he removed the ring from the box and slipped it onto her finger. It was the perfect size. Somehow, she was certain he'd found that out on the internet, too. When he stood up, Sam threw her arms around his neck and kissed him.

She was stunned to hear the roar of applause coincide with their kiss. When she finally pulled away and looked around, she was surprised to see they were surrounded by people. Her new boss was clapping enthusiastically with tears in her eyes. At some point, the entire accounting department had come out to watch the proposal unfold. Sam had been so wrapped up in the moment, she hadn't noticed anything but Brody.

"Get out of here," her boss said with a smile. "You're the first assistant I've lost after only six hours."

"I'm sorry," Sam said, although she was unable to hide her grin. She rounded her desk to grab her things, sweeping up her silver bud vase and rose last. Then she slipped her arm through Brody's and walked with him out of the building.

Once they reached the street, they stopped. "Where are we going now?" she asked.

"Anywhere you want."

"I want to go out to lunch."

Brody smiled, but she could tell he was nervous about the prospect. He wasn't going to be comfortable overnight. "Okay. How about that place across the street?"

They headed toward the crosswalk and waited for the light to change. As they passed through the crowd of people, Sam could feel Brody tense beside her. There were some stares, but Sam clung tighter to him and they kept moving. Outside the restaurant, she stopped and turned to him. "Are you okay? Is this too much for your first day out?"

The tension eased from his face as he leaned down and kissed her. "I'll be fine. I can do anything if you're

with me. Besides, I've decided that they're not staring
at me because of my scars. They're staring because my
fiancée is so damn hot."

Epilogue

Christmas Eve

"I don't know what to wear," Sam said from the depths of their closet.

Brody sat on the mattress and shook his head. "It really doesn't matter. We usually wear whatever we feel like. Something warm," he suggested.

"It does matter!" She flipped through several outfits and frowned. "I'm meeting your family for the first time. I want to make the right impression."

"My family has been so concerned about my love life for the past ten years that I think they'll love you on principle. No matter what you wear, they're going to adore the beauty that tamed the beast."

That was sweet, but it didn't make her any less nervous about facing the Edens and their clan of super-successful children. Sam emerged from the closet with an outfit held up to her chin. It was a plaid wool wrap skirt and cream sweater that she would pair with tights and knee-high boots. "What about this?"

"It's great."

She could tell he was humoring her. Sam carried the outfit back into the closet and came out with another one. This one was a red sparkly sweater with flowing black palazzo pants. "What about this?"

"It's great."

She dropped the outfit to her side. "You said that about the last one."

"They were both great. Really."

Sam sighed. "You're no help at all."

Brody shook his head and got up from the bed to approach her. He wrapped his arms around her waist and tugged her close. "You're beautiful in anything. I actually prefer you in nothing. But you could wear an ugly reindeer sweater and it wouldn't matter. You're so fashionable, you'd probably start a new trend of ugly reindeer sweaters."

He leaned down to kiss her, and Sam felt her nerves finally start to fade. She melted into him, letting the latest outfit fall to the floor. Brody's hands glided over her back. One slipped beneath her top and moved to unsnap her bra.

"Oh, no you don't," she said, twisting from his grasp before he could succeed. "We're going to be late getting to your parents' house as it is."

"Then finish packing so we can leave!"

"Fine. The skirt," she decided.

"Fine." Brody smiled, and she realized he'd tricked her into making a quick decision.

Sam was stuffing the last of her things in a bag when she heard Brody's cell phone ring. She recognized the

tone now as his brother Xander's—"Hail to the Chief."
It always made her laugh when she heard the different
songs he chose for each member of his family.

"Hey, Xander," Brody answered. "Are you at the
house already?"

There was an extended silence. Sam zipped up her
bag and rolled it across the room to where Brody was
standing. The expression on his face was not what she
was expecting. His face was blank and stony, his eyes
boring into the wall. Something was wrong. Hopefully
nothing happened with his parents. Brody had told her
his foster dad, Ken, had a heart condition.

"Are we certain it's him?" Brody said at last. "So
Wade was wrong."

Sam wished she could hear the other half of this conversation. She could only put a reassuring hand on his
arm and wait for the call to end.

"I'm not blaming him. I...I had just hoped we had
that problem dealt with last year."

She could hear Xander's muffled voice on the phone
but couldn't make out the words.

"We'll be there in a couple hours. We were about
to leave when you called. Okay. I'll see you shortly."

At that, Brody disconnected the phone and flopped
onto the bed. Sam sat down beside him. "What happened? Is everyone okay?"

"For now," Brody said. "Xander says that the local
news has reported the discovery of human remains at
the site of a new resort being built. On the land my parents used to own."

Sam let his words sink in. "Is it...*him?*"

Brody nodded his head and took her hand in his. "It
has to be, although I'm sure it will take the lab quite

a while to confirm an identity. I was hoping this day would never come, but I'm pretty certain someone has finally unearthed the body of Tommy Wilder."

* * * * *

A sneaky peek at next month..

PASSIONATE AND DRAMATIC LOVE STORIES

My wish list for next month's titles...

In stores from 18th October 2013:

2 stories in each book - only £5.49!

☐ To Tame a Cowboy – Jules Bennett

& Claiming His Own – Olivia Gates

☐ The Secret Heir of Sunset Ranch – Charlene Sand

& Yuletide Baby Surprise – Catherine Mann

☐ Expecting a Bolton Baby – Sarah M. Anderson

& One Texas Night... – Sara Orwig

Available at WHSmith, Tesco, Asda, Eason, Amazon and Apple

Just can't wait?

Visit us Online

You can buy our books online a month before they hit the shops! **www.millsandboon.co.u**

101

Join the Mills & Boon Book Clu

Want to read more **Desire**™ books?
We're offering you **2 more** absolutely **FREE**

We'll also treat you to these fabulous extras:

- Exclusive offers and much more!
- FREE home delivery
- FREE books and gifts with our special rewards scheme

Get your free books now!

visit www.millsandboon.co.uk/bookclub
or call Customer Relations on 020 8288 288

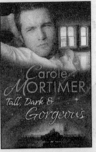

Meet The Sullivans...

ONLY £3.99
Over 1 MILLION Books Sold

BELLA ANDRE
The Look of Love

THE SULLIVANS
Over 1 MILLION books sold!

BELLA ANDRE
From This Moment On

THE SULLIVANS
Over 1 MILLION books sold!

BELLA ANDRE
Can't Help Falling in Love

Over 1 million books sold worldwide!

Stay tuned for more from **The Sullivans** in 201

Available from:

www.millsandboon.co.uk

1113/MB444

The World of Mills & Boon®

There's a Mills & Boon® series that's perfect for you. We publish ten series and, with new titles every month, you never have to wait long for your favourite to come along.

Blaze®
Scorching hot, sexy reads
4 new stories every month

By Request
Relive the romance with the best of the best
9 new stories every month

Cherish™
Romance to melt the heart every time
12 new stories every month

Desire™
Passionate and dramatic love stories
8 new stories every month